BIRDS OF PARADISE

By Cedar G. Elkheart

First Paperback Edition, February 2023

Published in Bellingham, Washington

ISBN
979-8-9856615-1-4

All artwork by Cedar Elkheart
Published 2023 by Cedar Elkheart.

Throughout this book, you will find subscript numbers attached to the end of words, like this$_A$. This lets you know that you can turn to the QR Code Index in the back of the book and search for the number in the index, and you will find a QR code. It allows you to scan a code which will bring up a link on your device. The codes in this book will link you to my website, where you will find maps, paintings, and other assets that will enrich your reading experience. The book is still a complete work without these additions, do not worry if you don't access these resources. They are organized in such a way that they do not adhere to a numerical order. Scanning them ahead of their queue will only serve as a spoiler for yourself! This is an experiment, and I hope it will bring your fiction reading into a new dimension!

To do this:

Bring up your phone camera. Those with older devices may need to download a QR code reader app.

Point your camera at the QR code, hold it steady, and tap on the code on your screen. A link should pop up after a few seconds. Tap this.
It should take you to a specific page.

Let's try a specific example, I will attach a QR code below. Try scanning it, and it should take you to a secure page. The rest of the QR codes are at the end of the book, in the QR Code Appendix. If you are having trouble, you may need to download the app for Dropbox, where the files are hosted.

Sample QR Code "A"

Please enjoy these new ideas. I will do my best to maintain these codes indefinitely, but the internet is a confusing place and I get older every day. Printing is expensive, and I want to be able to share more than text in my stories. If you like what you see, please consider checking out my other books, Youtube channel, patreon, and other sections on my website. Thank you!

This is a work of fiction. Some characters, incidents, events, and settings in the story are inspired by my personal commissions as a backcountry and frontcountry guide for various companies, resorts, ventures, parks, and expeditions throughout the Four Corners Region and in the National Parks system. All such inspirations have been altered beyond recognition out of consideration for the respected groups and should be taken as a cautionary tale, and nothing more.

I want to make this abundantly clear: **_this story did not happen._** Do not search newspaper archives looking for it. Do not ask around town. And most definitely do not try to infiltrate the Maroon Mesa Resort. They've changed their name, anyway.

In the dual interest of preserving an unspoiled story, and more importantly preserving a sense of agency and safety among my readers, please only read the rest of this paragraph if you wish to be warned about the content of this book. Otherwise, skip to the next paragraph now. This book tells a story that needs to be told, and is based off of personal experiences and experiences of those around me. It includes references to human trafficking, drug and alcohol abuse, violence, terrorism, the pandemic, and late-stage capitalism. If these things may upset you or cause painful memories and/or feelings to surface, please close the book and seek professional help if warranted.

This is a small scale work and was done with the budget of an outdoor professional. That is to say, not much. It would be greatly appreciated if the reader could contact the author if they notice typos, blunders, or mistakes, want to say howdy, had a moment of connection with the work, or have any cold soak recipes to share. The author can be reached at elkheartendeavors@gmail.com.

Like the entire continent of North America, the landscapes in this story were violently colonized. These stories are intergenerational, convoluted, and often intentionally obscured. Here, we only briefly mention those that came before. I encourage you to delve into the complicated history of these places, and those that have stewarded them for tens of thousands of years.

These people include: the Navajo Nation, the Southern Ute Indian Tribe, the Hopi Tribe, the Las Vegas Paiute, the Ute Indian Tribe of Uintah and Ouray Reservation, the Ute Mountain Ute Tribe, the Kaibab Band of Paiute Indians, the Paiute Indian Tribe of Utah, the Pueblo of Zuni, the Rosebud Sioux, the Moapa Band of Paiute Indians of the Moapa River Reservation, the San Juan Southern Paiute, *and others.*

I encourage all readers to investigate their home, and where it falls on native land. https://native-land.ca/ is an excellent resource that hosts an interactive web map that allows you to search your area to determine what indigenous group or groups existed in specific places before colonization. It even allows you to organize by languages and relevant treaties, and works anywhere in North and South America.

Table of Contents

For my dead friends Andre, Alden and Roland.

"Society is like a stew. If you don't stir it up every once in a while then a layer of scum floats to the top."
— Edward Abbey

...and the good parts sink to the bottom, where they get burned.

ACT I

THE HOME RANGE

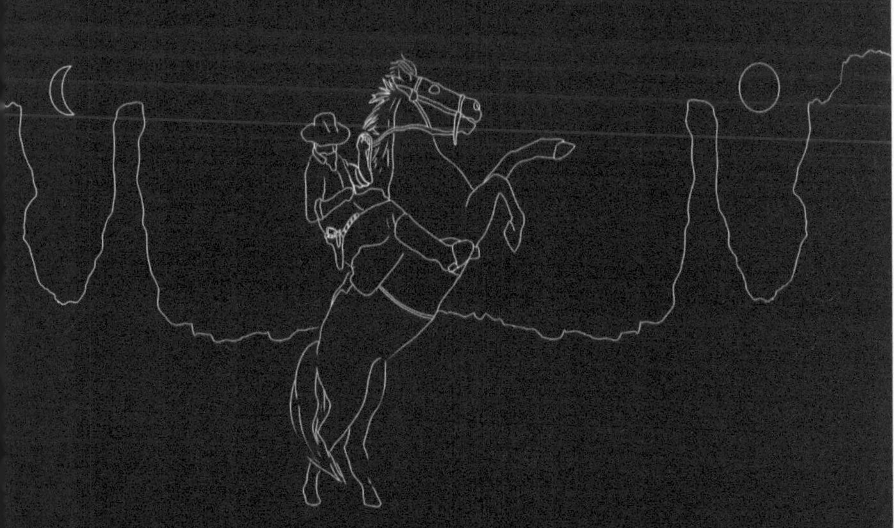

Chapter One || The Hand of Justice

Sometimes it's hard to remember that there was a time when we were all here together. Most often, it feels like

When I was a child, I would watch out the window at the two lane street. And, wait for two cars to approach from opposite directions. Strangers on separate missions, facing one another for a brief moment, and then losslessly colliding.

Uninterrupted momentum.

For a pocketful of seconds, they overlap, sharing the road and the sky, and they may never share anything again for the rest of their lives.

I moved here from Vermont. Even though I repeat that every day to new clients, the sandstone theater makes it easy to forget. My boots grip the entrada like I've always been here, and the sagebrush laughs at me assuming that I could leave if I wanted to. You don't end up in the desert by accident.

In the case of my clients, they landed here by recommendation of a 'Top 10 National Parks You Have To Visit' webpage, or more commonly by a travel agent whose headset is probably augmented into their skull by now.

Some are kind, and ask me about myself. They ask where I went to school, how I know the area, and almost always about where the secret spots are. As a general rule, it is a crime punishable by exile, excommunication, and sometimes execution for a local guide to share knowledge of such places. And as a general rule, it is a custom for the client to ask for information about such places and to swear that they aren't like the others, that your secrets are safe with them.

Mill Creek is the latest stronghold to fall. One week it was a paradise just outside of Moab that the working folks of this town could escape to find waterfalls, ruins, petroglyphs, pictographs, shade, and real bona-fide freshwater outside of the Colorado. The next week, some guide or local had let it slip and a geotag allowed social media to become saturated with the van life at Mill Creek. Jumping pools now bubbled up with the children of tourists who learned how to cliff jump on a tablet encrusted with Cheeto dust (and promptly had to have traction pulled on their shoulders). Algae slides now played host to selfie stick holding visitors projecting their being onto video and using their camera as a lit beacon to send them into the world. The once glittering teacup pools now hold gas station coffee cups and used diapers (only slightly less effective than standard naval mines in the effort of keeping folks out of the water).

Some guests are less kind, and spend the majority of the tour trying to convince you of their wealth. The funny thing is that this sort of guest rarely tips. Sometimes we get tips in other ways, like inside stock information that we can't afford to invest in, or the bottom of a bag of chips. I'm just happy to take people outside, but for old time guides who have families to support like Don, tips like that can drive a person mad. You try and listen to a CEO whose net worth is two hundred and ten million dollars talk for forty-five minutes about the $15,000 bottle of wine he's going to have with dinner; specifically how the whole restaurant staff gathered around to watch him open the $10,000 bottle of 1968 Chardonnay last night because they were excited, so he can't imagine how excited they'll be tonight, then fail to tip both the restaurant staff and myself. Working this job for as long as I have, I've learned that there's a few different types of rich. The boaters with purebreds, the ones who won't look at you while they order their meal, the zealots with the doomsday bunkers, etc. The type of rich I'm talking about isn't happy with having everything they need and more, but seems to chase happiness by working constantly and inefficiently to try to convince others that they are, in fact, happy. The effect is similar to that of a child in your care approaching and explaining unprompted that 'I didn't do anything'. Sure, kid.

All manner of wealth are greatly accepted at Moab's
premiere luxury resort, the Maroon Mesa: Where
Sandstone Meets Serenity. Though, I will say that the
length of the owner's smile grows when the credit
card in question is made of metal and not plastic.
It isn't like we see them but₃ or 4 times a year,
anyway. When they do show up, a quarter of the 60
person staff is sure to get fired and a laundry list
of nonsensical tasks are added to everyone's plate.
This spring, they had us paint all of the handrails
and steps on the property their favorite color: black.
This wouldn't be so bad if the color scheme of the
place wasn't a facade of wood, and if our summer
days weren't regularly above 110 degrees. Someone
complained about the painting and pointed out the
obvious safety hazard, and was fired on the spot,
then escorted off property. The turnover rate here
is so high that after working and living at the resort
for a year and a half, I have the fourth longest
tenure. I've outlasted generation after generation
of HR staff, entire management regimes, and a
constant stream of employees, at least one of which
commits suicide or dies here each year. The average
employment period for employees and managers is
three months. In the 21 years since the resort has
opened, the owner has hired and fired 34 general
managers. The only people I haven't outlasted
are an engineer with a fascination for bugs and
nothing to lose, a vehicle mechanic with a love for
geology, and the owner themself. Hire & fire, hire
& fire...With the right kind of gall and perseverance,
employees can sometimes push through the period
   where they're most likely to get fired. That
⬤━━━━━▸ is, if they manage not to quit from the

mental and physical load of working here. One of the best roommates I've ever had is a living testament to this.

Manuel arrived here from Peru on a warm and cloudy spring night. I had been working, manning the guide office on the night shift in case one of the 12 in-house guests decided they wanted to book a trip after their heads hit the pillow. I got a call from my manager, who at the time was filling in for three other managers that had recently been fired. "Manuel is here," He said.

"Who is Manuel?" I asked into the radio.

"Your roommate? Did they not tell you again?" He said, defeated. Each day in the books here appeared as a wrinkle on his face.

"Did you expect them to?"

"Not really," he laughed. "Listen," his tone switched. "Your room looks pretty bad, so we're gonna put him up in one of the empty guest rooms. I need you to clean that up tonight so he can move in tomorrow morning, okay?"

"What do you mean? I spent all morning cleaning that space,"

"Housekeeping said it was too messy for him to move in, so no hard feelings but I need you to clean it, okay?"

"I don't understand,"

"I don't know, I'm just passing it on, I gotta go,"

I took one of the UTVs back to employee housing, only a mile away from the guest rooms. My bedroom door was opened, the light left on. The door creaked open and I saw every one of my belongings thrown onto my bed, stacked like some design for a Moab garage sale. Broken glass littered the floor, the charging block in my wall outlet was bent out of shape. Once sealed letters I had been waiting to send had been opened, their envelopes scattered on the floor. The window was open, too, and the screen had a cannonball hole through it, but that was already there, if I'm being honest. Underneath the pile of all of my earthly possessions were my solar panels, weighed down by at least 300 pounds of gear, equipment, clothing, food, and maps. That was the cherry on top. Or, bottom.

"Hey dude, yeah. I guess you saw," Eric, our other roommate, hangs off of my door frame. The night auditor. He's off today.

"Did you see what happened?"

"Yeah, the head housekeeper lady and a bunch of guys came in and told me they were getting the place ready for a roommate, I thought you knew."

"No, I didn't."

"Yeah, they were, like, reading your mail and stuff. They were pointing your rifle at each other and stuff, too."

"Jesus,"

"Yeah. When you tried to tell me how bad that housekeeping lady was I didn't really believe you, but," he shrugs. "Sorry, man, that blows," he walks away into the kitchen. I pick up my rifle from where I didn't leave it and opened the chamber.

"You didn't try to stop them?" I call.

"What?" Eric replies, distantly.

"Nothing," I say. I should count my blessings. If I had been a little bit more careless and didn't hide my ammunition, I'd be in handcuffs right now for manslaughter. This place, man. My hair will be gray by the time I leave here. But I stay, because I don't have another choice. Because if I leave then the others who come here won't have anyone to warn them. They won't have anyone to help them survive.

I take photos, a lot of them. I clear out the broken glass from between the two twin beds, which are set up in the style of an old married couple leaving room for the holy spirit: exactly 10 inches apart, just enough room for you to shimmy in horizontally. They couldn't be any wider; the stucco walls make sure of that, and the room isn't large enough to rotate them in the other direction. I checked all the spots where I had hidden ammunition, they hadn't found any of it. What they had found, though, was a few hundred dollars in cash tips that I left on my desk. I marched down to my manager's place and showed him the evidence, he didn't know what happened. Didn't know how to react. Didn't know how to fix it. He asked why I didn't lock my room. I told him that I had asked four times for a key, but I was told that none existed. Apparently none ever had. Then why, pray tell, install a lock without a key?

On my way to drop the UTV off I met a man with a suitcase. He wasn't a guest, I could tell that much just through the headlights.

"Hey, are you Manuel?"

"Yes, nice to meet you."

"I'm Birch," we shook hands. I explained what happened, and that he could come move in now if he wants.

"No, really, it is no trouble at all. I don't mind. Just happy to be here," he

smiled.
How long does it take to get to Utah from Peru?
More than a few hours. He's been kicked out of
housing before he even moved in, and still meets me
with kindness. "Are you doing good?" He says.

"I'm okay, thanks. Do you need help with your
bags or anything?"

"I am good," he said. His accent isn't one
that I've heard before.

"¿Hablas español?"

"Si, " he said, then proceeded to rapidly fire
off an inquisitive series of sentences that fly right
past me... and I thought I was fluent in Spanish prior
to this conversation.
Some time passes and I learn more about the man
I sleep less than a foot away from. I learned that
he grew up cooking at his uncles restaurant near
Lima, where they specialized in all different kinds of
ceviche. I learn that he knows 100 ways to cook an
egg, and that he likes to flex his culinary muscles.
His hiring must have been swift and easy, then, a
stereotypical target for the resort. Foreign, highly
skilled in one field and willing to accept low wages.
And no family nearby to come calling if something
were to happen to him.

A month after he arrived, I walk from the
main lobby to where the kitchen and dining room
are inside the main lodge of the resort. I make a
point to swing by and hang out with Manuel often.
Sometimes he'll even cook me something. Today is
different, though, because it is the first day that we
take a lunch break together and sit in the museum
lounge on the top floor of the building. Directly
22   adjacent, we can hear the sounds of the bar
  ━━━━→ and the kitchen. He has worked in the

kitchen his whole time here, but he had never paid
much mind to the area immediately outside the
service door, which led to the museum lounge that
nobody used. Here, all manner of western style
art and artifacts made from non-western artists
found homes. Massive vases that are now luxurious
mansions for Hobo Spiders, Eratigena agrestis, who
underwent a name change from Tegenaria agrestis
in recent years. Happy to have them staying with
us. Pewter statues of rodeo champions tossing rope,
forever suspended in a loop through the air. Here, it
looks like the funnel spiders have made a trampoline
of sorts, maybe for after hours use. I don't know, I
still haven't received my invitation for that club.

 Not unlike most museums, here can be seen
a myriad of ill-gotten artifacts. Stolen indigenous
patterns rewoven by descendants who share 1/64
blood, one of John Wayne's revolvers from Saddle
King, spurs that some insignificant rancher wore a
hundred and fifty years ago.

 "Can you imagine," I say, "You spend your life
with cracked lips trying to carve out an existence
here, and five generations later your bloodline
is dead. The only thing you left behind are some
footprints in the crypto and brass spurs?"

 "Yeah, but think about all the thousands of
people before that, who left nothing," Manuel says.
I think for a moment.

 "Do you want a legacy?" I ask.

 "A what?" he holds his hand out.

 "Like, this," I point at the revolver. "Even
you know who John Wayne is. Do you want people to
remember you after you're gone?" I ask.

 "Yes," he pushes his lips together.
"I would be happy with just my family

23

remembering me. My children, if I ever create them, but I have got to save some money and complete marriage first."

We lean on a display case, peering down at rusted bullet cartridges and a collection of pottery shards that lovely, mindful clients have brought to the front desk over the years.

"I'm surprised there's not more," Manuel says.

"Usually they keep them, even when you tell them not to," I say.

"You don't stop them?"

"Even if they pick it up in front of me, the best I can do is educate them, then scold them, you know? I'm not going to report it or anything. That's what that guy, Jared, did? I'm sure Chef has told you that story by now. The one where he confiscated the pottery pieces his guests stole and tried to report it, then the owner found out and got him taken away?" I say. He nods, as if he's heard the story before.

The plexiglass encased paintings on the wall draw his eye next. A great deal of them romanticize the property, showing herds of wild horses running in front of guest rooms, treasure hunters peering down from a nearby cliff, Dome Plateau, and a whole flock of birds. A whole wall in this museum is dedicated to the owner, with portraits of them on canvases as large as twin sized beds from every birthday since they were a child. The wooden rafters criss-crossing the high ceiling were neglected from cleaning duties, and several real bird's nests are tucked away on the rafters. We determined that the most likely cause of this was that whoever used to clean this space had been fired a long time ago, and never passed the duty on. We agree that it looks better this way.

"I also wanted to ask you about that," he points at an inaccessible recession up near the ceiling.

"What about it?"

"What is it?"

"I'm not really sure, but I can tell you what I've heard. I think that's the original owner's. There was a chest that was there from when he was a little boy. Had a big lock on it. Some old photographs, an old sled. Chest was probably empty now that I think about it," I say. "Apparently there used to be a spiral staircase leading up there, but they removed it because after the property sold, people kept coming into the museum drunk and falling off of that unsecure ledge," I say.

"That is a big drop."

"Yeah, at least one story. I heard that a guest broke their collarbone falling down it with a ranchwater in their hand. The broken bone probably isn't why it got removed," I say, toeing the ground-off bolts stuck into the floor.

"There is barely enough room up there for a display like that," He says.

"That's why they fell off I guess," I point to the eye level painting of an older woman who looks like the dean of some pay-to-graduate school. She wears a dark robe, indistinguishable from that of a judge's save for the addition of a lace cloth at the neck. I slide the vented plastic glass around the painting open and point my headlamp at the top. I notice a stain running down the portrait, a whitish aberration covering the forehead of the woman. I pocket my headlamp again and close the case.

"Ranchwater."

"Tequila and lime do not leave stains like that. I have repaired paintings before, in school." He says.

"Yes, but you're forgetting that this resort has to leave the owner's trademark on everything," I say, pulling the pen out of his apron pocket and showing him the logo. I point down to the logo on his shirt, then flick his nose when he looks down. He smiles. "I'm sure that it's hidden in our contracts somewhere that we have to get tattoos of the place if we accept a salary position."

"I still don't understand, the glass that the drink was in had a logo on it?" He asks.

"No, my friend. They used to dye all the drinks red," I say. He tilts his head. "Well, Maroon." He nods, looks at a few paintings, then touches a wooden support column that leads up to the cornered platform above.

"Too high for a ladder. Is there still anything up there?" he asks.

"I've climbed up before. There's a bunch of spare parts, pipes, broken vents. Nothing important, and mostly things that are too big to bring down without a rope or a staircase anyway. There's roof access up there, if that interests you," I say, thinking of the dead space. The triangle shaped corner deck is tucked up against the upper roof of the main building we stand in. The area up there is larger than the house I grew up in. Excluding this specific angle it is otherwise completely swallowed by the vastness of Maroon Mesa.

We turn our attention back to the glass cases.

Peacock feather earrings with sterling silver hooks sit in a glass case on the wall. $985...

per earring. A glass jeweler's case holds a

set of fake sheriff and sheriff's deputy badges, made
of either silver or gold and priced at around $2,000
each. Manuel and I eat french fries while we look
down at the case and talk cowboys. We even double
dip into the same honey mustard. It turns out that
sleeping 10 inches apart every night eliminates most
barriers in friendship.

He points into one of the glass cases and stops
chewing.

"What's that?"

"Oh, that's the hand from 127 Hours," I laugh.
He stares at me, hard. "You know, the movie about
that guy that got stuck out in that canyon?" He looks
puzzled, but becomes horrified when I explain the
rest. "He cut off his arm with a multi tool because
a rock fell on him. Trapped him, kinda. Threw a
tourniquet on and climbed out of the canyon and
escaped. I think he lives in Aspen now. Anyway, the
Park Service had to bring out a winch to dislodge the
rock and get the arm out," I say. The forearm and
hand sits, papery and mummified next to a piece of
jewelry that would cost me two month's income to
buy. Manuel sweats.
"Here, see," I open the lid on the case and toss the
arm at him. He steps back, but catches it with wide
eyes. "Still less heinous than pretty much everything
else here."

"It is…lighter than I thought," he smiles.

"That's because I made it out of paper
mache," I say, and we laugh. He chops me over the
head with the rotting hand, then articulates it to
feed himself a french fry. He tucks it into his sleeve
to appear cohesive, then shakes my hand and laughs
when it pulls off.   27

"Need a hand?"

"Very funny. I wonder what Aron would think of that," I warn.

"Who?"

"The owner of the arm,"

"Yeah," He steps forward, and looks into the case from the side. "They are all just unlocked?"

"Yeah," I say, lifting and dropping the doors on a few of the adjacent cases.

"Why do not people steal these things?" He asks.

"Something I've learned here is that only poor people steal stuff like this, and it's usually because they need it. If rich people were to steal these things, it would be because they want it. But that's what they have those metal credit cards for. Besides, once you stop stealing for your basic needs you go a lot bigger," I gesture with my arms.

"What do you mean?"

"You'll never get the kind of filthy rich that our guests are by stealing jewelry like this. You either have to inherit the money and spend your life cultivating it, or you've gotta hurt people," I say.

"There's no other way to get that kind of rich?"

"I don't think so. And I don't think you'd be happy, either, even with all that money. Personally, just give me a fast million and I'll happily enjoy the rest of my life making a full time job out of figuring out who's hospital bills to pay, who to send to college. I'd probably eat fries every day and maybe even get my boots resoled," I say, lifting my foot to show him the peeling rubber. He has a big smile on his face.

28   "I think I would pay for everybody in my family to go to school. I would buy them

a new house in a new place. I think I would invest
the rest, and then use it to make more. Then, when
I am old I would donate it all," he says, grinning at
a painting. "Okay, maybe I would spend a little on
myself," he says, we laugh. He takes a step back
and sighs, then looks at me. I tilt my head. "I have
something to ask you, and I don't know how to ask
it."

"Just say it. I won't let you hurt my feelings,"

"Are you sure? No matter your answer, you
can't share that I asked."

"Yeah."

"Promise?"

"Promise," I say. He sighs, looks back and
forth between the paintings and myself.

"There is," he starts, clasping his hands
together. "These-" he begins again. He closes his
eyes and shakes his head. "I know something about
these paintings."

"Okay," I say, crossing my arms and leaning
on a jewelry case. He opens up one of the glass
protective panels over the canvas, squeaking the
hinges as it pulls away from the painting of a bird.
He points to the bottom corner, where it reads
'1757', and a signature. I stay quiet, waiting for him
to continue.

"The truth is that this is not the first time I
have come in here to look at these. I have known
what they are for a long time. I recognized them
almost right away when I arrived," he says. "I want
to ask for your help with something," I nod. "These
are stolen," he says, pointing around the room.

"All of them?" I ask, wondering what he might
be getting at.

29

"Probably, but I am not a historian

on all of them. I know specifically about these," he points to the others. I wonder silently how and why he has seen them before. "Six in this room, it is all the same. I don't know how to say it, like... ah," He looks around for his answer. "Like chapters. They go together. They are from the same book?"

"Like pictures at the beginning of a chapter?"

"No, like, uh," He looks around again.
This is one of my favorite pastimes with Manuel. I think he enjoys it like this when I flutter in Spanish. Though, there is considerable disparity between our two secondary languages.
"Like the whole book." he says.

"Like a series? Like a compendium?"

"You know, like Spider-Man 1, Spider-Man 2, Spider-Man 3,"

"Those aren't books,"

"They are like comics, right? It is all—" He holds an invisible ball between his hands and tries to explain.

"Like the same, but not. Like together but different. Like siblings," he says.

"Oh, that's cool," I say. He nods, then runs a cloth from his apron down one of the long frames and wipes the dust off. "These are expired,"

"Expired?" I ask. He rubs his palm on his forehead.

"They should be in a museum. Older than both of us combined," he says. He walks to another, this one depicting a Kingfisher on top of a dead cottonwood branch. The colors were souring; yellowing and aging in this exposure. He is right. The corners are cracked and dried, the kingfisher
30   depressing into its backdrop. Everything here
has a price tag on it, even these paintings.

"This has to be a joke, right?" I ask him.

"No, I would say even more than that,"

"Are you serious?"

"That is why I had surprise when there was no security alarm on this," he says. I count the zeros on this painting alone. 3.1 million dollars. No dollar symbol.

In the restaurant here, they don't even have prices next to the items.

"With all of them together that's-"

"18 million dollars," he says. We take a step back and look at the paintings together. They aren't even that good, to be honest. I personally couldn't do better, but I have friends that could.

"Is that a lot of money for the owner?" He asks.

"I doubt it. Last year the resort netted 23 million. And this isn't their only property."

"Where else?"

"I know they were trying to start one out in Zion but they're getting a lot of pushback from the town. They've got the other resort in upstate New York, and the restaurant in the city that only serves fries and steak. They own a couple minor league sports stadiums too. I think they also own one of those rehab camps outside of Salt Lake," I say. He shakes his head.

"How can someone have so much time?"

"They don't," I cross my arms. "That's why this place is the way it is. There's so much potential here. I see it, I know that you do, too, and that's what everyone says right before they quit."

He leans in close to me. I expect a love tap, but he quietly asks a question.

31

"Do these security cameras have

microphones?"

"Mm-mm. If they did there wouldn't be a single employee left here. They don't check them, either. They're always on, not motion activated. I've been in the back and watched them go over footage before, from when that old cook got into a fight with the old GM? The process takes hours and hours and they already don't want to pay people for their regular jobs. We're fine. Besides, all we're doing is talking about them, it isn't like we're spitting on them or something," I say. He nods thoughtfully and cracks his neck, then looks at me.

"What if I want to do more than talk about them?" He asks.

"What do you mean?" I ask. He purses his lips. Starts, then stops. He takes out his cellphone and takes a flash photograph behind one of the frames, then shows me. He pinches in to zoom in on another one of the tension alarms in the very center of the frame.

"And this is what I want help with. I told you I worked in Clearwater before. I know someone from a museum there who will purchase these," I harden my gaze. "I understand if you are not interested, but you are always complaining about your job," he says. It is true, with three degrees and a medical certificate I make $6 less an hour than an entry level McDonalds worker, not that there's anything wrong with that job. We look at one another in silence for a moment.

"I should clock back in," I say. "Thanks for lunch."

"Manuel, can I ask you something?" I say, now that we've both clocked out and are in our bedroom. The broken solar panel sits against the wall. It was for the top of my car, but I have yet to rig it up.

"I think I know what you will ask," He says. He lay on his bed, his head at a tight angle while he slays zombies on the computer's trackpad.
"Did you mean to say that we should steal those paintings?" I say, my butt on the edge of the bed. I hear him pause the game, but he doesn't look up from his computer.

"I don't think it is stealing if they are already stolen. If you took my telephone and put it in your backpack, then I took it back, is that stealing?" He asks. I sigh.

"That's different. Stealing those—taking those—is genuinely crazy. You get that, right? Like big trouble. If the owner finds out it was us they'll ruin our lives in court if they don't have us killed. That's more money than we'll make in our entire lives... than we could ever make in a hundred lifetimes," I say, looking at my socks.

"That's why I asked you. That was not my first time seeing those paintings. You've been in this place longer than anyone else that I know. I know I could not take them without you and not get caught," he says. I nod to myself. "Bringing them back to a real museum is the right thing to do. That's who the buyer is, a curator that is interested in preserving them."

"Why can't they just buy them from the owner?"

"People have tried. I have a whole report on them I can show you. They're assets, they won't sell them unless they're in trouble and need the money," he says.

"I can't imagine the kind of trouble 18 million could get you out of," I say. Why does he know so much? He nods. "So your buyer pays us the price of the paintings, just for delivering them?" I ask. He nods again. I look at the floor. Wind ruffles our curtain—a bedsheet tacked onto the wall.

"What about after the resort? Once we get them out of Moab."

"I can organize all of that so we will not get caught," he says.

"Well, what is that supposed to mean?"

"I can't say much more unless we want to do it. The person we can sell it to can organize everything, to make sure we have everything we need...

"Look," he says, folding his hands on his belly. "I am not going to ask you how you will get them off of the ranch.. I will trust you with that, but I need you to trust me that I will take care of the rest."

"I looked up art theft earlier. If we get caught and they want to prosecute, which they will, we'll either be working off the fine for the rest of our lives, or we'll be in prison. And again, that's if they don't have us killed," I say.

"We will not get caught. Just some simple planning. They do not have any idea that the pieces are stolen. Everyone that comes here is too rich to need that money anyway, like you said. Also, the alarms are all the same, I checked the other paintings while I was dusting. The buyer will supply us with replacement fakes. All we have to do is replace them in the frames and deliver the product. If we work together on this, they will never even know that it happened,"

"Even still. Clearwater is like 2000 miles away,"

"About 3,000 kilometers, yes. And we could not fly, I—I really can't say more. Just let me know if you are in. Are you in?"

"No," I say.

"Okay, my contract is up in 11 months and then I go home to Peru. I know yours is up at the same time. I will wait to hear from you until then," he says, baiting me I suppose.

"Was that a threat?" I say, standing up and toward the door.

"Just remember that I know where you sleep," He says, smiling innocently. He unpauses the game and the groans of the undead once again fill the room.

"Are things gonna be weird between us now?"

"Not unless you make it so," he says.

Chapter Two || The Architect

Manuel and I walk back into the museum, where the gift shop and the exhibits are the same thing. We sit on the rim of the cheap pool table and unload our backpacks. His laptop, his soda, his headphones. My watercolors, my water, my headphones. Here, a promotional pamphlet for the resort lays crumpled in one of the corner pockets[16]. In the corner of the large room stand two suits, the general manager and the food and beverage manager. They work diligently with some paper, rubber rollers, and about a hundred bottles of wine in front of them. They eye us intermittently, but allow us usage of the space. For all that we pay for employee housing, functional utilities aren't included.

"Who are you gonna call first?" I ask.

"Probably my parents," He says, and is speaking to them through the webcam a moment later. I decide to try to illustrate the managers working with the wine, but I've got to wade through awkward and repetitive eye contact first. Even if I didn't have headphones in, the blatancy of the subject of their conversation could not have been more obvious. With a special, copper handled tool they peel the label off of one bottle and toss it into the trash. The presence of recycling drop slots across the property and insistence of both managers and staff might give the impression that Maroon Mesa recycles, but as one of the fortunate souls who gets to take out the trash of our esteemed guests, I can assure you that the cutouts with the fancy plaques labeled 'recycling', 'compost', and 'landfill' all chute down to the same pesticide treated trash bags. The most common thing to find in this trash is food, usually barely touched. As you can imagine, Manuel and I's grocery bills here are quite low.

I look from painting to painting, the illustrated birds seeming to look adjacent to me. Asking. When I look back at the managers, they're drying the bottles and putting salvaged labels from the empty and more expensive bottles on them. This is common practice. They've only been caught once, when a visa worker accidentally relabelled a $10 bottle of pinot noir as a $240 bottle of chardonnay. The guest who ordered it was a NASCAR driver, here to celebrate a victory. Their grandmother came to celebrate, and that's who caught the slip up because of the color difference. Now, only managers are allowed to relabel the wine. Manuel ends his call and takes off one side of his headphones. After asking how the call went, I relay the NASCAR story. Over the past few weeks I have been taking every opportunity to educate him on the vast folklore, drama, and politics to help him keep afloat in this place.

"Wow, but not surprising to me," he says.

"When my old friend Monty used to work here, they left the alcohol locker open one night,"

"It is a whole locker?" Manuel asks. I lower my voice, he matches my tone.

"Mhm. Lots of cash, too. From all the cash sales."

"Like how much?"

"I don't know, maybe 10 duffel bags? We didn't count it. I don't want anything to do with that, it's probably blood money," I say.

"Blood money?"

"Yeah, like dishonestly gotten,"

"Is not that everything around here?" Manuel says, smiling.

"Pretty much. Anyway, one night they left it open so Monty and I took pictures of a bunch of bottles and pictures of the inventory sheets," I say, he looks over at the managers. "They don't write it down anymore but they used to keep a written record on paper of how they relabel and what the markups are," I say. "You know how a markup of like 60% or something is usually around normal at most restaurants?" He nods. "Guess how high their markup is here, on things that haven't been relabelled?"

"200%," he shrugs.

"Over 500%. We put it into a spreadsheet and everything." He takes a long inhale and looks at the birds on the wall. A few bottles clink in the background. He grabs a loose cue ball and bounces it off the felt near my leg, where it softly ricochets and drops into a hole.

"And you do not want justice for that?   39
You do not see this as an opportunity to set ━━━◖

things right, get a little bit of revenge?" he asks. I
swallow.

I shake my head. "Nobody wins when you're
playing for revenge."

"Then justice," he says firmly. We look at one
another for a moment. I nod.

"I'd lose my job,"

"You would never have to work again. You
hate this place anyway,"

"But I have the chance here to reach such a
rare audience. When I take people into the parks
I get to teach them, you know? For most of these
people, the time they're on vacation is the only
time they get to interact with the natural world. If
I lose this job, then I give that up and the cycle just
continues. They take their private jet home, buy
their fast food and their plastics, and don't teach
their kids that unless this all stops they're not going
to have children of their own," I say, and exhale
hard. Dust from the pool table becomes airborne.

"I apologize,"

"No, I'm sorry. I'm not upset with you."

"I know," he says, then sneezes. "but think
about all the people you could teach with that
money."

"I'm thinking about it."

"Okay," he says. "I'm going to call my sister."

I sketch the managers, finding the average
of their movements to express. They know that I'm
looking at them, but I don't think they grasp the
concept of art in the same way that we do.

Manuel speaks for a few minutes. I'm by no
means trying to eavesdrop, but I catch the word
'pintura', and he looks at me. I gesture at my
watercolor, and he smiles and nods, then

quickly looks away. I wash my brushes in my water
bottle and put them away, then give my girlfriend,
Wren, a call. She's been leading backpacking trips
with a highschool camp across the country, but just
wrapped up for the season and has been working
on art projects of her own. Manuel and I's calls end
around the same time, just as the general manager
walks up to us.

"Can I have what you made please?" she
says to me, holding out a hand with thick fingers.
She's three times older than both of us, with a thick
accent and a name that nobody here can pronounce.
Most of us would have bothered to learn how to say
it correctly if she didn't act like this all the time.
She smells like she just finished a paintball game
where the pellets were filled with pricey cologne,
but the starched and tailored suit says otherwise. If
a stray particle of dust landed on it, she could have
snapped her fingers and had one of her assistants
appear with a lint roller.

"You know that you are not allowed to take
pictures up here, I thought you were smart enough
to interpret that this wouldn't be okay either," she
says, pulling the still wet paper from my hand and
shoving it into her pocket. Evidence, I suppose.

"Well there's never anyone in here,"

"That doesn't mean you can just hang out
up here. This is the first and last time. Do you
understand?" she demands. Manuel and I grab our
things and leave, coughing from the nearly visible
cologne fumigation.

"Let's stop by the back office," I say, crossing
the lobby and into the destroyed back area. Loose
wires hang from the ceiling, the blanched
white walls each have test splotches of

wildly different and unmatching colors. It has been under constant remodel since before I arrived. Here, in the deepest bowels of the building, is where the architect's office lay.

 "Hey man, you busy?" I ask.

"Come on in my friend. Hey Manuel. Have a seat, you guys want some water?" He asks kindly.

"I'm good man, just had a question," I say.

"Is it about the light fixtures?" He says, putting his palms on the desk. "It's gonna be another few weeks, maybe more."

"Why, what happened?" Manuel asks.

"Nobody in Moab wants to work for us anymore, because the owner never pays them. We have resorted to finding another company from Grand Junction that will drive out here to do all the work. But we have that water leak in the owner's suite that they're fixing, and it takes them an hour to get here, an hour to drive back, and an hour for lunch so they're barely working a full day. I finally managed to repair our relationship with one of the contracting companies in Moab after I pulled some strings, even sent a muffin basket, but," He throws his hands in the air, "guess who never paid them?"

"Wow," Manuel says. "Sounds stressful,"

"And then I get blamed for everything," says the architect.

"Well I hope they gave you that raise that reflects the stress level" I say.

"That would happen in a world that values us," He smiles. "How is everything going? Did they fix that broken window in your apartment?"

"No, they said they'd come check it out again last week . Not a big deal though... I just wanted to ask you something about the lounge area upstairs,"

"Yeah, what is it?"

"Well…" I explain what just happened, which riles up the architect. " But, I actually wanted to ask you about the security up there, because we were dusting earlier and we were pretty afraid we were going to set off an alarm and call the sheriff or something,"

"The sheriff is still here from earlier," The architect says. "Over by the owner's suite. They won't tell us why,"

"Huh," we shrug.

"But I'm not surprised you didn't set anything off. I've been warning them that there's no protection measures up there, but if they listened to me about things like that it would be much more expensive to run this place," He takes a sip from a glass water bottle, with horizontal lines to mark the capacity and with encouraging messages, like 'almost there!'.

"Is there anything else aside from the security cameras though?"

"They're tied to the proximity sensor, to save on power costs they are turned off unless the sensor goes off. Like those security lights that everyone in the suburbs has." He rolls his eyes and huffs, then points at the bags under his eyes. "They bought the cheapest plan we could find and guess who keeps waking up in the middle of the night when the alarm goes off?"

"Dude," Manuel says. "That is annoying."

"Yeah. I wish they would hire a security guard. Checking alarms wasn't in my job description…but then again neither are half of the things I am in charge of."

"Why does it keep going off?" I question. "I heard an alarm the other night while I was walking, that's why I'm asking," I say, trying not to sound too eager.

"An alarm? You shouldn't have heard anything outside, its a silent alarm," The architect says, furrowing his brow. His cell phone buzzes on the desk, he silences it without breaking eye contact.

"Maybe it was a fire alarm that I heard," I shrug. He looks at me for a moment.

"Wouldn't be surprised," he says. "That system was due for repair 11 months ago, and so was the security system. I think there's something wrong with the sensor for the cameras, I'm near my wit's end with it. Every time it goes off it calls the sheriff's department, the night auditor, and my phone; and the stupid software glitches my phone until the police put in the passcode to unlock the unit. The problem is that we have mice up there, and dust, and who knows what else, so it's gone off four times this week already. I already wasn't getting enough sleep, but now..."

"Dang man, I'm sorry. That sounds super frustrating," I say. He nods.

"Did it go off just now, while we were up there?" Manuel asks.

"No," the architect shakes his head. "It turns on when the night auditor clocks in, turns off when they clock out. That way it isn't going off all the time."

"Hm," I breathe, maybe a little too loudly. "Well, we're gonna go make some pasta. Come by if you get off anytime soon,"

44   "Thank you. It was nice chatting. Sorry I'm so-" He shakes his palms next to his

temples. "You guys know how it is."

"That we do," Manuel says.

"See ya later," I shut the door and we walk outside, then casually bump fists.

Chapter Three || Irv the Indian

I wipe the sweat off of my face with a blackened rag and toss it next to the UTV$_1$. The engine croaks and sputters. With a flathead screwdriver, I scrape red mud off of the air intake and then hose down the dirt on the hood. The water from the hose leads with black, thick sludge for a moment before becoming a tannish clear and vaporizing into the only bit of humidity in the whole state.

"You know, we've got a massage in two hours. You should just refund this trip," the client says, with his skin tight t-shirt and shorts exposing him to more solar radiation than he can handle, but he won't know that until tomorrow. I'll probably find his Ray-Bans with his clothing in the trash after this tour, too, because he didn't listen to me or the waiver, and they'll end up dirty and scratched. He holds an iced sports drink in his hand and doesn't look at his wife.

"Birch," someone says from around the building. The front desk manager waves me around. He sweats in his three piece suit.

"What's up?" I ask, trying to scrape the slippery tractor joint lubricant from my palms while he speaks. I thought we'd have switched to the electric UTVs by now.

"The schedule says you're supposed to be on an Arches tour right now, is that right?" He holds out a tablet in front of me with one hand, shielding it from the sun with the other. I puff air out hard.

"Yeah, but they were 30 minutes late for the 5 hour tour, I told them they had to reschedule because I had a UTV tour I was about to leave in. The morning tour, you know? They arrived as we were leaving property."

"Buddy, you can't do that, that's a $5000 tour."

"I'm triple booked today. Nobody else could come in?"

"You're the only one on the schedule, everyone else is sick," he says, leaning back. "They just came in and yelled at me, then my manager yelled at me. We have to do better,"

"What, you just want me to pick? How am I supposed to decide who's tour to cancel? I can't be everywhere at once. Do you want me to just merge all the tours into one?"

"Just cancel the tour that is least expensive," he says. "This UTV is only $800. Drop it and get your act together and get those people to the National Park. They were waiting with their backpacks on. I told them to come back in 10."

"How am I supposed to know which tour is the most expensive when there's one number they're
48   quoted before they get here, one number we
━━━━ give the travel agents, a different number

on their portfolio, and a brand new number that their card gets charged for? And why is that my job? I'm a guide," I say, feeling the sweat bead up at my hairline. A family walks into view with vibrant, sleek backpacks slung over their shoulders. The manager looks at them, then back at me.

"Excuse me, I've got a tour that I paid for that is already 15 minutes behind schedule," the client says, arms crossed, brand new waterproof hiking boots planted firmly on the drive. The manager touches the radio piece in his ear, and says

"Okay. I need to get back inside. Cancel this tour," He points at the UTV. "I need you to unwind this web of overbookings today and cancel what you can't make. You've got another Arches after this one. Get on the computer in the reception office and call and cancel with the guests."

"I'll do my best," I say, hanging my head.

"That's all I'm asking for," he says. "And you understand that things are pulled tight? If you can't show up for me now..." He trails off. "I don't know that I can ask you back after this pay period," he says, and waits for a reply.

"I still need to take a lunch," I say. He hands me a 20% off coupon for the on-site restaurant from his suit pocket, then slaps me on the shoulder and walks back into the main building. The restaurant doesn't open until halfway through my second tour, and even with this coupon it will cost four hours of working to get the cheapest thing on the menu. I walk back to my UTV clients, who throw their hands in the air and demand an explanation.

"I'm working on it, sorry about that," I say. "I just need to check us out inside, I'll be back   49
in a couple of seconds. You can get in the ——◄

UTV and get all settled, alright? And we'll go out for an extra hour or two to make up for your time that I've wasted. Sound good?" I extend my hand. The patriarch shakes my hand. Cold and wet from the drink, but confident.

"Thanks, we knew you'd come through for us," he says.

"Be right back," I grab my backpack and jog inside the side entrance, where the array of offices sit among the properly designed but half built structure. Behind the first painted plywood wall, I hear the owner's voice berating the retail consultant about how the design of the storefront doesn't reflect the theme of Maroon Mesa, apparently it's 'not modern western enough'. A cup, presumably full of pencils, drops when the owner says if it isn't handled by the time they are back in September there will be serious repercussions.

The door to the next office over pops when it is opened. The swollen paint on the door releases and peels like onion skin in the heat. Balls of dust blowing on the floor as the harsh fluorescent light angles in. The industrial sized fans back here blot out the sound of the stressful video call happening adjacent to me. Large footprints in the dust lead me to the broken office chair, where one armrest dangles like a lure. I lean down to turn on the computer tower, but a dim blue light already ignites the recessed button. The sweat drips off of my brow when I lean over the keyboard, falling onto the 'D' key. This, among a few other keys, have been wiped clear of dust.

I sign onto our booking system, where I learn that I am actually quintuple booked for today and should currently be in five different places, none of which are my sleeping pad. The system denies me access to guest contact information, so I log out of the default account and try to switch to the admin login. I try the password that was given to me a month or so ago, when I was told to make a spreadsheet of employee contact information and emergency contacts. You know, normal things that you hire a park guide for. The passwords had all been changed. I try the password from a month ago one more time on the administrator account, but it fails. Though muffled, the electronic shouting from the adjacent office rattles the walls and my psyche. I stare at the keyboard for a moment, then tap one of the keys that had been cleaned from someone's fingerprint. Then, another. Incorrect password. I try a different combination. Incorrect password.

After a minute of failed passwords, I grab a scrap of paper from my pocket and a nearby pencil, and organize the letters to tackle this strategically. My job may depend on it. DETAINER? There can't be that many anagrams of this word. My own fingerprints and dripped sweat make the work harder than it would have been if I approached this a bit more carefully from the start. RETAINED. That makes a lot more sense, but is incorrect. Maybe this 'F' wasn't from me. I drum my fingers on the desk, the person from the office next to me walks into the hallway in tears and calls someone on a cellphone. "Hi mom," they sniff. "Yeah, everything is fine. I just wanted to hear your voice," We make eye contact. I give them a questioning thumbs up, which they mirror. I nod and shut the door to give them some privacy. The letters play on the page as a puzzle; some crossed out, others circled. ⬤

FINETRADE.

"FINETRADE?" I whisper to myself. The admin login opens up. The page freezes on a massive spreadsheet document with names of people I don't know. I try moving the mouse, but it skips around the screen erratically. Not enough processing power. I type on the keyboard and an error sound comes from the speaker. I try typing a few more times, and end up holding my finger on the space bar for a few seconds before giving up. I look at the guest list on the screen in front of me, which dates back a few years and seems to include far fewer guests than we host. It even has Catherine Beaker on here, that girl that went missing after a rafting trip through the ranch. I didn't know she rented a room here, though. Thank goodness she wasn't one of my clients.

The rates sure have changed, it looks like she paid over $30,000 for her stay. Maybe she was in a suite. I haven't seen it, but I've heard that some folks rent out a room for a few weeks and explore the area, or sometimes to shoot a movie. I've also heard that the whole place has been rented out before for 'music video' shoots and weddings.

The computer catches up with my inputs and rapidly accepts them, rocketing the screen all over the spreadsheet to red and green columns, hundreds of names, and finally settles on overwriting someone's name with dozens of spaces. I scratch my head and try to click the 'undo' button, but the screen freezes again from the size of the document. I hold down a few keys and force close the window, then open up our booking software to find those guest contacts.

"Hey, is this Ms. Clark?" I say.

"Speaking,"

"Hi there, my name is Birch, I'm calling from Maroon Mesa. How are you doing today?"

"Alright, thanks,"

"The reason for my call is that I'm scheduled to be your guide for a trip this evening, but-" the cheap door flies open with a flurry of knocks. The general manager stands there. My eyes water from the smell of her perfume.

"Ah, Birch. I need to see you in my office right now," she says, bracing her arms on the doorframe and filling the passage with her body.

"I'm in the middle of a phone call," I say.

"I don't care," she says, stepping forward and reaching for the phone handset. I grab the base of the landline and wheel backward.

"With a guest,"

"Uh, hello?" the phone says.

"Sure you are," She says, reaching for the phone again. I dodge her and shoot her a look.

"I'm gonna have to give you a call back Ms. Clark, I'm so sorry about that. Can I have a good number to reach you at?"

She reaches behind the desk, ripping the phone cord out of the wall. I slowly put the handset onto the receiver and hand it to her. She breathes heavily, putting her hands on her hips, looking at the computer screen. I blink.

"Everything alright?" I ask. Her head swivels to meet my gaze. She kneels to try to turn off the computer tower, but only succeeds in ejecting a CD from the disc tray, which spins on the floor loudly. She closes the tray and looks up at me.

"How do I turn this off?" she asks.

"The power button right there. It's

53

like a circle with a line on it," I say.

"I know what a power button is, I just didn't see it." She presses the button, then unplugs the computer from behind. "Let's go,"

We walk to her office upstairs through the museum and down two hallways. She opens the heavy wooden door to a room full of photos of horses. It smells like the mall.

"Have a seat," She says. "What you just did," she pauses, clasping her hands on the clean desktop.

"What you just did was against company policy and you should know better. I have the signed employee handbook that clearly states the boundaries."

I interrupt her, "I'd like to hear what happened, from your perspective. From mine, I was following direct instructions from a manager to get onto the computer and-"

"Save all of your questions for the end. I'm talking right now. First of all, you left a guest outside waiting for you for over an hour,"

"What?" I ask.

"I said I am talking right now. If you want to interrupt me while I'm speaking then you can see yourself out and pack up your things right now," she says. I sit back in the chair, clamping my tongue between my teeth. "You know better. You know not to leave guests waiting. And I find you back there on a personal phone call? I thought you were better than this. I thought you had a future here, a career, but someone who thinks they can browse the personal files of managers is," she pauses, "is simply not someone I want to be in charge of. I cannot have you walking around being that kind of liability. A liability to me, a liability to your peers."

She stops, looking for something to rearrange on the desk, but it is completely empty. She looks back at me, eyes open.

"If I could have a chance to explain that I was doing what I was told-" I begin.

"Oh, for Pete's sake. You're fired. I want you off property by," She looks at her watch, "by 8:00 PM tomorrow night. Get out of my office." I stand up, sling my bag over my shoulder, and leave without saying a word. I walk back out through the hallways and museum.

I take a second to myself, I slow my breathing, wiping a tear from my eye and the sweat from my brow. I slow down, making eye contact with one of the birds in a painting. The room is devoid of other people, as usual. I slide my hand behind the frame, pinching the canvas in the corner. The tension alarms are all disabled. The painting is small enough that it would mix with all the other things I'll be throwing in my car. I step backward, looking at everything in the room. If I could get these things to a fence, I'd never have to worry about my student loans again. I could eat organic. I could get sunglasses that aren't cracked.

I walk around the second floor until I get to the dining room, where a few guests eat.

"Birch, sorry, no employees, you know that," the host says to me.

"Don't worry about that," I say, walking past him and into the kitchen. "Manuel," I call. He looks up from the line and sees my face, then throws down a towel and jogs over to me.

"What's up, what is wrong?" He asks, putting his hands on my shoulders. We go inside the
walk-in cooler. I sit on a giant cheese

wheel.

"I got fired," I say, putting my head in my hands.

"Oh no, I am so so sorry," He says, his palm on my back.

"So stupid. I don't even want to talk about it," I say.

"We do not have to. Do you want me to make you lunch?" He asks.

"I think I'm just," I say, looking around the cooler. "I'm just going to have this for lunch," I say, throwing a bunch of avocados into my pack. He laughs. I take a breath, then exhale and puff out my cheeks. We look at each other for a moment in the pale light. "I'm in," I nod. He suppresses a smile.

"Maybe you should think about it more," He says. "Sometimes emotions can, you know,"

"I want to do it tonight. Then I'm out of here,"

"No, my friend, I am afraid that we need to plan more. We do not have a plan, I have people I need to call,"

"What about tomorrow?" I ask. He smiles, then breaks posture.

"Let's talk about it in a week, you call me. I want to make sure that you are ready for this. I need to know this is not a rushed action," He says.

"When I was younger, my older brother blew out my birthday candles and I got so mad at him that I threw the whole cake at him. And it fell in the dirt. And nobody got to eat the cake," He says, then picks up a few tomatoes, a bunch of bananas, and a cucumber and puts them in my bag. He gives me a
56   hug. "I just need to finish prepping for the next
━━━━ shift and I will be home. I will help you

pack, okay?”

"Okay," I nod, "Thank you". He pulls out his phone as we leave the cooler, I go back out to the UTV depot. My client stands through the open roll cage bars on top of his vehicle. He throws his arms wide.

"Is this place for real? Are you for real? You've been gone for over 20 minutes, man!" He shouts while people look.

"I'm so sorry," I plead. "Someone had a—a fit in one of the offices and I needed to deal with it. Everyone's okay now, but I couldn't give them the kind of help that they need," I say, tapping the medical cross on my bag. "I just got off the phone and an ambulance will be here any minute. I'm so sorry for the delay," I say.

"Oh, jeez. I hope everyone's okay," he says. "We can just reschedule,"

"No, no, please. You've been waiting so long and you paid for this, I'm gonna make sure you have a fun time, alright?" I say.

"Yeah, alright," he says, yielding. The family nods. I pull out my key ring and unlock the vending machine, a cloud of cold vapor spills out onto the ground. I grab them each two drinks, and one for myself before closing the machine and leaving my key in the lock. I give the patriarch the vehicle key and explain how to drive, check helmets and seatbelts, and tell him how to get to the trail the most environmentally friendly way.

"Wait, I thought we signed up for a guided tour," the matriarch says.

"You did, ma'am, and I'll be joining you in just a few minutes," I say, pointing to the other UTV.

"I've got it, honey. I've watched Westworld and I was a Boy Scout," the man says. "I'm...sure I can find my way. This isn't my first time in the backcountry," he assures.

"...Okay," she surrenders.

"You feel safe going alone?" I ask everyone. Thumbs up across the board. "Well, then I'll meet you back here when you're done. Just watch your fuel and your map," I say, handing him a new and glistening folded trail map. He rejects it with a wave.

"I'm sure we can manage," He says, holding up his phone with a GPS app open.

"Your signal is going to die as soon as you're off property," I say matter of factly.

"Nah, we've got a new plan that connects to the satellites rather than the cell towers,"

"Okay," I say. "Make certain you stay on trail, avoid the cryptobiotic soil, and keep it slow." I stealthily pass the map to their teenager in the backseat, who nods. "Alright, have fun, be safe," I say. The engine roars and they tear off of property, still audible for another minute as I walk the dirt drive back to start packing.

As I am walking towards the employee housing complex I hear the familiar screech of tires. I spin around to determine if I'm about to be jumped, but it's just Dallas, my loan officer, here again to collect money and make sure that I fully understand the predicament that I'm in. Of course, I already know the predicament I'm in. I owe money and I don't have the money. I try, unsuccessfully, to wave him off.

"Hey, Birch, I know you saw me," he

says, driving next to me and leaning out the window. My clothes hang loosely on me, the sun bursting through any UV rating. I can hear the AC blasting inside of his vehicle. "You can hop in and we can chat about it if you want,"

"No thanks," I say. I was sent to collections about a month ago for some of my student loans, and a loan I took out to get a dental crown put in a year ago. At the current interest rate, the amount I originally borrowed is thrice overshadowed. Even with the loan forgiveness program, not everything is covered.

"Come on, man, I hate driving out here as much as you hate seeing me," he says. Almost home, just a few hundred feet to go. I spin around and start walking the opposite direction, his tires skid on the gravel. He does a 5-point turn to avoid driving his washed sedan into the ditch. When he catches up to me again, I turn to face him while I walk.

"Then stop coming out here," I say. "I don't have the money, man, can't get blood from a stone,"

"That's your CR-V over there, right?" he asks. I try not to make any expression, and turn in the opposite direction again. He does another k-turn and catches up to me, accelerating then cutting me off. He jumps out of the car and runs around the front, squaring up to me. I lower my sunglasses.

"Listen, today is really not the day," I say.

"You just got off of work," he says, pushing me in the chest. I put my hands in the air, weary. "Where's all that cash going?"

"Uh—to food, maybe? Ever considered that a loaf of bread out here is $10?" I say. He's from Junction, maybe he doesn't get it.

"Listen, they want me to teach you a lesson this time, because clearly you didn't understand me the last three times,"

"Dallas, I know you're not that kind of guy," I say. "Just go home, tell them you couldn't find me," I walk around the car and continue to my cabin. He knows which one is mine, already.

"I can't do that, because I'm trying to build a career at this agency,"

"Seems like a respectable place to work," I say over my shoulder. He grabs my backpack and spins me around. I take a deep breath. Just a few more paces and I can lock the door behind me.

"Give me your tips," he says, holding out a hand. I flip my pocket inside-out, showing him some dryer lint, some pocket sand, and a cool rock, then fold it all back in.

"Didn't make any,"

"B.S.," he says.

"Here," I say, handing him the coupon I got earlier that day. He reads it and scoffs. "I get paid tomorrow, for real this time. Come back, meet me at my apartment at the same time. I'll write you a check." I don't even own a checkbook. "Go enjoy that coupon and I'll have your first full payment tomorrow. Okay?"

He considers it for a moment, his hair gel crystallizing in the dry heat.

"Fine. But if you don't have it tomorrow, I'm taking everything you own," he says, getting back into his car. I turn back and continue my walk home. I'm tired of him knocking on my window in the middle of the night, waiting for me after tours and 60   leaving notes under the door. Maybe the best part about getting fired is that he'll have no idea where to find me.

What a day.

I look forward to seeing Manuel later. I could really use a friend.

...

I brush a lizard out of the cargo space under the hatch back of my car, and place my second to last backpack in. A single, weak light walks onto the property, waving slightly in the still visible heat shimmer. The sun set an hour or so ago, but the caked soil and rock is still hot enough to fry an egg. The light looks like it pauses for a moment, then continues. I wonder about it for a moment. Near a good climbing wall or boulder area headlamps are common all night long, but the sort of people that stay here don't actually like being outside. They just get their pictures and leave. Manuel comes up behind me and tosses the last pack in.

"I sometimes do not understand you," he says, smiling.

"What do you mean?"

"I mean every single bag you have packed is a backpack," he laughs. "You only have two shoulders". I smile back at him.

"Are you ready?"

"Yeah," he says. As we walk further from the main property, the wavering light gets closer until we discern a set of figures holding a cellphone's flashlight onto the ground.

"Hey!" someone shouts sharply. "Mr. Guide." I stop moving and pull my headlamp out of my pocket in reflex to the aggression. My spotlight overpowers the phone light to the point that I'm not sure if theirs is even on. It is the group I sent out earlier. They're covered in red dust, their brand new pants ripped at the hem and their skin bright pink either from sun or sand. Other than that, they seem unharmed. One of the kids wears a messenger bag with a full water bottle in the pocket, the patriarch holds a cola in his hand and cellphone in the other. "Your fuel gauge needs to be adjusted," he says. I blink.

"I'll...make a note of it," I say. Manuel looks at me. "Where's the UTV?"

"Nice of you to ask," the matriarch spits. "We ran it to empty, but you failed to tell us that it isn't like a car. My truck can drive another 15, maybe even 20 miles once it's on empty. That piece of junk just died and we ran it into a rock."

"Is everyone okay?" I ask, aiming my light at their feet. They keep the cellphone light pointed at me, holding it quite squarely. Maybe they're recording for their disaster vacation blog.

"No thanks to you. We're going to be reporting this to your manager, I hope you know that," she says.

"No, please don't," I say, and notice her cradling something in her arms. I point, "Is that pottery?"

"Barely," she scoffs at the quality of the piece. "I don't think it's real. It's got those baby corns from the Chinese buffet, but they're all dried up."

"Where did you get it?"

"Some cave near where we crashed. We're getting dinner now," they start walking.

62   "Restaurant is closed," Manuel says.

"Of course it is," the patriarch shouts,

then launches his phone into the air with a grunt. It oscillates, the light blinking like a beacon as it arcs below the starry sky and cracks down on a rock somewhere in the darkness. The light blinks out.

"Stealing artifacts is a federal crime," I call.

"It isn't stealing if the person who owned it isn't alive anymore. Besides, you never warned us about it, you're supposed to be our guide," the woman says. I cross my arms.
"Even if the maker isn't alive, you're stealing heritage. I know that we covered that in your paperwork because I'm the one who wrote the document. We talked about it this morning, and you asked me how much 'wiggle room' there was in that policy. Remember?" I appeal.

"Well, that was for the guided tour. We went on our own," she says doggedly. I take a deep breath. Manuel and I start walking in our original direction. "If you report us," the woman calls after us, "I'll know it was you and I'll make sure your manager knows everything that happened."

I spin on my heels and say, "Yeah. They might even consider firing me,"

...

Reaching the water cistern only takes a few minutes of uphill hiking. The corrugated cylinder shack has been neglected since its construction, having been allowed to rust. The oxidized steel is a likeness of the sandstone in both appearance and chemistry.

"You remember Gwen?" I ask.

"Yeah," he says. "She used to come here to smoke with Mike." I toe a roach

and a handful of cigarette butts on the ground.
"Maybe she's been here recently. Maybe not. Mike's
been gone for, what?"

"A long time," he says. We keep trekking
up the access road, the resort getting smaller and
smaller behind us. It is a waxing gibbous tonight,
more than enough light to navigate by. We cross the
still warm La Sal Loop Road and slip between two
dunes. The bluish starlight turns some rocks purple
and others gray. I grab a piece of cow parsley and
tuck it into the corner of my mouth to suck on,
savoring the salt. Here, the cross road terminates
at the western base of Anasazi Mesa. At least, that's
what our official interpretation for the guests says.

On the USGS maps, this is either Parriott Mesa
or Zastrow Mesa, named for one of the first white
families to migrate down from the Great Salt Lake
and settle in Moab. What appears to be a social
trail diverts around the perimeter of the mesa, but
is blocked with a sign. The acrylic paint is faded
and sand blasted, but still reads 'TRAIL CLOSED- NO
TRESPASSING'. I run my finger along the grooves of
the paint, thinking of my old friend Monty, who held
the brush when we made this sign.

We continue around the western wrap of the
monolithic rock, to where it opens in a rectangular
recession too perfect to be geological in origin.
I've tried my best to determine if the owner of
the resort owns this mesa, too. The records are
incomplete, but I'm sure the answer lies somewhere
in some hidden vault.

Cylindrical holes the size of water bottles
reveal the nesting place for the dynamite that blew
  open this cave, but we aren't supposed to
explain that during the tour. No, these are

'rock quivers', where the natives supposedly kept their arrows. The collection of curved sticks leaning on the wall and purchased javelina furs on the floor tie the room together to be the hunting room, where the Ancestral Puebloans would decompress after a hunt. In reality, the mining equipment that was used to clear out this uranium prospect sits rusting a few hundred feet away in the sand.

We continue along and straddle over a pony wall that Beet, Monty, and I built out of wingate and entrada sandstone many seasons ago. We arrived after dark and built the wall as an act of overnight protest against the resort's tour route into this specific part of the desert. Instead of removing this destination from the roster as we had begged for, they paid off the newspaper in town to toss out our interviews and assigned this route to other resort guides instead of us. At the time, I thought we were lucky to not get fired for the incident.

Tucked behind a casket sized boulder is the opening to a small cave with a white metal sign bolted straight into the rock. It reads 'PROPERTY OF THE OWNER'. Obviously. We walk into the cave and I hit a switch on the wall, a switch that I previously refused to hit ever again. Electricity crackles and a single dim light bulb comes to life on the ceiling[20].

It illuminates a railing preventing us from walking further, and another sign that reads 'The Body of Irv the Indian'. A few paces beyond that, at the edge of the light, is indeed a body. Slumped against the wall, they wear deerskin clothing covering browned and mummified skin. We both grimace at the sight and look away. The walls are covered in modern carvings, swastikas, phalics, names and years. I find one from the owner, and another, and another. Each time they visit, they make sure to bring their friends up to the cave and make their mark. Ever since half of the guides refused to do this tour, very few folks make their way up here despite it being marked on the complimentary map.

"So much blind destruction," I mumble, looking at the scene with my hands on my hips.
"I do not understand how this can be legal," he says. "Or respectful,"
"I don't know that it is," I say, staring hard. My heart feels heavy. "We tried,"
"Uh huh."
"With the wall, and the trespassing sign. We tried to stop all this. But we failed," I say. "There were tire tracks leading all the way up here, running over the crypto. We really did try," I insist.
"That is what is important,"
"How do you know that it's enough? I'm released now, but all..." I gesture, "this is still happening. Still going to happen as long as people can make money off of it. I've had about enough of it," I say. Manuel nods, and helps me hop the railing and carry the body outside.
"It is very light,"
"It's plaster."
"Huh?"
"Plaster. Fake. Made it a few years ago because the owner wanted to impress their in-laws. They would have fired me if I hadn't. How do you think I did such a good job on the fake hand in the museum? This was my practice piece," I explain.
66   In the full light of the moon, the illusion is
━━━━━ broken.

"I can now tell it is a fake, but that does not make it any less frightening," Manuel says. Standing back and staring intently. I disrobe the plaster mummy and roll the deerskin up. I set it in a crevice to grab on our way back. I try to pry off the bolted signage with a rock, but the owner used bolts far stronger than the Forest Service's. I settle on breaking the lightbulb and bending the sign at the corners.

"Even though the body is fake, the granary in there and the pottery shards are real. People lived in there," I say, seething. I pull off my belt and use it to strap Irv to my back as we begin a more vertical ascent of the mesa. More than once, we have to hand the plaster body back and forth during a tricky chimney or exposed slope.

"Just go up," Manuel cheers me on. After an hour or so of sweat, we summit onto the flat top, 800 feet higher than the cave we began at. "How crazy is it that the cave is still right below us?"

"Pretty crazy," I say, keeping my distance from the edge. The junipers wave in a light breeze before the desert turns still again. We walk forward, toward the edge that faces the mighty Colorado River. Only a few crickets chirp up here. A bighorn sheep quietly moves from the sagebrush cover to a mound of yucca rising from a pedestal. Our heels are silent as we tread forward on the caprock to the furthest edge. We carefully sit down and swing out legs over the side. "I wonder how far a paper airplane would go if you dropped it from here?"

"Probably right into the owner's suite" Manuel replies. The angle of the mesa top allows us to see the main lodge and a few of the buildings for the resort, the yellow street lamps twinkle around the circular Maroon Mesa. This, too, was renamed once the owner's family purchased the deed to stolen land many decades ago. The rooms built into the side of the mesa are the luxury suites, a week's stay there would pay off all of my student loans. And, I have a lot of loans. The owner's suite rests on the side, partially built into another once inhabited cave that now hosts a kitchenette. Important to note is a sporadic separation of architectural styles based on the owner's moods at the time of conception. While the main lodge, restaurant, and museum are all reminiscent of cookie-cutter ski lodge construction, the guest suites boast modern pueblo stylings. Atop the mesa is one of the three gift shops on property, all reflective of helicopter-lifted imported granite to support the gothic style that the owner insisted on after a death in the family blessed the resort with fresh inheritance to spend on more buildings, but not enough to pay for the upkeep of the old ones. More on top is a swimming pool and a pay-to-view scope are also found. Nobody carries coins anymore, so it now accepts cards. (only metal ones). Beyond all this is the river, stifled by its frame but proud and true nonetheless. One shade brighter than the water is a class IV rapid at the edge of the resort's land. The whitewater is barely visible from this distance, revealed only by looking directly adjacent. During the recession, tourism decreased so poorly that the resort decided it was necessary to detonate a mining charge on top of the cliff, sending boulders down into the river and creating the Maroon Rapid System. We name children, paintings

68   we create, and pets. If you create something, do you always get to name it?

To our side, a lone cloud drifts over the city of Moab. Streetlights catch on the white surface, yellowing it in the deep navy sky. Further in the distance is Castleton Tower, where a collection of headlamps descend and head to the approach parking lot for the night. Further still are the La Sal mountains, where my soul is from. Headlights coast across the face of the snow capped mountains. Larger than the mesas in the low country, they are here by many orders of magnitude, but are many millions of years younger on the grand scale. Sharp peaked and smart, these mountains are still adolescent and chipper.

I used to dream that mesas like these were the clear cut stumps of some ancient and giant species of tree. I long to climb that tree in a multi-pitched way, to follow the path of the water through the veins in the bark, hollow spaces as big as stadiums and roots as big as subways.

"Okay, I think this is about as private as we're going to get unless you want to drive up to Peale tonight," I point at the mountain.

"I have been thinking about it all the way up here," Manuel says, untying his shoes and retying them. "I do not want your choice in this to be clouded. I need to know that this is really what you want and, please do not offend, you are angry right now," he looks at me and waits.

"Maybe I am," I nod my head, and look at Irv. "Irving is a Scottish name. Not indigenous to here."

"Perhaps Irv was named after a relative or friend of the owner?"

"I don't know. But I hear you," I say. "How about this, we can talk again about it in a week, but for now we make a plan?"

"That sounds good," Manuel says. We discuss options for what seems like hours, picking apart catch-22's in between shooting stars and dreaming about the differences we could make with the money. Dead ends work themselves out until we've got a solid plan laid out. "Let's go over it one more time?"

"The crew is seven people. You, me, Mike Hawk, Beet, Wren, Carson and Monty. In one week's time, pending I don't change my mind, you'll quit working at the resort and I'll pick you up at the corner. We'll visit the respective parties and ask them to go on a whitewater trip, where we'll ask them if they want in or not. For the actual heist,"

"Heist?"

"Like, stealing something valuable," I say.

"I know what the word means. Seems a little...dramatic, right?"

"I think it makes it seem more exciting. In any case, you and I gather the paintings and meet Mike at the river with a raft. We raft down and beach on river-right, then hustle up Salt Wash Canyon. At the top of the canyon, Wren is waiting with dirt bikes. We divvy up the paintings in poster tubes and go offroading through the back side of Arches, until we get off property at the Sunshine Wall. We keep going east, through Yellow Cat and the Poison Strip until we reach Cisco, where we trailer the bikes, get in a van, and drive to Clearwater to sell the paintings."

"That is right. The take is 18 million dollars," he says.

"Before expenses."

"Right."

"So if there's seven of us, we each get about 2.5 million," I grin.

"Before expenses," he smiles. We grab each other's wrists and pull to stand up. I pick up Irv and bring him to the edge of the cliff, a starry breeze catching my shirt.

"I hope that he blows right down to the resort and breaks the owner's window, so the next time they're on property it is full of ravens and dust and spiders," I declare.

"Maybe even some rain, too. The scare would be enough satisfaction for me."

"Ready?"

"Ready."

We launch the naked, plaster Irv off the cliff.

The updraft famous for carving this landscape causes him to spin wildly and blow off course. By squinting, we can just barely make out the body shattering distantly, silently, on the rocks below.

Chapter Four || Top of the List

We got our hiking shirts from the thrift store in town, and I saved the heavy green pants from that Halloween store in Grand Junction Colorado that I had visited a while back. The embroidered patches came from a local artist friend that I probably shouldn't name here. They didn't even charge me, because they considered our mission an act of community service and designated it as providing a measurable benefit to the guiding community as a whole. For us, it is exclusively for entertainment purposes. However, as we stand in the hot sun I can't help but wonder if we could use this scheme as part of the master plan. Any real ranger would be foiled immediately by our lack of equipment, our untrimmed jaws, or our general jovialness that seems to evaporate at once upon signing your soul away on a government employment contract. Perhaps the only factor that could break the illusion to the common crowd, though, is the fact that I'm wearing military—not NPS—boots, and

Manuel wears shiny black kitchen shoes. If it were Halloween, I'd have gone the extra mile to wear a pair of handcuffs on my hip and a nametag on my chest.

We may be breaking the law, but I sleep at night knowing that all of this is in good fun and is part of the way of life. I'd be hard pressed to admit it, but I really do believe that both parties, rangers and guides, that is, enjoy the give and take relationship. We put a log in the mouth of a rock to make it look like the silhouette of Yogi Bear to tourists. Rangers tramp up the cliffside to take it out of his mouth, but they don't launch the dried juniper branch down the cliff or into the river, they don't even break it in half so that we can't use it again. No, they just leave it on the ground just below where we placed it. We provide updates on the rockslides, the mudslides, the lighting and litter, and that guy who keeps playing saxophone for tips in the Windows Section. In return, they graciously construct and erect signage that helps make these things safer and prettier. Believe me when I tell you that I am no fan of signage or tickets, but I am also no fan of stepping on exposed human feces in the middle of the trail, with a nice toilet paper bow on top. We exist, two sides of a window, to keep this place and the people in it safe. A playful exchange of reciprocity on the busiest salt anticline in the world.

My friends and I had, on occasion, done many variations of the work that Manuel and I do now. Which involved a vast array of hijinks and pranks. Mostly harmless, occasionally profitable.

    Among my favorites was the sample testing booth, where we set up a pop up tent with walls and a desk inside hidden from view of the guests. Tourists then were selected by suspected income class, and the appropriateness of their outfits for the day. That is, those that appeared to be inordinately wealthy and wore brand new clothing would be selected for the operation. They would then be pulled aside and asked to put the contents of their daypack on the table outside of the pop up. On the grounds of 'prior incidents', food was pulled and sampled by my comrades and I inside of the tent, until we were satisfied that the snacks proved no threat to the park. I see now that all this serves me well as training for a mission I could never have guessed that I'd be partaking in.

The thing I hold used to be a CB radio, but is now doctored up to be a gross amalgamation that dips into all bands and is held together by drops of sodder and masking tape. A large man with sweeping hair approaches us.

"How is your day going, sir?" Manuel asks.

"Are you a student or something?" he says, sizing Manuel up.

"No, I don't even work here," Manuel says.

"Maybe you should consider going back to Mexico," he offers. I hardly notice my friend's accent anymore, but even I know that it certainly isn't Mexican.

"Maybe you should consider moving along," I say, raising my eyebrows and the radio.

"Whatever man, I just wanted to know where the bathroom is," he says, sweat filling in the folded wrinkles on his face and dripping down into his sparse chin hair. He holds an empty sports drink bottle in his hand.

75

"You mean, the one right there?" I

point at the restroom a few paces away.

"Is there another one?" he asks, giving a mucousy cough.

"No," I say. Indeed, the line is sizable and the sun is hot. I think for a moment. "At least not here. You can drive back down to the VC, there's plenty of bathrooms there," I look at my watch. "They've just cleaned them, too."

"Is that an arch?"

"No, the visitor's center," Manuel says.

"You know everything, huh?"

"Listen, we are done here," Manuel says, shooing the man away. He huffs and looks out at the expanse of loose sand.

"If you go off trail by even a millimeter I swear that I'm going to write you a ticket," I say confidently.

"How much is the ticket?" he asks. I'm reminded that when the only punishment for a crime or injustice is a fine, then the rich are granted immunity.

"$500."

"Please, I paid that just for the hotel room," the large man says, headed to wiggle his way over the split rail fence.

"Alright," I say, attempting to convey some air of authority, "$5,000." He stops to look back at me. "I misread the zero." Manuel laughs. The man glares at me and joins the growing line for the pit toilet. Someone else approaches us.

"Hello, sir," Manuel says.

"Hello there. How are you doing today?" he asks.

 "Very well, thank you. What can I help you with?"

"Well, my wife and I were over at the Windows section earlier and I couldn't help but wonder who the artist is for the North Window?"

"Sorry, what?" Manuel says.

"We were just wondering who the artist is," the man asks sincerely. Manuel looks at me.

"On the infographic?" I ask. The man tilts his head.

"Pardon?"

"The signs in the Windows?" I ask. "With the trail history and statistics on them, the artist of those?"

"No, of the North Window?"

"The arch itself?"

"Yes," he says. "We went on a bike tour this morning. Our guide Don told us that the creator designed them after the arches she saw while traveling in South Africa. Do you know who I'm talking about?" I look at him for a moment, then at Manuel who is attempting to suppress a smile. "Come in Arches repeater," I say into the radio. It crackles and buzzes.

"Go ahead,"

"I've got a guest here, he wants to know who designed the North Window?" The radio is silent for a few moments.

"...She goes by Entrada. She's pretty old now. You know the Slick Rock club? She's a member there. A Slick Rock Member," the radio says. The man gives us a thumbs up and a thank you. I lock eyes with the man from earlier, who quickly looks away.

"Thanks, we've also got some guy trying to relieve himself in the crypto again at Petrified Dunes. What's your position?"

"I'm at Devil's Garden. Who is this?"

the voice on the radio says. It's her, we hop in my car and drive away past the long line. I roll down the window and glare at the man who seems to be doing a little dance to keep it together. We drive for a moment down the congested two lane road, until traffic slows to a crawl. As a visitor, you might think that the cause of this sort of thing was something unpredictable. In reality, it is just a bunch of smartphones sticking out of windows and sunroofs. I think back to the time I saw a young woman riding one of those single wheeled electric skateboards up this road. I remember she was wearing hot pink workout clothing and I recall being worried about her burning her skin. She carried nothing but her cellphone in one hand, a park map in the other, and the weight of fifteen cars crawling behind her in the no passing zone. There's a bike lane here, Don's tours would be impossible without it, but I suppose that she figured skateboards ought not to go in that lane. It only delayed my tour by a few minutes before my partner, Wren, pulled the woman over. We discussed the story in the radar room at the VC with friends, laughs, and coffee. All told, the woman had been staying with her family in town and, after traveling here from Ohio, they learned far too late that a reservation is now required to enter the park. Rather than turning back, she concocted a plan not only to enter the park, but to do so for free. Including the price of the citation, it would have been cheaper to book a tour to enter the park.

  We park in a littered spot. I pull out my minister's parking pass that I got for taking a one hour course online and paying $30. Weddings, baptisms, and funerals.

  A red pile of bowling rocks rests at the

base of the cliffside. The textured rock provides ample grip for plateau lizards of all sizes, and a complicated yet accommodating cave system for their prey. Atop the tallest rock in the pile, a rust colored canyon wren bursts into beautiful song. During my most recent interpretive hike, a particularly misogynistic client of mine learned that the song of the canyon wren is akin to that of a mythological siren. That is, each call of the delicate little bird is a bid for the wood eating termites in the soil to come out and approach. They speak the same language, it seems. We also learned that canyon wrens have particular taste in interior design, and are not very compromising in that matter. As we gaze at the bird, I ponder what a canyon wren even considers to be an interior? Anything below the cliff line? A particular layer of rock, or maybe anything within shadow when the sun is high? Regardless, I educated this client on the methods of gentle recorrection attempted by the species. You see, according to the lesson, if someone installs a structure on an area that the creature would rather see undeveloped, then a siren's song is sure to follow that directs termites to consume it. It works in a matter of hours, overnight sometimes. The two species have disassembled entire automobiles in this manner. I've seen it with my own two eyes.

      Wrens in actuality have a knack for accenting the very best that these cliffs and canyons represent: music, freedom, and respect. If you ever hear their distinct call, make the time to pause and look around. Locate your nearest boulder or pile of rocks. In a few minutes, you are sure to see the little creature pop up to a peak and sing their little heart out, before jumping down and disappearing among the stones again. Their wings grant them the freedom to be anywhere from the burnt cliff sides to the trees, but more often than not they choose to be humble and low. Falling into this way is dictated by a kind of innate respect the bird has for its landscape; to fly too high would be to be swallowed by a soaring bird of prey, yet to be exposed for more than a moment at a time would meet the same fate on the sand. It is just in that moment of daunting excellence, then, that the canyon wren dares to expose themself to spread their hopeful message despite the threat.

We hop into the back seat of the air conditioned pickup truck which sports the logo of the park against glossy white. I greet Wren with a kiss on the cheek. She stares intensely toward the Devil's Garden trailhead through binoculars, then passes them around. At the other end is a small family trying desperately to open the bear-proof trash receptacles. Although the designs are updated each year, so are the printed graphic instructions on the face of the devices.

Around here, we like to say that there is considerable overlap between the dumbest tourist and our smartest bear. After a moment, the family gives up and places the crumpled remains of their lunch on the ground: reflective foil wrappers, empty plastic bottles, a park map that someone wiped their nose with, and a pile of napkins. By the time they are five paces away the wind has blown the debris across the parking lot.

"Hey,"

      "Hey,"

"Hey," she says. "Doing more research

on your Index?"

"No," I say.

"What's that?" Manuel asks.

"I haven't told you about the Standard Index of Camper Vans?" He shakes his head. "It's still in the early stages of development, but my hypothesis is that by counting the number of camper vans in this parking lot and Delicate Arch parking lot, we can plug it into a formula and determine, roughly, the number of visitors in the park at any given time. For example," I say, doing a quick count, "there are 14 camper vans in this lot right now. Let's say there's 16 in the other lot to make an even 30, we then multiply that by a number to figure out about how many people are in the park."

"What's the number you multiply by?"

"I'm not sure yet," I laugh. Another person works against the trash cans. "What's your count?"

"Six in the last," she looks at her watch, "30 minutes."

"Not bad. Anyway, we're not here to do research. We have a business proposition for you," I say, explaining the operation in limited detail. We sit back and wait while she mulls it over silently.

"I like the idea, I really do. But, I'm just not so sure that it is worth the risk. I get that we practically have insurance on the operation because we're actually returning the items, but it still seems like we would be taking them away from the current owner. I think, if we could redistribute the money, then it may be worth it."

"You are more than welcome to do whatever you want with your portion," Manuel says. She continues to look at the trash cans.

"You know, I only glued one of those ⊢────◖

doors shut. That isn't even the one that everyone's having a problem with," she says. "Tell you what, I'll come to the rafting trip, but not because I've decided to help with the operation. Mostly just for the free rafting trip."

"That's good enough for me," I say.

...

The trail here opens up, our side dropping steeply down to a sweeping view of the desert below. But the heat of the desert couldn't be further from us, as the cool mountain breezes carry the sweet fragrance of chokecherries to Manuel and I as we walk into the aspen forest.

"How do you know he will be here?" he asks.

"Because she's here. Every year," I say.

"Does she move down the mountain like the others you told about?"

"Only when the freeze comes. We've got plenty of time." A fresh spring juts out of a cracked rock. We refill our bottles and enjoy the sugar tasting water, soaking our caps and splashing the sunburn on our necks and faces. We continue walking on the late cretaceous intrusive center, one of the many peaks that burst abruptly from the desert in Southeastern Utah. Like the Henry and Abajo ranges, the La Sal mountains within which we walk are mere infants among the geologic greats. These laccoliths dome skyward and punch a stark green into the tan expanse, providing shelter and food in abundance for those willing to rough it through the sandstone below.

"I still haven't seen any salt," Manuel says.

"There's some, but not much. That's

where the name comes from, though. Did you know that?" I say.

"What do you mean?"

"When the Spanish explorers were here, they saw the white caps on the La Sals in the summer, and named them 'Sierra de la Sal' because they thought it was salt. Obviously, it had a name before that, though."

"Who was here?" he asks, ducking under a branch. The spring drains down the pathway, making silty mud cover the broken stones that line the way. The forest populates quickly with singing aspen and woody shrubs trying their best to close our way. Some of the branches are bent; he's come this way recently, even if the spring has washed away his large footsteps.

"A whole lot of people. The main thought is that indigenous peoples moved in about 14,000 years ago, but who's to say? I certainly wasn't there,"

"Yeah, but who?"

"Paleo peoples, then Archaic peoples, then we start to see a more solid record through evidence that was left behind by the Ancestral Puebloans. Most people still call them the Anasazi, you've heard about that, right?" I ask. I turn around to see him shaking his head. I thumb someone's name scarred onto an aspen, then gently wipe my palm along the trunk. The powder in the bark sticks to my sweaty face to act as more sunscreen. "Anasazi is actually a Navajo word," I continue walking, "it means Enemy Ancestor, if I remember correctly. It would be like if the English word for Peruvian was..." I trail off. "I can't really compare it to anything. But, we shouldn't use that word. It is racist to start with,"

"And it does not even make sense. Did the Navajo hate them?"

"I don't know, I don't think so. The etymology of the word is unrelated to who the Ancestral Puebloans were,"

"What is it?"

"Huh?"

"The etymology?"

"Oh, I'll do my best here but don't make fun of me. There's a few ways to spell the word, usually starts with A-N-A or A-N-I, sazi. In Diné, the Navajo language, 'Anaa'' means an organized conflict, a prolonged fight, a war. Meanwhile, 'Ana'i' means a whole lot of things, but mostly seems to translate to someone who isn't Navajo, and is an enemy. If we put these two together, it might mean something like 'a non-Navajo opponent'. I think. And, 'sázi' means something like 'parts of a whole'. From what I've been told, 'sázi' is also used to describe a point of decomposition beyond skeletal, kind of like when the parts of someone begin to once again become part of the earth."

"So, Irv is now 'sázi'?"

"I think so," I say, grinding my jaw and sweating. "From what I know, the word 'Anasazi' was created when the very white settlers hired the Navajo to excavate archeological sites all through the southwest."

"What were they looking for?"

"I think mostly things to sell. Artifacts and corpses. I hate to say it, but Irv was real. You know, before the plaster Irv," I say. We both shudder. "There are many other words that describe the same people. Some make more sense, some make less. There's no way to pin it down. You can't define an entire culture by one word."

"Trust me, I know," Manuel says. "And how did you learn all this?"

"The museum in town, asking around, reading a lot of books and plaques. . So, who's to say how accurate any of it is? The descendants of most of these folks are still around, but the obliteration of oral histories and reschooling have ensured that little tradition remains. I feel like it is my responsibility to discuss these things on tours, and it would be wholeheartedly irresponsible to discuss them in a way that wasn't true, even if I was just ignorant to the truth," I say. He nods as the trail opens up to a steep, rocky gully with a stream gushing through the base of it. Here, the mud is deep enough to see his footprints from dawn. We diverge from the tracks and follow the gully for a moment.

I claw my way up a muddy slope and drag down a saturated but hard log that works just fine as a bridge across the gap. We straddle it and soak our pants, moving inch by inch across the log. The rocky stream rushes two stories below us. In all but the most unfortunate resolutions, a fall from this height would kill us outright. Once across the gorge, we climb a mossy, hard-edged rock.

"There's a killsite up here, let me go first," I say, topping out and rolling onto a large angled rock. I glance around and find it safe enough to stop resting my hand on the bear spray in my hip belt. The carcass of a deer dangles from a pine, where it had been impaled through the ribs some months ago. "It's clear. Come on up."

"What the—"

"Mountain lion. Nature's

refrigerator,"

"Right," he says. We keep moving, ascending to our flanking position when I see him. It isn't easy, but I can pick out the pattern of his DSLR's camouflage anywhere. The scar on his temple twitches in the mosaic of dappled light from the quaking aspens. Manuel and I crouch down and wait for a few minutes. I check my watch, the sun is high.

The distinct call of a belted kingfisher rattling as she takes flight, cuts through the woods. His fancy camera fires like a machine gun, his body swivels in a perfect and practiced arc. The kingfisher hits the water, then flies back up to the branches where she traipses around before settling on a branch. The steel blue of her head contrasts gorgeously with the rust colored button on her belly, she becomes nearly motionless once again, a mirror of her shooter. I let out a quiet and distinct whistle. To any other hiker, it blends in like spinach in a smoothie. To Monty, it means more. He slowly stands up and looks around, then replicates the whistle. We giggle and hit him with it one more time before revealing ourselves.

"Hey guys! What're you doing up here?" he asks, hugging both of us.

"Looking for you," I say. "You're still up here,"

"Yeah, shooting for the Post now," Monty says. His tall and lean frame overshadows both Manuel and I.

"Congratulations," I say. "Does it pay better than the resort?"

"In both sanity and wallet. But, still not enough. You know how it is," he says, grabbing a backpack from the bushes and strapping it on. "Still trying to break free from the stock photo world."   We begin the hike out together. "Most people still pay to have their photos featured, not the other way around,"

The canopy above us opens into an intersection, where our hiking path meets a narrow dirt groove. Without more than a moment's warning, Monty and I pull Manuel through the intersection as a mountain biker zooms by. A cloud of green bottle flies following in hot pursuit, biting at my neck and chatting up my ears.

"That reminds me, did you get the pamphlet in the mail about the race?" I ask.

"The Whole Enchilada?" Monty replies. "It's this trail," he points for Manuel's benefit. "Starts up here, goes all the way to town. About as long as a marathon,"

"Thank you for explaining," Manuel says. We duck back into the woods on the other side.

"Yeah I got it, but they were looking for riders,"

"Right, but do you have any idea how much money you could make if you posted up and took shots of every rider, listed them on your site? Easy couple grand if you camp out for the whole race weekend," I say.

"I tried that last year, only made a few hundred. Barely covered my expenses for the event. The real money-" he stops and snaps a few photos of something I didn't catch, then continues "is if you can get a sponsored follow. Basically follow a single racer through checkpoints, and snap action shots of them going over the toughest obstacles while they sport their sponsor-branded gear,"

"So why not do that this year? Last time I saw you, you mentioned you had offers up the wazoo,"

"Well, Old Faithful is good for a lot," he pats his telephoto lens, "but she's not up for that task. A lens that will take photos good enough for that kind of cake will cost about as much as your car,"

"Got to spend money to make money," I say. "Besides, the only way to do a sponsor follow is by biking the Whole Enchilada by-path shortcuts to have enough time to get the shots of the racers."

"Maybe you could rent the lens? What's the problem with the by-path?" I ask.

"I'd need a mountain bike,"

"I'm sure we can pull one out of the river. Or, maybe you can borrow one from Don's shop."

"I can't ride a bike, man," Monty says. "You said you came up here to find me, was it just to tell me about the race?"

"No," I say, exchanging a glance with Manuel. "We...came into some work recently. We've got an open spot and we're putting together a team,"

"Oh, yeah? This already sounds like it'll get me arrested," Monty laughs, fiddling with a button on his camera.

"Simple transport job. We take some valuables from Moab to Clearwater. You've got family there, don't you?" I ask.

"Just some old friends. Nobody I'd drive out there to see. I'm guessing these, uh, valuables don't belong to either of you?"

"Not really," Manuel says. "But that is the best part. They belong to the client already. Even if we get stopped, we're perfectly safe in court."

"I've heard that before. No offense guys, but I don't think I'm really interested. I'm lucky to have a clean record after what happened with you, Birch. I'm surprised you're already sold on this. Did you forget that we almost became permanent roommates?"

"I didn't forget. That was for a good cause, just as this is."

"Oh, hey boys," someone says, emerging with a basket full of pastel blue Oregon grape. Her gray-blonde hair falls to her shoulders, and sun kissed wrinkles pop out against the green.

"Hey, fancy seeing you here," I say, and give her a hug. She smells like my grandmother.

"A whole mountain range and we just keep seeming to bump hips," Monty says, and holds his camera away as he gives her a one-handed hug.

"I don't believe we've met," she holds out a hand, which Manuel shakes.

"I'm Manuel,"

"I'm Mountain Rainshadow,"

"Is that your real name?"

"Is Manuel yours?"

"I think we'd better keep going, we've got to be in town for a thing tonight, it was nice running into you!" I say, continuing. The others follow.

"What's the take?" Monty asks.

"Over six figures," I say.

"Who was that?" Manuel asks.

"Moab local. Don't worry about her," I say.

"And who's the client?"

"They're-" I begin.

"Confidential," Manuel says stiffly. We glance back at him. "A curator has a connection with the original owner of the valuables, our job is to return them. Then, we get paid,"

"And where are the valuables now?" ⸺◄

89

"They've yet to be repossessed," I say.

"You said this was just a transport job," Monty says.

"I did. If you want more of a cut, you can help us with the acquisition, too. No pressure. Help with as little or as much as you want,"

"You said this was a noble cause? Who are we taking from?" Monty asks, then looks at me. I smirk. "No, seriously?"

"Yeah," I nod.

"Of course. Who else would it be?" he throws his arms in the air, his camera dangling from a chest rig.

"Look, I really want nothing to do with them now that I've quit. That was one of—if not the— best decision I've made as an adult. Before you give me the whole spiel, I know. I know they're terrible. I know that nobody who's worked there deserves what the resort and the owner have given them. But," he presses his hands together, "I do have to say that stealing is not the answer,"

"And I agree. That's why we're returning previously stolen items to their original owner," I say. He's quiet for a minute as we approach the stream. "Do you two mind holding on for a moment? I've got to grab something" I say. They nod, and I grab a length of rope from my bag and secure one end to a nearby scrub oak, whose bark is wet from the mist. I tie the rope around my waist and lower myself over the edge of the gully, down until my boots fill with water. I welcome the icy cold spring against my veins, step out of the rope harness, and walk upstream a few paces. Here, a large boulder crashed down the mountain long before any of us had even been thought of. The La Sals

are young at 25 million years, children among elders
in the sandstone expanse that surrounds the isolated
range. I smile at the thought that this boulder, as
young as it is, could be older than all of humanity.

When it fell it landed smack in the middle
of the gully, creating a slippery bridge above me
and shade below. It shattered the integrity of the
gully's origin along the stream bed, creating a small
crack that forces the liquid down into a waterfall.
Under the duress of the drop, a heavy mist rises and
reverberates with the sound of the impact off of the
chamber walls. This is a holy place of reverence and
prayer for me. I wish I had time to stay. At this time
of day, the crack in the ceiling casts a ray of sunlight
down onto the rocks in an arrow, pointing directly
onto where I work.

I think for a moment this must be a sort of
tattoo for him, for this out of place rock. Sometimes
planned for months or years, or sometimes a few
seconds on the town with friends, tattoos are
made permanent in such a short time by skilled
hands. What skilled hands, then, created this ink of
resplendent light?

I carefully move a few algae covered rocks
aside, taking great care, and reach into a dark, wet
hollow. After a moment, I feel our cache and pull
out a small glass bottle full of sepia liquid, then
slide that into the bottle pocket on my bag and
gently replace the rocks to their exact position. This
space is both fragile and alive, two things I do not
intend to change. I whisper a few words of hello and
thanks, and harness up, then begin climbing out.
I rest for a moment by hanging onto an old, rusty
bolt. An old timer at the bar in town told me
that there used to be a canyoneering route

up here, but this and a few rotting wet ropes are all that's left of it. Someone else's failed business, someone's prospect or child's college fund exhausted because someone sold the gig for cheaper, and as part of a chain hotel bundle package. Business is like that here.

At the top, Monty grabs my cold and soaked wrist, hoisting me over the precipice.

"Get what you needed?" he asks. I nod.

"This is your way out, you know," I mention. "It is for all of us. No more loans, no more scraping by, no more ramen for every meal. We'd be able to afford healthcare. We could pay for school, not just for ourselves, but for friends, family. To the owner, it's nothing. Just a drop in the endless green river. But for us...man, how would you like to never have to work for a place like UMTRA again? You're good with money, you could even start your own magazine with that kind of dough."

"What's UMTRA?" Manuel asks.

"Old government project in town. I think it's the Uranium Mining Tailing Reclamation Act, or something. Basically getting all the radioactive waste from the nuclear bomb testing sites, stuffing them on cargo trains, and burying them way out in the middle of nowhere. I used to work there," Monty says.

"Oh, is that the train in town that goes by Corona Arch, and Potash?" Manuel asks. We nod.

"I hear you, man, I just don't like thinking about the legal repercussions. I mean, this is serious trouble if we get caught."

"As we said, it is perfectly legal," Manuel says.

"It doesn't sit right with me. And Birch,

you know just as well as I do that even if something is perfectly legal the owner still has enough financial power and pull to punish us for the rest of our lives. Think of how many lives the resort has already ruined. Just drops in a pool," he says, looking down at the trail as we hike out. I pass him a folded piece of paper. He takes it and puts it in his pocket.

"Think about it. Last weekend in August, we're holding an interest meeting. Meet that Saturday morning at the put-in for Westwater. I'll pay for a site where you can leave your car. It'll be a single night trip, bring camping and water gear. We're leaving at dawn. If you're at least a little bit interested, please make the time to show up. We'll iron out the details and make a solid plan. Sound okay to you?"

"I'll think about it," Monty says, pursing his lips.

...

Manuel and I aren't in camouflage, but we may as well be. The full moon shines down on us, a spotlight as we creep through the tall grass above Zion Canyon. A dry bone cracks beneath Manuel's heel. The warm August air breathes across the plains, shaking and shimmering the flora in melodious swells. The blue light shines down on us like we are underwater.

There, a bison. Two, no, eight, no, twenty something of them. Sleeping, breathing. They smell like hot cows. We make our way to the watchtower, following the trails of trampled plants. There's more than a handful of reasons to be quiet here. For one, we've just spent the last two or so miles creeping quietly.

For two, the feller in the watchtower has got an AR-15 with a laser on it, and a trigger finger that's shaky from nicotine.

For three, I don't think either of us would enjoy getting gored by a 1,800 pound bull.

"So people will come to try and shoot these things?" Manuel asks.

"Something like that," I whisper back.

"And Mike Hawk shoots those people?" He asks. I nod. A few stars show themselves as we creep along a dried tractor rut. The misshapen tread marks silently give way under our weight. The faint glow of his cigarette gives away his orientation easily. As long as we stay low and still while he looks at us, the moving shadows from the wind on the grass will keep us hidden. The process is slow, but will be so worth it. His black pickup is parked at the base of the tower. The ladder isn't what I was hoping for. Old, rusty, sure to be creaky. We take a few steps back and arm the weapon: a wrist rocket. I place the dry tea bag into the sling, and pull tension on the rubber cord. A nod. Manuel lights the teabag, a snap! and the little orb of flame soars up to the watchtower and hits the man on the back of the neck.

"Ah!"

Stomping.

"Who's down there? Huh?"

A gun barrel aiming down at us, and a barrel-mounted 50,000 lumen tactical flashlight in our faces.

"What?"

    "Hey Mike," I say.

"Hi," Manuel says.

"What're you two doing here?" Mike asks. Someone huffs and stomps in the now oppressive darkness.

"Can we come up there?" I ask.

"Yeah, grab a beer though? You can have one if you want. They're in the passenger seat." At the top, I hand him the warm beer. He puts the cigarette in his mouth and hugs both of us. We smile and wrinkle our noses at the smoke. The teabag (chamomile sleepytime tea) lay flickering on the wooden floorboard. "How'd you find me?"

"There ain't more than a handful of guys doing this kind of work out here, we just looked for the one who seemed to be defending his second amendment rights," I say. He laughs. Really, we've spent the last day and a half driving these fields and looking for his truck.

"And you? I thought your visa was up?"

"No," Manuel says. "Not yet. Extension."

"Well, shoot. My shift isn't over till dawn, but we should grab some breakfast or something. Are you guys just passing through?" Mike asks.

"No," we say in unison, then lock eyes.

"How would you like to go rafting with us? Westwater, a one-nighter," I ask.

"I don't know, man, I've got work every night for the next two weeks,"

"Can you call out sick?" Manuel asks.

"No, I-"

"If you help us pull a job, we can get you two million dollars," I say. He puts the rifle down against the railing and crosses his arms.

"Is that a joke or something?"

"No," I say. "With the old climbing crew."

95

"What do you think?" Manuel asks.

"I...don't know what to say. I don't really even know what you're talking about, man."

"We can't say more. We can't even hang around for breakfast," I say. "If you're interested in making the money,"

"I am,"

"Then meet us on the last Saturday in August, at the Westwater boat launch. Dawn."

"Alright you weirdo," Mike says, puffing. "Are you two going to disappear back into the night? It might be smart to let me drive you back to your car,"

"That sounds good," I say, and we each drop down the ladder. I make sure to stomp out the teabag. "We're parked by Checkerboard Mesa,"

"You haven't even told me what kind of job this is," Mike says.

"I can't say too much."

"Then say what you can,"

"We're returning stolen property. Transport from Utah to Florida."

"What's the hitch? That's a lot of dough for a transport job. Is it radioactive or something?"

"Not as far as I know," I say, looking at Manuel.

"It is not radioactive," he says.

"Then why such a high price tag?"

"It's a profitable run, taking advantage of an opportunity that's been presented to us," I explain.

"I bet you can't guess who we're taking from,"

"Who?" Mike asks, tossing the beer into the backseat. I try to pull the door handle, but it is missing. In its place is a rag with a wire bent through it. Inside the cab of the truck are empty boxes of bulk cigarettes, spent bullet shells, and a pair of women's underwear.

"Guess," I say, Manuel and I shove in to share the seat.

"No way man," Mike says, lighting another cigarette and turning on the truck. His lightbar flickers, strobing out into the field. He reaches under the steering column, tosses a handgun into my lap, and sticks his arm into the bundle of loose wires until the light bar projects a steady beam of bluish light in front of the vehicle. We begin driving through the tall and invasive ripgut brome. Massive beasts peer from beyond the cast of the light, some curious and others fearful. Mike grabs the handgun back from my lap and stashes it back into its holster somewhere under the steering wheel. "The resort?"

"Bingo."

"Gotta say, I'm not sure if you're brave for trying to steal from the owner, or if you're just dumber than I thought."

"Come with us and you can find out," I say.

"Think about how many cigarettes that could buy," Manuel chimes in.

"That is a good point," Mike answers, pointing out the window. A rotting bison lay just off the road. "Poachers," he says. "Let's see, I smoke about a pack a day. $9 a pack, two million will set me up for..."

"Six months or so," Manuel chuckles.

"Yeah, that sounds about right," Mike says. "What's the product?"

"I'll tell you at Westwater," I say.

"Okay, okay."

"On a scale from one to ten, how

interested would you say you are?" I ask. He thinks for a moment. Manuel and I adjust in the small seat.

"Ten for making two million, eleven for stealing from the resort, twelve for getting the gang back together, and a big fat thirteen for getting to put the owner back in their place."

"That sounds good," I say.

"I'd say you can count on me being there. Need me to bring some beers, anything for the whitewater trip?"

"Totally up to you. I don't think anyone would complain. Just no glass," I say. He nods.

...

As with most of the year, the temperatures at the Glen Canyon Dam near Page, Arizona are torturous. A few years ago when I first moved out here, I recall a traffic cone had melted onto the asphalt during the summer. That same year, a friend had worn a pair of soccer shorts when she got into her car after a long day. A penny had fallen out of her pocket in the morning and lay on the seat, baking, while her car sat in the parking lot and heated like an oven. When she sat back down, the metal of the coin burned her thigh so deeply that the profile of Abraham Lincoln's head was visible for two whole days. She counted.

Heat does not seem to deter the tourists, travelers, and residents from recreating in the green waters of Lake Powell. Consequently, it also heightens ailments pertaining to heat stress. This was my domain when I worked on the lake; search and rescue, emergency runs of water, food, fuel and parts, emergency repairs,

and answering distress calls on my little company
pontoon boat. They called me a pilot, but the most I
ever piloted was a 90 foot houseboat. This was also
an integral part of my job, instructing the tourists
with minimal water experience on how to drive
the behemoths. After just my optional 40 minute
instruction, I was required to hand over the keys
and let the guests venture into the man-made lake.
The frequency of the formerly mentioned part of
my job often depended on the success of the latter
mentioned. These duties and more were shared by
my old friend Carson, who walks out to meet us near
the barbed wire fence. In filthy clothes, he asks
the guard to open the gate to let us onto the crest
of the massive structure. The armed guard scans
his government ID at a kiosk and waits a moment,
a doorway in the fence opens and we greet Carson
with handshakes. He is our age, but years of teenage
labor bagging charcoal and a love of fireworks seem
to have permanently darkened the skin around his
eyes. He is cheerful, as always.

"Sorry about the parking fiasco," he says.
"Things have been real cinched around here lately,
I'm sure you've heard,"

"No, what's going on?"

"The Goodmen? That terrorist group? Last
week we had some fool down in engineering say
that he was one of them, that they were planning
to plant some type of bomb at the base of the dam.
Should've kept his mouth shut. Now everyone is
on edge and is suspicious of each other. With the
security update, if they come in here and try to
do anything there has to be bloodshed. I just wish
people would think before they speak," he
says, taking a deep breath and fiddling

with something in his pocket.

Just then, our old friend Mike Hawk appears from behind a concrete pillbox that I guess must be filled with controls and levers beyond our comprehension. I go for a hug, which he halfway delivers with one free hand. His strong form is unyielding even when met with affection, it seems.

"Didn't think you'd make it," I say.

"Well, Carson and I had some catching up to do. Poachers tend only to come at night, anyway,"

"Where'd you park?" I ask. We walk over to the edge of the dam, where he points to his truck wedged below a loose mass of sandstone and onto a lapping bed of silt far below. Anyone who hasn't had experience in a vehicle with him would think to question how he wedged the clunky old thing where a truck has no earthly business being. Or—better yet—how he had climbed up the steep cliff without spilling his drink.

"Aren't you worried about your ride sinking into the silt?" I ask. It was a long drive for all of us, but I know that he's got to be back by dusk. He shakes his head.

"Drought is only going to get worse, water level is only gonna go down," he shrugs. "Besides, I got that eBay winch we put on it, remember?"

"Yeah, but I don't see any trees to anchor to," I laugh. He smiles and shrugs again.

"Maybe I'll just wait a few years and drive it out through the wash," he suggests, then looks at the nearest guard as if he had said something that went above all of our heads. Carson shoots him a look, and a small plane flies low overhead,   the sound of the exhaust reverberating noisily ━━━━ through the canyon all around us. A few of the guards follow it with their heads tilted until the glare disappears, revealing a logo on the side. Air tours. The brief moment of tension dissolves back into the mind-melting heat of afternoon. I feel like an ant underneath a magnifying glass.

"What happens if the dam breaks?" Manuel inquires.

"Here's to it," Mike says, raising a tallboy inside a crinkled paper bag. He takes a drink and laughs.

"It won't," Carson says, putting his hands in his pockets. "Not without some sort of explosive intervention."

"But if it did?"

"Catastrophe," he states, then thinks for a moment. "Forty more days and forty more nights of floods. It would send a wall of water downstream and decimate Lake Mead, the Hoover Dam, you name it. And, all the people that live there. Not a bad plan if your goal is to seize the power infrastructure of the southwest. Once they have the dam, they've got a few million people with nooses around their necks."

"All the water from Lake Powell?"

"Not all of it, but most I should think," Carson says. I glance out at the bright green, algae filled water. This dam never should have been built. If you need a superstructure to sustain your livelihood, maybe you should live somewhere else. "Lake Powell is like the cash you hide under your mattress, pull it out when you need it the most— during a drought."

"We've been in a drought for..?" I ask.

"Almost two decades now. About the time we graduated elementary school," Carson says.

"You know," I say to Manuel,

"over 10,000 archeological sites were lost when they flooded the canyon from building the dam." Manuel's eyes widen, he leans over the side and looks down the spillway. Here, stained concrete drops down to a slush of sediment and algae blooms. A large plume of water jets out and pours down, limiting our hearing. Carson produces a vape pen and touches it to his lips, a ribbon of scars cover his hand. He blows out the smoke away from us, where the wind dissipates it beyond recognition. I wipe sweat from my brow.

"So, what did you three want to talk about? You drove all the way out here,"

"We've got an idea that I think you might like," I begin. I share most of the details while he maintains eye contact and listens quietly, unreactive. He hits his pen again, passes it to Mike, then grins.

"That sounds like a great idea to me, and you know I could use the money. But, I'm afraid I'm needed too pressingly here. As far as I'm concerned, that attack is coming. They keep saying that they're going to do something big, this ought to be it," he gestures around. "I am quite flattered, though,"

"You're welcome, I suppose. You can always change your mind. Just show up to the rafting trip,"

"I'll consider it, but I really don't think I'll make it out there. Thank you for the offer, I'm glad you thought of me,"

"Of course," I say. "When we first thought of all this we made a list of all our friends that we thought would be solid business partners in this endeavor," I say.

 "It is a serious business," Manuel adds.

"No kidding," Carson says.

"You were near the top of the list. Mike, on the other hand, I wrote lightly in pencil on the inside back cover."
"You make jokes, but I know you need me," he says, as if trying to convince me of something I already believed. He rolls up the sleeves on his t-shirt and kisses his biceps.
"I do not think guns are allowed on property here," Manuel says in a low voice. We grin, Mike fixes his posture and casually fluffs out his shirt to obscure his waistband.
The crest of the dam is deserted except for us and a handful of armed guards peering through binoculars, smoking, and reading the same signs that I'm sure they've read a hundred times before. We lean against the parapet on the releasing side of the dam, and after a moment we think better of it and relocate to the more scenic reservoir side.
"You remember that porn shoot?" I ask Carson, who laughs.
          "I sure do,"
          I tell the story to Manuel. Some years ago when Carson and I were both broke college students working the lake for the summer, we had a greasy looking man appear for a reservation of our largest, most expensive houseboat. The boat had been driven from a different marina a few hours away on the lake by another friend of ours who emptied all the floating latrines, and occasionally delivered boats. The renter's clothing matched the bill— sweatpants and a kimono— and he held himself above us all. He did, however, manage to talk down to us long enough for me to go through the paperwork with him. As expected, he declined my tutorial on how to use the machine,

navigate the lake, and the best spots to see the landscape in its entirety. I quickly ran through emergency procedures with him while he directed a much too large crew to load filming equipment onto the boat. Then came the oiled up and tanned cast of whatever monstrosity he was about to film. Carson and I reiterated that he had nearly tripled the passenger capacity of the vessel, and should really consider not loading every bit of equipment onto the rear deck, but everyone had already started drinking and the man already had the keys in his hand. Saving our dignity, we walked away and warmed up the engine on the pilot boat.

The houseboat clad with EDM music and silicone took off out of the marina, narrowly missing several other vessels and managing to maneuver straight over a fuel canister someone else had left in the water that morning. The propellers on the large houseboat engines shredded the can, spewing mixed gasoline and red plastic shreds all over the surface of the water. We weren't worried, this was on par for the course as far as lake visitors go. We got some ice water and waited for a few moments in the rescue vessel, turning the radio volume up and glassing the fading houseboat with a scope. They soon disappeared down the canyon and out of view.

It wasn't more than a few minutes before the distress beacon came in. In the meantime, we had radioed the fuel crew who isolated the spill with float hoses. We clicked the throttle into place, the hot air that hovered above the dark water drying my eyes out with increasing speed. The pilot boat circled around today's fuel spill mitigation efforts.

  Past the breakwater point, Carson punched the throttle causing me to settle deeply into my seat. This was a favorite of his—testing the horsepower of our recent repairs—and it had gotten the better of me more than once. The first time he did it, I was eating a vanilla soft serve cone in the co-pilot seat. The force of the wind acceleration from his driving whipped the dessert right out of my cone and caused it to spatter all over the outboard motor, as if a lactose intolerant seagull had dropped a bomb after the Superbowl.

I prepped our expected emergency supplies while Carson veered around water skiers and paddle boarders. Twenty PFDs (Type II), four life rings, and a raft for fourteen passengers that could inflate in 30 seconds with a cylinder of compressed CO_2. This was the kind they used in airplanes for water landings, I knew this because Carson and I accidentally dropped the packed raft off of the dock when he had tripped over a two liter bottle of soda someone had forgotten in our path. One surprise vessel and a write-up later, we now know to be prudent with the rig. Nearly to the beacon, I prep our medical supplies and throw my mask on. After tightening my own rescue PFD and harness, I climbed up to the lookout deck with my binoculars in one hand and radio in the other. A spray of polluted water crashed against the bow and sprayed me.

Carson jumped a wake and dropped the engine into idle when we came upon them. Dozens of naked folks laughing and splashing in the water, surrounding the capsizing houseboat as if it were a centerpiece in their film. Judging by the drones in the air, I suppose that it could have been. I piped onto the megaphone and tried to direct
everyone to swim toward the pilot boat

and away from the sinking boat, but only a handful
listened. The remaining handful were trying to
wrestle a bare chested kayaker out of his vessel
by using their bodies to overwhelm his center of
gravity. With a shout he went under the water and
disappeared from view. We killed the propellers and
began to hoist the cast and crew onto our deck,
and get them set up with blankets, towels, and
warm water bottles. We hadn't warmed the bottles
ourselves, but cleverly discovered that we could
keep them warm by the simple action of leaving
them exposed to the sun on deck. The fact that most
of the victims were extremely fit and lightweight
was to our favor; all the better for hoisting and self
rescuing. To our extreme disadvantage was the fact
that everyone seemed to be covered in some sort of
oil which left a sheen on the water and forced us to
wait until they had life jackets on to grip in order
to lift them into the boat. Many apologies were
had and I tried not to look too closely at anyone, a
lawsuit was the last thing I needed while trying to
work to pay for finishing school.

The kayaker appeared again, on the sideways
houseboat. Much of the cast of the movie chased
him as he ascended. Speedos, bikinis, and a whole
lot of tan lines pursued playfully, swatting and
calling. He laughed until he reached the very top of
the boat, the last part available to stand on, on the
windshield. He beat his chest as the vessel lowered
into the depths, cheers filled the canyon. On one
particular chest beat, the windshield gave way
beneath his bare feet and he disappeared from view
again. A chorus of worried remarks. Someone quickly
106 pulled out a bluetooth speaker and began to
play Taps. But, he could not be defeated;

he rose once again to the front of the boat, naked now, and began to climb the bow pulpit. At the top, he balanced carefully on the silver railing, holding tightly to the vertical antenna. Cheers and jump! Jump! Jump!

The kayaker placed his tighty whiteys, skid mark and all, at the top of the antenna. He jumped in an attempt to do a backflip down the three story drop, but only succeeded in a half rotation and landed face first with a crack. Dazed, the fuel of the applause drove him to climb back into his kayak and disappear into a narrow passage through the canyon. I wouldn't see the kayaker for a few more years, until we serendipitously wound up working on a ranch together in Moab.

"Anyway, I still got the scar from the windshield," Mike says, twisting his calf to show Manuel. "Kayak was about full of blood by the time I beached. Good thing there aren't any sharks in the Colorado," he says. "Except you," he laughs, tapping Carson on the shoulder with his can. We spend a few minutes catching up and telling our host about the latest mishaps and firings.

"Seems like every time I talk to you, you've outlived another generation of employees. You ought to be general manager by now,"

"Nah," I say. "That's the position with the highest likelihood to get fired and sued by the owner. You want to last at the Mesa, you keep your head down, let the boss take credit for your work, and don't complain," I huff. "Thank God I'm free,"

"Cheers bro, I'll drink to that," Mike says, leaning far over the cement edge and pulling another beer can out from somewhere unknown. He pops the tab and drinks the foam. The pounding in my head reminds me of how thirsty I always am.

"Well, I should get back to it soon. You know, it's not like the electricity is gonna generate itself or anything," Carson says. "If you still need that dirt bike equipment, it's yours. I don't have a ton of spares or anything, so the fit might not be the greatest on account that I can't fit anybody but the three of you in person,"

"I'm sure it'll be fine, thank you," I say.

"And—it might be helpful if we could take your spare set, since you will not be joining," Manuel says.

"Of course. You remember the combo?" He asks. I nod. "Good. Give me a shout next time you're out this way. If all goes well, maybe we could, I don't know..." he chuckles. "Buy a houseboat and sink it?"

"Sure, man," I say, shaking his hand. "Really, thanks for your help. It was good to see you."

"Don't forget about me, okay?" he wags a finger.

"Like I said, top of the list,"

...

The yellow rolling hills of Kansas have always been attractive to me, though I can't say I'd ever want to live here. Manuel and I are parked underneath one of 600,000 wind generators in the state. The highway is a few miles south of us, and still audible over the swoop swoop swoop of the turbine. I remember reading about this particular piece of land, as it was one of the last in the state to be taken by eminent domain.

Now, like all of the Midwest save a handful of golf courses, McMansions, and metro areas, it grows a palette of genetically engineered wheat, corn, and soybeans. Even most of the native habitats of the west have been tamed with starched agriculture. The wild canyon edges of the Colorado and Snake Rivers are now populated by the cliff dwelling root specialists, harvested by remote control vertical combines. My parents were the first to stop eating the 'traditional' durum wheat and start eating these new varieties that can withstand the storms, drought, and soil-air toxicity that comes with the modern age.

The hood of my car is propped open, a haze coming off of the engine block. On it sits an open can of baked beans allegedly made by a robot that uses the company's secret family recipe that has been passed down from generation to generation, if such a thing is possible.

"Do you think in another 100 years we'll have to engineer another series of crops to adapt to whatever we've done to the atmosphere by then?" I ask. Manuel thinks for a moment, looking at a large dent at the base of the turbine. Tire tracks from long ago pattern on the rutted depression leading to the structure.

"I do not think we will be around to see much of anything in 100 years, except a climate war."

"That's one way to look at it," I poke, "but on the other hand, look at what we've done. We've prevented ourselves from dying out where our ancestors surely would have starved."

"You say that, but you fail to consider that if it were not for the resourcefulness and genetic engineering of our ancestors we would not

be here," Manuel concludes. I nod.
"Fair enough,"

...

After Kansas, the drive down to Florida did not take us long. When we first set out, I inquired about the possibility of meeting with the original owner of the paintings. I was told that such a thing would be impossible. Part of their agreement, apparently, is that Manuel is the exclusive point of contact. The result of this is guaranteed confidentiality and anonymity between the two. I thought for a moment that Manuel might have a concern that he might be cut out of the deal, but his good company quickly reassured my insecurity.

Beet Turnipseed's apartment is in a run-down section of town, characterized by broken bottles, unemptied public trash cans, and more people sleeping on the street than inside of the apartments. It smells like old ham and cigarettes.

We have trouble finding a spot to park the car, but succeed in parking it at a fast food joint and walking. Having known Beet for some years now, the idea that a person like him could live in an urban neighborhood is on par with the idea that a glass of ice water might be discovered on the surface of the sun. Amid the concrete clashing with storm drains, I have a hard time picturing him growing up here.

I run my hand down the squalid buzzer next to the front door, pressing every button. Manuel gives me a funny look, and I shrug.

"Someone's always expecting someone," I say. A click and the filthy door opens, but gets jammed. I give it a tug and a bit of metal falls from the crack and onto the ground. In the stairwell up to the apartment, I step over someone slumped down and in a deep dream. We pass half a dozen lightbulbs on our way up, but only one of them is on—and in a dull flicker. I knock on his door, shifting in my boots. The floor sticky with cigarette smoke and spilled soda, two yellow eviction notices stapled to the door.

A little boy with wet hair opens the door a crack, several chains and locks preventing it from opening further. He can't be older than 10, he smells like soap. I crouch down at eye level with him.

"Hey—uh, is Beet home?"

"No," he says, slamming the door in my face. I look back at Manuel, who laughs silently. I knock again, he appears again.

"Are you sure he's not home? I saw his car outside," I say. The boy blinks, looks behind him for a moment. I can hear someone in the apartment. He looks back at me and shakes his head.

"Sorry, he's not home," and slams the door. I knock again, harder this time. "Go away," someone shouts from inside. Behind us in another apartment, a dog starts barking and a lady yells.

"I'm a friend," I say, kicking the door. I put over $800 worth of gas on my credit card to get over here. I'm not leaving because some kid says he's not home.

"Maybe we have the wrong address?" Manuel suggests.

"The kid didn't say we've got the wrong house, just that he wasn't home," I say, then turn back toward the door. "Listen, kid, if you don't let us in to see Beet I'm gonna climb up the fire escape and let myself in,"

In response, two more locks click into place behind the door.

"Beet, it's Manuel and Birch," Manuel says, knocking gently. The dog behind us continues to bark. We stare at the floor for a moment, wondering what to do. Finally, the series of locks click again and the door cracks open.

My friend's face appears in the crack, with a twisted expression of surprise. He shuts the door, undoes the locks, and throws it open. Before I can say a word, I'm wrapped into a hug and trying to breathe through the suffocation of his hemp cardigan.

"He thought you were from the bank," Beet says radiantly. "Well, don't just stand there, come in!"

"Thanks," I say, passing him sideways and kneeling down to the kid again. "Sorry, buddy. I didn't mean to scare you," I say, sticking out my hand for a handshake. "No? How about a high five?"

The kid looks at me distrustfully and walks over to Beet's side. The door is shut and locked once again. Beet's hand ruffles his hair.

"This is Carlos, he doesn't talk much. Why don't you go brush your hair? Use the new brush I got you, please, not the old one," he says, and the boy sulks off to a different room and shuts a door. The apartment smells like vinegar and bleach, we clearly had interrupted them in the middle of a deep clean. Laundry sits on the ripped couch in a garbage bag, a pair of yellow cleaning gloves are tossed into the sink. "Both my parents and I are all working two
 jobs, not much room between that to keep the place in good shape. Please excuse the

mess,"

"No worries, man," I say, leaning on the back of the sofa. The apartment is dark, the only light from the cloudy day filtering in through the window. "Who's the kid?"

"He lives down the hall, parents perpetually out of town. They've been gone...maybe eight days now? His dad's a trucker, I dunno what his mom does. He wandered over a few months ago and asked for grocery money. Poor kid was eating straight sugar because it was the only thing in the house,"

"Damn," I say.

"Yeah," Beet says with a sigh. "So, we've been trying to look after him, at least until school picks up again,"

"That's kind of you," I say.

"I suppose. I had to drop two of my volunteering positions, not enough hours in the day," he says.

"I know how that is," I say. Because his parents would be home soon, he takes us through the apartment to his large bedroom. The hallway is covered in framed photographs of him and his siblings, smiling at weddings and graduations. In a corner, a small dresser holds an array of Halloween photos of the family in costume throughout the years. A decade ago, I wouldn't be able to pick my friend out from the crowd. Now, a life of organic farming has cultivated him into his tall and muscular frame. Just like when I met him farming in Utah, he keeps his dark red hair short to fight the heat. Since the last time Manuel and I have seen him, his muted auburn beard has grown into immense swirls and length below his collarbone.

The illusion of my friend's residence ⟶◀

113

is broken when he welcomes us into his room, full of oils, flags, crafts, and wood. Now, only his bed looks out of place. I remember him telling me the story over the phone, about how he had snagged it from a nursing home that he was volunteering at. The hydraulics in the medical bed had finally failed after three decades of service, leaving the bed no longer adjustable. It turns out that being able to control the angle of the bed is occasionally vital to the recovery and stability of the elderly. For Beet, the bed was a major victory. Years of overwork at the resort had caused permanent swelling and nerve damage in his lower back. The abnormal swelling ensured that surgery could never be an option. To even attempt it may leave him paralyzed and out a few hundred thousand dollars, whether it healed his back or not. With a varying combination of orthopedic foam pads and braces, this bed allowed him to sleep for a few hours each night before waking up from the pain. He told me that his father occasionally helps him adjust the position of the bed manually, depending on the intensity of his condition, and what his work demands. I know he's tried his hand at office jobs, but the sedentary nature actually aggravates his condition.

On the floor next to the bed are crates of supplement bottles. I think most of them must be empty when I see the set of matching weekly pill organizers overflowing to the point that the compartments are prevented from closing. He invites us to sit on the floor pillows, I recall the stress of his last week at the resort.

Although his injury plagued him for a few weeks after it happened, he continued to work his hardest. I am unsure of exactly what happened, mostly because he refused to tell me the exact details. I do know a few things. I know that he kept up his work as best he could, but was called into a meeting with supervisors that had no hands in the soil. There, rather than lying, Beet explained that he was keeping pace the best he could, and trying to work through the pain because he did not want to let the team down. He held weight of all the greenery of the resort on his shoulders. Without him, the ornamental window boxes, the isolated plots of annuals, and the suffering flowers (the owner's favorite varieties) would wither and die. I was there the season prior when he advocated for planting organics, for planting resilient species that would survive without intensive labor in the harsh desert. Despite the fact that he lobbied for these changes even before his injury, he was shut down and told that there were no funds available to make these changes. He tried to explain that in the long run, these transitions would actually save the owner money, but was given his second written warning. A week after his proposal, the owner abandoned another Cadillac on property and exchanged it for the newest model. Beet was given instructions to drive it to the pit and bury it under the sand, just like last year's.

    At the meeting about his injury, he was told that his pace was unacceptable, but that is not why he was being terminated. The critical mistake he had made was failing to report a work injury, even if it was caused by incremental fatigue. The fact that he was not granted time off to see a doctor made no play. In the following weeks he fought, unvictorious, for unemployment. In his newly found time 115 off, he finally made it out to get his

injury evaluated and learned about his options, or
lack thereof. He was given a small variety of pain
relieving prescriptions, but without insurance he
would have to triple the income he was making at
the resort. These factors contributed to the making
of an angry man, homeless, in pain, and cooking
in the desert heat. Those days were long, where
we hiked out to bring water and food to Beet in
the wind caves. They asked us, but we refused the
supervisor's commands to water his plants. Instead,
all of us at the resort watched them wither as
steadily as Turnipseed's resolve.

It wasn't long before the heat got to him. It
never is. A month later, he did something that he
will regret for the rest of his life.

What was left was a husk of a man, broken
spiritually and physically. He said goodbye and left
on a bus with the few things the managers let him
take from his employee cabin. He went home to live
with his parents—what else is there to do?
The laundry bin on the floor is full of
t-shirts from the various organizations he's done
work at, when he can find the time between jobs.
Supplements and physical therapy and calisthenics
and yoga are a lot less expensive than unsubsidized
pharmaceuticals, but still not free. Light from an
essential oil diffuser shines off of his glossy beard.
I think, maybe, that the physical growth I see on
this man may reflect a cosmic growth within him.
I didn't want to drag him down into all of this. I
really didn't. For me, this operation comes with a
 guaranteed conclusion. Most of me thinks that
it could deliver the same to him. Although

he has grown and is many marks stronger than I have ever known him to be, the hurt still lingers behind his eyes. Do they have yoga classes that can guide you to release regret?

Despite all this, I see in his face that even in his youth he understands more than most will in an entire lifetime.

I explain the idea, and what it could bring for him. The money, the medication he could finally afford.

"I'm in," he declares, hands on his knees. "No need to say more, but can I still come on the free rafting trip?"

It feels like giving a cigarette to Mike. Like I might be helping a cancer grow. But maybe this could be his chemo. At least, I know that telling myself this story will allow me to sleep for some of tonight.

The nightmares will still come.

For all of us, I'm sure of it.

We're all veterans in the war against the resort.

Chapter Five || Westwater

Manuel and I sit on my ugly 14 foot raft at a camp spot next to the put-in for this section of river. He bounces on the springy thwart, rocking it back and forth on the gravel$_9$. I go through our supplies for a third time and reread our checklist. I draw a sketch of the trickiest rapid we'll face today, where 90% of our search-and-rescues take place. Then, I recheck the lines we will take on the map. Wren returns from the bathroom and rests under a tree, reading. I check my watch again, the ranger looks on from the netted porch.

"They've only got another hour to get here," I say.

"I still don't see why they will not let us launch after noon,"

"Lots of folks get stuck out here, a night rescue is much more challenging than a day rescue," I say, and toe at a piece of broken glass someone considerately left for the next camper.

A cloud of dust drifts into the sky

from the roadway, approaching. A few seconds later, Mike's truck barrels into the entrance and sends a plastic trash can whirling and rolling through the air. He honks, then pulls into the spot. Manuel points at the kayak on the roof of the truck. I nod.

Unexpectedly, a ragged backpack opens the passenger door and hits the dirt with a puff. Beet's ginger hair shines in the sun before he puts on his wide brimmed hat, decorated with constellations in silver and gold fabric paint. He tips it to us.

"Look who I found jogging through the sticks," Mike says, launching a huge case of beer into the raft. The weight of the impact ejects Manuel, who flops gracefully onto his hands and knees on the rocks. "Sorry, thought you were heavier than that," he says. We exchange greetings and load their gear.

"How far did you come? I figured you weren't interested anymore," I ask Beet while he pulls out a camp stove and heats some river water a few minutes later.

"I landed in Junction. You know the flight to Canyonlands was almost double the price? Mike and I linked up last night. Just another lucky hitchhiking day,"

"I don't know about all that luck stuff. Maybe it's all the volunteering you've been doing. Some good karma coming back around to you,"

"I need all I can get," he says sullenly, looking down to cover his face with the brim of his hat.

"Hey," I say softly, tapping his hat lightly with my finger. "You're not that man anymore," I state. "We all know that," I pick at my cuticles while I
120 crouch next to him. He doesn't reply. "Okay?"
━━━━━ I ask. "Listen, if this doesn't feel good

to you, please don't come. We've all got our own weights, but I don't need you carrying more than you can handle."

"That's the thing. I'm here because of the weight," he explains. He pours in the kratom powder into his warm drink and takes a sip, then pulls his knees close to his chest. I sit back and wait for him to explain. On the edge of my vision, Wren and Mike bounce a ball off of the raft to one another, Manuel sits in the shade of the passenger seat and reads something from the glove box, probably the user manual. He once explained that to get to know a new language, breaking down lyrics and user manuals were among the fastest methods.

"Can you say more?" I ask. A recently washed station wagon rolls quietly in and parks next to Mike's truck. Monty pops out and shoots a set of finger guns at me. "Let's pick this up later, alright? But I'm serious, I don't want you to come if you think it might make you lose progress on...whatever you're working toward," I say, standing up and shaking my leg.

"Enlightenment, my friend," he says, raising his metal mug. I clink my water bottle against it and take a swig. I palm the top of his head and greet Monty, who had apparently been driving from Moab with sunscreen already liberally applied on his face. The thumping of musical bass notes permeates the otherwise pleasant air.

"You got a little something," I say, tapping my nose.

"Don't worry, I brought enough for everyone," he says, swinging a backpack on. "Just finished working on a distribution map of skin cancer rates in the continental US. Guess what city is number 1?"

"Las Vegas?" Manuel shouts from the truck.

"No, nobody actually spends time outside in Vegas. Mow-Hab, baby. Capital of skin cancer and fainting tourists," he high-fives me. "You look surprised to see me,"

"He does wear his heart on his sleeve," Wren says, double checking the security and ice levels in our water GOT. The source of the bass notes are revealed; a group of folks wearing tank tops and with haircuts that look like mops round a corner. They carry inflated department store tubes with designs that look like frosted donuts.

"No, no, I didn't travel this far to listen to this," Mike says, shaking his head and standing up.

He brushes his cargo shorts and walks over to them calmly. I wonder at first if they might be having a conversation, but then I reckon that such a thing would be impossible over the sound of the music. Mike holds out his hands, and one of them places the medium sized bluetooth speaker in it. Calmly, Mike walks back toward the waterfront and places his legs shoulder-width apart. He cocks his arm and launches the speaker through the air like a spiraling football. It arcs gracefully and disappears with a white ripple. I glance, the ranger has seen. When she catches me looking at her, she walks further back out of sight. Saved her some trouble, I suppose.

"Nobody wants to hear your crappy music, just use headphones if you can't be away from your phone for more than an hour," Mike says. One of them drops their jaw in protest, but is pulled away 122 by another. They walk back through the parking lot.

We spend the next few minutes rigging without commentary.

"Thanks for taking a chance," I say. He nods and gives me a half smile. He crosses his arms and looks in the trees.

"You pulled me out of trouble before, I figured why not get into some more?" Monty smiles, then nods. "But, really, I thought about what you said, and I know that we can do some good with this. I just have doubts about whether or not we can pull it off,"

"I hear you. Let's load up and talk on the water," I say. The ranger comes over and double checks our permit, identification, and equipment. I suppose that, to her, all this talk seems to directly relate to our river trip.

"Have fun, y'all," she says with a wave and heads back into the air conditioned barrack.
"I think she was at the potluck last week," Wren says, then hands out the cheap life jackets that I've fished from the water over the years. Stitched together with love, these jackets still bear the scars of sun bleached nylon and bird feces. Most of us have our own, except Beet and Manuel. After a moment of consideration, Mike trades his personal PFD for one of mine on account of the pad designed to keep your head out of the water should you be knocked unconscious. Beet rips a fishing hook out of his vest and tosses it into the trash. While we tighten and check one another's PFDs, I step in front of everyone.

"Alright, thank you for coming everyone. I really do appreciate you taking a chance on this operation. I know you came all this way so I would hate to disappoint you with some news I could have given over the phone, but I really preferred to ask this in person," I say, checking over my shoulder to make sure the ranger remains inside. "First of all, no phones allowed on the trip due to the nature of our conversations and Mike's potty mouth. Second, no phones will be allowed on the operation itself," I say, opening a dry bag. "You can put your phones in here and I'll leave them locked in my car until we return from the trip. At that point, you'll get them back. If you choose to come for the main event, then you'll have to leave your cell phone somewhere safe on your own dime. This spot is paid for for the next two days, you're welcome to leave your cars here. If the cellphone thing is a dealbreaker for anyone, there's plenty of food and camping stuff in my car to last you until we're done with the river trip. You can wait here until we get back, no hard feelings." The gang swipes off their phones and places them into the bag. I lock it in my vehicle. I check over my shoulder once again, and lower my voice. With a gesture, everyone steps into a close huddle. The smells of sweat, sunscreen, and bug spray snap me to alertness. "I'm going to explain a bit about the operation, but I'm going to keep it vague. We're taking an asset from someone in Moab who stole it from our client a few decades ago. We're then going to transport it to Clearwater, Florida in a car," I explain, looking from face to face. The group sways, I feel the kind of gym-class closeness you feel from gripping a friend's back in this way.

"We're listening," Beet says.

"I'll be honest. The person who has the asset

now has great financial and political power in the Four Corners. If we are identified before we can deliver the asset, we will likely face prosecution. In such a case, I've been informed that our client will do their best to protect us and our innocence. This is a gray area in the law, and with that being said I'll tell you that there are no guarantees," I say. Wren nods, so do a few others. "We're going to take a stealth-based approach to this. If all goes well, the client will not know that the asset is missing."

"Until we deliver it?" Monty asks.

"Maybe ever," I say, and feel the impression of these words on the group. A bead of sweat falls from my brow.

"Does everyone know who we're stealing from?" Mike asks. "Can we just say it?"

"The owner," Manuel says. A few nods, Mike looks at Wren in a silent I-told-you-so.

"Just to get this straight, the plan is to steal an 18 million dollar asset from the owner of the Maroon Mesa?" Wren asks.

"Where Sandstone Meets Serenity?" Mike laughs.

"Nah, Where Your Vacation Meets Our Indignation," Monty says, poking a laugh out of everyone, even Beet. A moment of settling.

"Yes, that's the plan," I admit. "Now is your chance to walk away," I say, moving back to break up the huddle, but Monty pulls me back in. He pulls a slip of paper from his pocket.

"How much is that each? 2.5 million?" he asks, showing me the paper I wrote him earlier.

"It is actually more now," Manuel says, nodding seriously. Mike tilts his head.

"Carson backed out," I say.

"He did not back out, he just was

not interested," Manuel corrects me.

"That's right," I say. "Upon delivery, the client is prepared to pay us the actual value of the asset, 18 million. Divided between us is about three million dollars."

"Phew," Mike says. "Now I can buy a lifetime of cigarettes instead of just a life sentence worth of cigarettes,"

"Isn't that a little bit counter-intuitive? A lifetime of cigarettes?" Wren asks. Mike shrugs.

"Right, so," Beet edges.

"We will have some expenses for the operation, which I'll reveal later, so we'll need to split those evenly. The client has an accountant willing to help us with that matter, so we've set aside $50,000 to cover costs. Anything leftover from that will be reimbursed evenly," I say. Everyone nods.

"Any questions?" I ask.

"Who's the client?" Monty inquires.

"Can't answer that. Anything else? No?" I say. "If anyone wants to back out, this is your last chance. Otherwise, you are bound by one another to see this through. And, that's the only way we're going to pull this off. Together," I say. We all look from eye to eye. Monty makes a move, but ends up just stretching his ankle. He grimaces, I think, at more than the stretch. Wren puts her hand in the middle, each of us covering it.

"Trickle-down economy in three?" Monty asks.

"Two,"

"One,"

And we shout, pass high fives and toss the last of the gear into the raft. We grab the lines together and walk down the boat ramp, gently setting down my vessel into the river. The late-summer sun has boiled the water to turn it lukewarm and slower than I would like, but lovely nonetheless. Monty, being the tallest of us all, walks us out practically a third of the way into the channel before it is too deep for him and he muscle-ups his way into the raft.

...

  We beach for a moment on river right, where a magnificent sandstone wall curves with the river. It has got to be at least ten stories tall, with an outward curve that gives the impression of a petrified tsunami. We tromp over the loose rocks until we reach the wall, warm from another day of sun. The desert varnish here shines black against the red rock. Depending on what decade the guidebook you're reading was written in, you're likely to get a different explanation as to why it is there. But, nobody doubts its critical role in helping to preserve rock images carved by the first humans in this region. We first believed that some process involving exposure to the sun in a low moisture environment caused substances within the canyon walls to leach out, but now we know better. Getting its dark color from manganese, clay blown by wind adheres to the walls with help of the daily dew. Acting as a sort of glue, iron oxide joins the party with some silica. Often in the recessed cracks of massive walls such as these, we can find hanging gardens that provide eye-popping green in the otherwise drab colored landscape. Rainwater seeping through the sandstone helps to keep these plants fed, and their life helps contribute some of the organic matter that helps the desert patina dream become a reality.

We take turns, one by one, silently kissing the Good Luck Wall. My kiss isn't for good fortune on the rapid run; we are a skilled team with good muscle and know-how among us. Instead, I give a quiet prayer for our mission. My hands on the baking wall, I wish for safe passage and a few other things. Mostly, I wish for justice and I hope that our actions leave a mark. When I think that perhaps I've asked for too much, I step away and let Beet have his turn. He takes longer than anyone else, and presses his forehead on the rock. His expression combined with the tone of his whispers directs the rest of us to quietly retreat back to the water and leave him to pray in solitude.

The rapids grow in intensity and flavor as we continue down stream, to the confluence of the Little Dolores River. If everyone had arrived earlier, we could have beached and had lunch at the Dolores Waterfall, which is just a short hike away. Instead, we decide as a group to wait until after we exit Westwater Canyon for our sandwiches, chips, and kombucha. If you've been through the canyon as many times as I have, the hole in the first Class III rapid can be sailed directly around. Given his tardiness, peer pressure and a bit of chanting brings Monty to sit at the bow to 'ride the bull'. He holds on with just one hand, his long legs up in the air as we rotate and nearly get sucked into the hole, but spin backward and bump our way out without serious incident.

And just like that, we've reached the basement layer of rocks in this region. The Vishnu Schist, only visible in three parts of our world: here, Ruby-Horsethief, and the bottom of the Grand Canyon. Rocks, rocks, rocks, they're all the same in exactly zero ways. Up there with the old timers, these rocks are 1.8 billion years old. I take a moment and wonder who they've met, what they've asked, and what answers they've comprehended. We don't speak to one another in that sort of way, though. It is more sound than language, more vision than symbol. Even if we could hold a longer interaction, the messages that would be conveyed

I'm sure would be inconceivable to my juvenile mind. I thank them for what they've created here, so that my soul might feel nourished with my friends and so that my heart might beat quickly in anticipation. Further through the canyon is the most challenging rapid, Skull Rapid. There have been four rescue operations involving helicopters there this season alone. I have a small emergency beacon that can summon one, just in case. But, I don't think any of us have an interest in adding that bill to the pile.

Another attraction that we skip for lack of time is the Outlaw Cave, just a short walk off the side of the river. The story goes that this whole canyon used to be a safe haven for criminals back in the days of gunslinging and smuggling. Crossing the border of Colorado and Utah, this section of the Colorado goes through a canyon within a canyon, carving the only reasonable path in a particularly desolate section of country. No wonder they found privacy here. Today, we've passed several tour groups and paddlers and heard their entire conversations. Sound waves carry across water exceptionally well, especially in a canyon like this.

Mike and Manuel stand on the tube's edge on either side, causing extreme turbulence for the rest of us. Many of us have gotten good at surfing on a raft, playing catch from vessel to vessel, and keeping our balance. But, none have perfected it. They shove at one another and try to force a fall into the water. Manuel must have been training since the last time I saw him do this, because he knocks our usual victor into the water with relative ease.

Beet lays on the stern of the boat behind me as I steer. His chin rests on his fisted hand, his other arm dragging in the water. Wren pulls my pilot knife off of my PFD, where it lives in a clip mount. She gave it to me for my birthday last year. It has a nearly two dimensional design, being surprisingly flat, and boasts a few features such as a bottle opener, glass breaker on the hilt, and a blunt tip. The sides are still plenty sharp for slicing and dicing, which I mostly use it for. Some people think that a blunt tipped pilot knife is for self defense on the water, but for that purpose it would be rather pointless. She spreads some peanut butter on a banana while we approach the next section of river. Nearby, a bright green cataraft drifts idly by. Sitting naked on a groover is a familiar face, too far to start a conversation—the reverb would make it impossible. He waves with one hand and wipes with the other.

After Marble Canyon Rapid comes Funnel Falls, Monty's favorite. Here, there is not an inch of flatwater to be seen outside of an eddy. We fly straight into the rapid, and go down the short waterfall and into the deepest section of canyon. On river left is a small pool of water that our raft should barely fit into. With some grappling from the front paddlers, we manage to pull right into the space on the bottom of the cliff. Tall gray boulders surround us on three sides, and the roar of the whitewater caps behind us mean that almost shouting above the white noise is necessary. It was Manuel's idea—this spot—so that no passing boaters could hear our conversation. Even if they could, our position is directly upstream from Skull Rapid, so most travelers are occupied rigging their gear, setting up cameras, or scaring their clients.

"Okay, anybody not feeling wonderful?" I ask. "Let's take a quick WAM break," I say, pulling out my water bottle and raising it. Everyone does the same. "I'm grateful that everyone is here, and that we're going to make a difference,"

"I appreciate that everyone is being as cautious as we can be, despite the fact that we're robbing one of the world's richest and snobbiest elites," Monty says.

"And I, myself, am grateful for the chance to make a whole lot of money and distribute it like it was always supposed to be distributed," Beet says.

"I appreciate that we all bring our own strengths to the table," Wren says.

"And I appreciate that everyone came here. I know that this is a complicated thing. It really means that you are true friends, being here. It really means a lot," Manuel says, genuinely. If I didn't know him so well, I might mistake his tone for sarcasm.

"I'm grateful to spend my time with some real good people. I'm already having a great time and y'all haven't even made me rich yet," Mike says.

"That was a pretty good Water Appreciation Moment. Ready in 3, 2, 1, WAM!" And we clink our bottles, then take a swig. "Alright, down to business,"

"I don't see any Huns," Beet says, looking around.

"What?"

"Sorry, go on,"

"I'll go over the plan in more detail now, I know it is exciting but please save your questions to the end," I say. Monty pulls out an NRS strap, runs it through a D-ring at the bow, and ties us off to a boulder. Manuel grabs the communal dry bag and opens it, pulling out a manilla folder with some laminated sheets inside. The dry bag gets passed around in a circle, where all manner of snacks and sunscreen are pulled out.

"We're listening," Beet insists.

"Just thinking," I say. "I mentioned that there are some costs earlier, one of them is a truck that we'll need. We're still working on that."

"For all of us? Maybe a van would work better," Mike suggests. I nod with Manuel.

"You're right, we'll look into that. So we'll park the van at a friends house in Cisco,"

"Sorry, where's that? Is that the little town we drove past between Junction and Moab?" Beet asks.

"Yeah, our take out at the end of this route is right by Cisco, so you'll see it later. We'll also be buying dirt bikes for all of us and a trailer that will be hooked up to the van. We're not sure who we'll buy the dirt bikes from yet, maybe Don. That was the guy that was taking a dump in the groover earlier," I say. I elaborate on a few of the specifics and postings while they listen intently. Mike struggles to light a cigarette given the wet wind billowing off of the water.

"With the paintings in hand, Manuel and I will leave the museum and head for the shoreline, where Mike will be waiting with the rigged raft. When the two of us have all the paintings in hand, we'll use walkie-talkies to let you know, Monty. The whole time we're in there, you'll be at the cistern on the mesa providing a lookout with binos. I know you'll probably be distracted by all of Moab's wonderful wildlife," I poke, "but your job is to give us a heads up if anybody comes onto property; police, fire, anyone. We'll be setting off the alarm, there's no way around that. Once we radio you that we're done, you run down the hill and meet up with us at the raft with Mike. We secure the paintings, push off, and navigate the Maroon Rapid System. If it all goes to plan, nobody will even know that the paintings are missing. Once across the rapids, we'll beach at Salt Wash Canyon and deflate my raft, then stow it to pick up when we all return to Moab as millionaires. At the beach, Beet will be waiting with some backpacking equipment: packs, filtered water, food, sunscreen, etcetera. The five of us will hike the six miles up the canyon, and meet up with Wren, who is waiting in a ranger truck with a trailer. On the trailer is—"

"Dirt bikes?" Wren asks. Monty huffs and looks at the boulder.

"Why the sigh?"

"I told you I can't ride a bike," he says. "I mean I can, but barely,"

"Dirt biking and motorcycles are

totally different," Manuel says.

"Have you ridden a bike before?" Mike asks.

"Yeah,"

"Well it's impossible to forget. You'll be fine. If you're having trouble you can hop on the back of Birch's," he says. Monty nods, then takes off his sunglasses and cleans them without a word. Even with the wind and water cooling the canyon, the sun beats down upon my back.

"So we leave the borrowed ranger truck parked so that it looks like someone other than her used it and forgot to bring it back. The trailer is just...well, someone will get a free trailer I guess. We'll also grab a pick me up or two from the ranger truck. Coffee, sports drinks, energy bars, and a water refill. It is gonna be a loooong day. That will position us right where the canyon opens up, near Delicate Arch. We take the dirt bikes through the park north, through Cordova Canyon, then cut east through Yellow Cat and follow the Poison Strip until we reach Cisco. There, the van is stashed with another trailer. We load up the bikes on the trailer, and take off," I say, acting as if this were just another tour I had planned for a client. I know that a handful of us have been up through these trails before, myself among them, so navigation won't be much of an issue. Though, I do have my concerns about the change in the landscape since I've last been through. Landslides, rockfall, flooding. Things change in a second around these parts and often there isn't anyone around to report them for months and months. We could end up trying to take a familiar trail and end up boxed out, facing steep canyon walls that we'd need trad gear to ascend. At least we aren't trying to haul out gold bars.

"This seems overly complicated. Why don't we just take the park road out to the highway, then take route 128 to Cisco?" Monty asks. Manuel looks at him through the corner of his eye. "The more intricate we make this, the higher the likelihood that something will go wrong. What if we break down out there?"

"We will not," Manuel affirms, "we must take this path because there are security cameras at both terminations of 128. We are going to be obvious because of the paintings,"

"I thought nobody was going to know that this happened until after the fact, 'maybe ever'?" Beet prods.

"Ideally, yes. But we must prepare for the worst case scenario where we are being pursued and have been identified," Manuel explains.

"That sounds...condemning, when you put it that way," Monty says. "I guess on the bright side, nobody will be dumb enough to chase us through open desert while on bikes. They wouldn't be able to keep up with us, anyway,"

"Unless they take the owner's private helicopter," Mike says.

"Maybe we'll have to do some monkeywrenching," I suggest.

"Come to think of it, how are we gonna carry these paintings? Won't it act like a sail while we're trying to drive?" Mike asks.

"No, we have these tubes. Like, for posters, do you know?" Manuel says. The gang nods. "They have a strap and they go on your back. That is part of the reason that we need at least six of us   135
in the operation, to make sure that if one

of us drops a painting or loses it somehow, the rest still are delivered to the client. Though, they are virtually useless unless the full set is delivered. That, and there are many jobs to do. Many bases to cover to make sure that this plan will run smoothly.”

"Thanks for explaining that," Monty says. He throws a peanut into Manuel's open mouth on the first try.

"From there it's like falling off a log. We throw the paintings in and drive the van to Florida. We're done in 72 hours, home and retired in 96. Sound like a plan?" I ask. Everyone nods and cogitates for a moment. Wren looks at me, then Manuel.

"I just think that the risk might be too much for this operation. I understand that this is a life changing amount of money,"

"For more than just us," Beet adds.

"But I think we need to keep in mind the very, very real possibility of prosecution. I mean, from what I've heard the owner can ruin virtually anybody's life they want to. Even if they don't win in court, the owner has so much money that spending time hiring lawyers and finding time to go to court is no sweat for them. For us, that means we have got to get time off from our jobs and hire a lawyer. I don't know about y'all, but that would just about bankrupt me. Even if we win in court, the lost time and money would make it impossible to ever retire, and we'd continue to be wage slaves for the rest of our lives."

"Yeah," Beet says. Wren exhales sharply and folds her arms.

136   "It is not guaranteed, but the client did promise they would do their best to get

us out of legal trouble if the need should arise,"
Manuel reassures. She loosens up a bit, but from her
face I can tell that her mind is unsettled. A quiet
moment passes where Mike soaks his all cotton,
camouflage hat in the river, then splats it back onto
his head. The bucket hat droops and drips all over
his plain white t-shirt. Beet leans forward, toward
the center of the group.

"I would like to share a story that I think most
of you don't know," he says, his hands in prayer and
the tips of his fingers touching his lips. "I recalled it
whilst I was meditating on my decision to come or
not. Obviously, I'm here, right?" he asks, patting his
shoulders and hips, waiting for a response.

"Yes?" Manuel says with a cock of his
eyebrow. Beet was always doing this-talking as if he
were trying to bring about some revelation inside
of you. It usually worked, but even if he fails to
materialize the 'oh snap' moment within you, I love
how he can get anyone to stop and think, to slow
down for a moment and hang on every word.

"So, you already know the outcome. I think it
might be helpful to some of you," he takes a breath,
replacing his hands back where they were. "As a few
of you know, I had one particularly rough summer a
few years ago. They were overworking all of us to
make up for lost profits that...I can't imagine they'll
ever get back. Especially if we pull this off," he
says. He tells the story I've heard at least a dozen
times before. Each of us had made it a mission
to spread anti-resort propaganda at every chance
we got. Online reviews, recommendations while
working, but mostly word of mouth. One less person
giving money to the greedy owner makes the 137
rest of us just a little bit stronger. At least, ▸━━◖

that's what I tell myself.

The story he shares now is one of many in our collective arsenal of misery. It begins with a birthday dinner for the owner, nevermind the fact that their birthday fell several weeks prior. There was an arrangement among the luxury properties that aligned along a carefully placed sequence on the calendar; the owner could travel day by day to all of the properties in all of the different exotic parts of the world, being treated to a fresh birthday dinner and celebration for multiple consecutive weeks. It was our turn to hold festivities at Maroon Mesa, and the owner was coming from the highly esteemed Colorado Property. Best behavior, pressed linen, and superior service were of the utmost priority, especially considering the preceding venue's performance (the PR team had hired influencers and generated bots to post about the event online, just to make sure everyone remembered to send their birthday wishes).

Having only been at the Mesa for a few months, Beet hadn't been told when he first arrived where he should park. After helping him move in from where he pulled over on the curb, a quick walk around the employee cabins revealed that no more parking spots were available. Nevermind the empty three car garage reserved for the owner, or the owner's sports car, offroading rig, or converted van (all covered in dust and hadn't been used once during my tenure at the resort). Also ignore the two entire parking spots taken up by the owner's various brand new mountain bikes, purchased through a yearly subscription and delivered on New Year's Eve each year, which I had to wait around in the cold to sign for. A gardener and landscaper by trade, Beet had done his homework and learned about our fragile cryptobiotic soil that everyone seems to trample wantonly. Not wanting to be a part of such a statistic, he drove toward the center of the complex and pulled into one of the many empty parking spots there, and walked to his new home.

A few days later, when he went to take a drive into town after work, he found his windshield plastered with resort-issued tickets, and a parking boot on his tire. Being at the resort for as long as I was, I became a sort of liaison for new hires to help them get on their feet. The Mesa is remote, and many of the people joining the team are there on visas and don't have a way to get into town except to walk through the desert. Beet brought the tickets to me—over $2000 worth in less than a week—and we appealed to the general manager. We learned that the hiring manager had failed to email Beet a parking pass to be printed. Unfortunately, you see, there was nothing that he could do. His hands were simply tied. Beet either had to pay to have the car towed to a friend's place in town, or pay the fine. No matter the decision, this had to be resolved before the owner arrived for the birthday bash. At the time, I wondered if there would be clowns or superhero actors in nylon costumes. This was already immature beyond my comprehension. At the rate that the daily tickets were adding up, it was a literal, numerical impossibility that his wages would ever catch up to pay for even half of the current balance in time. The car was a jalopy, he's the first to admit that, but it was his only guarantee of independence from the resort now that he had signed his lease. Without it he was stranded, with no way to get food or prescriptions from town, and no way to take anything with him if he wanted to quit and leave. Outside of filling his backpack, of course.

We polled the whole crew to see if we could collectively raise the money to pay it off, we talked to people on the city council, we consulted online forums. This was perfectly legal on private property, it didn't seem like there was any way around it. We tried calling the towing companies in town, but most of them were occupied pulling scared tourists off of rocks they shouldn't have driven on top of. The rest, whose contact information we'd gotten from the architect, refused to do any sort of business with the resort, even from Grand Junction.

A few weeks passed without us reaching a solution. As is tradition, the owner took a skydive down and landed on their property to a blast of fireworks and sparklers despite the fire ban and other skydivers in the air. Knowing the jumpers in Moab, I actually imagine that they enjoyed the challenge of weaving around the projectiles mid-flight. A friend of mine was in ROTC here, but left before officially enlisting. Though, she always had dreams of being a paratrooper. The dreams were strong enough, apparently, that she became a skydiving instructor here. I wonder if she intentionally signed up for the same jump to celebrate the birthday each year, just to have a small chance to run a live combat scenario, however full of bright colors and shimmers it may be.

Beet and the general manager were both pulled aside, as the owner had spotted the car with the boot from the air. Beet was asked about 140 his 5 year plan. When he explained that he wanted to be at the resort for the long-

haul (as most of us bright-eyed new hires said), it made sense why he signed up for a one year lease despite never having been on property before. The fee to break a lease with the resort is $1000, more than both of our bank accounts combined at the time. Though, I don't reckon that I would've gone through with loaning that much money to a stranger, as we still were then and if I had that kind of cash. It must have been a high honor for him to receive two of his three strikes against him by the owner in living color. As punitive action, he was to hold the door open for the duration of the birthday party. This punishment didn't seem so bad when he first told me, many others had been through worse at the uncalloused hands of the owner, but my view on the subject changed when I carried the serving tray of tiny, soft boiled robin's eggs. Somewhere between needing to be punished and needing to be a functional part of the staff, Beet was being made to stand in the doorway holding a large pillar candle, lit, in each hand. In the dusky faded light, the bags of his eyes flickered hard and tormented. Surrounded by candelabras and a fake, styrofoam cake with lit candles, flickering electric lights, and fake ivy, he stood greeting guests who carried metal credit cards with credit limits worth more than our lives. The hot melted wax ran lumpily down the sides of each candle, searing the pink skin on his shaking hands. Piles of the creamy paraffin wax had built up around his grip, and oozed off the side of his hand, dropping to the ground and taking a measure of raw flesh with it. When I first laid eyes on him, he had been posted there for three hours. Just four more to go. I served the pastel colored eggs to
the clientele, who lifted them from their

black caviar nests and swallowed them shell and all.

It wasn't so much the pain, but the message that was being broadcasted by keeping him on display that chafed at my composure. Monty and I grabbed him quickly, propped the door open, and took him to the employee restroom. We flipped on all the faucets, which pumped unfiltered river water despite whatever the staff here tell the guests, and despite the official water quality report. With the white noise from the tan water, Monty poured a pitcher of warm tea over his skin to soften the wax, and gently worked the rest off with the back of his knife while I watched the door. Beet was silent aside from the occasional whimper or gasp when we removed a particularly tricky bit. The thicker layers of wax came off the most easily, practically cracked and provided more leverage, but the thin bits seemed to be the most painful for him. Would it be best to let him go the whole night with wax building up, and take it all off at once? Through the crack in the door I saw the owner approaching. What were they doing here? Everyone knows that the Golden Throne is in the suite, not here.

We rushed Beet into the handicap stall and locked the door behind us. Monty spun him facing away from the toilet, while he and I stood on top of the seat to make our feet invisible from the owner, who certainly was checking. Monty pushed the heel of his hand to his head, which made me realize that we had left all of the sinks running.

"I know you're in here, Beet Turnipseed. You've abandoned your duties yet again," a commanding voice from beyond the formica wall called. "I'm not playing around with you,"

Monty and I looked at one another,

wondering silently and then rapidly mouthing incoherent words to one another. Over his shoulder, I saw Beet staring down at his trembling hands. He was clearly in shock from the torture, but I didn't initially think the damage was this extensive. Peering closer I saw that his index finger had been degloved almost completely, his pale skin sloughed off and hanging by what looked like what remained of a slimy piece of chicken skin after a toddler had been playing with their food for an hour. White flesh and bright red bits mosaiced by a network of thin blue veins and a greasy sort of shine that I still cannot get out of my head. Perhaps the worst part of it all was the smell—tart cherry candles (owner's favorite) mixed with barbeque. I wanted to vomit. And, I almost did.

Monty put his hand on my shoulder and put a finger over his mouth, then jumped down. An open palmed hand behind his back told me to stay where I was. He gently ushered Beet forward and opened the stall door, blocking anyone's view of me with his large frame. Beet was given no additional strikes that night, provided that he scraped all the melted wax up with no tools but his remaining fingernails within the next 24 hours. Monty on the other hand, well, let's just say that this was his final shift. I'm forever grateful that he took that hit, as I didn't have a car to leave the resort in and would probably have just jumped in the Colorado River and seen where I floated to next. At that point, I had already racked up two strikes for trying to remedy similar punitive situations with my coworkers.

"It comes in handy at work now. I do side work at banquets for weddings and stuff," Beet says proudly, rotating his hands in the air to show off his multi toned skin. The spots of damage are lined by scars that tell the tale of dissolvable stitches and a lot of healing salve. The rapid transition in subject matter from his previous story to this one would have made anyone uneasy, but he navigates it with a finesse that makes him a pleasure to talk to about anything. "It helps with the hot plates, you know? Nerve damage blocks all the pain so I can carry them straight out of the dishwasher," he says. I think about the postcard he sent me from Mexico City when he went to get the procedure done: cheaper beer, kinder people, more affordable medicine.

Mike turns his head away from Beet's hands, but stares curiously out of the corner of his eyes, trying to get a good look so he can turn away for good. "But in a way that experience was eye-opening for me. What's the point of it all? Why waste my time working myself to death, breaking my body just to get someone else rich? I don't know if you know this, Wren, but once you're at the resort for 90 days they have you fill out paperwork about your will and your body," he says casually, spreading his arms out.

"What do you mean, your body?" she asks.

"I mean, they have you fill out paperwork saying that you'll have someone pick up your body within 24 hours of your death if you die or property, or otherwise they'll send you to the funeral home to be cremated."

"That sounds made up," Manuel says, eyebrows pressed together.

"No offense, but you weren't there as long as I was," Beet says.

"I had to fill that out, too," Mike says,

nodding with a puff.

"I didn't take it personally," Beet says, leaning back on the inflated tube. "I'd like to be cremated anyway. Just dump me in the river all on my lonesome, let my ashes mix with the water and erode the rocks away. I never understood the whole golden casket mentality. When my grandpa died, my mom spend $5,000 on his casket, only for him to be cremated in it."

"What's worse is when you don't get cremated, but buried in your casket," Wren says. "Polyurethane coated casket leaking carcinogens into the groundwater, not to mention the formaldehyde and god-knows-what pumped into your corpse just to keep you from rotting. Who cares? Nobody is ever going to see you again," she says, practically exasperated. I love her, and let her know with a smile.

"The suit or dress you wear in there is probably made of nylon, too," Mike says, looking down at his cigarette and smiling slightly to himself.

"Mhm, and your eyelids are glued shut with superglue, also made of plastic," Monty says. "I just don't get the point of it all,"

"Got to keep you looking good for the rapture, I guess," I conclude. Nodding, sipping water, tightening sandals and peering over the edge at the crawdads. Manuel shuffles the manilla folder he pulled out a few minutes ago, and places the laminated sheets on his lap. He struggles for a minute, trying to find comfort while keeping his knees close together to keep the files from hitting the bottom of the raft, and settles on resting the dry bag on his thighs, with the papers above that.

"I have given a lot of presentations in school, but this has got to be the weirdest place I have ever given one," he laughs. His tone is of a nervous comedian at some half-sold show, where the patrons are only there for the discounted drinks. Trying to win the crowd over. He's worth more than that. Still, both he and I seemed to feel as though we were sleazy salespeople, selling a product and then sending you through hours of funky hold music and transfers between departments so you could never speak to us once your credit card had cleared. We both felt a looming sense of guilt that pulsed under every conversation we had about the paintings. What if we landed everyone in prison? What if someone got hurt? Or, worst of all, what if we got away with it and lived with the fear of the owner discovering our swindle for the rest of our lives?

"Whatcha got?" Monty asks encouragingly.

"Not really a presentation, as it turns out," Manuel says. "Just pictures so you know what we are dealing with. A few maps to fill your mind," he says, passing around the pages. Mike and I wiggle the laminations so they wobble with that familiar sound, and giggle. We had done our homework, given the architect a bottle of wine from the cooler in exchange for the floorplan of the property (no questions asked), organized bulleted lists of supplies, materials, gas mileages, plotted distances on printed maps so we couldn't be traced after the fact.

"Look, I don't really care about bringing these people to justice. As far as I'm concerned, they can buy their way out of anything," Monty says, a few of 146 the sheets in his hand. Although he maintained a hard skepticism in his brow, I could tell that he was both impressed and comforted by the sheer amount and high quality of our research. "While this is a lot of money, many people have much, much more money than the owner and they don't use it for anything but themselves. I'm hoping that we can agree as a group to use our money to make a positive difference?" he says to philanthropic and gentle blinks. The sheets rotate through the group, changing hands a few more times while we study them.

"It is a lot of money," Mike starts. "I don't know what I'd do with all of it. But, certainly I'd like to have a little bit of fun. When I think of spending what is essentially the owner's cash on booze and fireworks and maybe even new tires, I can't help but smile," he says with conviction, unafraid of being looked at differently. To my surprise, the old Monty pops out for a moment.

"Maybe a little bit of fun," he laughs. "I've been tracking their stock. This year they exceeded in profits what it would cost to feed everyone currently in prison three meals a day for a decade."

"That's a lot of dough. What're you so worried about then?" Wren asks.

"At first I was worried about taking money away from the people working there, or costing them their jobs, but now I don't know." He wrings his hands. "Maybe that's just collateral damage. Maybe we can use some of our money to help those people get to a place where they are more secure. At least, that's what I'm going to do," he says. In the days when he first began distancing himself from some of the low-profile, low-profit schemes we would run he would often begin his opinion on one side of the spectrum, and work his way to the complete other side, to who he was trying to be. I feel a pang of guilt hit me again, particularly for him. There is a sense that I am urging him to be someone he tried for so long to defeat, someone that he'd buried a year ago when we went straight. None of us had ever done anything major, or even anything that a jury would side against (given the chance), but we had all done things in one another's company that were legally frowned upon. He's on the straight and narrow now. I hope that he'll use his money to find a job photographing what he loves, not bound to using his personal equipment and time to fulfill a contractual oath because that's what people are buying.

"Well man, even if that extra money is bypassing the workers and going straight to the owner, they've been running a serious deficit for years," Mike says, then pauses. When he realizes everyone is waiting for him to continue, he says "you know the standard breakdown-right? 30 percent food cost, 30 percent labor, 30 percent utilities and 10 percent profit, that is how 99 percent of restaurants operate. Only, the Mesa probably spends 60 percent on food cost because of all the bougie ingredients. Sure, it brings up the quality of the food but nobody in the world wants to foot the bill for genuinely handmade desserts and such,"

"You mean to tell me that the cheesecake-" I ask.

"Yeah. Every single cold serve meal, imported from a factory in Salt Lake. Don't look so surprised, why do you think half the menu is the same in all these fancy pants luxury resorts?"

148   "I guess all they say is 'homemade', and

⸺ 'in-house'. But, they never specify who's

home or house..." Wren says dramatically, as if this truth hurt her feelings.

"Not to mention the fact that they can't keep anybody in the kitchen for more than a month before they're fired or quit, but that's a whole different story," he concludes, quickly inhaling from his cigarette because he'd been away from it for so long.

"They must be getting money from somewhere else to help cover the cost of everything, right?" I ask. Manuel shrugs, locks eyes with me; he stares, hard.

"Yes, but what? Nothing legal or taxed, I am sure," he says, unflinching. From all of his English practice and reading, I occasionally think that he might be better than I am at the language, but here and there he will do something that just makes you itch, something culturally off putting like he's doing right now.

My raft sways as a wave passes beneath us and breaks onto the adjacent rocks. Made mostly of primary colors and sun bleached rubber, my raft is an amalgamation of journey's past. A thwart from the spring floods I recovered, part of a waxed tarp pulled from an eddy. Looking down, I admire my sew and seal job, running my finger along a jagged seam. This vessel must be made of at least eight others that had been destroyed. I wonder if it will hold up to the abuse of another season on the water.

"Speaking of, is this money taxable?" Monty asks. A few laughs. "No, seriously."

"You can marry me and then I'll give it to you as an untaxed gift, okay?" Wren says, smiling. "Thank you for your story earlier, Beet. I'm ready to lean more into this now that I know who we're up against. I had heard stories but—well—I always assumed that folks were using a healthy dose of exaggeration to make the point," she says. Monty leans forward, hands clasped in prayer.

"I'm with you, and thanks, Beet. I'm worried that I might be coming off like all I care about is the cash. Obviously bringing the owner to justice is a huge bonus to me, but I think it is probably best if we're all honest with one another, that's the only way any of this is gonna work, right?"

"Mhm,"

"Truth is that I could really use the money, just like the rest of us. In this economy? Who couldn't? All I know is that I'm tired of seeing their light pollution spill out. I can see it all the way up in my cabin, you know. That's gotta be 25 miles away and their stupid streetlights project straight into the sky, the only light for miles," he says, shaking it out of himself. "It pisses me off. I don't want anything to do with them, not to mention the legal repercussions if something were to happen. Can we just blackmail the owner? We can just take photos of the paintings on the wall, right? We can just say that we know they're stolen, they need to return them to their owner. Or...else."

"I've already asked the client, and they find this unacceptable. They need the physical paintings back," Manuel explains.

"Can't the police just get that?" Monty asks.

"It is a tricky business, often with matters like this, a little smoke and a priceless set of paintings like these will go underground. Lost forever,"

"Right, but isn't that our goal? To

get the owner to stop using them as insurance, collateral, whatever?" Wren asks.

"No, our goal is to deliver them to the original owner. Once they're back, our contact is prepared to file a suit against the thief, then the owner of the Mesa will be prosecuted."

"Maybe," I say. "The owner pays the salary of half the politicians in the state of Utah."

"And the other half?" Mike asks.

"Paid by the church," Monty says solemnly. He exhales and produces an alternate plan: "Okay—what if we talk to the FBI, or CIA or Men In Black or whatever. If these paintings really are worth that much, then surely a national agency like that would be interested."

"Again, I am afraid not. Our contact made it—what is the word—transparent? That this is a sensitive matter. We cannot reveal any information about the job to anyone not directly involved,"

"So let's get the police directly involved," Monty proposes. "I went to school with half those guys, they're kosher,"

"Kosher?" Manuel asks, looking to me.

"Like, clean. Honest, pure of heart," I say. Manuel sighs heavily, the same way he does during the dinner rush when a new wave of orders flies in.

"Not very kosher when the sheriff and the owner are having an affair. I have talked a lot with our client about this, and we agree that this investigation must take place outside of Utah as a whole. The police in Moab want to do the right thing, I know this for sure. But, it is hard to do the right thing when someone can ruin your life with a single word," Manuel says, sitting back.

"That single word," Monty says,

holding up a finger, "is exactly what I'm afraid of."
Manuel opens his mouth, then shuts it. The
laminated sheets have all made their way back
to Monty, who scratches his face and shuffles
through them. Behind us, a group of boaters pass
by screaming into the water without paying us any
mind. Beet takes a breath, and looks at Monty.

"Isn't that worth fighting for?" he asks. He
spreads his hands wide when he doesn't get an
answer. A few of us nod, Mike finishes his cigarette
and throws the butt into the water. Wren quietly
fishes it out of the eddy and puts it into our dry
bag dedicated to trash. In the heavy silence, Monty
closes his eyes and passes the sheets back to
Manuel.

Looking at his feet, Monty says "guys, I'm
not trying to make this harder than it already is on
anyone. We're all here for our own reasons. I'd just
rather die poor like the rest of the world than rot in
prison for trying to do what y'all keep saying is the
right thing."

"I hear you," Beet acknowledges, and pats
him gently on the back.

"I really hate to jump back into things as if
that did not happen, but I think you will want to
hear the whole story," Manuel explains. He skims
an additional sheet of paper, then chews on his lip
for a moment before continuing. "Okay, so—these
paintings were commissioned in 1757, made by the
hands of Cristóbal de Aguilar. He made many dozens
of portraits during this time, but what makes this
series of paintings unique is that they're of nature.
You all saw the sheet—yes?" he asks, holding up
152 a laminated page where the painting set is
illustrated, from the work printer that

never has enough toner.

"The six paintings of the birds were a commission, like most of his work. Any guesses who the client was?"

"George Washington?" Mike asks. He pulls out two slices of white bread from the cooler and lays them on his lap, delivers a dollop of bright yellow mustard and slaps on a few slices of baloney.

"First of all, how can you eat that?" Manuel laughs.

"You work in a kitchen?" Wren proposes, as if the expectation of a more refined palette should be self-evident. Through the many chefs and cooks I have known, it isn't altogether uncommon for their off-the-clock food to be microwave cuisine such as this.

"Not George Washington, whom I will never understand the obsession about, but a man named Albrecht Cossiau. As you sit on this raft, you may find yourself wondering just who this man is?

Many generations later, his great great great great grandchild would inherit many luxury properties across North America. One of which, is Maroon Mesa," he says dramatically.

"Where your vacation—" Mike says, through a mouth of baloney while he points at Monty.

"Is our indignation," he replies with a smirk.

"So this guy, Crystal Ball," Beet edges, waving his hands.

"Cristóbal, he makes the painting for Cossiau, who pays an arm and a leg for it. Way more than they are worth today, but we already knew that the owner is from old money. The paintings all have a desert theme, which he commissioned to be 153 duplicated as backgrounds behind all of his favorite birds. He takes them to a castle they bought from some old baron in Bavaria. There is some evidence that the Cossiaus pretended to be of royalty after purchasing the estate, but I will not go into detail on that. It sits on a wall in the castle for a few generations. Marriages, children, grandchildren, widows, etcetera. The money the family shared originally came from taxes and tax withholdings in the preceding centuries,"

"A tale as old as time,"

"Yes, well, that money eventually ran out—or was hidden—around 1929. For several years around that time, an economic depression in virtually all of Europe arose. Many people had to part with what was most precious to them, some even lost their children. Cossiau's family sold their collection of European estates and invested that money in the Americas to survive the depression that would soon hit here. Along with those sales went the majority of the contents of the estates, including our paintings. Then, World War II arrived and the paintings went underground. For a great many years, it was thought that they were gone forever, destroyed after so long by the Nazis. Fortunately, they were recovered after the war with many other artifacts and pieces of art that cannot even be priced. Rumor has it that they were stored in Adolf Hitler's Amber Room, has anyone heard of that?"

"Yeah," I nod. So does Monty.

"We can talk more about it once we are on our long road trip to the east with the paintings safely in our arms. For now, a brief description will have to do. The Amber Room is basically a sort of treasure room. The Nazis stole artifacts from all over during the war and put them into a museum in the heartland. Imagine it: the history and culture of so many peoples stolen and locked away under a genocidal regime. When the war finally came to an end, the city that the museum was in fell under an allied bombing raid. The Amber Room and its contents were reduced to rumors. The only reason the paintings were not destroyed is because a group of allied refugees managed to evacuate them during the bombing run, and took a wheelbarrow full of artifacts with them," he explains, putting away a few of the sheets and looking at us. We look back, expectantly. "The few items that survived were auctioned off to help raise funds to rebuild after the war. The current owner of the painting, our client, purchased the paintings and put them into proper display where they could experience ideal levels of light and humidity so that they might be preserved for centuries to come. This gallery was open to the public. Part of the public was another Cossiau descendant, who thought it necessary to break into the gallery and take back the paintings while on a ski holiday,"

"Sorry—" Wren waves a hand, "when did this happen?"

"1980s. They were too idiotic not to hire a professional. The grandparents of the current Mesa owner were caught on camera taking the series, and stopped once again at the airport. But they managed to get them all the way back to Utah, and hung them up in the 'museum'. There is also evidence now that the family is using the paintings as collateral for trade deals,"

"I don't understand how they weren't caught? TSA didn't stop them?" Beet asks, a little too loudly.

"Money may not buy happiness, but it sure can make a lot of problems go away," Mike says, licking the last of the mustard off of his fingers.

"Exactly. Bribed airport guards, destroyed video tapes. As far as the newspaper said, it was the Nazis that took them back once again." Manuel passes us another sheet, in German, that I can't read. "So you can see that our mission is more than recovering stolen property. Bringing them back into the public eye would deplete their value and make the Mesa owner look like a criminal."

"And publishing any evidence that we take from the resort would be an admittance of guilt. Even direct camera footage. All we are is a repossession team. Like I said, it's hardly theft at all," I say.

"There's pictures all over the internet of guests and celebrities in front of the wall. No matter how rich you are, that's not something it is easy to make go away. The owner is not that kind of rich. The kind of rich where you don't even appear to exist," Manuel says.

"Even though the owner might not try to prosecute over the paintings, we all know that all manner of guilt can be fabricated," Monty says. "I do feel better after hearing that, but we can't forget that there isn't a single one of us here who can't be bankrupted in a single day of court going toe-to-toe."

"I agree. I have always felt safer dealing with an enemy that I know, rather than one I do not know anything about," Manuel says.

"Thus the element of stealth?" Wren asks. "If

156 the owner figures out the paintings are stolen and has us arrested before we can deliver

them, nobody hears a word of the whole operation except our lawyers,"

"Assuming we can afford lawyers," Monty says pointedly.

"That's right," I say. "If we fail to deliver the paintings, then the owner will just pay for us to get charged for something else entirely and there won't be any evidence of the theft from the actual museum. We disappear into the annals of history and rot in prison. Or worse."

"It would almost be easier," Wren starts, "if we knew the owner was going to come after us for the paintings. Now, I don't know."

"No sense worrying about it. No way to predict it," Beet says. "You could be walking free one day, and the next you're getting hauled in for...a bank robbery in LA. Only, you've never been to LA."

"That's exactly how it would go down. Out of the dark, no way to see if it is coming,"

"But, if we succeed, then this would theoretically be enough proof to bring the owner and their family to justice, right?" Monty asks.

"Absolutely. Why do you think I'm here?" Manuel asks. Monty nods and relaxes his posture for the first time on this trip.

"All we have to do is deliver the paintings without getting caught and we're safe," Monty concludes.

"Where did you laminate those? There's no laminator at the resort," I ask. He shrugs.

"I do not know what this word means," he says. "But we can all take comfort that there are only a few other odds and ends that need to be filled out. Mostly logistics. And, no real loose ends."

"Great,"

"Awesome," I say. We all look from eye to eye and nod in agreement and comradery. We take a few more minutes to put things away and for Mike to eat yet another baloney sandwich. I produce the sketch I made earlier, showcasing it to the group before pushing off back into the rapid system[2].

Before us the raging waters narrow between high, gray cliff walls. The sound reverberates to a point that even shouting is futile. I stand up at the back of the vessel, knees bent, and survey Skull Rapid. In front of us sits a massive boulder, separated from the wall by a space of gushing water just a few inches larger than our paddle boat. This is the Rock of Shock. Hitting it will drain our speed. Without our speed, we are nothing more than a log rolling at the will of the current. Without any momentum, the deadly current present before us will not hesitate to suck us into a cove cut out of the right side of the wall. With a vicious whirlpool that currently cycles several junipers, a chewed up cataraft, a few PFDs, and a rotting cow, the consequences of botching this approach are monumental. I drop back down to my seat and J-stroke us onto the correct heading. If we get pulled into that cove, the Room of Doom, the only way out is a helicopter. Slick, unscalable walls sprayed with the green river's mist shine against the harsh noon sun, just visible between the channel of cliffs that present a baby blue sky. I swallow.

"All-forward!" I shout over the waves. Slaps on helmets and shoulders travel from the back to the front to compensate for the roar of the caps surrounding us. With unrelenting force, the river grabs us and we accelerate forward toward the rock. River center, hard cut right at the last moment. That's the plan. River left is a maze of jagged peaks peering like urchins. The two up front—Monty and Manuel—set the pace. All is in unison. All is aligned.

I stick my paddle in the water and brace at my hip, pushing the blade outward to swing us to the right of the Rock of Shock.

Too late.

The port side of the raft bashes against the rock, sending Beet onto its surface, reflecting the dazzling sun.

He puts his hands out to brace against it, but the algae cover surface makes him slip.

His helmet cracks audibly on the rock.
With a vacuum pull, the raft is ripped into the channel and down the drop.
Airborne, Monty plucks Beet from the sky and slams him down onto a thwart.

"Holy shit!" Mike screams. Beet scrambles to the edge and fishes for his paddle while I desperately try to steer us away from the cove.

"Paddle," I bark, "everything you have!"
The whitewater hurriedly ushers us starboard, the stern of the raft edging into the Room of Doom.
Beet finally manages to join in the paddling. Sweat, screams, howling. With his support, we claw our way out of the Room of Doom and float among the rise and drop of a smaller rapid that

159

doesn't need much steering.

"Oh my God," Wren says.

"Thank goodness we are not rafting very far with the paintings," Manuel says.

"Sorry, man. I turned too late," I say to Beet.

"No, my bad brother. I was looking over the side at these kind of fractal patterns in the whitewater, you know what I'm talking about?"

"Yeah," I laugh.

"I dropped my sunglasses and reached in for them, that's when we bumped," he says. A wave of relief washes over me. How can I expect to manage the responsibility that will come once we have the portraits?

A few small rapid systems shoot us out to where a ramp of talus makes a path to the top of a cliff. We eddy out in the bright green waters and rest, arms sore and aching. We tie the boat to a jug on one of the rocks and hike up to the cliff. From the bottom, Wren shoots me with an invisible arrow from her invisible bow. I muse the arrow striking me in the heart, and fall lifeless off the cliff into the chilly water below.

A few river miles later, we float lazily over to a sandstone cliffside. Here, millenia of birds, bugs, and erosion have made smooth handles in the rock. Often forming domes over the water, this is the very best place in Moab to boulder. Our group experiences failure after failure until Monty nearly completes the problem, but hangs upside down for so long that his arm gives out and he drops into the drink. Wren hops off of the raft and flashes it in half the time it took the rest of us to even begin. Beet pokes his bright red skin. Mike offers him some butter for the sunburn. He says that it helps the pain, but I rather think that he just wants to make a joke about lobster. Beet continues to poke at his skin and seems to take his burn personally, verbally condemning his lack of sunscreen and scowling as he cowers from the sun under all of our towels.

Chapter Six || To Live and Die in Moab, Utah

On the south end of town$_{17}$, Manuel and I enter a large garage that's been converted to a sort of bike workshop. Electric bicycles, used for tours, are lined up and waiting to be loaded onto a plated flatbed truck. Rebar welded and bent to accommodate the bikes is fitted snugly into 4x4 beams bolted onto the truck bed. Further back and being swallowed by weeds are a collection of ancient motorcycles and motorized scooters. Don, an old friend and quintessential Moab local, comes out to greet us.

"Long time no see, how's it going at the resort?" he asks. He, too, is a veteran. We lean against the truck and catch him up on the last year or so of Mesa happenings. "That's too bad. You two can always come work for me. We've got a new set of permits this year, offering like five new tours," he says.

"Thank you," Manuel says.

"We're actually working on something else. That big score I told you about over the phone?"

"Yeah," he says, folding his arms. "I kinda thought you had one too many at Woody's,"

"I'm happy to report that I was very much sober. And that a cut of our profits could be very much yours," I say. He smiles and leans in as we give him the framework of how he could help, while avoiding specific details.
"Yeah, I could make that happen. Gladly," he smiles kindly. "I do have a tour that day, though. But I don't mind. I've never been ashamed of letting my entrepreneurship endeavors blend into one another," he says, we laugh together.

"Alright, does a check work for you?" I ask.

"Yeah, but maybe after you cash in whatever it is you're doing? I trust you two, no need to invest before the fact. Happy to help,"

"Thanks, Don. I really appreciate it. This was one of the last big question marks on our plan," I say. We share a drink and hit the road toward Grand Junction, Colorado.

...

We pull off of the highway and onto the slippery sand trail of Willow Springs Road. The heat of the late summer is just starting to drop, since the sun disappeared behind the canyon about an hour ago. We've still got an hour or two of good light to work with. By working during this time of day we can manage to avoid the scorching rays that make Moab the skin cancer capitol of the USA. Short embankments rise up on either side of the single 164 lane road, sharp edges at their top corners reveal the scars of recent floods. A kind of ambient, indirect light encases everything in the valley in shadows, yet everything is still light.

We follow a paper map along a highlighted route, stopping every few minutes to annotate a potential obstacle. So long as the rain continues to hold out another few weeks, we should avoid any major landscape changes and be able to make it out this way. Once we pick up the motorbikes from Wren inside the park, we'll head into the desert and shouldn't see a single soul until we shoot back out to Willow Springs. The tracks between Willow and the interior of the park are rated red, the highest difficulty. Nobody who wants their off roading rig to survive takes those pathways. On a dirtbike, however, we avoid many of the major pitfalls that condemn normal vehicles. Sand pits are easily driven around. Large rocks are avoided entirely via the narrow passage that a dirtbike requires, and by throttling the motor we can easily hydroplane over the small strips of mud where springs enter the roadways. Even a total washout of boulders and sand is surmountable by carrying the bikes with our own brawn. The idea of simply taking UTVs from the Mesa for this purpose was not lost on me during the initial stages of planning. I know where the keys are, they aren't properly registered or insured. In fact, the license plates are custom ordered from a popular souvenir company (KRU$TBUST, M3SA, R3DR0K$, FEWLSP1L, & DYRTD0G), not to mention I still have access to the booking software. It would only take a few minutes for me to concoct a fake tour that they're out on. With all the disorganization and mismanagement, nobody would realize that the UTVs were missing. probably aren't anywhere that any manager knows how to get to.

It would be easy in terms of taking them, but the issue is that they aren't needed until we are on the other side of the river. Once we got them off the property we would have to cross a bridge, and the nearest bridge is on the north end of Moab which is out of the question; the second closest is all the way out at Dewey Bridge. Realistically we could cut through Dome Plateau, but if we follow that route we'd need a refuel before we get to our relay at Cisco. It just wouldn't work logistically.

For a moment I ponder the various hurdles we'll have to cross, and wish desperately for a backroom to tack photos on a wall and connect them with pins and red yarn. Maybe then all of this wouldn't seem so crazy.

Things would be simpler if it weren't for the installation of security cameras on every corner known to man. There's a set at the exit gates of the Mesa, then another at the intersection of Highway 128. Here, the outlaw Butch Cassidy once hijacked a ferry and rode down the Colorado with a small fortune in stolen gold. I chuckle at the way history repeats, and what this relation to the outlaw implicates for the rest of our operation.

Because of the coordinated inconvenience of the cameras, our only option to avoid producing video evidence is to travel through the park, along the route we now scope out.

We pass a large fifth wheel with collapsed siding and caved in roof, a victim to the windstorms. Manuel points to it inquisitively.

"Shai-Hulud, desert worms," I shout over the engines. He taps his ear through the helmet.

     "What?"

"Nevermind," I say, grinning quietly

to myself. A few years ago I had explored that trailer with a friend, who found the previous occupant's wide brimmed hat. Around the brim lay a rattlesnake skin pinned against the circumference. A woman lived there weaving and selling rugs for a few decades, but left for reasons unknown. Now, it holds a whole lot of graffiti, trash, and serves as a drop point for certain exchanges. We continue up the road and through cliffs impassable by pretty much anything except bikes or horses. Deep inside the park, we brake to a stop and kill our engines.

The two dirt bikes that we borrowed from Don ride loud, but smooth. Before heading out and making sure we wore good helmets, he told us how he pulled these from the quicksand after a festival and revived them. I weave around an oil slick from where some 4x4 rental probably stopped to eat lunch in their air conditioned cab. Although some parts require us to slow down or skirt around rockslides, the route seems easy enough to do for most skill levels.

"We look pretty tough in these," I say, admiring Manuel's set of acrylonitrile butadiene styrene (ABS) armor. We studied the material in school. Strong enough to curb heavy impacts and wipeouts. Strong enough to stop a sword...probably. On the horizon, sets of tourists slow down and completely stop in the center of the main roadway to take photographs of the arches. Further back, blue specks punched out of the rocks show me some of my favorites. I know from experience that they won't translate into photography. I take a sip from my hydration pack that rests in my backpack, the tube of water curled over my shoulder and clipped in near my collarbone.

"It is going to be a nightmare getting through that traffic with our parade of bikes," Manuel says, resting his hand on the jaw of his helmet. I nod.

"We'll only be visible in the park for less than a mile. And less than a half mile of pavement," I say, trying to reassure him. "Chances of anyone even seeing us are slim to none. We'll be faster than pronghorn leaping a fence,"

"You are right, but you have seen the way that some of these people drive, like they have a wish for death,"

"To live and die in Moab, Utah. Right?"

"Right," he says. A cloud of dust drifts across the landscape, lifting into the air, little pieces of floating micah dazzling in the sunlight above the canyon wall.

...

Further along the paved road sits the lonely little town of Cisco, Utah. With half the town in Colorado, you'd think that there might be a large cultural divide among its citizens. But, there isn't a huge culture of anything with only four full time residents. Sitting here on any given weekday will grant you the pleasure of observing the truck that imports 100% of the town's water, making deliveries to the four tanks. I hand over the check to my good friend Gina.

"Thanks, hope it works okay for you," she says, looking back at the van.

"I'm sure it'll be fine. Thank you," I say. "And you're sure it's okay to park it here for a few weeks until we're ready to pick it up?"

"Of course," she says. "I don't know that

you should share anything more than you already have," she says, then goes back into her general store with a wave. The white van will blend in well on the highway, once we ditch the trailer it is attached to. With a welded cage enough for double the amount of dirt bikes we'll be carrying, I imagine that we can resell it for a pretty penny once we're a few states away. Not that our profit margin wasn't high enough already.

Manuel and Mike stand at the back of his big pickup and slide a heavy crate onto the tailgate. With a shaped rock, Mike pops the lid and tosses it onto the dirt with a puff. We gather in a half circle around as we pass out and organize the dirt bike armor according to size, fit, and color. Among our equipment is also a few full size backpacking bags, and a few bags from Don that are designed specifically for dirtbiking. In them there isn't much room for more than a hydration pack and a side sleeve for radios, which gets distributed next. After a few minutes of quiet joking and shuffling, each of us has a set of equipment at our feet or on our bodies. From Don's rental inventory, each piece of equipment is numerically labeled which will aid in our effort to gather the armor and gear we picked out a few minutes ago. Manuel puts open palms toward us and speaks.

"Do not panic. We got these just in case, for intimidation purposes only,"

"Here," Mike says, lifting a canvas shopping bag and walking up to each of us. When the bag reaches me, I peer inside to see several black pistols with their serial numbers crudely filed off. I look at the weapon, then at Mike who greets me with a stern look. I sigh and carefully take one, thankful for the gloves I got a few minutes prior. He comes around with a second bag full of loaded magazines for the weapons. "Everybody take three,"

"We didn't agree on this as a group," I say. Monty and Beet nod in agreement.

"Look, see—" Mike offers, lifting his waistband to show a pistol near his tailbone and a fixed blade knife tucked inside. He rotates and pulls vertically near his belt, exposing a leather concealed carry holster with a small Derringer inside. Further, he kneels and lifts a leg of his cargo shorts up to show us yet another handgun resting on the inside of his thigh with an elastic strap.

"Are you afraid of someone?" Monty asks.

"No, just making sure everyone else is afraid of me. It's no big deal. Once you've got it on you for a few minutes, you'll forget all about it. Just for show."

"And who are we supposed to be showing these to?" Wren inquires.

"The resort, I imagine, if anyone tries to stop us," Monty says.

"Exactly," Manuel replies.

"If we get stopped by other rangers or the police, showing them these wouldn't just be a jail sentence," Beet says.

"It would be suicide," Monty concludes. "We have got to be careful with these. I'm not going to tell anyone else what to do, but if it comes down to it I'm shooting at someone's feet only. I refuse to hurt anyone," he says, putting his palms up. Manuel walks us through basic instructions on how to avoid accidental discharge, what to do if the weapon

  jams while you're using it, how to implement the safety and how to reload, and how to carry it safely. Most of us have had at least a little bit of experience in the past, so we don't spend too much time on it. Manuel has a focused look in his eyes. I wish he had talked to me prior to handing these out, because I would have protested. Perhaps that is exactly why he didn't. Monty and I spend time organizing our equipment inside of the van while others meander about. We organize it in old gym bags from Wabi Sabi Thrift Store, one for each of us. On the morning of, we'll each retrieve our own. Spare parts and gear for the second leg of the trip will be picked up by Wren in the ranger truck, so we can armor up before hitting the dirt track.

Beet combs the parking lot picking up bottle caps and broken glass from the sand, gently placing them into his wide brimmed hat. I admire his posture as he crouches, avoiding bending his back. Manuel has spread open several maps on the flatbed trailer and is carefully copying our route with a highlighter. Each of us will get a copy of the map in case we are separated, so we can rendezvous here in Cisco. Outside of Cisco and Moab is nothing but hours of empty, straight highway, rocks and sand. The expanse goes on for leagues and leagues, taking hours to reach the next human settlement even by airplane. Punishing sun, dirty algae filled water, no rain, no shelter, and no wild edibles. Getting left behind out here would be a death sentence.

Across the red and tan landscape one can seldom find a safe place to rest. Finding a spot with shade and friendly neighbors is a different challenge entirely.

Occasionally Gina, the shop owner, will let RVs and vans park in the lot overnight for a small trade or fee. Without turning around,

Mike gives a half hearted wave and walks off toward the lot in an effort to find some company, I am sure. Wren walks up the wooden porch and enters the general store with a jingle of bells.

...

"Hi Wren, how did it go out there?" Gina asks me. Her open carry bumps against the counter when she leans forward.

"Fine, I guess. As well as it could have. I—"

"I'm glad," she says, pushing her eyebrows together. "I think it is best if you don't say much more,"

"That's fair," I say, putting my hands in my pockets and admiring the glassware she has in a transparent cabinet. A blacklight illuminates the glass a ghostly green color. Radium glass, she explains. The radio on the wall crackles.

"—increased border security amidst a canopy of nationwide threats—"

"Any word on that?" I ask.

"No, they just keep repeating the same thing. Now they're thinking the insurrectionists are going to attack Washington again."

"And what do you think?" I ask. She pauses for a moment, leans back and crosses her arms thoughtfully. The sign on the wall behind her depicts a gun barrel pointed at the viewer, and says 'nothing in this store is worth dying for'.

"I think that if I were the Goodmen and I were planning an attack, I wouldn't make threats about it first. I don't think their plan is to actually attack anything. It's probably just a bunch of lowlifes in their parent's basement—who can blame them, with the housing market, shooting off sparks to get a rise out of people like we don't have enough problems in this country. Trying to cause fear and make everyone scared to go into town. Maybe they're firearm manufacturers trying to increase demand." She chews on her lip. "Course, if I were to plan an attack and I had to be public about it, you'd better believe I would send out a hundred identical threats that I never planned on following through with. That way you get the network going, get the National Guard all spread out, then you can hit harder in a less concentrated area."

"Did they announce a ransom?" I ask. The last few months have been advented by threats of varying nature and location, their only commonality being their origin.

"No," firmly. "I wouldn't sweat it too much, kid. Utah only has enough room for one religious group of whackos and they've been here far longer than the Goodmen have existed."

"Really?" I ask. "I was sure that I heard they have roots for at least a few hundred years,"

"And I'm sure that I heard their leader is immortal," she laughs. "Really. There's nothing to go after here unless they want dust," she says, taking the tea towel off her shoulder and wiping the particles off the glass display case.

"Uranium," I suggest.

"It's all been mined. Just cleanup operations where the old sites used to be. Trust me, there'd be a lot more digging if it was worth getting. From what I've read, the silos are full. Really, I wish you didn't have to worry about this sort of thing at your age, and I'm sorry you have to. The last couple of decades have been...ugh." she shakes her head. "I just hope things straighten out for my grandson."

...

"Hey Wren, can you come back outside?" I pop my head in the door and ask. Gina waves at me. I try to wave back, but let go of the door to do so and it nearly shuts on my fingers.

"Hey," I say, once she's outside.

"What's up?"

"I just talked to everyone else individually. I just wanted to offer a last chance to back out," I say quickly, hoping that she won't think too hard about it. She narrows her eyes.

"You're not a very good criminal; you've got too many feelings," she says, poking me in the chest.

"Look, I've never done a heist before," I say. She smiles gently and puts her arm on my shoulder. "I don't want anyone to do it if they're gonna regret it."

"I already told you that I'm in this. You already gave everyone a chance to back out. Half of the crew traveled across the country to be here,"

"Beet?"

"Mike had a long drive, too," she says. "What more do you want, a blood oath?"

ACT II

WHERE CATTLE HAVE NEVER ROAMED

WHERE CATTLE HAVE NEVER ROAMED

Chapter Seven || Overwatch

New moons are my favorite of the repeating set.
I've always been able to see well in the dark without
help. As I walk across the deserted ranchland, I
admire how the light from the stars is bright enough
to cast harsh shadows from the mesas of the valley.
The flocks of drunken CEOs and their mistresses
are easy to dodge, even in the stark absence of
any cover save the occasional patch of cow parsley
and sagebrush. My only real challenge is to avoid
crushing the cryptobiotic soil. To do so, I follow the
hoof depressions until my toes meet the wood at the
base of the main lodge.

Designed to look like a ski lodge, the timbers
used for construction were imported from the Grand
Tetons after a generous donation from a previous
owner. Although coated with an exterior sealant to
protect from the sun, the logs themselves aren't all
that slippery—especially with my climbing shoes on.
On the corners of the building, I-beams provide
legitimate structural support. I give this a ⸺●

light touch with my hand, but immediately discover that they're still hot from the day's exposure. I continue ascending the outside of the building without much difficulty[4]. At the crux, I find a set of rickety gutters clogged with cottonwood seeds. With a good tug, they'll rip straight off the building and clatter the 60 feet down to expose and likely kill me. I grapple over to the corner of the eave, and rest as I dangle for a second. I swing my legs to the side to gain the momentum I need, then strain as I barely manage to hook my ankle around the corner of the roof, and scrape in a heated effort. The strap on my backpack is caught, and it rips when I lean away from the gutter. I crimp my fingers onto an exposed screw onto the metal roof, panting as I roll flat onto the slick and slanted surface.

Uneasily, I stand with my knees bent. The metal panels buckle with a pop under my weight. My muscles shake from stressing them, I try to slow my breathing as I walk toward the apex of the roof. A popped and deflated balloon here, a pile of bird poop there. Not pictured is the array of solar panels that the brochures declare power the entirety of the resort. I take a seat on a chimney to rest and change out of my climbing shoes and into my boots. I continue walking toward the hatch that will grant me access to the lodge. In an instant, my foot slides on something slick and I go down, my hands preventing me from bashing my face. My palm feels red hot, and dark blood runs down my forearm from a sliced flap of skin.

"Naturally," I sigh, staring at it for a moment before it completely fills with blood. Holding it

against my hip briefly helps with the pain while I try to open my first aid kit with one hand. The stars watch me carefully, distant laughter and champagne popping in the distance to celebrate another successful merger. I inhale hard, looking for extra sensory cues. The pandemic robbed me of most of my smell, but at least I walked away with my life. I close my eyes and inhale, the smell of lobster and steak and beer and dust. With a tight bandage to stop the bleeding on my hand, I limp up to the hatch and shoulder my pack. I stretch my leg and roll my ankle in a circle; the pain will pass soon. Through my binoculars, I look at the dark water cistern nestled onto the distant cliff. Most of the others should be in position there, waiting for our plan to kick into action in a few hours. Monty should be keeping an eye out. It would be a great distance, but I wonder if he watched me slip. Thoughts of them abandoning the whole operation and leaving run through my mind.

A deep breath, a prayer for hinges that aren't squeaky, but of course it shrieks with a corrosive note when I lift it; this thing doesn't get opened more than once or twice in a year. I climb the short ladder down onto the dry-rotting loft where all manner of refuse and clutter is piled. Mike's old ashtray with a mountain of cigarette butts, torn underwear, needle caps, the backs of magnetic name tags. I glance at my hand; the gauze is red but seems to be holding the bleeding. Looking at it makes the throbbing worse.

 Although she won't be on duty for a while, I lean over the edge of the loft and peek at the proximity sensor, nothing more than a small white panel the size of a lightswitch. Thankfully, the cameras are all angled down and away from anywhere I could be seen up here.

Still, Manuel will meet me later and will briefly
be exposed. Tomorrow morning when we get the
paintings we'll also be visible and likely recorded,
but there isn't really a way around that unless my
surprise for Manuel works out.

After making sure the museum below me is
empty, I straddle one of the suspended rafters and
shimmy out to where I can stick my leg into the path
of the proximity sensor. The rough, unfinished wood
catches on my gauze, slowing my progress. Below,
smells of garlic and the clatter of dishes from the
adjacent restaurant echo. A stretched leg confirms
that I can reach it from here, I don't want to have
to fumble out here with a flashlight later. I wonder
how I will pass the time until morning, and I wonder
what meal Manuel is cooking in the kitchen below.
I take a quick look around at some of the paintings
we won't be taking with us. What draws my eye
the most is the set of the owner's paintings we had
visited before. Some large, some extra large, they
ascend and cover almost a full wall. As it was before
I left my employment here, many remain gathering
cobwebs and dust. Specifically cleaned are the
portraits of the owner themselves, and they appear
to be done by the same artist.

From up here I can see a few paintings that
don't have much light shining on them, deviating
from the most recent paintings of the owner.
Relatives, maybe. Some resemblance remains in
the nose and cheekbones, just enough to draw
hereditary lineage past the current owner's
rhinoplasty. Rumor has it that the handful of most
recent paintings look so similar because they're
  based off a photo from a few decades ago,
━━━━━ as the owner is determined not to show

they're aging if at all possible.

Still straddling the rafter, I grab another wad of gauze from my shirt pocket to tuck into my wrap job. While trying to shove it inside, the old pieces are forced out. Without much sound, I fumble and reach into the air below me trying to catch it, but likea pair of sunglasses in the river, it spirals down out of reach. I slap my leg in frustration, then consider dropping down to get it before someone walks in. It is at least a 30 foot drop, I'd break an ankle if nothing worse. I have my ATC, harness, and rope in my bag. In five minutes I could be down and back up. But, what if someone were to walk in to see a recently fired employee mid-rappel? According to a text from Manuel, the sheriff is already on site. No reason to test my luck more than I am just by being here.

Safely back on the loft, I take a look around to see if I can find anything interesting or useful. The post where the stairs used to be mounted holds old electronic panels from various appliances, nothing helpful. I sit and wait on the floor, safely out of sight of the occasional senator that meanders through the museum with a cocktail. I pace back and forth and take a drink of water. Should have brought a book. In the empty room, nothing but my own anxieties about the operation are here to entertain me. My watch shows the time; the night auditor will be on in a few minutes. Running hot, I can almost smell the detergent from the dishwasher trying to keep up as the restaurant winds down for the night. Chemical, different than before.

By crouching or laying down I am hidden in the shadows near the back of the loft, but now I stand. Dim display lights from below hit

my shirt, my heart beating quickly in my exposure, I
drop into a push up and crawl backward. Daring only
to let my eyes peek over the edge...could it be? The
owner berating someone from the kitchen, a new
worker. I recognize her, can't remember her name,
here from Brazil, was it? She's younger than me by a
few years, here to earn money over the summer to
bring back to her family. Maria Campos. That's it.

 She cowers away as the owner screams
something. She, too, holds her hands together as if
to conceal something before the owner rips them
apart and pins her wrist against one of the display
cases. The owner produces a cellphone and captures
a photo of her hand. In the flash, I see a small
bandage wrapped around one finger.

 "I don't know what you were thinking," the
owner spits. "You've been here, what? Two weeks?
That means it has only been two weeks since you
signed your contract. How could you forget so
easily?" Silence, a weep, and a slap on the cheek,
knocking Maria to the floor. I get into a plank,
then on my knee. There's a broken lamp base right
next to me. From this height I could—no. I handle
my pocket knife, then try to cool my anger. The
owner lets out a gasp, then shines a light. Their
hand has a tiny, almost invisible scratch, if I hadn't
been watching through the magnification of my
binoculars, I wouldn't have seen it. "You disgusting
little spic," the owner says, "your braces cut my
ring hand. I—and what's that?" marching over to my
bloodied gauze on the floor, I shut my eyes tightly,
wishing I were anywhere else, "you just throw your
nasty used bandages wherever you want? I've got
  news for you, this is my home. Not yours."

 "May I please leave?" Maria cries,

standing slowly and holding her cheek.

"You're going to go back to work and finish prepping for tomorrow's brunch. And if you speak a word to anybody about this, I'm going to make sure that you never see your family again. Entiendo?"

"I—yes. Okay, I'm sorry,"

"You ought to be much more sorry than you are. As soon as you're done with whatever Manuel has you helping with tonight, you're going to wait for me right here. Understand?"

"Yes, I am sorry, when I—" Maria starts, then the owner grabs her by the shoulders and shoves her back through the door toward the kitchen. She falls onto the floor with a yelp and walks away stifling her sobs. The owner huffs and does something on a cellphone for a few minutes while I back away silently, wondering what I just witnessed and wishing I had cut the chandelier or something. It is bad here-terrible. But very rarely is anyone that cares actually in a position to do anything about it.

I must remember her name. Maria Campos. Maria Campos. Maria Campos. I must remember. There is no consolation prize.

...

I wipe sweat from my brow. All of the heat from the lower stories and the kitchen rises to the loft in a dense, dry saturation. Speaking of saturation, I wrap an elastic bandage around my hand now that the bleeding has finally stopped. All it took was holding my hand above my head for an hour. With just a minute to spare before the night auditor clocks in, Manuel finally appears from around the corner, jogging quietly with a backpack and six poster tubes tucked under his arm.

With a wave, he throws a small stick up to me. Around the center of the stick with a bowline, is a series of shoelaces tied together to make a longer rope. On the other end, tied in a bundle, are the poster tubes that I hoist up. With a nod, he walks off and disappears. I tuck the tubes out of the way under an old children's desk and admire them. Same material as my camping mug: titanium. I undo the twist top on one of them and run my finger along the O-ring. Waterproof? At least water resistant. I carefully inch out one of the replacement paintings, I'm not sure which one it is, but it looks like a rather faithful reproduction. Although the canvas is rolled, I can see the raised texture of the oil paints in the copy.

A tap on my shoulder and I spin, drawing my river knife. Manuel smiles at me, laughing silently to himself. He is quiet when he wants to be, which is most of the time. This is only a part of what makes him a great roommate.

"I saw blood on the roof, are you alright?" he asks, gently grabbing my hand. I nod.

"Yeah I'm fine, just slipped."

"Need sewing? It looked like a lot of blood,"

"Stitches? Only one or two. I managed to stop it,"

"Watch it to avoid an infection," he says, then points to the poster tubes with his chin. "What do you think?"

"Pretty cool, couldn't have made them better myself,"

"Well I know that," he smiles, speaking in a hushed tone. "It is a good thing we decided to wait until morning to transport them. I just spoke with Monty on the radio," he says, turning down the volume almost all the way on his walkie then putting it next to his water bottle. "He said not a single car has driven from here toward Cisco in over two hours. I know he may not be the most committed member of the crew, but I have to say it was a good idea of his to wait for the morning. This way when we leave Cisco the van will blend in with the morning traffic in Junction. Even with the trailer, I think. I am still most worried about the traffic inside of the park."

"Me too, but I think it should be alright."

"All the influencers get there at dawn, though,"

"I know. Admittedly, it is a hard lifestyle..." I jest. He quickly puts the back of his hand on my chest and gets onto his stomach, then points. The owner has walked back into the room. I copy his posture, offering my binoculars. He leans in to whisper.

"I forgot to tell you we had a surprise visit," he says, tickling my ear and making me shiver. The sheriff walks in soon after, in an ill fitting uniform and with a swaying disposition. They speak too quietly for us to hear, especially considering the air conditioning exhaust is right behind us. The owner grabs the sheriff around the collar and kisses him without warning, pulling at his shirt and nearly bursting the buttons. Hands fly in places they shouldn't be, a grunt, a moan. Manuel and I slowly turn to look at each other with wide eyes. He puffs up his cheeks and feigns vomiting in his mouth, then gestures for me to stop laughing and to be quiet.

"Okay," the owner says loudly, shoving the sheriff back.

"I thought we were just getting

started?" he says.

"Save it for later, I want it to last this time. Go get the girl, the one with the braces,"

"Oh, no," Manuel whispers, then looks at me. The sheriff walks toward the restaurant while the owner stares at an empty fireplace and sips on a cocktail. We whisper rapidly, I fill him in on what happened earlier. He pinches the bridge of his nose. "She came in and told me about it, I told the kitchen manager," he says. I blink. "What was I supposed to do?"

"I don't know," I say, trying to think of something helpful and coming up blank. The sheriff reappears, escorting Maria. She stutters, hot tears streaking down her cheeks. I roll onto my side and pull out my cell phone, then start recording a video. Manuel nods in approval, then looks through the binoculars. They're speaking but I can barely hear them, I doubt it'll come out in a video. "I can't hear them," I say, pointing to my phone. Manuel shifts backward. I glance at him pulling a multitool from his belt and leaning into a mass of shadow somewhere further back. The fan from the exhaust skitters to a stop, Manuel carefully gets back into position.

"Ms. Campos, anything to say?" asks the sheriff, facing the young woman toward the owner, who waits expectantly with an empty glass. He locks his arm and pushes down onto her handcuffed wrists, behind her back. She yelps in pain. I go to stand up, but Manuel stops me with a hand on my shoulder. He leans close to me.

"We'll hand this video over to the client. It will help with the case, trust me,"

"They're hurting her, we can stop

this—"

"If you interrupt you'll compromise the mission," he warns, with the most serious face I've ever seen him wear. Down below, Maria pleads.

"We are in the United States. I wish to invoke my right to an attorney."

"There's nobody here who's going to help you. What do you have to say to your owner?"

"Your owner?" I whisper. "What the hell?"

"I wish to invoke my right to an attorney," she says, sobs wracking her tone before she stands up straight. "I wish to invoke my right to an attorney."

"Do you see a bodycam?" the sheriff shouts, standing an inch from her face. He towers over her, yet seems to fail to maintain a sense of authority. "Does it look like you have any rights here?" Frustrated, he grabs her hairnet and pulls backward. She stumbles, still holding her hair he circles back behind and yanks her to the ground. Manuel's eyebrows are pressed together, he strains to keep still. The sheriff rolls her onto her stomach and lifts her by her wrists, a cry of pain, showing the owner the bandaged cut. "You lost your rights the moment you didn't report a work injury,"

"We'll just have to see if anyone still wants you," the owner says, stepping forward with the drink. In the cup is nothing more than a few cubes of ice and a coffee straw. The owner spits in the glass, long and slow. I grimace at the thought of what that must taste like-cigarettes and taffy. With one hand the sheriff pries open Maria's mouth and holds it while the owner pours the bottom of the cocktail down her throat. She chokes and sputters, the ice cube landing on the floor.

189

"Should we make her lick it up?" the

sheriff asks.

"Don't be disgusting," the owner says. "Let's get out of here before closing, follow me." Smiling devilishly the pair drag a crying Maria out of sight and soon out of earshot. As soon as the coast is clear, we rapidly turn to face one another.

"What!" we both say in unison, then speak over one another so quickly that we don't understand a word from the other.

"Dude," he says, shaking his hands in the air. "I mean—"

"I know," I say, emailing the video to him on my phone, then turning it off to save the battery.

"She cut her hand while she was cutting fruit for the parfaits that are served with brunch, that is all that happened, nothing more,"

"They said she didn't report it? I think I heard about others getting fired for not reporting work injuries, then they immediately move off property," I say. Manuel thinks for a moment.

"Maybe they do not move out," he says. "Can you email that to me? I do not know how much good it will do. Others have tried to use video evidence before in court, but the owner won saying that there is no way to prove what happened before or after the camera was turned on. They could have antagonized before the recording started."

"You can hate them all day, but the Mesa has some fine lawyers," I say shamefully. I hope that all of this works out, because I most certainly would hate to put this place on my resume. I reason again with myself that we've taken nearly every measure possible to make our mission a success. After we
190 deliver the paintings and it hits the press, if
⬤━━━━ they figure out who we are, the owner

might try a hail mary to prosecute us for anything and everything the legal team can think of. I pray that the jury will see through this as a last ditch effort of someone who the law finally caught up to. While we discuss what we saw and Manuel sends the video to the others, the last of the night crew clocks out and leaves the building. We know Maria's name, we make a promise to ourselves and to one another to make this right once the heist is over. Right on time, the overhead lights shut off. The emergency exit lights cast a faint glow, reflecting off of the jewelry cases. I'm reminded of museum sleepovers I went to as a cub scout, running from paleolithics and into dinosaurs frozen in time.

I move back out onto the rafter and swing my leg in front of the proximity sensor, illuminating a small LED.

"Hey, Monty, come in," I say quietly into the radio.

"Go ahead,"

"Just triggered it for the first time,"

"Copy, starting the timer. Gotta say, it's almost comical that your plan is to just annoy the police so much that they won't do their job anymore."

...

"And that's 37 minutes," Monty says. "Two cars, perfectly average and ordinary in every way. You know Gwen, by the way? She says hey."

"What? Why is Gwen with you?" I whisper in confusion. We worked together several years ago, she's an old friend and Moab local.

"I...don't think she's gonna

remember this tomorrow. Nothing to worry about," he says.

A few moments later, the night auditor and the architect walk up the steps in the dark, shining a keychain flashlight onto the floor. Manuel and I scoot back, he shoves the radio in his coat to cover the dim projection from the screen.

"I am seriously so sick of this," one of them says, flipping on the lightswitch. "That one, blinking there," I shrink into my clothing, knowing that they're likely pointing or even taking a photo of the sensor just a meter away from me.

"Maybe there's a rat nest or something up there in the loft," the architect suggests. The light goes off and a flashlight beams at us, cutting harshly on the trim at the edge of the loft. I try to make myself flat and end up kicking a vent cover or something with a quiet clang. "Did you hear that?"

"Yeah, like you said. Probably rats," the auditor says. "Case closed. I'm missing the game and I'm going to have to come back up in a minute when the sheriff's department arrives, so if you don't mind," he says. The light points away and the footsteps fade. They are replaced later with a squad of people walking up and turning on the lights. Stiff, broad voices of sheriff's deputies echo through the vacant space.

"Rats, you said?" someone asks.

"Yes, sir, maybe, I don't know,"

"Pretty common this time of year, you haven't lived here long, have you?"

"No," the auditor replies. "How did you guess?"

192   "Well, we don't receive investigative training ———— for nothing. My trained ears noticed

that you were watching a game of cricket on the computer. Even though your American accent is good, it didn't fool me. Listen, it really isn't my department but with everything that's going on at the border I'd make sure you have your paperwork in order, if you can understand my meaning,"

"Yes, sir."

"The agents tend not to give much warning before they arrive," he says, another flashlight beam casting up toward us. "That's why they're getting more effective every year. That, or there's more prey to be caught," he says. Two sets of laughter. "Just looking out for you. You should set some traps,"

...

For a brief moment, I considered saying something to the deputies or forwarding the video somewhere useful, like The Times Independent. Manuel talked me out of it under the same reasoning as before. We need everything to go as smoothly and as quietly as possible. A single slip up here could ruin what we've been planning for months, and we likely won't get another shot at this. If anybody smells anything suspicious, the paintings are likely to go underground and off the radar for decades, if not longer.

This time it is Manuel's turn, he swings his leg out and scoots back to the loft.

"Monty, come in,"

"I'm here," he yawns.

"Mark round two,"

"Copy, starting a timer,"

We continue to replay the video

again and again on Manuel's phone, trying to pick
apart the dialogue to figure out some semblance of
meaning from the encounter. He eats a sandwich
and chips leftover from dinner, I pop open the
roof hatch and pick out constellations with my
binoculars. It isn't long before the radio comes back
to life.

"33 minutes, two squad cars. They're driving
pretty fast, your frustration plan must be working,"

"Copy, thanks," I say. Against the dirty
ceiling, faint blue and red lights dance. The same
officers walk back up with the night auditor, the
lights come on. We move further back into the loft,
well out of sight.

"Well, that's par for the course," one of
the deputies says. "Nobody here. Have you tried
checking the cameras when the sensor goes off?"

"I don't have access to the cameras," the
auditor says. Only the general manager does. "They
point at the merchandise anyway,"

"You might want to adjust those cameras
to see what is triggering that sensor. Looks like
you have a pretty spacious loft up there. It isn't
a long walk to the kitchen for a rat. Does it look
like everything is here to you? Anything look out of
place?" he asks. A moment of pause and footsteps.

"Nobody ever takes anything from here," he
says. "It's all fine."

"Yeah," the deputy laughs. "Lot of one of a
kind pieces. Be hard to sell any of this,"

"Yikes," I say to Manuel, who shakes his head
nonchalantly.

"Listen, here's my card. I wrote your case
number for this call on the back. Call the office
in the morning between 8 and 10, and ask

for me. My name's on the front. I don't have it now but I'll give you the information for a friend of mine who does pest control. I know y'all have had some trouble getting contractors to come out here in the past, on account of not paying them and everything, but my buddy can come out and at least confirm for you whether or not you've got a rat problem."

"Thank you, sir,"

"You're welcome. Happy to help. How are you liking Moab so far? Different from home?"

"Very different. It can be hard to get to town for groceries and things like that, but I have many American friends here with cars that can help me,"

"That's great. Any chance you started the morning coffee yet?"

"No, sir, I do not start that until 4:30. I could always make you a cup," he says.

"We'll just swing by the new chain coffee place once we're back in town. If that godforsaken alarm goes off again tonight maybe I'll take you up on it. Thanks, though," he says.

"What new place? I would like to try it when next I go into town,"

"Oh, I'd give you a name now and by next week it would no longer be the newest. Kind of a weekly tradition for the graveyard shift."

...

"So, Monty? Is that your birth name?" Gwen asks me. She appeared out of nowhere an hour or two ago and hasn't left yet.

"Yeah," I point at Mt. Peale, not much more than a riveted silhouette without a moon to illuminate her. A few friends and I have a recurring bet every year as to when the last bit of snow cap will disappear. Last week, the final cap of white melted off of the summit. It melts sooner every year. "I live up there,"

"A little bit on the nose from your parents, don't you think?" she asks, taking a toke from her joint. She offers me a hit, but I decline. I take a sip from my hydration pack, which is filled with iced coffee. Well, cold watered-down coffee at this point. Behind us is the water cistern, a reservoir on BLM land that anyone nearby can tap into. Further back on the hill approaching the mesa is a small wooden cross, bone dry and held together with a twist of cattle wire. It used to be a main feature of my tours, especially when we were on horseback. The scripted interp we had to share explained that the grave belonged to the owner's ancestor, one of the original settlers of the region. Although it is one of the distinguishing features of the Maroon Mesa region, that doesn't change the fact that the grave up there is from a rancher that was born in Colorado and died a hundred years before the resort here was even conceived of. The theft of identity is unacceptable.

I climb the side ladder on the rusted cistern, sliding a red piece of sheet metal to the side so I can peer in. With a small flashlight, I illuminate the stinking brown water. Mike climbs up and takes a turn.

"Gross," he says. "Even I wouldn't drink that,"

"I suppose I shouldn't tell you that you drank it every single day you were at work, put it into every dish," I say.

"No, sir. Bottled water for me,"

"Of course," I say. Beet sleeps slumped against a brick half wall, quietly snoring with his hat over his face. I turn and look back at the Colorado River, to our north. Almost a mile away is the main lodge of the resort, glittering obnoxiously in the otherwise crystalline hours of night.

"Do you know the story of the cistern?" Gwen asks mysteriously. I had met her a few times at community gatherings, but have never spent so much time adjacent to her. She's friendly, but I keep asking myself what she's doing out here in the middle of the night. This plan has so many facets that could go wrong already. I shake out the worry that she might be in on it somehow, and not just here because we happened to be at her smoke spot. She sips a cup of coffee, then frowns. Her dog, a chocolate lab, wanders around and lifts a leg next to Beet, then moves along to curl up next to his owner. "Hello?"

"No, I don't," I say, a little bit sharper than I had meant to. The video Manuel emailed me has me a bit on edge.

"You clearly don't want to talk to me, so I'll give you the short version. There was a body rotting in there five years ago,"

"Okay, sure," I reply. She finishes a joint and puts it in her pocket, then lights another one. She takes a puff and passes it to Mike, who meanders around with a beer in one hand and the joint in another.

"You don't believe me?" she asks.

"I believe you," Mike sings, giggling a little bit. "Bottled water all the way," he says. "I've been thinking about something clever to say to the reporters if we get caught, other than

197

'down with the patriarchy'," Beet springs upward with a shout, turning all eyes toward him.

"You alright?" I ask.

"Yeah. Nightmare," he says, then rolls back to sleep. I peer toward the lodge through my spotting scope, stabilized on a tripod. The squad car is still parked, its red and blue lights blasting into the night and illuminating the distant canyon walls. Procedurally, the lights shut off until only the headlights remain and the vehicle slowly drives off property.

"Hey," Birch says through the radio. "What was the time on that?"

"28 minutes. Only one car this time. No traffic, I guess."

"No more squad cars on property? Can you look around, looking for undercover cars, too," he asks. I look with the scope at every spot I can see from my current position.

"Yeah, all clear."

"Did the same number of police cars that arrived all leave?" he asks.

"Yes," I say, unsure of what he's getting at.

"All day?"

"All day."

"Okay, thanks," he says. "I was just wondering about that girl that got arrested,"

Chapter Eight || Grave and Imminent Danger

2,4,6,8. I count the sections of rope tied together in a loop that wraps down underneath my butt, then slide our descent rig off and reach for my bag. I pull out a handgun, which to an untrained eye looks identical to any real, working model.

"What did you bring a toy for?" Manuel asks. Golden light reverberates around the room as the morning sun clears the canyon wall.

"It was a surprise for you, a gift," I say, handing it to him. He inspects it and pulls out the magazine, touches the gas cartridge and cocks it. "I figured we could blind the cameras with the paintballs,"

"Very kind of you, thank you. Have you played much before? Paintball is very popular in America, yes?"

"Once or twice, birthday parties. One time a friend's older brother joined the Marines, he was home after basic training and played with us. It was pretty fascinating to watch how he played differently before and after being trained.”

"Looks like we only have six shots, and five cameras,”

"Yeah,” I say. "I could've brought a full size paintball gun, but it didn't really seem like a necessity.”

"Right, but it was clever of you. I was sweating about being on these cameras all night,” he says. "I better take the shots, if you do not mind. More experience with guns than you,”

"Mhm,” I say, trying to recall if or when he had ever mentioned shooting before. He handles it well, weighing it in his palm before taking a practiced stance and pecking off the cameras one by one. For the final camera, he tiptoes out onto the rafter above the sensor to achieve a solid angle before spraying paint on the lens to blind it. He locks the safety and puts the device into his cargo pants pocket, then looks at me. I clip the handgun that I was given to me earlier onto a belt loop of my pants. Last night I tied a length of webbing around the grip in absence of a holster. It swings a bit too loosely for my comfort.

"How do you feel?” he asks.

"I'm nervous,” I admit. "Scared,”

He nods, putting a hand on my shoulder. "We're going to change lives,” I nod. "Hopefully when we trigger this alarm the police will not even come this time, given the several false alerts. Even if they do, we have about thirty minutes before we need to be the heck off of this property. Nothing to be a scared of.”

"I've never done anything big like this before,” I say.

"It is not much more complicated than

planning a tour route. Maybe a little longer but hey, you get to spend time with friends, right?" he jeers, stepping back and handing me our makeshift descender. I slip it on and grab the large walkie talkie from the water bottle pocket of my bag. The building is virtually silent, save for our voices and the metal roof popping as the sun heats it. The night auditor should still be downstairs, but far out of hearing range. If things go to plan, he too will ignore the next proximity sensor alarm when it goes off.

"Monty, you there?"

"I'm here, loud and clear,"

"Sitrep?" I ask, feeling a bit silly and a bit like I'm in a theater production.

"Yeah. Traffic is backing up on river road, according to schedule. Lots of folks on their way to Junction by way of Cisco, we should blend in just fine. Looks like you've still got two hours before the restaurant opens, should be alone in there except the night auditor, I haven't seen anybody else pull into the resort. What else?" he says, his voice getting a little quieter. "We've got a pleasant eastwind caressing us up here. Quite lovely."

"And Mike?"

"Mike hiked down and joined the head housekeeper for a midnight snack last night. The elderly lady with black hair? He left her house maybe an hour ago, I saw him head down to the water with the raft and paddles."

"Gwen still there?"

"No, she took off. Morning shift at the coffee shop. Beet and I are ready to go at your signal,"

"Okay, thanks. Wren, you copy?" I ask.

"Go for Arches Repeater," she says, static and muffled due to the geology between us.

"Very funny. Are you on schedule?" I ask, beginning to shake a bit and feeling queasy.

"Yep, all good on my end. Send me a signal when you start the canyon run, then I'll get into position. Backpacking bags are all set to go,"

"Copy, thanks," I say. Manuel fixes the last bit of his gear and slowly nods at me, then gives a thumbs up.

"We've got this," he says confidently. I take a few deep breaths to calm my breathing, then lift the radio one last time.

"Anybody not ready?" I ask. Silence. "Okay, dropping now. Over."

"May the Force be with you," Monty says.

"And stay gold, Ponyboy." Wren says. Manuel tilts his head and smiles.

"Let's do this. After you,"

"Rope," I whisper, throwing the rappel line down to the wooden floor with a slap. I sit on the edge of the ledge, then swing over the side and hang freely beneath the rope, looped through the rafter above me. With a quiet clang like dull windchimes, the poster tubes around my shoulder settle down. I slowly loosen my grip on the rope, letting it feed through my uncut hand, heating up and quickly burning without a glove on. My handgun dangles freely below me, pointing in every direction and spinning like an angry ghost is holding it. A kink in the rope, I shimmy and it unravels, a twist rotating me until finally my feet hit the floor. I glance up and see the proximity sensor's LED lit up. At eye level, I see through a crack in the door that a light is on in 204 the kitchen. Must be from last night, nothing to
━━━━━━━ worry about.

"Everything okay?" Manuel asks from above, sitting on the ledge.

"Yeah—" I say. "Just—untangling," I lift the heavy rope over my head, stepping through the mess and yank it free of where it was caught on my bag, trying not to make an absolute racket with the poster tubes.

Audibly, the kitchen door opens. I freeze, then spin around to see the sheriff's eyes meeting mine.

He looks just as surprised to see me as I am to see him, holding a pile of pastries in the crook of his elbow and a ceramic dinner bowl full of cereal and milk. He makes a confused sound and glances at the gun swinging from my hip, then drops the bowl and reaches for his waistband.

The bowl shatters instantly, sugary puffs and 2% splattering in every direction.

I jump backward, but swing on the rope forward, slamming into the sheriff who puts me in a chokehold with one hand. I let the poster tubes fall to the ground in a great clatter and wave my arms, frantically trying to prevent him from putting the gun to my head.

A heavy tug at my waist and I am pulled away from him, straight under the rafter. The rope caught at my feet, moving up toward the sky as I scurry over the line and look for cover somewhere—anywhere.

I think of the gun on my hip, but I am

severely behind on the draw and I would just get
shot—

A heavy lamp from the loft rockets down, catching
the enemy in the forearm and knocking his pistol
to the ground. He looks up, then at me. I throw my
backpack at his face and dive for the pistol.

He makes a yelp as the air is forced from his lungs,
I spin and see Manuel swinging from the rope and
connecting with the man's chest. He falls to the
ground, his head making audible contact. My friend
quickly meets him there, wrapping the dynamic rope
around his neck and pulling tension. I rush over.

    "He's unconscious, look," I blurt, faster than
intended. Manuel stammers and pulls the rope off
of him. We catch our breath and fall back onto our
bottoms. I grip my hand into a hard fist, feeling
fresh blood from my wound saturating my elastic
bandage, but no pain. "Is he dead?"
    "No, he still has a pulse," Manuel says after
checking. "Someone probably heard all that. Let's
check him real quick and then get out of here,"
    "Nobody was supposed to get hurt," I say.
He starts rifling through the man's pockets. "Check
him? What do you mean? Don't shake him, watch
you don't twist his neck," I say, then start helping.
Manuel pauses for a minute at his shirt, which was
untucked and stained when he walked out of the
kitchen. He rips the badge off of the fabric and
sets it aside. The unconscious man's jaw opens and
hangs loose, his face has a series of freshly scabbed
scratches running down it.
    "Did you scratch him?" Manuel asks.

"Mm-mm."

"Me either. Look at this uniform," he says, picking at the fake pockets with two fingers and looking at me. "Look familiar?"

"What does that mean?" I ask, knowing the answer. They are the same set of pants we purchased from the Halloween store in Junction, to play a prank pretending to be rangers. These are cheaply made nylon with a fake hem and fake pleats. He picks up the badge and grabs my arm, dragging me over to the display case. He points inside, at the jewelry for sale and the souvenir sheriff's badges, the gold one being an identical match. He looks at me with a look of grave concern, then takes out his phone and begins taking photos of everything while I empty the rest of the stranger's pockets. I unearth his wallet, with a license from Pennsylvania and not Utah, an empty carton of cigarettes, wrappers from the mints served in the lobby, a citation booklet, a wet $20, a pair of torn women's underwear, and a strange looking brochure. I take photos of everything, and leave his belongings with him except the brochure, which gets shoved into my pocket.

Frantically, we pack the rope into my backpack in a tangled heap and open the plexiglass paintings. The pressure sensors, small spring loaded brackets, fall out of place and onto the ground.

"Fakes?" I ask. He nods. "Look at this, fast," I say, handing him the brochure. He studies it, his eyes darting all over the page before he shoves it back to me.

"Do not lose that, keep it somewhere safe," he says, meeting my eyes to confirm my understanding.

"So does this mean every parking ticket I've ever paid to that guy has been a fake?" I ask.

"Did you pay in cash?"

"Yeah, ugh," I complain, helping to remove the framed paintings from their cases and lean them against the wall. With one hand, I wiggle the radio free from my bag while I use a small flathead screwdriver to free the canvas from the wooden trim with the other. Lifting the radio to my face, blood drips down onto the floor.

"Monty, come in,"

"I'm here, we're in position,"

"Great, we just had a run-in with the sheriff, or—I don't know. Someone came and drew a gun on us. We've got it under control but I need you to tell me immediately if you hear sirens,"

"Loud and clear?" he asks.

"They can be distant or muffled,"

"No, I mean I understand,"

"Okay, thanks. We'll be out as fast as we can," I say, shoving the radio back into the water bottle pocket of my bag.

"You're bleeding," Manuel says, as we pry the kingfisher painting off of its frame. On the back, taped with masking tape, are several sheets of paper with various names, phone numbers, addresses, check marks and X marks.

Here, the hotline to call for questions about the process.

The phone number for the resort. Are they really that bold?

We gape for a moment, recognizing both Maria Campos and Catherine Beaker. Manuel shakes his 208 head heavily.

A new voice cuts into the room.

    "Hello?" it says. We grit our teeth and continue as quietly as we can. "I heard something break, is there anyone up here?"
    I hold my hand out at a distance, preventing the blood from dropping onto the artwork. Footsteps. Manuel gestures frantically.
    "This is the sheriff," I state in my most commanding voice. "Everything is under control. Do not enter the museum. Go back to your desk and I will fill you in momentarily."
    "Uh-okay? I'm going to go let the general manager know that you're here again. She thought that you left."
    "No, do not do that," I say quickly. No response. Footsteps headed away from us. We resume our work, me working with one hand and Manuel gracefully deframing the set. I open up my medical kit and put a blue latex glove over my injured hand so we can work faster.
    With a seemingly practiced ease, Manuel frames the fakes while I carefully roll the originals into the tube, a sheet of glassine paper preventing the paint from rubbing against the now wrapped canvas. With a twist, the water sealed tops lock into place. We lift Manuel's finished work back into the plexiglass mounts, then pick up the fake pressure sensors. We try to get them to stay in place for a moment, then think better of it and throw them into Manuel's bag. This entire reframing process is done in a fraction of the time that museum protocol dictates, but still takes far too long for my liking.
    "Hey," the radio clicks. "8 minutes left on our average time." Monty says. "Just

letting you know,"

"We are so screwed," I pant, rushing back over to the injured man to check his pulse.

"Stay focused, Birch. We are only running behind because of that," he says, looking at his watch. I do a quick pat down to check for any blood and in case we missed something, but find nothing. With my gloved hand I pick up his handgun and eject the magazine, then brace the weapon against my thigh to cycle it and eject the chambered bullet which hits the ground with a glimmer. I lean back and lob the gun up onto the loft where it clatters to a halt. No desired outcome other than confusion for whoever finds him. That, and so he can't gun us down through the window if he wakes up soon.

With everything in order except for the incapacitated assailant, we walk quickly for the kitchen door, trying not to make more noise than we already have. From a side door, the general manager appears with a preceding energy of anger.

"Hey! What are you doing?" she shouts in her thick Bulgarian accent. Her massive, heavy frame takes up the full doorway.

"We're just working on some stuff for school," I blurt out. Manuel grabs the back of my collar and yanks me backward into the kitchen, we sprint through and trip over a serving table full of dishes someone had moved. A tray of wine glasses shatter onto the tile floor in a painful screech. From the floor, I see the cart was moved to open the pastry freezer. Manuel is up in an instant, meeting the manager as she throws open the kitchen door screaming. With a swift forward kick from my friend, the door swings back to hit her. She throws it open again. Manuel backs up quickly, bumping into a cooler and a prep station. He reaches back and pulls out the paintball gun, a bright burst of blue paint impacts her on the heart. Marching at him, she is at least a foot taller and easily double his weight.

"You are so fired, Manuel," she jeers. He launches the spent gun at her face. She leans to the side and it bounces off of a fire extinguisher. He reaches an open palm out to me, I throw him one of the poster tubes and dive over the prep station, landing on my shoulder and rolling to avoid cutting my other hand. I grab the fire extinguisher off the wall and pull the pin.

"Oi!" I shout, she spins and gets a cloud of noxious powder shot in her face. Through the haze, I barely see the edge of one of the titanium tubes swinging and making contact with her temple. She stumbles and falls against the wall, coughing out white powder in a plume. I vault back over the prep station and sprint for the door with my partner, practically falling into it. We land against a railing on the third story of the building.

A second of silence, outside, a bird chirps. The fire alarm blares, I glance at the bright red push handle on the door, declaring this an emergency exit. Through the blinking light, like a camera flash, the large manager's silhouette moves through the kitchen toward us with unpredicted speed. Manuel grabs my sleeve as I hold my breath and reach back into the room, pulling the fire alarm on the wall.

A second series of alarms activates, buzzing my ear. I back up into Manuel, watching jets of foam rocket out of the vent hoods and quickly filling the room. We slam the door and beat the handle with the bottom of one of the tubes, but it does nothing. I jump down the stairs several at a time, falling and dropping several tubes over and over again until finally we reach the ground level and run across the golf course quicker than my legs will carry me.

...

"Jeez, Monty, you run track?" Mike asks as I drop from a jog to a walk. He sits on the edge of the ugly raft, one foot inside and one foot dangling in the water, sneakers and socks on both feet. A lit cigarette rests in his hand.

"In high school. Just keeping up my metabolism," I admit, proud of taking responsibility for my figure.

"A question for you two," he says, turning his head to make sure Beet, who is lounging in the water, can hear. "Do you think the hot tip of this cigarette can pop this raft?"

"Mm, no." I say.

"I do, and for the last time, you probably shouldn't try it," Beet says, then wades a little deeper.

"Think about it, it would pop a balloon," Mike offers.

"But I think the only reason it pops a balloon is because it heats the air inside so much that the elasticity can't handle it," I say. Just then, a pounding of footsteps on the sand behind us. I turn to face the resort, bursting forth from the rocks like a parasite. On the edge of the golf course I see Manuel and Birch cradling the poster tubes they mentioned, tripping and falling all over themselves over prickly pear and sharp yucca. Immediately behind them is a smaller framed person, one of the new visa workers I think.

"Beet, get in the boat," Mike says, throwing his cigarette into the water. "Now,"

Beet sloshes over and hops in, then tucks the paddle blades under the thwarts where they can be easily pulled out. I toss my bag to Mike and get my feet wet, ready to help however I can. The three runners reach the embankment, which crumbles under their collective weight and drops them a meter into the wet shallows. They scramble to their feet and run at us, throwing their gear and themselves into the boat.

"Hey, you can't take those! You can't launch here either, this is private property!" the worker says. They're young, like they might still be in highschool. New here, too new to recognize any of us except Manuel and maybe Birch. He clips on his guide PFD, the only one we brought because of its utility; CPR mask, knife, and whistle. We put the radios and a few other things into drybags for safekeeping, which are then clipped to the thwarts.

"Look, miss," I say. "You're getting how much? Probably $7 an hour because they're covering room and board?"

"That doesn't matter," she says defensively.

"It does, actually. Maybe you'll figure that out later. Look, we're leaving. Sorry about all the confusion," I say, when movement on the embankment catches my eye. The general manager, the one of my nightmares, pounds into the cryptobiotic soil. She leaps over the drop, her weight carrying her down onto the sand.

"Monty, get in the boat!" someone shouts. I turn around and begin pushing the

213

boat out of the shallows and closer to the center of the river, where a deep channel runs and the current picks up. On all sides, bright red canyon walls stare at us beneath a bright blue sky. To my terror, the manager strips her outer layers that are covered in what looks like melted marshmallow and baby powder.

"Get the list! The list!" she shouts at the visa worker, who looks back in confusion. "The paintings! The tubes!"

Overweight but muscular, the manager pounds toward us while the visa worker runs back toward the resort. A hard thump on the back of my neck and a shove forward, the momentum I already had tumbles me down onto my knees in the water. I stand back up just in time to receive another blow on the cheekbone, and manage to block the next by diving down and swimming a few feet away. Surfacing in the waist deep water, the raft is picking up speed away from us.

She reaches into her vest pocket and pulls out a small blade—either a letter opener or a dagger, then trodges toward the raft.

"She's gonna pop us!" someone yells, I run through the water until my muscles burn like acid and finally catch up, hitting her on the side with the back of my fist and getting swiped at in return. The nose of the vessel is being pulled into the fast moving water, I hold onto the perimeter line with all my might as the riverbottom stones roll beneath me. I try to dig my toes in somewhere, but repeatedly move to dodge the slow but heavy swiping of the blade-definitely a letter opener.

214   Birch throws the cooler full of our lunches at her, smashing her face and sending BLTs

floating. He jumps out of the raft and tries to pull her attention off of me.

"Get in the boat!" he screams, face bright red to match the blood streaming down his arm and dyeing the water.

"Summer teeth," Mike says, throwing a paddle through the air to Birch, who catches it with one hand and swings at the manager from a few feet away. She dodges the first swipe, I deliver a solid punch to her kidney, he finally connects the blade of the paddle to her jaw, then takes another swing, meeting the aluminum shaft to her skull. She staggers forward, he swings again and again, making contact twice with her mouth and bending the paddle 30 degrees from straight.

"Some'r in your mouth," he says, then chops downward for a decisive blow, "some'r in the water."

"Let's go," I say, my muscles straining to hold the raft in place for him. He leaps paddle first, Beet dragging him in over the side. The manager sways in the water, clutching her mouth and wailing. I try not to look and muscle up into the raft as it is finally allowed to catch the current. "This is specifically not what I signed up for,"

"I know, but we're in it now," Birch says. The bow of the boat gets caught in an eddy as Birch gets into position with the guide paddle at the stern. We all paddle forward, he steers the stern around to catch the current and push us into the waves.

"Look," Beet points.

"No way," I say, rubbing my hurting cheek and checking for blood. Covered in sand, mud, and water like all of us, the manager sprints at full 215 speed, outrunning us in a parallel route along the shoreline. Mike stands up and cracks his knuckles[12]. "Birch, direct us next to that dock," he says, with such conviction that Birch doesn't hesitate or question. The rest of us gape in horror as a thousand thoughts of what the next moment might hold race through my head. Manuel is at the bow, trying desperately to tie the poster tubes to the raft with a cam strap. "Are you trying to get killed, old lady? The resort isn't worth all this. We learned that a long time ago," Mike shouts over the roar of whitewater. Still, the manager pounds into the dirt and runs for the disheveled old dock we are about to pass.

"Too close, man, too close to the dock," I say, not sure if our guide can hear me, or cares. The manager runs at full speed onto the dock, preparing to jump down onto us, the dry rotted wood gives way on the last step. She stumbles, her ankle catches, her mass lands with the weight of an anchor at the rear of the boat.

The front of the boat recoils into the air without warning.

"Ha—" Manuel yelps as he catapults through the air and disappears into the whitecaps.

Mike grapples with the manager in the center of the boat, we toss and turn at unpredictable angles as we pass the chunk of rock that marks the beginning of the Maroon Rapid system. I crawl through the manager's legs and over the thwarts, trying to get to the front of the boat where I can find Manuel. Why didn't we pack lifejackets?

I reach the front of the boat Band hold desperately onto the chicken line, getting blasted by a wave and nearly going over myself.

"I don't have any power, I can hardly

steer, hang on," Birch screams. I see the tattoo
on his ankle and pray it to be true: RIG2FLIP. Are
we capable of staying afloat through all this? I feel
like I am drowning even though oxygen surrounds
me. I choke and push the water out of my nose.
There—black hair bobbing a few meters away. Beet
trying to paddle at the front. A glance back, a fist
fight between Mike and the manager, a tooth goes
flying. The raft bucks upward, then down as we skim
around a hole, I watch Manuel's body get ripped
downward like muck at the bottom of a drain.
I reach for the throw bag at the stern—he's used
it to tie the posters. No time. There's another at
the bow, I can use it to throw a line of rope at him
and reel him in. I run along the perimeter tube
and allow myself to faceplant in order to get there
faster. Lean back to avoid an overhanging ledge that
nearly decapitates me. I unclip it from the D-ring
and dive over the thwart, feeling my stomach drop.
Just downstream, the horizon of water disappears.
Even experienced rafters know-and fear-this route.
Portage to avoid it is the standard ever since this
rapid formed. I look back at Birch, face bright red
and equally colored blood spilling all over the raft,
sloshing back and forth. He looks woozy, his face
trembling with focus.

Beet paddles with ferocity, panting like a
madman.

"Stop, I will give you a hundred dollar gift
card for the paintings, right now," the manager
pleads to Mike, breathless. The boat slams into a
rock, nearly knocking them from standing. Mike's
face contorts in confusion, then he prepares to
deliver a haymaker.

"Minimum wage, *maximum rage*,"

he shouts, the power of his blow railing straight through a defensive block and making complete contact with the manager's brow. He goes to deliver another haymaker, but the manager ducks under and plows into him, raising the letter opener to stab. Mike grapples, the blade slowly reaching closer to his neck.

"Don't you understand? If I let these get taken, the owner will kill me anyway!" the manager screams.

I jump and slam my weight into the manager, but only bounce off against her mass. Birch struggles to steer, digging deep and failing to maintain any sort of control against the terrible approach and near complete lack of thrust. This route is challenging even with a good set of paddlers and adequate planning. Upstream behind us, Manuel's head pops out of the water for a gasp of air, he frantically grasps at a wet rock and fails, sucked underwater again. I glance downstream, the roar of the drop filling my ears along with my heartbeat.

I stand up and prepare to hurl the throw bag toward Manuel. Birch stands up and pulls the pilot knife from the only PFD we brought. He reaches forward and slices at the back of the manager's knee, then tosses the blade to Mike. In the momentary absence of a guiding rudder, the boat spins out of control and bounces like a pinball from rock to rock. Beet looks at me, his face ghastly white. The blade of his paddle has snapped. More plastic in the river.

"Biggun' Drop coming up," Birch shouts, the boat headed toward another rock sticking out of the water. The manager takes another jab at Mike, sticking him somewhere in the ribs. Beet stands up and runs the length of the vessel, jumping with his feet forward just before we plow into the massive boulder. His heels connect with the manager, he drop kicks, sending her off the raft and into the rock. With such momentum she had no hope to slow down by sticking out her hands, they slip immediately as her knees and elbows tear open on the cheese grater surface.

Remarkably, she rolls off the boat and toils back into the raft with a thud.

Mike lifts her up by her collar. "Do you know what this place has taken from me?" he screams, his voice cracking. A flurry of blows with the hilt of the pilot knife. The front of the raft meets the apex of the waterfall. I launch the throw bag into the white caps to our rear, where it hits Manuel straight in the head. As gravity gives out beneath us, I see his hand wrap around the neon yellow cord before he disappears out of view. I roll backward as we drop, my stomach in my throat, the poster tubes flying like kites. With furious strength, Mike throws the manager over the side. With horror, I watch as she flails helplessly in the air until her spine slaps into a boulder. She bounces off. We slam down into the pouring foam, her limp body slapping next to us in the water.

I reel in the line from the throw bag as quickly as I can, until finally Manuel's wrist is in my grasp. I wrap my arms under his armpits and lean back, yanking him into the boat on top of me. Immediately, he vomits clear water on my chest and apologizes, then goes into a coughing fit sputtering up water. Next to me, Beet recovers and grabs a new paddle, heaving and shaking his wet hair. Behind, Birch climbs back into the raft and spits.

Mike grabs the general manager's ponytail like a mass of seaweed, then leans in close.

"Mike," I warn, loud enough for him to hear. We've cleared the worst of it, Class I and II from here until Salt Wash. He lifts her head out of the water and presses his face near hers.

"If you breathe a word of this, I won't only kill you, but your whole family too. Understand?"

"Mike. Pull her in the boat," I say, and Beet helps him. In the end, it takes the strength of all three of us to pull her up, I'm not sure how Mike threw her like that earlier. She coughs delicately, her nose broken and bleeding out onto her chest.

I grab Birch's backpack and pull out the med kit, throw on gloves and begin working on her. I open her mouth and sweep two fingers around her tongue, pulling out fragments of teeth and place them respectfully in her breast pocket. I wrap the SAM splint to form a neck brace, noting the rapid bruising on her collarbone. Birch makes hard eye contact with me: she isn't looking good. With Beet's broken paddle and some webbing, we stabilize a most likely broken leg, then wrap gauze around her still bleeding elbows and knees. "This is most of our medical supplies,"

"We can re-up from the ranger truck,"

"Wouldn't that be federal larceny or something?" I ask.

220   "We're already there, bud. Make sure you save some of those supplies for us," Mike

says, trying to light a sopping cigarette and holding his rib tightly.

"I'm going to use whatever I need to in order to help her," I say. "And I'm not having that argument with you."

"Whatever, man. I just saved all of our lives,"

"You could have taken hers," Birch says. Mike doesn't reply.

"He did what needed to be done in the moment," Manuel says, laying on his side in a pool of foamy puke. With a rise and fall in the boat, it gets sucked through the self-bailing holes. "I'm not sure what happened, but it looked like it could have ended up a lot worse. It looked like she was trying to kill you."

"Maybe," Mike says, then looks away. I toss a wound packing kit to him.

"Shove that in your wound, how deep is it?" I ask. He throws the package back at me.

"Use it on her. I'm fine." He gives up on the cigarette, tucking it behind his ear and pocketing a lighter.

"Don't be a tough guy," Beet says, pushing his glasses back on and securing their strap tightly to his head.

"I'm fine,"

I help Beet with the only other remaining paddle, in an hour we reach the river bend at the entrance to Salt Wash Canyon: a towering channel cut perpendicularly through the canyon wall. Taller than skyscrapers, hotter than Hell. We beach and yank the raft onto the sand. Beet and I, being the most physically sound, drag the manager out into one of the only spots of shade next to a tall log 221 of driftwood. Birch looks across the river at the rapids, then hunches with his hands on his knees.   He wretches, Beet puts his hand on Birch's back in solidarity.

Manuel collects himself and tries to work out a kink in his shoulder blade. Mike brings all of the equipment out of the water and begins to deflate the raft.

"Hey, wait—" Manuel says, pinching his face.

"I thought we were supposed to take this stuff with us?" Mike says, still bent over manually depressing the air valve instead of locking it.

"We have lost a lot of time," explains Manuel.

"Carrying it will slow us down, maybe we can stow it underneath some rocks."

"Under where? All I see is dead cottonwood," Beet says.

"Underwear," Mike giggles.

"Shut up, dude." Manuel says sharply. We can roll it under a log and get it later.

"I hear you, but consider that that raft would be physical evidence that would link us back to the crime," Birch says, walking up to the group. In an exaggerated gesture, Mike displays the wreck of a general manager on the shoreline. "Not just a witness statement,"

I recall the races we ran with it a few years ago, and the sparse competitions we entered. Not to mention it's one-of-a-kind construction made of Birch's whirlpool trash recovery hobby. Posters of this thing-and us in it—are on the wall in half of the restaurants in town.

"Okay, so are we taking the raft?" Mike asks, still bent over. Nobody replies. "I'm packing up the 222 raft and paddles, somebody please stop me if I don't need to be doing this," he says to the ground as he pushes the rest of the air out of it. Beet collects the remainder of the paddles and helps me drag the manager through the mouth of the canyon and into the shade of a healthy cottonwood. Above us, a robin stares and sings. I prop her up against the bark, head angled downward in case she vomits. A quick jog away are the backpacking bags Wren left here. I peer up, trying to see the upper edge of the canyon wall, then back down at the sets of footsteps in the dry sand, leading to the river and back through the canyon, into Arches National Park. "How do you think she got the backpacks in here? There's five of them, probably 40 pounds each, and that trail takes 7 hours to hike." I ask, pointing with an open hand. Beet shrugs, then smiles looking up at the sliver of blue against the amber yellow of the sandstone. I put my hands on my hips and huff.

"Oh," I realize. "*Wren.*"

"Trippy, man," he smiles.

I grab one of the packs, mine, and bring it over to the manager. We had bought (and packed) enough supplies to deal with an emergency like this. The process of that was dreary and only served to heighten my worries about the situation—why would we ever need half of this equipment? When sitting adjacent to this broken body I'm grateful for every ounce of bandages and every foot of gauze. I pull off the old, sandy and soggy bandages-more full of water than anything else—and dry her off before replacing them. I work alone in this endeavor, the remainder of the crew struggling to roll the raft to a size that will fit in one of the backpacks. One of her eyes is bruised and already swollen so badly that it can't be opened, the other is a deepening red and inflamed more with each minute that passes. I speak to her as I work, telling her what I'm doing to ease her fear. Still, she moves no limbs and only breaths softly through an open mouth. When I've done all I can to patch her up, I grind a small painkiller between two river stones and fill a water bottle cap, raising it gently against her lip.

"I have a dose of acetaminophen mixed with this water. It's going to taste like licking a battery but it'll ease your pain. Can you stick out your tongue if you want it?" I say quietly. Her tongue pushes out of her mouth, I tip the cap of the bottle. She swallows with a wince and coughs dryly, having exhausted the river water that was inside of her body. I follow up by slowly pouring more water for her, which she takes sip by slow sip. Manuel points at his watch, looking at me. The sun is higher in the sky, but thankfully most of our hike will still be in shade. "I'm gonna check your pockets to make sure you're not gonna shoot me as soon as I turn around," I say, patting her down. I pull out a sandy phone, water dripping out of the charging port. Dead. Inside a small coin purse I find her wallet with ID cards and credit cards. The group approaches me, but stands at a respectful distance. Mike stares at her with curiosity, the rest are polite enough to focus on me.

"What if we send her downstream on the raft? In a few more miles she'll end up in town anyway, way faster than anyone finding her here," Birch offers.

"You could have mentioned that *before* we packed it up," Mike replies.

"Course, there's another good whirlpool and a big strainer before reaching Moab. Nevermind," 224 Birch says. Mike collapses the few paddles that remain and straps them to the exterior of our bags, then reorganizes all the gear to make our hike easier. I pull out our emergency beacon, reading the back: TO BE USED ONLY IN THE FACE OF GRAVE AND IMMINENT DANGER: FACE ANTENNA TOWARD UNOBSTRUCTED SKY.

"Not the beacon," Mike moans. "What if we get stuck out there? Arches is a big place."

"We've studied the maps," I say. "I know what I'm doing, even if you might not be able to handle the geology out here."

"We might need it later," Manuel says. "She is in bad shape, not gonna make it," he says. Beet and Birch remain silent. I collect my thoughts before speaking with conviction.

"I'm activating the beacon. She is my patient and if she has a chance to evac she'll make it. I know she works for the owner, and has seen us, but I think your threat hit home, Mike. She's not going to say anything," I say. Sirens, distant, from the road across the river.

"No—"

I pull the antenna out and press the SOS button with an audible beep. Like a camera flash, the light on the beacon blinks intermittently along with another beep. I place it on her lap along with her driver's license, then write the time on her forehead with a permanent marker. Taking out my hydration pack, I lean it against the cottonwood next to her and clip the mouthpiece near her lips.

"Just suck on this and you'll get water. That beacon will sound off for 48 hours, but Search and Rescue or someone else will find you well before then. There's a flare gun at your hip, all you've got to do is pull the trigger when you see someone, it'll most likely be a helicopter.

In any case, aim it at the sky." I lean back onto my toes. "I'm putting my trust in you," I say. Through a tiny slit, her iris looks back. Soon, she won't be able to see. With a gentle touch of reassurance, I leave her.

"You just gave away half of our supplies," Mike says flatly.

"I wouldn't have had to do that if you didn't beat her within an inch of her life,"

"Hey, it's done. Mike protected us, you protected her," Beet interrupts. "It's done. Let's drop it, okay? Now shake hands."

We do, glaring at one another, then crack a smile. Can't let the stress get the better of us.

"Despite how badly I wished I had one when we were in the water, I sure am glad we did not pack life jackets," Manuel says. "Already too tired for this hike,"

"I hear you," I say, clipping my hip belt on and tightening my load lifters. Due to the fact that my bag was nearly empty after giving away the majority of my supplies, someone stuffed the raft into my pack when I wasn't looking.

"Anybody not ready?" Birch asks. Idle looks, water sips. The canyon stretches before us, magnificent and damning. Now that we've set off alarms, a team of rangers could be waiting for us at the other end. I linger a moment behind the others and stare into the turbulent whitewater with what could be my last view of true wildness and freedom.

Chapter Nine || Bootlegger Canyon

In the ranger truck that I borrowed without asking, I disconnect the radio and plug it back in. After the call that the rest of the crew was beginning their hike about two hours ago, the appliance refuses to relay any signal.

Utter silence, despite the displayed channels and adequate reception. Seeing Don's vehicle coming toward me, I shut the door and wave him down. Of course, I wouldn't be very easy to miss.

The shining new tour van gleams in the harsh light, pulling our rusted trailer that couldn't be more opposite in matters of beauty. Like a woman in office, as our president foolishly says. The gravel rumbles under the heavy tires, the sunscreened faces of his tour group gaping at me behind tinted and polished glass. On the back window I see a star spangled sticker in all American red, white, and blue. It reads 'Trump Peed in the Groover'. I grin and wait for him to put it in park. He opens the door and steps out, wide brimmed hat nearly blowing off of his head.

"Are we getting pulled over?" someone from inside asks.

"No, just—making sure all the arches are still there," he says, then shuts the door. "Hey. Sorry I'm late, had to argue with some lady that she couldn't leave her dog locked in her car while we were on the tour,"

"No worries, glad you came. I tried to reach you on the CB, but my radio seems to be locked up,"

"It's probably all the 5G," he jokes, throwing 4x4 blocks behind the wheels to chuck the trailer, then disconnects the hitch. "So you're just gonna leave this here? Don't you need a trailer to put the bikes on at the other end of things? Wait–don't tell me–I don't wanna know."

"It'll be here. The boys should be coming out of the wash in just a few minutes. It's yours if you want to pick it up after the dirtbikes are off of it, later today,"

"Really? That would almost feel like stealing," he says, shooting a knowing smile from behind a set of sunglasses. In the reflection, I see myself in my Class A uniform, and once again question what on Earth I am doing here.

"Not an imposition, just swing by later and take it. Thanks for the delivery," I say.

"Well gee, thanks,", tipping the brim of his hat, then pointing a thumb back to his rig. "Don't let the boys get too crazy, and be careful. Ah, you know what you're doing. Later,"

"Have a good tour," I say, worried that I might
  make it on the social media story of some vacation-brained visitor just for being a

part of the NPS. I put my face mask and sunglasses on, just for good measure. Briefly, my mind crosses the details I wrote in for my PTO request, wondering if I fictionalized to the point of arousing suspicion. This truck was left empty in the depot, whoever was on watch must have forgotten to sign the keys back in. I'll be back in a week or less, with nobody the wiser that I didn't spend my time in Tahiti picking mangoes.

...

Hours later, I still sit in the bed of the pickup and eat my last apple. Juicy and delicious, but with too many food miles to think about. In my mind I sift through the banana box of food in the van, baking outside of that shop in Cisco. If given the chance, I think I would eat the whole bunch of bananas we packed... I consider swiping an apple from someone else's pack.

Someone with more on their mind may find it cause to worry that I haven't heard a peep from the radio, and that the gang is running over five hours late. In fact, we had expected to make it past Junction a few hours ago. Now, the sun prepares to set over Elephant Butte and park traffic picks up. The truck, trailer and I wait well off the beaten path, on a short dirt road leading to the opening of Salt Wash. Far off, the windshields and mirrors of thousands of automobiles idling in touristic procession shimmer.

The dull and abrasive sound of the oversized trucks and converted fans is interrupted by the deep drumming of a helicopter. The sound intensifies as it flies over the Fiery Furnace, a rock formation defined by red knobby spires. I recognize the vehicle—the Search and Rescue chopper. They fly low, making sand airborne and harassing the sagebrush. It arcs over me, I hold onto my hat as it continues toward Salt Wash Canyon, flying in the empty space between canyon walls toward the river. Below, the boys emerge from an embankment in a jogging rush. Something isn't right about their gait, and through a pair of binoculars I see the helicopter fly beyond them and around a bend in the sandstone wall. Someone is being supported between two others, but the heat haze makes it impossible to tell much more. I make myself busy preparing for the distress, opening the trauma kit from the truck box and putting on gloves.

"What happened?" I ask when they arrive. Mike, who was being carried, falls onto the hot sand clutching his rib. He yelps and rolls into the shade cast by the truck.

"He got stabbed, the big idiot," Manuel says, in a tone a little harsher than what would normally be considered joking.

"Just lost my breath," Mike pants. The blood on his shirt is mostly brown and dry thanks to the warm air. I drop down and swat his hands away, cutting his shirt open with trauma shears. A small slit the size of a staple oozes slowly.

"He lost some blood, not too much," Monty says.

"Guess I'll be out of work for a few days," Mike breathes, then coughs. He sounds like he's swallowed a pint of heavy cream and then immediately did a set of burpees. That is to say, truly awful. In record time, I patch him up and wrap an elastic bandage around his whole torso. Next to me, Birch addresses a wound on his hand and is also smeared with deep red. I grab his wrist and look at the flap of soggy skin while he changes out of water soaked gauze.

"What did you do?" I ask.

"Wish it was cooler, but I just slipped on the roof," he says. "No biggie, I'm fine,"

"And the painkillers—" Mike says faintly, his eyes closing and head lolling.

"How much blood, Monty?"

"I—I'm not sure. Maybe a pint. It's been slow but he didn't want to go back and wait for the helicopter," Monty says, admiring the dirtbike equipment I organized and laid out for everyone in the bed of the truck.

"What do you mean, go back for the helicopter?" I ask.

"Long story, they're evacin' the GM," he says. "She came after us, water and-well, Mike's fists, took quite a toll."

"Only room for one in the 'copter, anyways," Mike says, fumbling with his words.

"We tried to leave him for dead, we really did, but he just wouldn't quit," Beet muses.

"Would somebody please put a goddamn cigarette in my mouth," Mike asks, his head unsupported and rolled down for his chin to meet his collarbones. Manuel takes the pack from Mike's cargo shorts, then sticks a still wet cigarette into his mouth. He stands up with a smug look while Mike sucks water out of the filter and spits brown tobacco paste onto himself.

"When I feel better I'm gonna get you for that one," he says, laughing quietly and wincing at the pain.

233

"Obviously we can't keep going. We're way behind schedule anyway," I say to the group. Beet is already putting on his equipment.

"We already talked about it. He wants to keep going," Monty says, the rest nodding. "Leaving him out here would be a death sentence, dropping him at the hospital would land him in prison in the same town as the owner."

"I disagree. I think if we gave him some supplies and a bike he could make it in the open desert just fine," Birch says.

"Not in this condition," I argue. "He needs a transfusion,"

"No I don't," Mike says, rifling through the jump bag. Pill bottles rattle and splints fall onto the ground. He takes a handful of painkillers with a full bottle of water.

"That wasn't aspirin, right?" Monty asks.

"In fact, I guarantee in about 30 minutes I'll feel way better than any of you sorry sunburned losers," still looking through the bag. All of us discuss alternative plans: camping overnight, calling 911 for Mike. In the end, we end up standing around him while he waits for the painkillers to kick in. While unsupervised, he had apparently grabbed an emergency hip injector to combat anaphylaxis-you know the kind.

"Don't-" Monty reaches, too late. Mike sticks himself with the auto injector on the inside of his thigh, then throws it over his head and into the bed of the truck. He gets on his hands and knees, then stands up shaking his head. "Did you seriously just inject yourself with that?"

234   "Yeah, adrenaline, right? I feel great," Mike smiles, then touches a spot on his

abdomen where his sweat had kept the blood wet. He paints a line under his eyes and glares at the traffic.

"Dude," Beet says.

"Really, I'm okay. We don't have time to chill," Mike says, then gets busy putting on his equipment. The rest of us follow suit. He takes a spare longsleeve from behind the driver's seat and downs another bottle of water. I slide on knee and elbow protection, some of the others wear full armored suits the color of olive and sand, spray painted and stuck with dust. We quickly pack all the equipment up, taking extra medical supplies to rewrap their wounds in the van, and painkillers for the road trip. I take the key to the truck and tuck it behind the sunshade, leaving the door unlocked. Nobody will know we were even here, except for the paltry bag of landfill-bound medical waste I carry in my small backpack, tight to my back with just enough room for the water bladder full of warm electrolyte mix. Like the others, I keep the handheld radio they brought me in the side pocket. Some carry the larger backpacking bags that remain, apparently they left most of them down in the canyon once they had to carry Mike. Included in these is a set of emergency blankets and a few down puffy jackets, just in case. Birch's raft somehow made the cut, which Manuel carries in his bag along with a few collapsed paddles.

We distribute the titanium poster tubes evenly between us. If anything goes wrong, we're supposed to consolidate to keep the whole set of paintings together. Without words, I wonder if they made any critical blunders, such as forgetting to swap the paintings. We roll the dirtbikes ⊶━━━◗

235

off of the trailer and line them up on the side of the service road, then go over the plan.

"So just follow me, okay? I know it sounds complicated, but like we said before, all we're doing is connecting a series of off road trails to get us from here to Cisco without being seen. You don't need to remember the name of the trails, just stick together and we'll be in Cisco in about two hours. Then, we load up the van with the bikes, and drive to Florida. Easy, breezy," Birch explains. Many of us are skeptical of his condition and constitution, but to my surprise Mike looks completely fine. In fact, he looks as though he just received a raise and a free case of beer in the same afternoon.

We fire up the bikes with a roar of exhaust, then put on our helmets while they idle. Monty kindly walks behind each of us, running a spiraling cable from each of our radios into the sides of our helmets. He stands in front of us and speaks.

"Radio check," he says. We all repeat his words: nods all around. Over the rumbling engines, I think I faintly hear a beep and distant words from the truck. Dreadfully, I saunter over to shut it off so it doesn't kill the battery.

"—intended for the individuals who have commandeered truck 12. This is the park supervisor, we-" it continues, I click the button on the side of my helmet to transmit the message to the others. As it speaks, their heads turn to me in horror. "—will not be tolerated. The vehicle has been remotely disabled and is being investigated by a team of rangers. Remain in the vehicle and put your hands on the steering wheel. Failure to follow these instructions will result in charges including fleeing the police, evading arrest and—"

"What do we do?" Beet asks frantically.

"We ride," Manuel says casually, kicking into gear. I reach in and shut the radio off, then run and hop onto the bike. Immediately, we accelerate and head west. We should only be on the pavement for a moment to cross onto the other side of the park and connect to the offroad trail. Sagebrush and tumblewood fly by without time to focus on them and soon we approach the road leading to Delicate Arch, looming like a pair of cowboy chaps in the yellow light. From our left, two ranger trucks (the whole force) come barreling down the road.

"Ah-we're gonna cut left," Birch says through the microphone, then turns hard and kicks up a cloud of dust.

"What are we doing?"

"Plan B. We'll cut south through the Windows Section and west at Balanced Rock, to link with Willow Flats Road. They're faster than us, if we go the other way they'll overtake us. We'll make it," Birch says. I wipe the dry dirt from my visor with the back of my glove. Monty, in front of me, veers around a rock and wobbles to regain control. We head south over barren entrada, over fire red lichen and tufts of prairie grass. We stand up to allow our knees to compensate for the rough terrain. Though I'm hardly doing cardio, I find it hard to keep my breath in my lungs.

We nose onto a social trail and fly toward the main attraction of the Windows: North and South Arches.

"We're not going through that," Monty says.

"I think you may be wrong about that," Mike shouts.

"We have to-" Birch says. "Too many———◄

people to drive around it, we have to get to the road,"

I look to my left at the primitive trail, full of strollers and fake service animals and the elderly. He's right. Unfortunately.

Through the arch, Birch's silhouette goes airborne and bursts into the golden colors of sunset. The others go before me, yanking the throttle, and go airborne over the harsh incline. My tires catch, I stand and lean forward and open the throttle. My tires disconnect from the ground and I fly over a pile of fast food wrappers, over discarded water bottles and forgotten sunglasses. I land with a jolt, Monty still wobbling in front of me and holding on for dear life. The crowd shouts and dives out of the way, others turning their cameras to face and record us. Still standing, we ride down the steps that were once ADA compliant, dropping more than rolling, and finally get down to the parking lot and solid ground.

The congestion is typical and ludicrous. Entourages, lifted trucks, a limousine. Windows down, everyone trying to capture the brilliant dusky light that evokes the pigment from every inch of entrada. We weave between the cars, between wheelchairs, jumping into the one way and banking hard to follow the curve of the road. Everywhere—cameras, bucket hats, cellphones, selfie sticks, plastic bottles. Grateful not to be wearing my uniform or anything identifiable, I rev the engine warning an influencer to clear the way.

"Stick together, clean line," Birch says. "We're still in it, no no *no*,"

The two ranger trucks from earlier are rapidly approaching with their lights and sirens on, moving to block our path to the offroad section. Audible even through the padding in the helmet, even over the roaring engines, the sirens reverberate off of the rocks in every direction and hone in on us like a tractor beam. I stand up to see over the other helmets. The entry, a narrow channel, is blocked off by a truck. No way onto the backup path. Onto Plan C.

Birch leads, swerving onto the main park road and nearly getting clipped by a sedan. I'm in last place, the civilians are pulling to the side for the most part and getting out of the way. Emergency horns blaring and the smashing of metal behind me as one of my coworkers plows through a car that wouldn't move. A month ago we were at a meeting together.

We rocket past a pair of bicyclists, weaving through cars and rumbling on the median and shoulder.

"Where are we going?" someone shouts, their voice distorted and quiet behind the blood rushing through my ears. Each path before us dead ends, unfolding but never releasing. The Great Wall. The Three Gossips.

"Highway, we'll turn out and take the highway past the Sunshine Wall and go off road from there," Birch shouts. High rocks on all sides, our once abundant options rapidly diminishing to just one. "Shortcut through Park Ave!"

He cuts to the right across from Courthouse Towers and onto a sandstone wash, day hikers diving out of the way while they snap photos of the fiery rocks.

"Are they filming a movie—" I hear, whipping by a man about to launch a drone.

The trail inclines, our motors

239

shaking between our legs, we slow down and tactfully ascend the set of wide steps up to the parking lot. Painfully slowly, we drive up the rock staircase. Slow enough even for the tourists to make eye contact, to get out phones and snap photographs. Monty slips, hops off his bike and holds the throttle and handlebars while he runs up the path. At the top it levels out in a parking lot, he hops back on and we continue our race through the standstill traffic.

We gain headway at the last stretch of park road, a narrow switchback without a shoulder for anyone to pull out of the way. We drive on a narrow strip of asphalt, ducking under extended mirrors on lifted trucks and swerving to avoid roadside litter being tossed out. Finally at the bottom of the hill, we open our throttles and fly past the VC, past where that woman was decapitated when I was an intern, through the roundabout and the fee station. We move toward the intersection of the park road and Highway 191. Traffic on the highway only creeping, but on the shoulder—

"Sheriff's office!" Monty yells. Red and blue blazing, reflecting. A white SUV drives out from between two vehicles and clips the front of Birch's dirt bike, he rolls onto the hood of the vehicle and down to the ground like a ragdoll. Second in line, Manuel, turns too sharply and wipes out, sliding with his bike to slam into the front tire of the vehicle. Beet dodges and yanks his brake, skidding to a stop just in time. Monty tries to turn but wobbles exponentially, losing control and driving into a UTV waiting in traffic.

240   Manuel screams, scrambling to his feet and ramming his body against the door of the

police vehicle before the single officer can open it. Mike–there he is–hops off his bike and helps Birch back onto his.

"We stop here and we'll never see the light of day. Keep going," Manuel demands, pushing all of his weight into the door. Monty crawls out of the UTV, kicks the door hard, and points to Birch.

"Birch, take my bike," He says, then throws me his poster tube.

"No, what are you doing?" Manuel asks. I wrap the tube around my shoulder and make eye contact. More police lights coming from town. Rangers halfway through the switchback. No time. Birch ditches the wrecked bike, then hops on Monty's.

"Are you sure about this?"

"Finish the job." Monty says, producing his handgun. The SUV window rolls down, the last glint of sunlight shepherding us into a purple and orange twilight. A yellow stun gun points out toward Manuel, who rips it from the cop's hand and throws it onto the road.

"We gotta move!" Mike shouts, revving his engine. We all look from eye to eye. Get back on our bikes.

"Ride up the sand hill, ride the tracks to Shafer Trail," Monty instructs, diving for cover behind an electric car. "Potash! Go!"

I try to think of something to say. Anything that might be kind or acknowledge his sacrifice, which may be his life. He didn't even want to come.

"Monty, I–" Birch says, thinking the same.

"No time to be sentimental, we need to move!" Mike hollers in my speaker. Birch and Monty exchange a hard and definitive nod, and we cut across four lanes of congested highway. Across the street, Moab's famous sand hill: a landslide inclining several hundred feet up toward a ledge. Our tires kick plumes of sand, catching the very last bit of sunlight while children and parents grab their greased sleds and move out of the way.

We stand and lean forward to keep balance, and sit back down once we reach the top. The railroad tracks. Right. The railroad ties bump bump bump underneath us, police trucks down in the valley, stopped.

"They got me, *do not stop—*" Monty's voice, tweaking, on the radio. "Looks like I'm going to the Outer Darkness, fellas-"

"Monty, are you hit?" Beet asks. No response.

"Reply if you can hear us," Manuel says.

Nothing.

"Listen, we're going to head into Canyonlands, Island in the Sky," Birch says, his voice vibrating with his shocks. And we rocket along the rail tracks for miles and miles, but still two, then three trucks follow us on the road below.

"I don't think we're gonna get out of this one," Beet says.

"Then we drive until we are out of gas," Manuel says.

"I have a plan," Birch says, but none of us find this reassuring. Truly, what else are we to do except follow?

We drive to the drop-lot for the Rocky Mountaineer, veering hard into the park entrance road.

242   "I hope everyone has their park passes," I say, smiling to myself despite the

critical audience reception. On the dirt, we have a maneuverability and speed advantage. Out here on the pavement, the police vehicles rapidly close the distance and are nearly on our tails.

The fee station for Canyonlands National Park whips by us, we grab the brakes and turn hard onto Shafer Trail.

"Hang on tight, stay close. This is a tricky road even when you're going the speed limit," Birch says. I glance back, a white SUV drifting onto the washboarded road and struggling to hold control. As we move forward, I swallow hard and risk a look down to my left. We're driving, descending, the rim of a massive canyon. Falling from this height would give you enough time to write your last will & testament before hitting the bottom. The road is only one lane, and a narrow one at that. Traffic here at the top is jammed, of people watching the sunset and taking photos and picnicking in the middle of the path. Hopefully that'll slow them down, I think.

We drive around the tourists on the sloped embankments, picking up speed and lurching forward when we grip the brakes to slow before a turn. The perimeter road circles and switches back, we move quickly. The sun finally blinks out, the definitive shadow projecting and rising vertically against us as we descend as quickly as we can. On a turn, I look back. Three ranger trucks, they must've called in the iSky team. The drone of the engines in my face, this is getting old rather quickly. A crack behind me, the ranger truck in the back slips, blue and red lights dancing in the dust clouds. The white pickup's wheel disconnects from the edge of the road. Too wide. In suspended animation, it rolls forward down. The front

243

sinks like a lead fishing weight, slamming into the lower switchback like an anchor. Colossal impact. Sandstone$_{14}$ fragments and an explosion of dust. Still, it leans forward, falling over itself even as the path beneath it gives out. The tailgate somersaults, falling to the next level and crashing. The vehicle tilts and continues to roll downward in a horizontal spin, picking up speed and escalating with the rest of the landslide.

"Did anyone else see that?" I scream.

"Yeah,"

"We should stop and give aid," I say. There's no other way out of this.

"That ranger is dead, honey," Birch says.

"Stay focused, there are still two trucks after us," Manuel interrupts. I shake my head, grateful to not have seen the accident in more detail. Two dead, is this worth the price? How many more have suffered and died at the hand of the owner? I recall the video of Maria.

In a minute, we drive by where Thelma and Louise took their final drop. Maybe we'd be better off doing the same. There's no way we'll make it now that we've killed an officer of the law.

We hop back onto the railroad tracks where the road ends, at the potash plant, and drive back toward town. Missing railroad tie. Tumbleweed. Tire drop. We get off the tracks and follow the road back to town. To the left, Gold Bar and Corona Arch.

"Hey, let's cut through the tunnel by Corona, it'll save us some time," Mike suggests.

"No way," Manuel says.

"Tunnel is too long, not enough oxygen, all the diesel fumes from the trains get stuck in there," Birch says. "You'd choke to death.

We're too slow on these things," he says. Water next to us.

If we could just get on the other side of the Colorado, we'd be able to get through to Hurrah Pass. It would take a long time, but we'd eventually be able to—

"Ugh, they're still on us," Birch says, looking back. Sky darkening. We leave our headlights off. We weave around Poison Spider Mesa, past Williams Bottom and the crater known as Project U.M.T.R.A. The massive loop almost brings us back to where we started, almost back at the highway near the Arches Visitor Center. Blue lights headed toward us. Red lights behind. Spotlights next to mirrors. I wonder what they might find.

"We're cornered," Beet says in a panic. We drive forward at full speed, fully aware that we are no more than bugs and the polished boot of the law is about to stomp us. The snare closes.

"I-Ah—left! Back on the tracks!" Birch yells, turning and tearing through the cryptobiotic crust until we get back on the railroad tracks.

"I don't know if you noticed," Mike yells. "But we're going in circles, and the circle is getting smaller!"

"I know!" Birch screams back in frustration. In the blur of oscillating lights it becomes impossible to determine how many vehicles are on us now. Suddenly, the tracks turn right, into a small channel through the rock. We follow the tracks into it and lean back, taking my sore hand off the throttle and stretching it out. The others do the same, slowing down in the comfort that there's no longer a road running parallel to us.

Canyon wall blurring by on our right ━━◀

side, death drop on the left. Giant angled boulders collapsed and dispersed intermittently. Ahead, a boxed out canyon with a pitch black arch in the center. Tunnel.

And, a black being on the tracks. We swerve around the solitary cow.

A harsh and artificial light hits my back and casts a long shadow forward. Helicopter. I risk a glance backward.

"*Traiiiiin!*" I scream, the massive locomotive pushing just a few meters back and gaining rapidly.

"Pull over! Pull over!"

"Up that rock, go!" Birch instructs, veering off and riding up a rock the size of a house, angled like a see-saw. We follow and clench the brakes. He jumps-or falls-off of his bike at the top, it continues down the other side and onto the tracks. Horn blaring, the dirtbike is reduced to rubble in a matter of seconds. I look up, through the narrow canyon at the road. Backed up traffic, sets of police lights headed for the park. A helicopter—the SAR copter from earlier, or backup from Junction?

Beneath us, the cargo train flies past at full speed, metal thunder. Open wagon train cars billowing past, full of tannish rubble. We dismount and gather in a line at the edge of the rock. Mike's kickstand doesn't properly engage, his bike leans to the side and then tumbles down onto the track and is ripped apart.

"I hate to say it. I *really* hate to say it," Birch begins. "But I think we gotta jump."

"I agree," Manuel says.

"Me too," Mike joins.

246   "Anybody not ready?" Birch asks.

"Make sure you lean backward to land

on your butt," I say. "That's where the armor is the thickest,"

Flashlights back from the way we came. Either side of the tracks. Dozens of them. No other way.

Beet and I shove the last of the dirtbikes down to be annihilated by the train. Through our helmets and without looking at one another, we hope the police will assume we were pulverized too. "The posters, we have to drop them otherwise they will be crushed under our weight," Manuel says, we all pass ours to him. Quickly, he drops them down into the bin of a train car and they get whisked away.

We grab hands in a line and sneak closer, toes over the precipice.

"Just like cliff jumping," I say. "Three, two, one-"

And we leap, the weight of the helmet helping to lean back. For a brief moment we exist between rock and rubble, the man made machination traveling beneath us in a current. The impact is jarring and immediately painful, knocking the wind out of me and denting my armor in dozens of places. My head smacks hard, the pain bouncing around my skull. Without these protections, that fall would have undoubtedly killed us.

"Listen up, leave your helmets on," Birch says rapidly. "We're going through that tunnel, I don't know how long it is. You need to start breathing quickly now to build up oxygen in your system, and hold your breath as long as you can. The train exhaust will fill that tunnel and in one breath you'll be unconscious, in three you'll be dead."

From the looks of it, Beet doesn't

need help hyperventilating and was halfway there without coaching. I heave and huff, fogging up my goggles.　　　　　The inky blackness of the tunnel sweeps over us all at once, our recumbent bodies nestled in jagged piles of stone. I reach out my hand to feel for someone, anyone. Another gloved hand meets me and squeezes in the consuming darkness. Bumps underneath. Jostling debris. Elastic digging at my knee. Chinstrap getting tighter and tighter.

Underwater. I'm swimming, that's all. Tendrils of a death-black being come from the cracks beneath me, ensnaring my limbs and my neck, willing me to become part of the water bottom. My abdomen flinches, my throat tightening painfully.

I slowly release my breath to ease the discomfort, lungs deflating, my chest flat and the architecture of armor tenting atop.
The hand—mine? Squeezes harder. I open my eyes and see no light, not even reflection. What feels like smoke pressurizes the impossibly loud space, sinking through the fabric of my clothing and through the pores of my skin. My abdomen seizes rapidly, I writhe my feet in agony as I fight my own biology.

Whiteness and neon fireworks at the edge of my vision, the hand pulling. Then, I have to. I must. A sharp inhale. Toxic fumes like swallowing steel wool entrusted with razor wire. I hold it in, hold the smoke, freezing in position until the buildup is too much and my lizard brain takes over. I inhale again, acid, and go into a coughing fit. The sound drops out around me, just blood rushing through my ears. Trying to cough up a sea urchin, spiky with needles embedded in my lungs.

248　　My helmet is ripped off and a twilight blue sky above. Birch and Beet, I reach for him and he hugs me. In the background, Mike coughs and tries to stand, but falls back down. We take a moment to regain our composure.

"I've smoked more than the Marlboro Man, and my lungs still couldn't handle that racket," he shouts.

"Everyone, get together so we don't need to scream," Birch says, we crawl to the center of the car, I peek up and look out. High rocks on both sides. I look up and see Corona Arch halfway up the cliff, and get a glimpse at Bowtie Arch as well. That must make this Bootlegger Canyon. The train turns hard to the right, running adjacent to the road, which runs adjacent to the river. The turn rocks my body, I cough.

Manuel rips through his backpack and throws a map to Birch, who works on unfolding it in the high wind. I lend a hand and spread it out before everyone, I struggle to read it in the dying light. Manuel takes out a cellphone and begins typing furiously.

"No cellphones, that was rule number one," Mike says, slapping the phone out of his hand. It goes flying, spins into a chunk of rock. Devastated, Manuel picks it up and shows Mike the screen, which now blinks primary colors behind a spider web of glass. Broken.

I study the map, tracing and retracing with my fingers and praying that my eyes deceive me, that I just can't read it right.

"Are you seeing what I'm seeing?" I ask. Birch nods, and informs the group. In about a mile, the train tracks end on the map. Beyond that, a few river bends and 100 miles of open desert before the Arizona state line. Then, the area surrounding the Grand Canyon and a whole lot of nothing. We go back toward town and face a lifetime in prison, or worse at the hands of the owner. We go into the desert and run, we won't make it more than a few days. Really, the choice is already made for us, by the owner. Manuel leans forward and looks at us with a frown.

"Not so kosher, huh?"

Chapter Ten || End of the Line

I learned once that a train like this one going full steam can take over a mile to stop. Once the brake is applied.

With a terrible metal grinding the locomotive slows down, fear and sound echoing through the canyon. New moon above, sparks below. This last section of train tracks has a dirt road on the left, then the river. On the right, a dirt road, some kind of processing plant, then a steep canyon wall. As we slow to a halt, a stream of police vehicles file in, their lights casting on the water and walls like we're in an aquarium.

On the side of the chemical plant, an inspector drives slowly up in a white pickup, then parks. Birch shuffles next to me. I fear for Monty, but I can tell that we all feel almost giddy from the adrenaline.

"That's a railyard bull, just as bad as the owner's police," Mike says. "Maybe worse. They'll kill you without an excuse, hide the body way out in the middle of nowhere,"

We speak for a moment about our handguns. About hijacking the train, or perhaps even bribing the driver with untold wealth. But where would the driver take us, except back toward town? This is the end of the line.

Doors shutting, spotlights coming on and flashlights moving our way. Under Manuel's leadership, we creep forward toward the boxcar linked in front of ours. A refrigerator car, based on the looks of it, metallic sides and a cooling exhaust sticking out of the top. I clamber up to the top, 5.8 on a tough day. Resting on my belly, I help the others climb up. Mike needs an extra hand, and winces when he rolls over the corner. No red on his shirt. Yet.

I am grateful for the darkness of the stars when we lay flat. Under a full moon we'd be lit up like corpses fresh from a graveyard. As close to the center of the boxcar as we can get with our heads pointed to the side to reduce our height, our lower backs are pushed into the still warm aluminum emanating the echoes of the sun.

The beating sound of another helicopter. We're made. Hands sliding slowly, grabbing one another and squeezing. I see it approaching, green and red blinking lights. It flies low, ready to land. What a fool I'll feel like when that spotlight beams down on us, laying here like we drank the punch, like a group of paper angels all filthy covered in blood and sweat and dust.

And it passes us. I see the star of life on the bottom, it heads toward the landslide we caused. Maybe that ranger, whoever it was, survived. A professional courtesy, they call it. From one first responder to another. Tax dollars spent flying you to Grand Junction even though your only sign of life is the still warm blood in your muscles.

A group of police walk by, toward the engine of the train a few cars ahead of us. The motor turns off and hisses. Doors slamming. Distant speaking, annoyed. Getting closer. A beep, a sliding from the car we are on top of.

"As you can see, we've got an urgent delivery here. Not a very long half life, so if you'd like to be the one to report to General Montgomery what took so long, then I'd be happy to hang out. I hear you, I do, trust me, no *really*," the voice says insistently.

"I was a bull for over 20 years. All I'm trying to do is secure my pension, I'm sure you know what that's like. To your worry, if anyone *is* hiding on the train there's no way they'd survive out there. You know as well as I do that you can walk from here to Mexico, no roads or nothin'."

"Part of our job is to investigate collisions such as the one you reported. Additionally, it's more of a matter of national security than—"

"You're gonna lecture *me* on national security? No disrespect, but I don't see any city cops being followed by an unmarked van when they go out for the grocery shopping," the conductor (I presume) says.

"What we're saying is that this could be the attack we've been anticipating. You said it yourself that you are transporting special cargo to a sensitive area, lieutenant."

"Yes, and I'll be certain that we undergo a full security screening upon our arrival to the base. I know this isn't your area of expertise, but you should know that terrorists don't hitchhike ——◀

on traincars.”

"And the accident, then?”

"Undetermined. I’ll be reviewing the footage after I unload, you’ll get a copy of my incident report. Though, I’ll warn you that there’ll be little more than black highlighter to read. Now if you’d please let me get on before we all get radiation poisoning,”

"Erm, yes.”

"I’ll go slowly. If it were me, I’d position a man on either side of the tracks while I drive by.” the conductor says.

"Very well.”

Drive by? Is he unloading potash at this chemical plant? Out of the corner of my eye, someone climbs the side and shines a light into the rubble cart we moved from. I hold my breath and lay still, they leave. More doors, a siren gets louder and then stops altogether. The train creaks and creeps forward. Flashlight beams on either side. Why, how, is he driving off the tracks?

The edge of a light catches the toe of my boot, I do not move a muscle.

"What’s that?”

"Not sure, looks like a tenderloin.”

"They had it coming, one of the bastards sprained John’s wrist,”

"That’s a solid nine months off for him. Let’s double back and see if we can piece together their bikes,”

"We gotta wait for the coroner to piece together their bodies first,” someone chuckles. "Coffee while we wait? It's gonna be a long night.”

     No kidding.

The light spins away. More doors

shutting. The train accelerates away from them, away from Moab and into the desert. I turn to face Beet.

"Where are we going?" I ask.

"I don't know, Wren." We continue to pick up speed, the wind and vibrations rustling us loose, shaking like sand on a subwoofer. All at once, we crawl and jump back into the rock pile and try to figure out what just happened. More important to me is where we are currently headed. I peek my head up and see the police lights still flashing, but rapidly fading. At least two miles away now. I climb back on top of the refrigerator car and look forward. The massive headlight of the train casts harshly forward, free range cattle running off the tracks. And the tracks—expanding ruler straight as far as my eyes can see. Straight through the canyons, away from all civilization.

"So there's a track, then?" Beet asks.

"Of course, did you think we were hovering?" Mike replies, ripping off his armor and checking his bandage with a headlamp. Looks good.

"How are you feeling?"

"Like I'm playing someone else in a movie—like—I don't know. I keep on thinking I'm going to wake up in the back of my truck," he says. We nod in agreement. I feel foreign, occupying a role and body that I wasn't meant for. Birch and I move back onto a flatcar. It smells like a mine, wooden crates with stenciled lettering on either side and a narrow hallway between. The gang moves into this space. There is room enough for us to sit or lay if we want to, but the effort of processing the last few hours forces most of us to take to pacing back and forth with the wind whipping through our hair. I tie mine up.

Between two boxes to block the wind, Beet starts up his camp stove and makes kratom for his back pain and to calm his nerves. Manuel and Birch study a map, weighed down with rocks on top of one of the crates. I look on one of the sides, stamped with a fallout logo. Everyone has noticed this symbol pervading on the cargo, it would be near impossible not to. What other option do we have but to be near it, other than breaking our necks jumping off the train?

We come to the consensus that we're stuck as long as it keeps moving forward. The next time it slows will be our opportunity to jump off to avoid the security checkpoint the conductor mentioned, whatever that means. I'm not entirely sold on the idea, though. I know that there are checkpoints and refueling stations often enough, and sometimes a great distance away from any place that we might find a way out of this mess.

In a moment of dismay, I pinch myself hard. Eyes open. Still here.

"Do you think he's dead?" Birch finally asks. We look at one another, then at him. There is no answer to give that might ease him into a resolution. His death would be final, but at least we would be anonymous. Our criminal selves dead to the world in a horrific train car accident. I see the weight of Monty's life on his shoulders, pressing down, etching a finality that can't ever be erased, even in the absence of a conviction. Equally as condemning is his survival. We could be internationally blacklisted, wanted for grand larceny, evading arrest, assault 258 and battery, attempted murder,

"Yes," Manuel breaks the silence. "We

will honor him when we get out of this. Best not to think too much about it, it will only slow us down."

"That's a little cold," I say. He nods.

"Cold but productive,"

I sit on the rumbling ground, my sweat soaked outfit chilling me to the bone in the rapidly blowing and relentless current of air. Beet offers me a mug of something, which I refuse. I feel like I've just finished a marathon, I lie cold and wet on the metal ground and wish time would pass faster, to reach a resolution no matter what it may be.

In my discontentment I hardly notice Birch moving to sit by my side. I put my head in his lap, he hands me a cellphone with a big play button on it.

"I'm confused," Mike says. "I thought we agreed on no cellphones,"

"It looks like you and I are the only two that didn't bring ours," Beet says. "Not much to do about it now,"

"Wishing for a little in-flight entertainment. Who knows how long this route is?" Mike huffs, crossing his arms and leaning against a crate. "Sorry, man. I thought it was a security issue. Like a national security issue. Didn't mean to smash your phone anyway. I'll buy you whatever phone you want once we have the money, okay?"

"Thanks," Manuel says halfheartedly, looking up at the stars.

I look at the video recording from the loft. Maria getting a drink poured down her throat. I look away, up at Birch.

"Don't forget what we're fighting for."

Chapter 11 || Residual Dread

The hours pass, and then days. Nights spent huddled together, wind roaring in our ears and stealing our heat. Even the daylight hours are not necessarily warm. Ultraviolet rays shining down and baking any exposed skin, but the warmth leaves quickly and incites a constant shiver that chisels away at our calories. Already too few[18].

The food ran out yesterday, and my teeth hurt from the protein and granola bars. These days I think they've got the same amount of sugar as candy bars, just different marketing. Wren paces back and forth trying to stay warm and succeeding only in aggravating the looming sense of anxiety and doom that prevails in the group.

Years ago I led a backpacking trip through the Maze District of Canyonlands, contracted through Maroon Mesa. We completed our route on time, my clients satisfied, all goals on my performance review either met or exceeded. The van that was supposed to pick us up failed to show. I'll spare you the details of those nights, just know that I sacrificed my personal backup water to keep the obese CFO of a large corporation from complaining. The fact that he had dumped half of his water trying to clean his sunglasses made little difference to his demands.   This lesson and a few others have made me both diligent and paranoid in equal measure when it comes to carrying water in the backcountry. Usually this leads to a heavier load than is necessary, extra time rigging, and deliberation among my crewmates. Occasionally, as now, it pays off. We've got a few days' supply left, at least. And a backup water filter.

        The first night we checked the news and found nothing, as expected. Only a small article discussing the ongoing traffic nightmare, and how the city may allocate tax funds to expand the road system yet again to accommodate the load and to bring more transit near the new chain hotels that pop up every few weeks.

No news on Monty.

Obsessive water packing.

Nervous jokes about cannibalism.

        That is to say, no news on Monty, and I fear the worst. If not for my water packing, the rest of us would be dead come tomorrow. If we don't eat one another first.

Beet seems to walk with an aire of guilt himself, looks passed between him and I in silent understanding. Let it happen. We let it happen. It would not have happened if we hadn't tried all this. No, we made it happen.

Manuel spends his time reading the laminated sheets he brought, some of the same ones from the river trip. He studies the map, too, and borrows our phones to check for service, but they're all dead now from the baking days and freezing nights. The map is perplexing. By all accounts we are quite literally in the middle of nowhere. I read once that the furthest point away from human civilization in the continental United States is somewhere in the direction we're headed, but our collective bearing details little more than that. We've exited canyon country proper, and head into the flatter desert of the far south, characterized by lumps of sandy rock and green deposits of copper and gypsum. We saw an airplane yesterday. Cruising altitude but probably just as lost as us, given the distance from any city or place where someone might be able to purchase an airline ticket.

Much of our banter involves the conductor of the train. It was a woman's voice. We discuss her story. *Lieutenant,* the cop had said. Manuel thinks, critically, that she is a government officer delivering precious cargo on a strict timeline. Before that, she might have been in the Civil Air Patrol, or perhaps a Girl Scout. According to Mike she's an insurrectionist herself, and we're carrying top secret military cargo that is to be used in an attack against the federal government. To me she's just doing her job, and it's best not to think much more about it than that.

We're headed to some base, I guess. She's

got to be taking us somewhere, because she has human needs too. Of course, as Beet suggests, she might be an android wearing synthetic silicon skin. The government has droids for tasks such as these, he's sure of it.

Then there is the question of the driver's endurance. We haven't stopped, and only slowed slightly to accommodate for a bend in the railroad tracks. We settle, assuming that she must have a co-pilot in there, along with a few dozen MRE's (that we'd all really like to get our hands on) and a full bed and bath. Perhaps there's an old RV buried inside the control cabin. Or perhaps it is one of the newer Solpilo models. That is, self piloting and fully automated. No traffic to deal with, perfect technology to be used on a railroad. Although it is continually reevaluated, many of us consider it a good decision that we didn't attempt to hijack the vessel. If this continues and our water supply is threatened, drastic measures may come into play.

A prevailing discussion this morning was focused on how the Glen Canyon Dam was supposed to be near Lion's Park in Moab. To a fresh ear this sounds like urban legend, and in retelling the story I am transported back in time where my audience must take my word as truth in the absence of the ability to search the internet or even an atlas or guidebook. The clients I guide do not adhere to such story-driven focus, instead I am often cut off by an updated statistic or new article mid sentence.

  The dam is true, though. I speak of Matrimony Springs and the ancient ladder near

Dewey Bridge, both scars of the white surveyors that evaluated the canyons. In the end, the sandstone in Moab was too soft to accommodate a dam. Imagine it, though. Imagine Lake Powell being in Moab instead, sinking Moab's indigenous ruins instead of those near Page, Arizona, and submerging the sites of so many resorts and hotels. I kid myself pretending that these businesses wouldn't have simply built on the shoreline instead of in the riparian zone adjacent to the river.

We hop from train car to train car. Initially it was dangerous and terrifying, but now it has become more or less a form of entertainment. Mike and I play catch with pieces of rock atop a box car, watching how the wind affects it as the train goes around a curve.

We've discovered that the train has 132 cars on it, 133 if you ask Wren. She's the only one that has traveled the full length of the thing. Counting the sections as we go around bends only allows us to count part of the vessel. I haven't been, but I am told that the rear of the train has another diesel engine as a caboose, facing the opposite direction. From our front end view we can easily see four diesel engines currently working to haul us, so I can logically conclude that wherever we are going, if we go back the way we came we'd ought to be without cargo in these boxes. Most of what we have now is dump cars full of rock that even I can't identify. Definitely from Moab, and definitely a little funny looking. Yellow and green tints to some sort of sandstone is my guess, but beyond that I have no idea. A few more refrigerator cars are intermittently dispersed throughout the machine. Wren tells me that when she made it to the caboose she saw through a small window a bed set and a case of military rations stored neatly. For the return trip, I suppose.

We're wishing hard for some sort of bathroom, but so far we've dedicated one of the rubble cars to the cause. #1 trickles down and disappears. #2 is to be done only on a rock that you can lift yourself, which gets thrown over the edge. I consider my constant displeasure at the poorly dug catholes and toilet paper that tourists (and sometimes locals) leave all over the desert. I know that our scat will only be mummified out here, left as a source of confusion for future anthropologists. This is precisely why I'll be donating some of my profits to help pick up all the human feces around town.

Mike's injuries seem to be stabilizing. That's what I think, anyway. He seems to think himself to be too much of a man to share any details beyond that. My hand is getting worse, despite my best efforts. The bleeding has stopped but beneath the flap of skin is a constant and unnerving yellow ooze that soaks whatever bandage I put on top of it. And, I've put on a great many. The pain was an intense burning but has reduced over yesterday to a dull, swollen aching.

Still more time is spent sharing and discussing the anecdotes that I normally present on a guiding trip. I've driven the Shafer Trail before on a 4x4 route. The angle and drama of the road has always made my heart quicken, I never thought

I'd be in my first high speed chase on it. I speak of
potash, the nearby potash plant and the vibrant
blue pools evaporating in the desert. They harvest
it with water, mixing it with blue dye to quicken
the evaporation process. The facility the train
stopped next to is the point in which it is processed
into a marketable form, and sent on a train to be
packaged elsewhere. Of course, we're headed the
opposite direction than the processed potash goes.
Pharmaceuticals, pots and spoon holders. Ceramics,
cleaners and detergents. But mostly it is made into
fertilizer. You've probably heard the name of it
before. What we modernists call it now, anyway.
Pot-ash-ium.

A great deal of our time is spent staring at the
titanium tubes, or otherwise focusing intentionally
to ignore their presence. We spoke of opening them,
but in the end decided it was a bad idea considering
the wind. How brutal an ending to this tale would
be, to have a painting blow off the train and all of us
die jumping off whilst chasing it like a runaway kite
on the beach.

And so Manuel studies his sheets and literature
and printed slideshows, and comes to us around
what would normally be mealtimes. Instead,
we hold WAM breaks. Or, Water Appreciation
Moments. Appreciating friendship, appreciating the
resources we have and the story we'll be able to
tell. Appreciating freedom and time off of work.
Appreciating everything we have left. Trying not to
think about the ebbing hunger.

At these mealtimes he shares what he spent the
previous hours studying. An oral presentation
to the class. At least that still feels normal.

I think that our inability to do anything might lead us to act as casual and goofy as we are. Maybe if we pretend everything is normal, Monty might come back and everything will be alright in a week or two.

He speaks of Adolf Hitler's Amber Room. The Eighth Wonder of the World, they used to call it. We talk about who the allied refugees might have been that stole our painting set back, if they might have been anything like us.

"So Cossiau is the owner's old last name?" Beet asks.
"No, they changed the family name after the second World War." Manuel explains, cross legged in the flat car. "Some branches of the Cossiau lost all their finances, all their wealth, during the wars and the owner's great grandparents did not want to be associated with them. Naturally, they fled as a group to the United States and took advantage of the refugee program here, and the wealth that came after the war. They had money held in savings and things like gold, which they brought with them. They used this money to buy real estate from farmers and ranchers who had run out of money during the depression, and to buy the farms abandoned by their owners who died overseas. They built on top of these properties into the resort system that exists today."

With the aching hunger making us irritable, we host a small meeting. There it is decided that we ought to do something to remedy our situation, considering that we have no idea what the journey ahead might look like and we are all beginning to feel fatigued from the lack of calories. The gears in my skull behind turning and I try to recall an old formula. With remorse, Mike shares a candy bar he had been hiding in his boot, melted into a glob that we take turns licking off the wrapper.

What's more is the great suspicion that befalls me when I begin making a recipe. The recipe itself is not what draws attention, but rather the fact that I know it by heart, and must have in the past been in some situation that demanded its memorization. I start by shifting the large rocks in one of the haulers (not our restroom car) and make my way to the bottom. Here, mounds of the whitish potash still wait in the corners, accumulated from vibration and out of reach from whatever dumping procedure they use. To make it, I employ my skills from the detention school I went to during a youth I'd rather not talk about. I will not share most of the recipe here... For reasons of national security, as one might say.

After heating the ingredients (which we conveniently had in the form of electrolyte powder and a few other odds and ends, including Manuel's broken phone) in Beet's Kratom cup, I pour them into a plastic water bottle and stick the wire and trigger in place.

The journey to the caboose takes well over an hour, hot metal containers make it uncomfortable to crawl, but the power of hunger overrides the pain. We leap down onto the narrow walkway, just a thin railing separating us from the rushing ground below. The door is about the size of a large gym locker, too small to fit more than one person at a time. There's a small panel of bandit glass at eye level, about three centimeters thick and certainly built to resist bullets. I think about the windshield on the back, but that would surely be more reinforced to resist tragic bovine impacts. I rest the plastic bottle on the sill, and Manuel's cell phone next to it. The two connected by a thin charging cable that I owe Wren a replacement of.

The fuse takes less time than I expected, which could have been an issue in different circumstances. With a barely audible explosion and a puff of smoke, the glass is blown out of its panel and falls onto the ground. Not shattered, just chipped and bent a bit. I reach my arm inside and undo the lock, swinging the door open. The smell of a subway inside, metal and steam and diesel and rat poop. The view in every direction has been spectacular. Outlined by the frame of the windshield takes it to another level. Two captain's chairs, all manner of switches and levers and buttons. A small door with a toilet symbol on it, unfortunately locked. An emergency brake lever the size of my arm, which might work if we need it. Digital screens, black and stained with fingerprint oils. Solpilo logo next to a laptop which is somehow fused to the operator desk.

What we came for sits before us in a sealed cardboard box, which we tear into ravenously. 30 Meals Ready to Eat, MREs. Brisket entree. Spaghetti with beef and sauce. Chicken a la king.

Without waiting for the integrated heat pouches to warm our meals, we slurp them up like wild dogs to a carcass. The first to vomit-Manuel-does so over the side of the train, then comes back for more. Beet follows in second.

On Manuel's insistence, we carry the rations back to our site, where we plan to stay.

He explains that we will need to see as far ahead as we can in order to jump off before we reach whatever security we're headed to. We'll lose that visibility from the back of the train. We measure the distance of the cars, and figure that the train must be over a mile long, too much time for a spotter to be posted, and to give adequate warning.

We've got enough food for a few more days at least. Maybe over a week if we are careful.

Nestled in a pile of rocks, we craft a makeshift fire pit and have an extremely short fire, burning the cardboard to punch back at the chilling night winds.

"So, did you end up sleeping with the head housekeeper?" Beet asks. "You two have never been friendly, and you *did* stay there all night." Mike smiles and looks toward the stars, playing with his shoelaces.

"My dick has led me to places I wouldn't go with a gun, my friend."

All the talking and idle time might lead one to think that we would get tired of one another. Temperaments show occasionally, the fatigue of the trip and the uncertainty eating at us all more feverishly than we consume our scant meals. More often is the sense of comradery, of family, that prevails and fortifies my constitution.

"I've never been on a train like this before. Even though I'm constantly either freezing or burning, I'm excited for the chance to be here," Wren says, more to herself than to the group.

"A *train* like this before?" Beet asks. "Or never been on a train like *this* before?"

"Uh-a train like this. A cargo train," she answers, laughing.

"Has anyone?" Manuel says.

I turn to face Mike in response, who is already staring at me with a wide smirk.

"Well, there was that one time," we laugh.

...

The endless desert unfolds.
Spires, pronghorn, mesas.

There is talk among the guides of what may lay far out into a desert such as this. A place devoid of all water or anything classically valuable aside from raw beauty and the absence of mankind.

Few have traveled here, yes, but I would wager that *nobody* has traveled perpendicularly to the way the railroad goes. Why would they? Early humans certainly wouldn't have: no water. A few short exploration trips, surely, but probably not much more than that. The Spaniards wouldn't, there's no gold or minerals to be found among the endless shallow dunes.

There are rumors of a cove, of a place where mankind has never set foot. A place absent on all maps, censored on satellite images. A place where nobody should ever go.

...

The barbed wire fence comes into view after the third day. The sun has set an hour or so ago, the sky overtaken by a deep blue and the sliver of a white moon. The train billows past too quickly for us to read the yellow and black sign posted. A break in the fence just large enough for the tracks. The train already slowing down.

From atop a boxcar, dark outlines ahead. Hills, maybe a mountain, a few lights shining down. A checkpoint.

"Time to go, checkpoint ahead," I shout.

"Finally, time to stretch the legs," Mike says.

"Make sure you take everything with you, we do not want to leave any evidence behind," Manuel says, putting the last of his armor back on. We're packing out all the food wrappers, the only evidence we've been here will be a puddle of urine at the bottom of the rock pile and a missing window. The bandit glass is somewhere a few hundred miles back; Beet tossed it like a frisbee in a bout of boredom.

I put my armor back on, feeling the stiffness of the nylon lining that's been dried with the salt from my sweat.

We swing our feet over the edge, having meant to jump before we even went through a single fence. Now, we pass a second set of fences with some sort of hydraulic gate, only open temporarily. We lean over the edge, a good amount of space between us. Mike jumps first, staggering on the landing but remaining upright. Next is Wren, who intelligently throws her bag before herself and lands gracefully. I jump and try to run forward to match the speed of the train, but face plant into the sand. My mind rattles, my brain feeling as though it were still up in the air somewhere.

Manuel pulls me up by my backpack, already running back toward the fence. The others follow us, it's only a few hundred feet away. When we arrive I see that the height of the fence isn't the issue, all of us are more than capable of climbing virtually any height.

273

Rather, a small panel box that I

recognize from my days at the detention camp. A small transformer inside and a wire passing through, electrifying the fence. Signage posted every few paces confirms it. There exists a small gap between the still zooming train and the electric fence. Without speaking, we shimmy through it in a procession.

As the last of the train cars flies by, I try to get a glimpse of the damage we caused but do not succeed. There is a momentary lapse between the passing of the caboose, and when the gate slides shut as it was programmed to do.

"We should've just waited, no sense in risking our noses like that," I say.

"No way to know," Beet reminds me. He isn't looking good, deep purple bags beneath his eyes and cheeks pulled in too tight under his beard. He looks like a ghost in the moonlight.

We walk beyond the perimeter fence, and through the gap in the secondary fence. It seems to only enclose a small area, the fence itself only running a few hundred meters into the desert before terminating completely.

"For cattle, maybe?" Beet offers.

"For cattle," I say. Better not to think too much about it. Putting a lid on it is better than leaving the mystery open to rot in our minds. I wipe the sweat from my brow, then shiver.

...

Heading back the way we came brings us atop a short hill, granting us a view into the shadowy darkness. The tracks lead into little more than a few pinpricks of light, and then nothing.

However, we quickly discover an intersection of track, with four possible directions. We know which way we came, and which way the train went, which leaves us with a much too long discussion and two more possibilities. Wren and I take the path to the left, the others take the path to the right. We'll meet back at the intersection before dawn.

I adjust the strap on the poster tube, making it more comfortable around my neck as we walk. The quiet eats at me, making my ears ring after so many days on that train. This track is easy to walk on, almost a pleasure, compared to some others I've used. The sand fills in all the cracks between the railroad ties and I don't have the fear that I'll break my ankle if I look up. In doing so, I see more stars than I've seen in my entire life. I'm comforted by the thought that they're always there, even if they might be invisible due to the light pollution. I wonder if the soldiers out here appreciate what they see, where they live. I wonder if anybody joins the military these days to 'see the world'. The climate wars take them to the most remote regions of the world, the last possible places to find petroleum for the big American trucks and platinum so we can all have a new model of cell phone every year. I finger the crumpled up pamphlet in my pocket.

A light breeze pushes the finest dust into a cloud, drifting through the landscape like a fog. It is cool, but not cold. The sand emanates heat upward. Warm, but not hot. As all things, balance.

"You doing okay?" Wren asks me, gently touching my hand.

"Yeah, feeling a bit ill today,"

"I can tell. Still thinking about him?"

she asks. I don't need to respond. My nonanswer is confirmation enough. My hand throbs.

We walk for hours more, without a hint of dawn. The track must be endless, or repeating. Perhaps we've walked past that prickly pear more than once.

The cryptobiotic soil typical of Utah isn't here. At least, I haven't seen it yet. Just an expanse of free flowing sand.

The track stops, my step falls into a pile of loose sediment beyond the last beam. The rivets are here, the end of the rail itself clearly manufactured to end here. Forever waiting for the next segment to be imported.

We kick around the loose sand for any tools, or perhaps extra pieces of the rail and come up with nothing. With nothing more to do, we continue in the direction the tracks ought to be going, a level and flat walkway presented before us. Before long, it catches my eye.

Ahead of us, pyramids. Atypical of Egyptian architecture, not Peruvian either. Narrow and tall, almost like spikes towering above even the largest skyscraper I've seen. We approach one, made of some kind of tannish metal I've never seen before. Still warm from the day[6].

Before us they unfold, visible only in the negative space they produce between the stars. The sand blows between them, sounding like two bedsheets being rubbed together.

In awe we continue forward, a growing sense of
residual dread leaking from the towers themselves.
There are no words, no explanations. Only a million
questions and an agreement not to ask any of them.
We turn from the monoliths and walk back toward
the intersection. I pluck a section of saltbrush,
chewing on the teal colored petals and let the
salty saliva swish through my mouth. This feels like
a night of first connection. A first time spent diving
deep with a new friend, a new lover, or unlocking a
new depth to a relationship already developing.

I could walk forever.

Chapter 12 || The Sins of Our Fathers

Wren and I decided it best to keep the details of our discovery to ourselves. To be revealed at some later date, some midnight fire or chatty corner of a mid-river raft. The others found something of interest. Something of promise.

As it was told to me, they went around a bend and a shimmer on the horizon came into view. A collection of lights, like what you'd see on the side of a mountain or at a hotel complex from way up in an airplane. We rested in a pile of boulders, covering our skin to safeguard our heat and resting our heads on backpacks. Troubled by the monoliths, I took the first watch to contemplate their meaning, if any at all. Then I think about how we got here. I don't want to think we are dumb or careless. The radiation symbols on all the train cars were obvious to us and occupied a subliminal part of our minds, creeping out only when we tried not to think of them. We didn't speak of it on the train, and we won't here in the desert simply for the

279

fact that we reached a group consensus from the moment each of us first saw the symbol. As Beet would say, nothing to be done. Acknowledged.

Beet awoke several times throughout the night in a run, trying to get to his feet but coming to his senses and slouching back down before even getting to a full stand. He panted but couldn't get back to sleep, and eventually took guard duty from me. An exhausted, fevered sleep gave way to an exhausted, fevered morning of rough hiking.

Now, we finally reach the place. From the rail, we hop onto an old wooden train platform, the beams practically begging to be oiled. Old lamp posts, old mailboxes. Everything beginning to give way under the constant barrage of solar radiation.

We move into the abandoned town, packs heavy on our backs but lightening by the day. The houses with a type of siding I've never seen, cars from automobile museums parked and rusting away in driveways. Everything is as if I am looking through a postcard, back decades to a time when the Iron Curtain shrouded every window of the mind. There are no mannequins, as one might expect. Perhaps there used to be, or perhaps this place is just for structural testing.

The detonation tower sits on the edge of the town. Metal criss crossing like a radio tower and a small bit of scaffolding at the top. It wouldn't look like much to most people, but live in Utah long enough and you can begin to understand the secrets that the silent desert keeps.

A full scale suburb, completely intact. The windows in place, every door unlocked. Houses   hot without any ventilation, and smelling like sunflower seeds. Smelling like my treehouse when I left the door shut in August heat.

Empty fridges, empty drawers, empty stomachs.

"Not that I'd want to eat whatever would be there, anyway," Mike says. "Gelatin-tuna-casserole, or something,"

The post office is of special novelty, parcels and envelopes lay on the counter like a display table at a wedding. They've probably been there longer than we've been alive.

The streets are asphalt, but are decayed from their original state into a cracked mosaic of different heights and angles. Let's just say that I would never push my wheelchair bound grandmother through this pathway. The edges of the road have slumps of sand blown across.

Manuel and I stand back to back in the middle of the main street. A thousand ghosts watching from empty windows, our friends watching from a bench beneath a faded American flag.

We step exactly ten paces away from one another and draw our handguns, shooting only an instant apart.

Far from my feet a ping of dirt shoots up, I seem to have missed him entirely.

Stupid, yes. Foolish and a little bit self indulgent. I find it challenging to admit that the grief and anxiety that has been building up is released through the gunshot, even if minutely.

At the intersection of the town we see all manner of traffic signs, with faded colors and fonts that we don't recognize.

My mind drifts for a moment and I'm back on training wheels, riding through a pastel colored Safety Town...And then I'm back

281

in Arches with Manuel. Heavy wool pants from the costume store, fake badges on our chest. He stands with a stop sign that they use (and we took) on road construction sites to control traffic. We only did this on days with slow attendance, and only to folks we knew could spare it. The truck or van rig would stop at his signal, I'd jump out from a bush and loot the solitary vehicle for anything that might be loose and unsecured. My main targets were loose lunch coolers and beer. My mind wanders to the sheriff and that golden badge...

From a rooftop, Mike points out beyond the town.

"Looks like there's some trucks over there. Maybe a building, or maybe-actually I think that's just a big truck," he grins, the hard sun bouncing off his oversized shirt. I wonder what happened to the truck Wren borrowed without asking. He makes fake binoculars with his fingers, and looks through them. We stand on the street, looking up at him like he's some kind of prophet.

"You know, if we're really that lost, maybe we can find a piece of sandpaper," Beet says. "Use that as a map."

From above, Mike continues.
"Looks like a whole different set of train tracks, and lots of rocks to creep around in. A big hill way out that way, and-I'd almost say that one over there's a mountain. Definitely some buildings on that thing. Looks like a small lake over there behind those rocks. And-woah," he gasps, cupping his hands over the sides of his eyes.

"See a pyramid or something?" Beet asks, smiling. Wren and I look at each other. No way to know.

"No, some kind of…rocket?" Mike says. "Like a missile or something, just flew on the railroad track and exploded against a wall. I swear I'm not making this up," he says.

"My bet is on aliens, at this point," I say. Beet strokes his beard and nods at me, as if I were on to something. I find myself wishing for my binoculars once again. A victim-like Monty-of poor planning despite our very best efforts. We brought two sets in case one got lost or broken or somehow separated, but they somehow both ended up in Monty's backpack. Just like chewing gum, which is also sorely wanted.

"How far is that mountain with the buildings?" I ask.

"Mmm-at least a day's walk. I only say there's buildings because of the—the glimmer. You know, off of open windows. Otherwise it looks like any other chunk of rock out here."

"And the…rocket?" Manuel asks, hesitating.

"A mile or three, I'm coming down now. I feel like I'm inside of an oven," he says.

We take shelter inside of one of the homes, one that might belong to a nuclear family. Bedrooms painted for one boy and one girl. To my surprise, the doors actually have functional locks on them.

After a few hours of slowly exploring the house and having a fight with the world's dustiest pillows, the sun finally drops behind the rocks and we're encased in a yellowy and warm light, perfectly mellow. We sit around the table like a perfectly normal family. Dad's just come home from work, Mom's been working on dinner. How was school? Fine, thanks.

We dish out the MRE's, which are

rapidly dwindling. We can make them last another day or two if we ration carefully. I take a set of dehydrated beef and pork patties, gummy and a bit too much like eating leather for my pallet. But I swallow because I'm hungry. Mike eats what will be his fourth package of chicken a la king, unanimously despised by the rest of the posse. Wren places a few empty glasses on the table that she pulled from a display shelf. Another set sits on the shelf behind us, tinted slightly green. We all know what this means, the classical art of uranium glassing. In the clear and clean glasses she pours from another hydration pack, finishing it off.

"To...Nuketown, U.S.A.?" I ask, raising my glass. Clink.

"Think we're in California? I've always wanted to go to California," Beet says.

"No, we couldn't have gotten that far this fast. Besides, that's the wrong direction," I say. "I think."

After dinner we lick our wrappers clean and put them into Manuel's bag, the trash bag. Carry in, carry out. All of our maps are spread onto the table, a pen and paper come out. The family dinner turns to look like a war room. In a way, I suppose it is. The war on the resort, on capitalism. As a collective we try to illuminate how we got here, what canyons we may have rode through, and what rivers we may have passed. In the end, we haven't even the foggiest clue how many miles we've traveled. There were simply too many bends in the track. Too many micro adjustments of speed, and of heading. Maybe the conductor was right, and there's no logical way anybody could survive the trip. Maybe we're already dead, staving off the reaper with a pitchfork of hydration packs and MREs.

At night we drag the ancient mattresses together in what would have been the girl's bedroom. We grimace at the cartoon ponies painted on the wall and the hot pink paper peeling at the corners. The little dolls and the ballerina music box. Most of the homes are like this, empty except for a few exceptional details. Perhaps placed there by some scientist intending to study what remains of a music box after the detonation of an atom bomb.

A few feet from one another, on the ground, slumped in a corner chair. Like a sleepover.

"Think this is Area 51?" Beet asks, looking straight at the ceiling. His glasses on the nightstand reflect the stars outside the window. Empty ceiling, not even a light. Just a lamp on the desk over there.

"Yes," Wren answers, snuggled into me, but far enough away not to impose on the group.

"Really? Actually?" he asks.

"Obviously. Where else could we be? This is clearly where they keep all the enslaved aliens from Roswell," she says, the muscles in her cheeks rising to a smile.

"Obviously," Mike says from the chair, smoking a cigarette with his eyes closed. He turns his head and blows out the window.

"To what end?" Manuel asks.

"Well," Wren begins. "They need the aliens to make the microwaves. Not just the waves themselves, but the machine that we call a microwave. There's a factory out here, probably on that mountain Mike saw. Any microwave that ever has been built, or ever will be built, was constructed with grubby pale fingers by intergalactic refugees," she says with fervor. A brief second while everyone considers this possibility.

"*Duuuuuuuude*," Beet says, clapping his hands together softly. With that, I close my eyes and smile, knowing I'm surrounded in a family home by the people meant to be here with me.

...

The following day is made productive by searching for the lake Mike saw from the rooftop. We considered investigating the 'rocket rail', as we've come to call it, but decided it best to avoid military patrols if at all possible. We're likely wanted criminals, after all.

The trip leads us to a rocky outcropping and a rise of stone devoid of sand more miles away from town than we had intended. An arroyo, perhaps. A large body of water might be nearby, if we're willing to search for clues and spend some calories in pursuit of it. The pathway leads back to a much larger pile of rocks, which we clamber over and wind up dropping into a fine bit of country that reminds me of the Needles District of Canyonlands National Park. Here we have all the rocks, but no trees except for the occasional defiant juniper. Rock piles everywhere rest against mountains of cohesive sandstone. In one section I slide down a shadowy rock to investigate a splotch of yellow. At the base of the hill I find a dried and cracked river bed, reaching far out into the tannish haze. A fly bites me on the back of the neck, I fight back too late and end up slapping myself without any casualties.

I walk the cracked riverbed and approach the bit of yellow sticking out from the collapsed embankment. The passenger side rear corner of a yellow Datsun sticks out. I know the model—I'd built it out of plastic pieces from the hobby store when I was a kid. Must've gotten here from a flash flood ages ago, come from who knows where.

After climbing back up I relay the discovery to an unamused and heat sick audience. We take shelter in the rocks during the worst of the sun and emerge later in the day to continue our journey. My boots feel like there's a fire in them, my feet blistering in my sweat soaked socks.

This area was all under water once. The basin of a prehistoric ocean. I turn my eyes toward the baby blue sky and picture schools of fish and even a dolphin or two. Over time the waters have receded, filling in massive lakes and then rivers and then streams and then trickles and then mere puddles. And now, dust.

The suspected arroyo leads us a few miles to a few cracks in sandstone with a few inches of stagnant water collected in them. The edges round from erosion, all manner of bugs and algae inside. This isn't the first time, and it's far from the last. A cowboy jacuzzi, we call it. Big enough to stick your feet in and plenty warm.

"Just make sure you don't stick your ear in, you can get a brain-eating prion-parasite thing," Mike says to Wren, who fills an empty water bladder from the puddle.

"*How* would I accidentally stick my ear in, Mike?" Wren asks, irritable from the heat like the rest of us.

I scratch at my sunburned and red skin, feeling feverish and clammy. We brought all of our equipment with us on the off chance that we found a town out in the rubble. That, and we didn't want to leave evidence of our presence, having put everything back precisely where we found it.

Our exploration takes us to the edge of this mound of rocks, to a crater so big that the moon might be able to fit into it. Embedded in the sandstone are a variety of fossils-snails, trilobites, perhaps even a squid if I use my imagination a little bit. We walk through an archway carved by wind, the stone on either side holding the ribcage of a fossilized whale. Vertebrae the size of my head above on the ceiling, the rest of the creature lost to time.

In the center of the crater is a patch of grass, green and tidy with bees buzzing about.

There are tales of a place like this in the Maze District of Canyonlands. The perimeter of the crater is the best for climbing in Utah, maybe even in North America. But descending the crater walls and walking to the center, even the edge of the grass, is a sin. There are places out here respected by even the most vile, selfish humans. Even by the thugs who carve their names into rock, who throw their litter on the road. A place where it is understood that no human being should ever set foot, from the dawn of our species unto time immemorial. We have a name for it.

Where Cattle Have Never Roamed.

We hike on.

Weary from the heat, our muscles like

deflated balloons, we round a corner and freeze. A wandering sheep stands idly chewing on a lump of grass. She looks at me with blank eyes and bleats. Her wool is overwhelming, filthy with red dust and three times the mass that it should be. She hasn't been sheared in two years or more, by the way she looks. Mike is the first to produce his pistol, aiming it at the animal. With a look of peace, Manuel shakes his head at Mike and pushes the man's handgun down with a benign palm. Manuel slowly pulls out his own handgun, the lot of us covering our ears and standing behind his firing line. He pulls the trigger, we wince. The animal's neck jerks to the side, she starts running and slams straight into a rock wall. We rush over and put our hands on her, struggling to feel any muscle or bone beneath the massive cloud of wool.

The bullet hit directly in the temple. Not a hunter's shot, but a deadly one.

She seizes up, a leg kicking in a last defiant motion before giving out. Knives out, Mike, Wren and I set to work with shearing her. The mound of wool produced is more than I thought. Filthy, full of ticks and mites and fleas and burrs. It smells foul, like a gym sock mixed with a specific cheese that my clients often brought but I was never permitted to try.

Each of us grabbing a limb, we haul the sheep over to a wind cave. It goes deep into the rock, the air is cool and damp. I feel a sense of excitement mixed with a welcoming from our newfound shelter in the mess of spires and domes. Then, we set to work on the butchering process.

Beet gets started collecting the bone dry timber outside, building a fire near the mouth of the cave. Along the ceiling near the opening is a runway of dark stains, running deep into the cave. Mineral deposits from flash flooding. Must be.

I have to admit that I was at first hesitant to bring my bushcraft knife. Such a big blade would arouse suspicion, despite how regularly I use it for daily tasks. Once I crossed the threshold of carrying an illegal handgun with the serial number filed off, a knife didn't seem so bad anymore.

We cut the meat into cubes and skewer them on sticks, holding them over the hot flames. The sizzling and the smell penetrates my very being, exciting the most primal part of me. After a week of military rations and sugar bars, this meat feels like being bathed in nourishment. Warm grease runs down my chin and through my beard, the tender mutton breaking apart between my molars. I break the bone between two stones and suck out the slick marrow, wishing only for salt.

After the feast we slump against the wall and start to fall asleep lying together, the sun not even set. I kick off my boots and peel my socks back. My skin is wrinkled and pruny, the fire kisses it. I lean against Beet, he puts his arm around me. Mike lies in front of all of us, his head on Wren's shin as a pillow.

...

I awake a few hours later to the sound of amiable laughter, stifled to a low volume in consideration.

at the mouth of the cave, the others sit

cross legged and reclined around a fire that has died
down.
small flames and embers paint their faces and
the cave wall a deep crimson, the light reaching
backward and being expelled before it can
illuminate where I lie.
pack rat droppings next to me in the sand. beyond
them, the smooth mouth of the wind cave frames
a navy sky and the sandstone garden beyond. a
blanket of stars.

     I stand up and crack my back, wiping the
grease from my lips with the back of my hand. I've
always wondered what it is about eating before bed
that guarantees your hunger once you awake. I walk
up to them, and stop to admire an intricate mural
of indigenous markings. I have seen ones similar
to these before, but never in such a great number.
children's handprints at eye level, parents holding
them up to reach.
red and white pigments, firelight. I take comfort in
knowing that we aren't the first to take refuge here.

     "...and because he painted most of his
portraits after the subject has death, it makes sense
that he did not get a lot of fame in his time. I do
not know from experience, but I think that sitting
still in front of a painter for hours or days may
create friendship, you would remember the painter.
A strange choice for the Cossiau's to commission,
really strange for them to ask him to paint nature,"
Manuel says. Everyone listens intently. "They were
inspired by their trip to the western United States,
but if you look at the paintings they do not make
much sense. For example, the wren nesting in the
sandbank. They are all like this—nonsense.
Just rich people wanting things to look

good."

"Fine work...for a man named Crystal Ball," Beet says. Behind him on the ground are the paintings, each taken out of their tube and laid delicately, as if this were an exhibit.

"Morning," Wren says.

"Hey,"

"There's more mutton cooked if you're still hungry," Mike says, passing me a kebab. I take it and pop a piece of the skewered meat in my mouth, gummy but juicy. in the dim light I pour over the paintings. the burrowing owl, digging a tunnel inside the ashes of a retired fire pit. it looks at the viewer guiltily. perhaps the fire pit was built on top of her home, and she's just digging it back out. it may be that she feels guilty for needing to live among the ashes. I get the sense that she's flustered, quietly angry at the camper for building in such a place. then, I look closer and see the singe mark on the tips of her feathers. conceivably, this is just black oil paint applied a bit too liberally, and nothing more. just my imagination.

I lean in, really looking at the paintings for the first time. the great blue heron rests on one foot, reflection in the still water of a deep and cool canyon pool. a crayfish has crawled up and gnawed away at the bird's ankle, which is a ruby red. the great traveler, moving wherever she wants, wherever there is food ready for the taking or easy hunting. yet, a vice at the ankle, a chain. she could eat the crawfish in a heartbeat, destroyed with the powerful bill and a providing a meal that is practically free.

292

━━━ why does she sit, being chewed on?

Chapter 13 || Molar

The following evening we depart our sanctuary after tearing apart the fire pit and doing a bit of housekeeping: filtering water from the puddle, cooking all the meat, and dressing wounds.

My hand throbs near constantly now, a creeping supply of pus protruding. My veins near that hand bulge and highlight in pink, tracing upward toward my elbow.

"Yeah, see? So it works in both Spanish and English," Manuel says to Mike. "¿A dónde van los gatos cuando mueren? Pur*gatorio*. Or, where do cats go when they die? *Purr*gatory."

"I don't get it,"

"Well, you don't speak Spanish, so" he says, trailing off into silence.

I hear the beating of wings, and pause to give thought. It takes the others a moment to realize that I'm trying to listen, before they also stop walking. *Beat, beat, beat, beat, glide.* Familiar, I know that bird. But who? A burst of energy, then a respite as they coast toward their branch. I smile at the familiarity of this methodology, and wish to be in the gliding part.

Then, I see him coasting between two small juniper trees, some kind of scrub-jay. A charming blue color against the oppressive warmness of the rocks all around us. There are a few here, traveling in a small group as normal. His belly is gray, and filthy, and looks ragged.

What are they doing way out here? I shake my head, I don't even know where I am, and learning that we're within their range narrows it down minimally. Not to mention that the chances of someone coming all the way out here to catalog what few birds are present is extremely slim[19].

We pause on the hillside before walking closer. A line of rail, razor straight and terminating at a half wall.

At the end opposite the wall, a concrete pad and a few dark squares that are too far to discern. The idea is that the pad side may hold clues as to where we might find a way out of this place. Those trucks Mike saw had to come from somewhere, after all.

There are enough boulders and shattered rocks running parallel to the rail line that there would be adequate cover, enough even for all of us to comfortably sleep in should we need to.

The evening sun is gentle on us tonight, low and orange in a cloudless sky when we finally reach the tracks. Black burn marks on the half wall, made of reinforced concrete with a metal ballistics plate on the burned side. Looks like something you'd see on the front of a tank.

Black pieces of hard confetti cover the

ground so densely as to give the visual impression of mulch, but the poignant smell of rot and creosote tells me otherwise. The smell brings me back to cleaning the grill at the resort. There was a time when the head chef banned all cooking oils in response to a food critic that thought the meals were too fatty. A look from Manuel and Mike shows me that their olfactory senses brought them back there, too.

Beet squats and examines something, then picks it up to show us.

"I think this is a molar?"

"From who?" Wren asks.

"You think it is human?" Manuel replies.

"I don't know, pretty worn down," I say. We look around more and see irregular patches in the black litter, where rakes and shovels had clearly removed the duff. The sand is exposed in these spots, vaguely the size and shape of a kayak, or a corpse.

White pickups coming from the mountain in the distance, a plume of dust behind them.

We take cover among the rocks, stowing our bags. Our unprecedented level of grime aids in our camouflage. The trucks arrive at the far end, a dozen or so men in khaki camouflage ambling about and messing with equipment. Big heavy rifles slung around their shoulders, I wonder if they ever see anyone out here. If there are any humans to be afraid of. Could be that they're just afraid in general. Heightened security in response to the recent terror attacks. Can never be too careful. Once again I find myself wishing for my binoculars. I hope the police gave them to Monty's dad, at least. They're probably just going to sit in an evidence locker for the rest of time.

We munch on some of the half dried meat and try to fight away the flies while we hide among the rocks and pass the time. A highly defensible position, should it come to that. We could stay in cover and prevent them from using their rifles until they're so close that our handguns and knives would be the preferred tools. Of course, all we have are dirt biking helmets and a distinct absence of kevlar or plate carriers. There really isn't any question about who would win that fight, and I'd rather not kill someone else's child.

Once the sun sets they set to work. The sound of a compressor reaches us, then some kind of air wrench. A low droning sound, then of a fuse being lit. A high pitched hissing followed by a thunderous clap that makes me shudder. We peek out, a small railcar with a cylindrical tube attached to it rests against the reinforced wall. A seat is atop it, a roasted torso steams inside a set of buckled restraints. More black litter is thrown around, in large chunks rather than a fine spray. Two men take a small machine, almost like a khaki snowmobile with desert camouflage, to the wall. One of them hops off and attaches a line to the railcar, then they tow it back out of our sight.

"The insurrectionists have been threatening to target military facilities, maybe they are prepping for that," Manuel says. We try to figure out a way to get a cellphone back on to record, knowing that there would be no way for anyone else to logically believe us without hard evidence. Several more incidents follow at much the same pace: rocket, detonation, retrieval. Conspiracies of execution, murder, war crimes and military court.

    At last they seem to break for lunch, but the sound of footsteps causes me to peek my eye over the lichen covered rock. A single soldier pushes the rail cart out next to the wall, then another joins him. It is rotated 180 degrees now, the contents of the seat replaced. Tan skin and black hair, head lolled to the side. Hands and feet strapped in. A bulletproof vest, and then a ballistics helmet is placed upon their head, unmoving. A small cube is positioned onto their lap with an antenna on it, one of them pulls out a clipboard and marks something down. They walk away.

We've gotten used to covering our ears now, some with our hands and others by wearing their helmets and earplugs that we brought. The explosions, like this one, come without warning. Not much more than a pop, a screen door slammed in the middle of the night. The body is ravaged, the bowels spilling out in a brown slew. Almost immediately the flies around us migrate over there, sensing dinner. The soldiers reappear, unclip the body, and throw it onto the dirt.

Another, then another. Different explosive charges, same model of helmet and probably the same caliber of bullet proof vest. Notes taken both before and after, the bodies rolled off the chair and dragged away from the track. Murder after murder. This process takes hours, most of the time filled with words too quiet to hear, and details too distant to make out. Boredom overtakes once again, we throw pebbles against rocks, just to watch the physics of them bouncing.

A white pickup drives to the half-wall, three men jump out and unroll huge black trash bags, placing them in a pile next to the bodies. Procedurally, they pick up the pieces and try to match them together, then zip them into the bags.

Body bags, Manuel explains. Thick vinyl. The soldiers pick up the body bags from either end, like you'd carry them if there was a regular corpse in them. But, the chunks of the bodies migrate together in the center of the bag, forcing the soldiers to take a step closer to one another and carry them with their faces close together, only a foot apart.

They lay another body bag onto the ground and rake up the larger pieces, black and lumpy and dispersed. A shovel comes out, the pieces put into the last bag, then loading them all into the bed of the truck. The men sit on the tailgate and deliver two slaps to the frame, it drives away. A procession of red taillights head toward the mountain along the horizon, the first stars appear. We crawl out of our den and walk back near the wall, onto the waste.

The rake and shovel prints are more well defined in the still desert air, fresh boot prints and blood sprays. They got most of the corpses, but not everything. A fingernail here, a piece of cartilage there. And hauntingly, an eyeball with the muscle attached to the back of it. Beet touches it with his toe and we turn away and bite our thumbs when it jiggles like pudding.

     "Looks like they missed a spot," Mike says, ducking behind a rock and walking over.

He holds a jet black L-shaped thing at arm's length, flies buzzing incessantly around it.

"Is that—"

"A human foot," Beet says, covering his eyes and then peeking through his fingers.

"What do you think, size 8 or 9 shoe?" Mike says, then pulls on a plastic tag tied around the largest toe. "Lily Bitsillie, age: 48, cause of death: cardiac arrest,"

"Pretty extreme heart attack," I remark.

"And there's a logo on the bottom of the tag that says...no, that can't be right. Just a coincidence,"

"What does it say?" Manuel asks impatiently.

"Property of Cossiau Medical Donations."

"What?" Wren asks. Manuel looks at me, asking with his eyes. I stick my hand in my pocket and touch the brochure, not time yet. A light panic passes through the group, trying to connect the dots.

"It has to be a coincidence, there's no other explanation," Mike says calmly.

"Best not to think too much about–" Beet begins.

"Would you stop it with that?" Wren interrupts. "Sorry,"

"It's fine," Beet says. "I just don't know what to make of it. No sense torturing yourself about the unknowns, be at peace with them,"

...

And so we walk toward the mountain. Not on the road, but next to it. The night takes over and as we approach I can see the distinct domish shape of it, but with the absence of trees or water of any kind I have a hard time calling it a mountain. We hash out an escape plan dealing with their imports and exports, working with what little information we have. The walk drops us down a few dozen feet in elevation, we walk on the cracked surface of a salt bed, what was once a massive lake.

Chapter 14 || AbomiNation

We sit curled close together, in the shade under
a jumble of rockfall. Spiders and lizards share
the space with us, Mike nervously swats his neck
when he remembers this fact. Our approach to the
mountain last night was a wild success. No military
patrols or checkpoints or spotlights. Not even
security cameras. That we can identify, anyway.

The 'buildings' on the side of the mountain
seem to be little more than geologic anomalies;
sandstone blocks sheared off at hard angles. Near
the summit we spied a radio tower, but only because
of the red light that briefly came on during our
approach. This morning a convoy of three military
transports left and drove eastward on a dirt road.
They remained in our view for over an hour. There
was a brief conversation about walking this road
out, but that was stamped out when Manuel drew
attention to the fact that one of the three trucks
was a fuel transport. Wherever they're going,
their petrol tanks need to be refueled

several times before they will get there. Taking the risk of walking that road might be too much for our bodies to handle. On the plus side, if we are pushed too far or someone gets hurt, we could always surrender to the military and get blown up in a rocket chair.

Just now, Beet chimneys down to our position with an excited expression.

"I found a cave, and a door I think,"

"You *think?*" Manuel asks, smiling.

"Yeah, come check it out. Should at least provide more shade than down here," he says, climbing back out above us. We follow a goat trail up to a crack in the rocks, I bend my neck to fit through and have to take off my bag. The interior of the space is about the size of a large SUV, enough for all of us to fit. A small crack of sunlight comes in through the entrance, its path visible in the bleached rock on the opposite wall.

Beet goes to one of the walls and lifts a rock with his finger, revealing a cavity beneath it. A plastic top, on hinges. Something you'd hide a key under in your garden. Beneath is a dusty keypad, new in condition except for the layer of silt on top of it.

"I just don't know what it's for," he says, looking at us. I walk over to one of the walls, curiously flat and lacking any sort of layering or cracking. It feels like it had been sprayed with some sort of adhesive and then stuck with sand to blend in.

We decide not to push the numbers, but determine that this hints at a large interior space. Perhaps it is an emergency exit, or a smoking spot where the scientists take their breaks.

The breeze up here is pleasant. We continue our hike—more of a climb—up to the summit in search of an entrance. At the top, a huge radio tower. Support cables extending in three directions, Mike adds a cigarette butt to the collection up here. A box the size of a refrigerator, painted tan with splotches of brown, humming. A large vented platform near the base of the tower, faint current of air pulsing out of it. And, a metal hatch.

To our delight, it is unlocked. I get down onto the hot rock and peer inside while Manuel holds it open, but all I see is darkness. Opening it all the way might squeak the hinges and give away our position, and it will definitely spill hard sunlight into a decisively dark space. We decide to wait until nightfall, encamped on the north side a few meters down. At one point we hear a metal clanging and Mike perks up, sniffing wildly like a dog. Tobacco.

Another clang. I check my watch, we wait until the sun has been set for a few hours before entering. I wonder to myself if this is still considered breaking and entering, or if there's a more frightening name for it. Would I still be tried in civilian court?

The hatch opens without a screech, well greased. The rungs on the ladder are textured, I'm the first to go inside. The tunnel is just long enough that I become bored of moving my body in this way, I hit the metal grated floor and look around. We're at the end of a passageway, a singular long hallway stretches out before me. Dim red lights in protective cages line the walls. I point a single finger up to my friends and tiptoe down the hallway. Doorways without doors on either side, bunk beds with breathing bodies in fatigues and t-shirts. Machine guns either leaning against the wall or tucked under the sheets. Neat and orderly. Snoring. The end of the hallway opens up to two more pathways. I double back and wave my friends down with a finger over my mouth[10].

They come down smoothly taking care not to let their backpacks drag against the wall. We creep past the barracks and guess at which hallway to take, standing straight and rolling our feet. Acting like ghosts.

Locker room, communal shower, toilets with no stalls. A locked door labeled 'armory'. We search diligently for a map of any kind, to find either the cafeteria or a way out. And still no footsteps, no cameras.

After exploring all pathways on this level, we finally dead-end at a door marked 'LAB-02'. There's a keypad next to it, but the sliding blast door pushes open easily. It takes us down a flight of steps and through another doorway into a sort of vestibule, lab coats, hazardous material suits and rubber boots folded neatly on a white bench.

"Mask up," Manuel says, pointing to a docket on the wall that is reminiscent of the news during the first years of the pandemic. I put mine on, as do the others excluding Mike, who apparently had not brought one. He takes a spare KN-95 from a box affixed to the wall, Beet finishes by tying his bandana over his face. Manuel tightens a serious looking mask with black Spanish labels.

The walls here are a metallic white, too, like the interior of a spaceship. The last one in is Wren, who spins with a gasp when the door electronically shuts behind her. Mike shows his teeth in embarrassment, his finger still hovering above a touchpad. Valves on the ceiling open up, spraying us with a mist that smells like vodka. A click, and a door on the opposite side hydraulically opens.   Beyond, a catwalk that follows the perimeter of a large room, a metal grated set of stairs goes down. Fluorescent lights noiselessly illuminate the space. The way we came is locked, and we are in this deep already. Why not continue on? We take the steps down to the main floor, a mechanical clicking almost creating a rhythm. A rod runs the length of the room on either side, curtains sectioned off into segments. I draw back the curtain slowly, looking inside.

A man on a ventilator, tubes stuck down his throat. Probes strapped to his head, his eyes open and staring up. The next curtained section holds a similar secret, and the next. Mike comes up to me with a clipboard, one from the foot of a bed where they are kept for each patient.

"Look," he says, peeling back several sheets, each a new patient. He points to a familiar name$_7$.

"Catherine Beaker," I mouth, quietly.

"The girl that went missing from the resort?" Wren asks, coming over and examining the sheet.

"She must have passed through here at some point,"

"It's more than coincidence," I say. "It has to be."

"What do you think, then?" Manuel asks. I take a moment to collect my thoughts, walking around the room and reading the patient files for most of the patients here.

"They're testing a new drug on them," I say, pointing to the charts.

"Aero-sol?" Manuel says, then nods in understanding.

"Looks like they're testing a new vaccine against Cable Pox. Everyone here's been administered it, then exposed to the virus," I say, showing them the paper evidence. We pass it around, gaping, some more surprised than others. Reading the paper over and over, I try to recall high school biology class from the recesses of my mind. An aerosol, administered through the ventilator that somehow penetrates the stem cells and strengthens the immune system to make the patient immune to the virus. That's the hope, anyway. We remove and bag a sheet or two from each chart, pulling from the middle, then replacing the clipboards where we found them.

A hiss. The decontamination chamber we came through has been activated.

Doors on all sides of the room, we pick one and run as quietly as possible. Rotate the strange handle, sliding the blast door open and then shut behind us. A small window of bulletproof glass lets us see back into the main room, nobody yet.

Someone gasps behind us. I spin and draw my gun.

Cages. Cages with human beings in them. Six of them, slumped against the grated metal walls and perfectly still. Nobody moves, Beet's breath fogging up his glasses from the mask. The bodies are malnourished, their lips torn and dangling above and below the mouth, corresponding smears of dried blood and gnaw marks near the locked cage handles. Ripped fingers and ripped bare feet, stained blood in half circles and footprints on the cold floor.

I lean in to look at one of their faces,

the tip of the nose rotting off. Syphilitic ulcers dotting the skin all over, pus filled blisters covering the face and exposed tendons along the arms. Medical gowns soaked in multiple types of fluid, all smell undetectable beneath the breathy smell of our masks and the massive vent at the back of the room.

I step closer to it, blades the size of a kayak paddle and casually pumping air out of this space and up somewhere, probably near that vent we were all hanging around.

We look from eye to eye, I check the slit on the door to see someone walking into the main room behind us. A short man with a receding hairline gets on the floor and looks underneath a desk, then checks several drawers before finding a pair of reading glasses and laughing at himself. He walks away in socks.

I let the air out of my lungs and try not to breathe too much, despite the ventilation. The door into this room is heavy, designed to be locked shut both manually and electronically. Manuel carefully removes the clipboard from a holder on one of the cages, pointing out a specific line to me. Late stage Cable, I've seen it before. But only on the news. Normally people don't last this long unless they're being kept alive by artificial means, which most people can't afford.

That's probably a blessing. He silently places the clipboard back after stealing a sheet near the back, and looks expectantly at me. I give a thumbs up and we exit the room.

Beet pushes his hands together and narrows his eyes, looking around in confusion like someone stole his shoelaces without him noticing. In stunned silence, we check several adjacent rooms accessible from the lab.

A stock room full of extra medical supplies and printer toner, not much else. Except for the swinging double door that we quietly push through. Inside, sleek metal walls and ceiling, lamps hanging down and casting harsh white light onto examination tables. The wall a mosaic of vault doors at varying heights, like a grid.

A morgue. We've all seen photos of them before, but being inside one for the first time allows a tugging battle of eeriness and demanded respect for those that lie here. We look for more documents, more patient files, but find few on display. A desktop computer sits at a small table in a side office, white tile walls to match the floor.

"I suppose that they are relying mostly on paper to document everything," Wren says. Manuel nods, saying

"That way they have no reason to fear being monitored or probed." He bends down at the side of the desk and tugs at some wires. "It is not connected by ethernet cable. Only to the wall. Same thing with this printer, that way they can print without releasing the patient files to any external network. Clever,"

"Clever," Mike says. "Or maybe they can't get wifi inside of this hunk of rock,"

"Yeah, maybe," I say. We still speak quietly, as if someone inside of the body vaults might awaken and tattle on us.

"I guess that would explain the lack of video surveillance," Wren says. Beet nods thoughtfully, looking at the puzzle in his mind.

"Guys, sorry-folks, come look at this," Mike says. The rest of us go over to him, where

he's opened up several of the receiving chambers.
He points to the toe of one of the corpses, which has
a tag on it.

"What is with you and feet today?" Wren asks.
He shrugs. The name is not one that I recognize.
Cause of death: major infection—ovarian cancer.
Manuel pulls a roster out from a pile of papers,
finally matching the name on the tag.

"She's scheduled to go out tomorrow on
'range two'," he explains.

"Another flesh firework," I say.

"That's a good metal album name," Mike
comments.

"Can you check the sheets that go back?" I
ask Manuel, who holds a plastic binder full of rosters
dating back several years. "May of last year,"

He flips to the page, I scan it thrice to be
sure.

"Okay, June?" I say, he flips the sheet. For
each month there are only about a dozen patients.
The winter months have the highest number of
deaths, most of them from heart disease or some
form of respiratory distress. That makes sense in
the context of the virus. Under June I check once,
twice, my eyes weary and having trouble focusing.
On the third sweep I see her name: Catherine
Beaker.

"That was the month she disappeared,"
Mike says. He should know, they were friends and
he was hounded by the police for weeks after she
disappeared. Eventually a note showed up at the
resort, a resignation letter written to the owner.
The handwriting was cross examined and verified
with the journal she had left in her employee   313
room. She had moved out of state to   ←———

somewhere she didn't want to share, apparently
with a girlfriend. She and I had spoken once or
twice, sat next to one another at a gathering with
a bonfire. Hoodies and cheap beer. She worked in
the restaurant, a server. Her family situation wasn't
the best and she needed to get out of Chicago, go
anywhere but the midwest. She had posted her
resume online, shortly after a recruiter from the
resort reached out and she was on her way with
nothing more than a single packed suitcase. She is
a kind person, someone you might routinely borrow
a pencil from and that exists only when you look
back to revisit your yearbook. She probably feels the
same about me.

Felt the same.
Mike and I never subscribed to the corroborated
handwritten letter. It was published in The
Times Independent, a front page story of quality
journalism, detailing what might have happened
before and after Catherine ran away with her
girlfriend Kennedy, whom none of us had ever met
or heard of. He no longer works there, but it is
important to note that the writer of the story left
town for good with a brand new car about a week
after it was published.
        She had confided the same secret in both
Mike and I, something she was unnecessarily
ashamed of and not ready to openly claim: she was
asexual.

        We walk to yet another push door, opening
to a long hallway. We look around along the wall
314   for more clipboards or binders of information.
━━━━━━━ We make the decision as a group to begin

taking all the physical evidence we can carry in the form of paperwork.

"We need recent information to prove that this is still happening," Manuel says. And so we search for paperwork regarding bodies before they get to the morgue.

Along the walls we do not find it, but instead find fire extinguishers and safety data sheets for various chemicals I've never heard of in bright yellow binders with hard black lettering. The place is well lit and sickeningly clean, I worry that in my grimy state that soil and grease will fall off of me or my equipment and leave a trail.

Not to mention the now rotting meat that we all carry in our bags. We truly did our best to dry it over the fire, but the absence of any real wood with which to build a drying rack made that plan irrelevant.

On either side of the seemingly endless hallway we find small labs, which in my limited experience are not useful for anything elaborate or enduring.

At the end is a large service elevator, so big that it could accommodate a smaller sized vehicle or several forklifts. We do not take it for fear of giving ourselves away. I take a minute to appreciate the miracle that we've not really run into anyone yet.

There is a set of fire stairs adjacent, which we take. It continues down in a square, but we take a side door that allows us to access a catwalk. The room—hangar—is massive and cold. The walkway is solid metal, I lean over the railing to get a better view of what is below me. Crates and bins, like the rest of the room. Steel cables are mounted to the railing, suspending the entire platform many stories high. The height makes me dizzy.

"They must've mined out the interior and used the rail cart to transport the debris, then left the rubble on either side of the train tracks," Wren says, pointing out a pile of disassembled rail in the corner. Near them are two military personnel transport trucks, canvas stretched and covering the beds. On the furthest wall is a garage door big enough to fit several of them at the same time.

Loading carts and forklifts. The trucks are some distance away, and above them is a sizable air duct, all part of the robust ventilation required for a laboratory of this caliber. With enough hounding, the group convinces me to pry open the ventilation shaft adjacent to us and try to climb through it, in order to get a better view of the trucks and to see if there might be cargo already in them.

The vent cover comes off easily and I shed my backpack, preparing to crawl through. I don't get more than a few feet before my clothing gets caught and torn on the hundreds of self tapping screws holding the shaft together. Not like the movies. No way I'm getting through that without bleeding to death, especially with my hand mostly out of commission.

Instead, we resign to descend eight flights of stairs until we reach the ground floor. We open the push door as quietly as possible, but the hardware on it does not make the process easy. Crouched, creeping. The space seems expansive and so much more dangerous from the ground. Perhaps this would have been an easier task if we had left someone up on the catwalk, if our radios weren't dead and full of sand. We sneak alongside a pile of cement pipes in great condition and peer through

the pallets of construction materials in storage,
trying to see where those unnerving footsteps are
coming from.   Two soldiers meander in
the center of the room, a great distance of open and
smooth floor around them. It would be a good place
to play dodgeball.

Their rifles are slung around their sides. One
of the soldiers, about our age, slinks from foot
to foot, spinning and staring at the ground in an
elaborate display of boredom. There aren't even
any rocks to kick. In a few minutes they are gone
through a door, to another part of the base.

We need to get back before the scheduled
vacation days for most of our crew run out,
especially Manuel and Wren. Not returning to work
would only serve to make them suspects in this case.
Our food is nearly gone once again, our water almost
empty. We have to make this work somehow.

With the only patrol on duty out of the way,
we follow along the massive hangar door until we
get to the trucks. A helicopter rests in storage, a
minigun mounted on small wings and rotors folded
together. Wheeled pallets of bombs, crates of
mortars and ordinance. The trucks have a paint
job matching that of the uniforms here-digital
camouflage broken by gray stones. All different
shades of brown. Manuel makes a run for the cab,
but I grab his arm.

"We absolutely cannot steal one of these," I
say, trying to be firm but knowing that I still need to
convince him.

"Do not worry, my bro. I am just checking for
evidence. I do not have American license anyway,
remember?" he whispers, laughing. I let him   317
go, he opens the door gingerly and climbs

up.

The spacious cargo area is full of crates, confirmed on closer inspection to be caskets. With a nearby crowbar, prying them open is a piece of cake. The same body bags we saw earlier are inside, it smells of window cleaner and melted plastic. A white label containing the patient information is glued to the bag near where the head should be, but often isn't.

Some of the other crates smell more pungent, which creates a convenient symphony with the scent of our own sweat and moldy mutton that we've been slowly getting used to.

The Peruvian appears with an unorganized stack of forms. For more cover, we all climb into the transport and sit on the caskets, preparing for another one of his presentations.
Instead, we get a mash of thoughts, propositions, and theories.

He sits on one of the wooden boxes, crossing one leg over the other and opening the binder. The cover reads 'Forms: Intake'. He reads a few pages before closing it and looking up at us.

"The good news is that this truck goes to a big city, if we can hide in it then we should be able to hop out. The bad news is that these coffins are headed to a government crematorium. I put my head in my hands. The only way we can sneak out of here on the truck is *inside* of the coffins; a fact that nobody has said aloud but that we all know.

A clanging and a door opens up somewhere, then shuts. Peeking my head out, I don't see anyone. Maybe someone else forgot to get their glasses.

"We should probably figure out our

plan," I say.

"Clearly there isn't much left to figure out," Beet says. "Hide in the caskets and escape when we have a chance."

"We'll need to wait until we are stopped before we can get out, otherwise we might just hop out in the middle of the desert, and we're back to square one," I say.

"Seems like we'll need some way to escape," Mike says, feeling the growing stubble on his chin. "How about this: we get that case of smoke grenades over there," he says, pointing to the storage bay. "We use the roster thing to figure out which casket will get burned up first, and we fill it with smoke grenades and flares and stuff. Then, when they take them all in to be cremated, they'll burn that one first and it'll blow up, giving us a veil of smoke to escape through..." he spreads his hands as he says this, his eyes full of imagination. A soft chuckle from Wren.

"Your heart is in the right place," I say. "But I don't plan to see the inside of a crematorium in my lifetime. Seems way too risky,"

"Not even after you die? We're running out of room to bury people, you know," Beet says, happy this topic has been brought up more than once on our trip.

"I don't know, man," I say impatiently.

"Well," Wren begins. "There's nothing stopping us from getting out of the coffins once we're on the road. We wait until we see pavement, at least, then jump. They don't know we're here,"

"They will once they see half of their paperwork missing," Manuel says, shoving the binder and sheets into his heavy backpack.

Nobody speaks for a few moments.

"That's the plan, then," I say.

"The paperwork says that they are due for the next pickup at 1300 hours. I do not know how far the city is, but I imagine the drivers will be here soon. We should get ready," Manuel says.

The coffins are already nailed, so there likely won't be an inspection involving prying them open, but they'll likely do a count and make sure everything is in order before leaving property. Someone needs to hide in a crate that isn't nailed down. We have the conversation, nobody perking up and volunteering until Wren raises her hand.

"I'll do it," she says altruistically. One by one, we crawl into the pine coffins. The wood is still wet from manufacturing and probably coated in all manner of chemical nastiness to preserve it, despite the fact that it is to be incinerated. Mike struggles to fit his backpack with the raft inside, but manages by manipulating the bag into a pillow. We stow all the poster tubes in a separate casket, being too large to fit inside our own. Underneath me is the slippery body bag, abnormal chunks of human flesh and organs sloshing around. It feels like a waterbed full of garbage dispenser muck. I stash my backpack between my legs and get my last glimpse at the fluorescent lights. Wren kisses me on the forehead. "Goodnight, sleeping beauty. See you in a few years," she says, putting the lid over me. The nails holding it together are from a nail gun, sliding easily into their relief holes with the right pressure from above.

The smell of rot is suffocating and permeating, through my clothing and skin. This is a closed casket funeral.

Chapter 15 || Departures

The worst part of it all is that it isn't totally dark. There are cracks everywhere, but still my breath fails to escape and I am forced to inhale it over and over again, each time with a lower concentration of oxygen. When it was time to depart, there were voices but I could only hear half of the conversation. More cargo loaded on top of us, heavy boxes that rattle. Something about shipping, something about improper delivery and reallocation. When the voice was gone and the engine started, I tried to push the lid off in a panic. I only succeeded in pushing myself further down against the sloshing corpse beneath me. I achieved peace only by closing my eyes and pretending to be in darkness, pretending not to see cracks of light, the contents behind them vague and blurry. We're alone back here. I think.

And hours of this. My throat is dry and sore when I swallow, which I am doing a lot because I'm thinking about it. I manage to jam my good arm downward and reach the hose on my hydration pack, which meets my lips. I've had to pee for an entire day it feels like, so maybe more water isn't a good idea, but I can't help myself. I bite down on the mouthpiece and suck, but nothing comes out except warm air. Then, nothing. I've vacuum sealed it myself.

I've drifted in and out of sleep, awoken by the vehicle shuddering as it goes over a rock or some such thing. I think about the others, if they're awake or if they've managed to relax enough to get to sleep. I wonder if Mike is trying to smoke inside of there, hotboxing himself. Maybe he's opened the body bag to share the cigarette. I shake the thought out of my head, focusing instead on if Wren is trapped, too. If she has cargo on top of her, she can't get out to help us.

Traffic. Pavement. Horns, airplanes. Voices, laughter. The air brakes grind to a halt, then we accelerate again. I sigh at the relief of asphalt under the tires. I used to joke with my guests before my 4x4 tours. After the tour is over you either *need* a chiropractic adjustment, or you *no longer* need a chiropractic adjustment. That feels like a lifetime ago, like someone else's story.

I close my eyes and I'm Monty, bleeding out on the asphalt surrounded by shouting and german shepherds barking furiously.
 Then I am him. I'm underground, being lowered by my friends. Not the friends I died for, but for the ones who actually bothered to show up to the funeral. Surely it would have happened by now. The casket hits the bottom of the grave. A rapping on the top as my father sprinkles the first pile of dirt onto the lid.

We keep driving, the sound of air traffic gets louder and soon I cannot hear myself think. The truck stops, it smells like tar.

Someone is inside moving things around. I hold my breath, the condensation from the wet wood and my breath beading on the ceiling of the casket in the hot summer air. A pause outside, quietly I pull out my pistol and point it sideways, barrel against the wood. To shoot through, through the wood and the gut of whoever opens this. That would be the only way out. There's a round in the chamber. The safety is off this time.

The resort has done things, ruined lives and killed people. I knew this, but now I understand it to be true beyond personal experience. The owner has ruined a battalion's worth of lives for their own gain. To take one more life in service of bringing the resort to justice, is that worth the price? Am I ready?

I am ready. The handgun is black and heavy in my palm, I rest it on my hip. I hold it with my bad hand, the throbbing incessant and greedy. I'm sweating all the time, my face and skin flushed red with sunburn and fever.

A kick on the side of the casket. The crate is pushed off from above. My finger on the trigger. A lifetime in prison if we can't get out of this.

The lid lifts, a gasp. I pull the trigger.

Wren's face meets mine through the gap. She slides the lid back quietly. I tuck the gun back into my pocket and crawl out, she hasn't seen. The safety was locked, thank goodness.

I help unearth the others and glance outside of the transport. Most of the crates that had been loaded in here sit a few meters away on pallets, asphalt everywhere. Airplanes, helicopters. I look out and see a terminal, strong people with high visibility clothing and hearing protection, waving passenger planes as they begin to taxi.

"Where are we?" I ask, grabbing the poster tubes and handing them out. My joints crack painfully, my entire backside saturated with sweat. We reset the coffins where they were.

"I don't know, but we have got to move fast," Wren says. Through an eyelet on the canvas, she looks outward. Copying her, I see a passenger jet with its guts open, cargo bay unlatched. "There's a small trolley down there with a few baggage carts behind it. Looks like they're loading the luggage from the plane onto it."

I look through the eyelets on the opposite side to see a military cargobob, the crates from our truck being loaded onto it. A handful of soldiers carrying them, two with flight helmets in the cockpit.

"It's moving," Beet says frantically, getting ready to jump out of the truck.

"Anybody not ready?" I ask, Manuel leaping out of the vehicle before I finish my sentence. We follow, the overwhelming sound of the engines all around us more than covering the slapping of our shoes. The tug vehicle has three luggage carts behind it.

No way we could all hop in and hope not to be noticed by the military on the other side. We run parallel to it, keeping our heads down below the top level and glancing around nervously. I look forward, the tug doesn't even have side mirrors. We do a half-jog along the utility vehicle, hoping we are moving swiftly enough to not be seen.

And if we are seen, hoping that whatever our next move is will put enough distance between us and the military that we'll make it out of this unscathed.

"Put your gun away," someone says.

We're headed straight for a building the size of a stadium, an unfamiliar skyline beyond and tan control tower to our side. I look down and slap my hand onto the side of the luggage trailer, grabbing so I won't lose it. I took my mask off in the casket, we all did. There's probably a thousand sets of eyes watching us through the mosaic of glinting windows, from the airplanes, from the watchtower. Faceless and condemning. We might be on someone's social media story. The whole country is on edge because of the attacks, nobody would think twice before considering us terrorists out on the runway like this. There's probably crosshairs focused on my cowlick right now. I shut my eyes so I won't see my own brains splatter in front of me.

And the cart slows, only a few paces from the building. Receiving doors open, for the baggage of this passenger flight to be transported. One after another, with open hatches that have conveyor belts going into them. We run, in a rush, and pick one.

"Don't get split up!" I try to say, but the words don't make it out of my mouth. We dive onto the same filthy belt, years of luggage grime built up. The sunlight disappears behind us in a shrinking square until we round a corner and it disappears entirely. Someone grabs my hand, someone else grabs my foot. A headlamp—Beet's—turns on and shines on the black carpeted walls all around us. We go through another bend and through a set of plastic flaps. The beam of his light whips wildly from side to side. Conveyor belts full of luggage and skis and golf clubs going in all directions and at all angles. It smells like machine oil and the air is hot and stiff, like the inside of a tissue box.

Our belt stops abruptly, if it weren't for the railing I'd have tumbled over the edge into black nothingness. It jerks to a start again without warning, through another set of flaps and we accelerate forward. A barcode scanner on the wall, a red laser line scanning my flannel shirt. A flash. A souvenir photo for the world's most dangerous amusement park. The conveyor goes over a set of gnashing metal teeth, the bottom of an escalator that eats shoelaces. We get into a crawling position and raise our limbs to pass over it, in my weakened state my good arm fails to hold me up. I drop, hitting my face. My elastic bandage is caught and unwinds as we are ushered away by the machinery.

Suddenly, bright light. We're on a baggage carousel, dazzled by a crowd of people eagerly awaiting their bags. I jump, my legs acting as springs, plowing through the gasps.

The others follow, we stand in the terminal, I catch a logo: Harry Reid International Airport—LAS. Poster tubes in a jumble of hands. Manuel makes a run for the payphone against the wall but is yanked away by Mike. We hide among the crowd and push through, bursting out the glass doorway. Cars idle, waiting for passengers. There, a yellow taxi, an SUV big enough to fit us all. We pile in and slam the door behind us before anyone can get a good look at our faces.

"Go, go!" Mike shouts. The driver activates the meter and turns around painfully slowly, raising an eyebrow.

"We don't do that anymore. Where are

you going?" He asks calmly.

"Baby shower—my wife's in labor and we need to get to the hospital, that's what I'm trying to say," Mike stammers.

"Mhm, which hospital?"

"Uh, *Marty,* I think you mean the hotel. We need to go to the hotel," Beet says, his voice reserved and mirroring the driver's.

"She's having an at home birth—" Wren says, frowning.

"Yes, yes. The hotel," Mike says. The driver pauses, apparently deep in thought.

"Mhm, which hotel?" He asks.

"17 Main Street," Manuel says.

"There's an extra 20 for you if you step on it," I add. He sighs remorsefully and puts the vehicle into gear, then takes off.

"Can I bum a cigarette?" Mike asks the driver, leaning forward.

"No. No vaping either," he says, then leans back with a free hand and slides the plexiglass divider shut between us.

"What's 17 Main Street? We don't even know what city we're in," I ask, spinning my head over to Manuel. He shrugs.

"In the USA there is a Main Street in every town," he says, as if he hadn't given his clever solution much thought.

In a minute we travel down a wide road, white buildings and neon signs projecting from every direction. The pyramid, the Eiffel Tower and the Statue of Liberty. The only place in the world where all of these landmarks are together, other than an atlas. Then, the Bellagio, the Venetian, Caesars Palace and the MGM Grand.

"Vegas, baby!" Mike hollers, rolling down the window and sticking his head out like a dog. A cloud of dirt and insects puff out of his hair and get sucked into the wind. The poster tubes rest safely on our laps.

...

After getting dropped off, we almost immediately hailed another cab from a different company so as not to arouse suspicion. Beet had to go and drag Mike back, who had become enamored with the flyers littering the streets of half naked escorts making a competitive living for themselves.

"Stay focused," Manuel had said, playfully slapping him on the cheek. Mike already had at least five of the flyers in his hand and was looking at them like trading cards.

"We can't just come to Vegas and not—" he paused, looking around and searching for the words. "—not do Vegas things."

After protesting nonstop for fifteen minutes, the driver stopped the vehicle and as a group we told him he either needed to shut up or get out. And so he passed us his poster tube, grabbed his backpack and hopped out with a smile and a wave.

We spent the night in a dingy motel that I'm pretty sure was featured on one of those remodeling television shows but has since gone downhill. We all showered to wash off the filth. I've had my share of extended backpacking trips and their subsequent Showers of Glory, but this was different. First layer to come off was the sand, so prominent in every crack and crevasse (from the diving and squirming about that we

did) that it clogged the drain and had to be cleared
with a chopstick from the takeout Thai food that
we ordered. Next was the brown silt that had
turned virtually into a tattoo, adhering to my skin
and refusing to come off until I scrubbed with a
toothbrush and soap wrapper.

More was the little pebbles and bits of
seashell that had somehow worked into my most
private areas, betraying a strict legacy of exclusivity
and regality that I've worked hard my entire life to
maintain.

Most disgustingly came my hand. I peeled
the last bit of gauze that had survived the conveyor
belt massacre and it fell into the sink with a clink
of hardened pus. The wound has grown larger, deep
red at the edges in a way that makes me think of
a glowing stoplight at night. The flaps of skin have
grown as well, pale and separated and hanging like
damaged gills from my pruny palm. The slit itself is
ochre and widening, a trail of liquid streaming when
I poke at it. I take one of the plastic bags meant
for the garbage in the bathroom and put my hand
into it after replacing the gauze, then secure it with
rubber bands. My thoughts drift to Monty. Is he stuck
underground in some constricting plastic sleeve,
buried and choking in the vacuum?

There was a conversation before dinner about
being less conspicuous. Clean and shaven, we look
more like we belong in Nevada than Utah. With our
hair combed, we practically seal the deal. In the
end, we tossed the dirt bike armor in dumpsters all
across the nearby strip mall neighborhood complex.
As a souvenir, I'm not ashamed to say that I did hold
on to a bracer for my forearm, only to help
keep the new elastic bandage in place.

I was told that I look ridiculous, like I'm trying out for a part in some apocalypse movie. But, the plastic bracer stays.

Now, we wait for Mike at the world's largest Chevron gas station, further out into the desert and finally away from the abysmal city. The payphone is on the side of the shop over there. It is night and the massive concrete pad is lit up with harsh white lights. A light wind and not much traffic, I meander around the 96 pumps and wait for my turn.

Manuel is the first to call. He said he was calling his parents, but immediately breaks out into rapid Spanish and I can't catch more than a word or two. Though, it doesn't seem like an amiable conversation.

Next up is Wren. I try to give privacy, but the lot is huge and devoid of any traffic except for the occasional visitor, who stops a good distance away to refuel. No reason to drive near us, I suppose. She calls her family, and offers what sounds to be good advice to a sister. I know she's homesick; we all are.

I try not to think about the fact that I've got nowhere to call home, except the sand. Nowhere to go back to.

With the money, I'll pay all my debts and rent a cabin somewhere for a few months to organize how I'll donate the rest. Monty's family surely deserves some.

I pick up the phone, covered in smog dust and fingerprint oil, and put in a coin. I dial Gina's number, which I had made sure to memorize before we left.

"Cisco,"

  "Hey, Gina. I don't know that I should say much but its me,"

"Who?"

"With the van. I just wanted to let you know that we won't be making it back there any time soon. We're a good ways away. I just wanted to say thanks, and—and that you can keep it. Title's in the glovebox," I say. A static echo on the other end, her breath while she thinks.

At the edge of the property is a heavy handed darkness and liminal contrast from the barrage of security lights on each pump. Intermittently, sets of headlights pass by. Mike emerges from the darkness. He holds up bags of fast food in either hand, like he's just kicked a winning goal. He smiles at me, a lit cigarette burning brightly in the corner of his mouth. Lipstick on his cheek. He comes from the direction of the tractor trailer parking, where the long haul truckers park to sleep. Mike Hawk, the lot lizard.

He approaches and takes the phone out of my hand. When I open my mouth in protest, he pulls a hamburger out and pretends to stuff it in my mouth. I grab the food from him and walk over to the others. Over my shoulder, I hear him speak.

"Hey, it's me. Can you just hold onto it for a few weeks?" he asks, looking around. "A few months? I'll be there to pick it up. Yeah, love you too," he hangs up the phone.

I pass off the bag of food to the others, and return to the payphone. I've been dreading making this call, but it needs to be done. Can't eat until it is. I dial Monty.

Straight to voicemail. I try his dad's number, who I've used as an emergency contact in the past.

"Hello?"

"Mr. Montague?" I ask.

"Yes, who's this?"

"It's Birch. I'm calling about Monty," I say.

There's silence on the other end. What sounds like a newspaper being put down. I hold my breath. He sighs. "I-I just want to tell you that this is my fault—" I say, my voice breaking. My throat clenches and I hold back a sob, moving the mouthpiece away from my lips and looking at the dark sky. A glimmer of stars.

"How do you mean?" he asks, sounding irritated. "Matter of fact, you ought to keep it to yourself. The trial is at the courthouse tomorrow if you can make it. He's just being kept in town, do you want the number for the station? Why are you calling from Nevada?" he asks, his voice old and gruff. I hold the phone away from me as he speaks, my mind jumping from one point to another as I try to keep up.

"The trial?"

"Haven't you got the paper? I figured he would have at least called you," he says.

"No...I—I've been having trouble getting the paper delivered lately," I say, feigning. Technically the truth.

"Here's the number for the station," he says, listing it out. I pop a permanent marker out of the first aid kit and write the digits on my arm.

"Thank you, goodnight Mr. Montague," I say, trying not to sound as confused as I feel. I look over at the others, waiting for me before they eat. I hold up one finger to let them know I'll be there soon. Beet gives me a thumbs up.

"Grand County Dispatch,"

334   "Hi—erm, I was wondering if you could connect me with Cameron-uh, Montague?"

I ask, shooting in the dark. They had that poster in school. Aim for the moon. If you miss, maybe you'll land among the stars. Or end up drifting in the infinite void of outer space. The operator breathes out of her nose, a professional laugh.

"Are you his attorney?"

"—yes."

"Sure," she says. A click comes out of the speaker, then a dial tone.

"You are attempting to reach a receiver in the Grand County Correctional System. All phone calls will be recorded for the safety of the public and our officers. Do you accept these terms? Press 1 for yes, press 2 for—"

It goes on hold. I wait for a minute, then two. I start to wonder whether she just went on a lunch break, but I stay the course.

"Hello?" someone says.

"Monty?" I stammer, not believing it.

"Birch? What the hell?" he says. Even through the phone, I can hear his smile. He's angry, too, though. The same tone used when we took a game too far and someone ended up getting hurt.

"I can't believe it's really you," I say. "I can't believe you're alive."

"Yeah," he says. "Me either. It was stupid for me to stick with those felons for as long as I did. Should've reported them as soon as I had the chance," he says. I push my eyebrows together, my heart sinks slowly down. My stomach feels full of mud. Is he serious? He continues.

"I'm sure they're dead, so at least I can take solace in that fact. Nobody survives getting creamed by a train like that."

"...yeah." I say, trying to think

of something clever to convey my message and discover if my feelings ought to be hurt. More specifically, if I've lost a friend. "Why didn't you report those guys?"
He takes a second before answering. "Well, they threatened my life. I know I never told you this, but they said they'd kill me if I spoke a word of it to anyone, especially the cops,"

"Oh," I say. I definitely didn't threaten that. Maybe Mike did, as a joke. Manuel could have, if he was in the heat of the moment. Still, I have my doubts. "Well, I talked to your dad and he said I should let you know that we stopped by that... enchilada food truck you really like out near Vegas," I say. No sense in lying about where we are, they can trace the call. Where we're going, on the other hand...

"Uh, okay?"

"We're still on our way to Eugene. We just got a little sidetracked, but we're hustling because—" I scramble, trying to tell the story. My exhausted mind can't generate the words in time.

"Ope, I gotta run. We should be there in a day or two. Eugene, I mean,"

"Thanks for calling, I guess. Good to...know you're having a good vacation," he says, smiling. Or did I make that up in my mind? Is my timeline too ambitious?

He hangs up before I can say goodbye. I walk over to the others and give them the news. An uproar of protest, excitement, and crossed arms. What do we do now? There's no way we can get there in two days. He's alive, he's guilty, he's

going to court. We have got to prove that he's innocent before he testifies against us. He

won't. Yes he will, he doesn't want to get locked
up. They'll offer him a plea deal, no question about
it.

And we take a breath, wordlessly agreeing
to enjoy the meal before figuring out how to get
east as quickly as possible. The food is still hot.
Hamburgers and french fries, salty and greasy
and probably with some sugar hidden in there
somewhere.

We sit on the ground, the pumps against our
backs. The stained concrete does little to dirty
my already filthy clothing. Across the pavement,
skitters. A mangy looking stray dog walks amiably
toward us.

"Hey, buddy," Beet says, tossing a french fry.
The pup stiffs it, then walks away.

"Makes me a little concerned as to what I
am putting in my body," Manuel says, laughing a
little bit. "Speaking of, you never finished your
proposition,"

"That's right," Beet says. So if the
recommended diet is 2,000 calories a day, and
there's 365 days a year, I need to eat 730,000
calories a year,"

"How are you doing that in your head, man?"
Mike asks.

"So let's say I live another 60 years and die
an average death. That's about 43,800,000 calories,
really not that many when you think about it. We
learned in school that petroleum products are
extremely energy dense, high calorie. If I remember
correctly a gallon of gas has about 30,000 calories. I
would only need to drink like...1400 gallons and then
I'd never have to eat again. Think of how much
faster I would be backpacking."

"Technically speaking, I think you'd never have to eat again after drinking just one gallon of gas," I say. We laugh and finish the meal, throwing out the plastic containers and saving the greasy brown bags as a firestarter. I tie my bootlaces again in preparation for our long walk.

"Oh, I almost forgot. We're ready to leave whenever," Mike says, dusting off his pants.

"What?"

"Yeah, I got a driver that's willing to take us to Nogales. A little far south, I know, but it'll get us a good ways east, too," encouragingly. We look at one another with relief—we are all tired of walking. Sore heels, full bellies.

"How?" Wren asks. He grins and points to the lipstick on his cheek.

Chapter 16 || Dead to the Court

I hang up the phone in disbelief. After the collision and what I read in the paper, I didn't think there was any way they could have survived that. Not only survived...but escaped somehow. My jaw still slack, I follow the deputy in a trance, mind focused on where they might be and if they're coming to rescue me. I don't expect a breakout with guns blazing and a helicopter escort. I only hope that they can deliver the paintings and secure legal protection for me.

I sit in the cell by myself. There are a few others in adjacent cells, but they sit quietly and mind their own business. The Moab jail isn't much more than a drunk tank. No major crimes happen here, and if they do the trial is usually from somewhere else because folks don't tend to be *from* Moab. I am one of the few. From what they tell me, tomorrow I will be tried at the courthouse here in town, just a block away from the nonprofits here, the redeeming pockets in our consumerist town.

"Oi, you. You know the owner of Maroon Mesa?" the deputy says, peeking his head in through a door in the hallway. I look back from behind bars and nod once. "They wanna see you, that okay?" I nod. "Holler if there's any trouble, or if you want your lawyer,"

The security door opens, the owner and a personal assistant walk in, staying well away from the bars. They look at me for a moment and huff, then begin speaking.

"I suppose you can understand why I'm more than a little bit frazzled. The schedule rotates annually, I know it has been a few years since you worked for me but that's not really an excuse to forget when I'm on vacation," the owner says.

I laugh, I can't help myself.

They both scoff. The owner is always on vacation, once you consider that no actual management comes through their office and every bit of legitimate decision making is the responsibility of the managers at each resort. The owner only makes decisions to make things align more with their personal vision, which more often than not ends up disrupting and shutting down the plans of the professionals that are hired to do the work. You know, the people with education and experience. If a word is spoken about this process, a non-disclosure agreement and meager severance is sure to follow. Then, the outspoken lawyer that contacts you when you try to file for unemployment.

    "If things had gone a little bit more south out there, you'd be in a nice comfortable bed,

surrounded by people who want you," the owner
says. I frown at this. "Too bad they already booked
you," they say, looking down their nose at me, as if
I were something that needed to be focused through
glasses that aren't being worn. I shake my head
slowly.

"Leave me alone,"

"Oh, you'll never be alone again. Not
when you're eating, not when you're sleeping or
showering, not even when you're on the loo." I
guess a word like *shitting* is too uncivilized for a
person of this caliber. "You're going to rot, Monty."

...

"Hi, I'm Mary Barclay, I'm your public
defender," the woman says loudly, sliding down at
the metallic table and handing me hot coffee in a
paper cup.

"Thank you," I say, taking a sip and struggling
to swallow. It must be from a vending machine
in the hallway or something. She manipulates
a messenger bag and two purses, as well as her
own lidless coffee, with an ease that shows daily
practice and commitment to routine. She slides a
small energy drink over to me and a bag of peanuts,
bigger than an airline serving.

"So how you doin'?" she asks, speaking louder
than is necessary. "Are they treating you okay?"

"Yeah, I mean—jail is jail, right? As well as I
can be,"

"Yeah, but I know who you're in trouble with.
Just wanted to make sure nobody was 'forgetting'
your meals, or anything,"

"I'm okay. The owner came to visit

me last night," I say. She pauses, her upper lip tilted, like she's watching a fish being gutted.

"And how did that go?"

"As well as you'd expect," I say, smiling a little.

"Well I'll talk to the deputies and try to make sure they don't allow that to happen again. You know how things are though, everyone's family it seems,"

"Yeah," I say, resolute. She lays some paperwork out in front of me, and pulls out two yellow legal pads and pens. One for her, one for me. "Alright, sweetie. Now I'm just going to ask you some questions to start out with, then I'll ask you to tell me the whole story. Try to keep it linear, cohesive. Remember that I don't know you, so throw in details if they're important, but remember that we don't have all day. First, are you active LDS?"

"No, not anymore," I say. I wasn't raised that way, I adopted it for a brief time in high school and early college. Never believed in the higher power, but always believed in bringing community members together under a common banner.

"I'm asking because the security footage shows you shouting something about someone going to the Outer Darkness," she says, looking at me with a slight smirk. I smile back with my eyebrows raised. She giggles a little bit. "I'm ex-LDS too. When I heard that on the news I knew I wanted you to be one of my pro bonos for the year." She flips a page.

"Extremist religions these days, seems like they're either getting people put on watchlists or elected."

344   "No kidding," I say. She seems like a good fit for me. Even if she turns out to be a

terrible lawyer, at least she made me laugh and at least I don't have to represent myself.

"Okay, start from the first point that you think might be relevant, and tell me everything you feel comfortable sharing. Your secrets are safe with me, lying now will only hurt the case."

"You sure you won't tell?" I ask, looking around the concrete room. No cameras, no bugs. Just a metal table, an overhead light, and two chairs. Oh, and a door.

"I'm positive. I'd lose my license if I did." So. I tell her everything, from all the messes I made when I was a kid to meeting Birch to him and Manuel finding me in the woods, and all the details of the heist. I trip over my words when describing what happened to the manager, but she listens patiently. I ask for news about her, but nothing ever surfaced. Not yet, anyway. I tell her about the phone call I got yesterday, about how my friends are trying their hardest to deliver the parcels so we can prove that this whole operation is a big misunderstanding. In the end, she looks at me with wide eyes, her page wet with ink and her pen practically smoking.

"Okay, not the wildest thing I've heard. You and your friends are quite the adventurers, though. Maybe after all this is over you and I can revisit our attorney-client privilege, because I think this would make an interesting book,"

"Alright," I say, sitting back. She scribbles for a few minutes, her phone rings. She checks it and hangs up the call.

"Sorry about that. Okay Monty, can I call you that? Based on your record and the evidence that they have, I can tell you from my experience that this doesn't look very good for you," she says, looking at me, waiting for a response until I finally force one out.

"Okay."

"I know your friends are supposed to be rescuing you and everything, but to me it doesn't seem like people who are involved in this kind of thing are very good friends, and I personally don't know that we should count on them riding in to save the day, because that may or may not happen. Are you with me?"

"Mhm," I say. Maybe she's right.

...

At the arraignment and bail hearing, I stand quietly next to my attorney. The judge appears, looking fair and tall in that classical black gown. Mary leans close to my ear.

"I've not worked with this judge before. I'm from Monticello, not sure if I told you that. Let's hope her pockets aren't lined with the owner's gold."

"Cameron Montague, the prosecution proposes that you are charged with the following: Reckless Driving, Aggravated Assault, Aiding and Abetting, Burglary, Conspiracy to Commit Burglary, Aggravated Robbery, Disorderly Conduct, Disturbing the Peace, and Vandalism," the judge says. Something about hearing my name at the beginning of all that cuts into me, like I'm being called out in front of the class and sent to detention.

Mary requests bail for me, even though I can't afford it. The judge says that she knows I am a guide, and that she believes that I could run off into the desert and the court would never see me again. The fact that I have a record apparently only solidifies this point.

My lawyer asks her to reconsider, considering that I was a model prisoner during my time in juvy, I've never skipped bail, and there are at least two incidents in the last year where I volunteered of my own accord to help clean up the river. The judge holds her ground. I hold my breath.

...

The trial begins before I even feel like I've been imprisoned for long. Though, each day of boredom feels like an eternity. Someone mentioned something about it being moved up the agenda because relevant parties were in town. As much as I hate the peace and quiet of the inside of my jail cell, I'd be more than happy to wait for my earned turn. I am not special. There's no reason I should be granted special privilege just because someone got paid off to change the order of the hearings. The longer this trial lasts, the better chance I have of my friends coming to liberate me.

She brings the paperwork to me with the schedule on it. All the pieces of evidence to be used, all the witnesses.

"It says there that I stole family heirloom jewelry, should we correct that?" I ask. We discuss it for a moment.

"I don't think so. Since the jewels are worth less than the painting. Did you hear what I said? Keep your eyes peeled for anyone that looks funny to you. We don't know who the owner has hired, who's been bought off. There's got to be at least one in here, there always is in cases regarding resort properties. Could be the judge. Could even be me," she says, looking at me with an iced face. She breaks with a smile and a wink.

I show her the video that Birch emailed to me. Of Maria, of the choking. I can't even watch the whole thing, I hand her the phone and look away. The audio of her gagging on the ice from the owner's drink makes me writhe in my seat. She replays the video, then asks me to email it to her. I do, and she takes my phone back, sticking it into the depths of her messenger bag. I didn't get a chance to check the 30 missed calls from my dad and 100 other notifications.

"This is going to be difficult to hear, but we'll have to deal with that later. We just need to focus on Monty right now, not trying to get the resort in trouble. If we pull that card, it will just look like we are grasping at straws because you're guilty. Do you know how 50% of people die in the water?"

"How?" I ask, folding my arms.

"They die trying to rescue someone else that was already drowning, and get pulled down with them. Let's stick to the plan we made. I know you're hesitant to...tarnish the legacies of your friends or what have you, but this is a good plan."

"I don't want their reputations ruined if they decide to return. I don't want warrants going out for their arrest," I clarify. "I know that they're alive now,"

"Right. Sweetie, I advise that you keep that to yourself unless you're directly asked," she says. I wish they hadn't called to tell me they were. Had to give me the hope as I'm trapped in here, helpless to 348 do anything about it and with an added burden of guilty knowledge.

     "Couldn't we just explain the situation?" I
ask, my hands chopping the table. "Explain that
they're trying to get to Florida, that if they get
there with the paintings then the client will provide
legal protection? They're supposed to be hiring a
defense team if anything should happen, they'll
have all the evidence—irrefutable—that this was a
legal operation to take back stolen property."
     "Listen-" she says, closing her makeupped
eyes and then looking genuinely at me. "I know that
you just want that so badly to work, I know. But
at the end of the day, civilians aren't allowed to
just go around repossessing property in the United
States. Not without warrants. That wouldn't even
be up to the local police. If there's property in
Utah that needs to be repossessed by someone in
Florida—assuming you can prove ownership—then
the whole case gets escalated to a federal level.
Okay? It would need to be prosecuted by the federal
government. I hate to say it, but even if your friends
make it, then they're still going to get charged,
they'll still have to prove it was an authentic
operation. That is, if your friends were even being
truthful with you. It's been more than a few days
and it seems to me like they've left you hanging, I'm
sorry. Let's just keep that whole painting and client
business to ourselves now. If we make that argument
and your friends don't make it then we'll seem like
a sham, like we're willing to lie to get you out of
this. You have to keep being honest with me, and
be honest with the court for the justice system to
work, okay?"

...

The courtroom feels smaller, being here as an adult.
Like revisiting a childhood bedroom. Same blue
carpet, same baseball trophy, same fluorescent
lights beating down.

My lawyer goes up and speaks to the prosecution and
the judge, up at the judge's bench. They've been up
there for more than a few minutes. Deliberating, I
guess.

I peek over my shoulder at the crowd chatting
quietly to themselves. People of all classes here,
unusual for a case in Utah, no matter how public.
Mostly white. Among them are a collection of well
dressed men and women in the back. I recognize
their faces, but they remain nameless. Features
changed with the tints of age and adolescence. From
my old temple.
        The longer I look, the more people I recognize
and the more eyes come to meet mine. I wasn't
sure what to ask about, for fear of looking foolish
in front of Mary. So I go with the tropes and search
for earpieces: I find only hearing aids. I search for
watches with radio antennas: I find only used sports
watches or gold pieces worth more than my father
and I combined.
        Half of the nearby city of Blanding has been
imported here to be my impartial jury. My family
lived there several generations ago, part of the
original settlement. Nobody that is from there knows
me now, just echoes of my bloodline. I hope they
can be impartial. The case has blown up publicly. I
look at the black and white newspaper on the table,
 a photo of the wreck at the Arches intersection
and photos of me being hauled away in

handcuffs. My black eye has healed by this point, something that won't help the case. They said it happened when I was ejected and hit the UTV, even though I was wearing a helmet. Mary said that we shouldn't mention it, since some of the deputies that arrested me will be on the stand later as key witnesses. A gaggle of photographers and reporters wait outside the courtroom. I had to stare downward in shame as they hounded me when I first came in. White signs with block letters: 4X4 OUT THE DOOR and a caricature of me smashing a UTV with a sledgehammer. If I get out of this, I'd like to have that framed and put on my wall. Half of the people here hate me for attacking someone inside the inner ring of wealth. The other half praise me for making a statement against the classism and exploitation present throughout the Four Corners Region, and the resort industry. Still another population of people celebrate me for reasons I do not understand. Mary comes back and sits down next to me at the defense table, furthest from the jury. The prosecution sits closer, two men in gray government suits and conditioned hair. I roll my shoulder muscles, feeling the cheap nylon suit from the thrift store. The sling holding my broken and casted arm presses against my abdomen under the jacket. My pants too loose. They don't fit, the hem is held together with my father's clothespins.

 "The sentence for just the aggravated robbery charge is 5 years to life. Not even to begin mentioning the other pile of charges they want to slap you with," she says. "Listen, if we lose this— and we might—you're never going to see the light of day again. They're offering you a plea deal. If you plead guilty now, they'll give you the minimum sentence for each crime."

"No way," I say immediately. "At the minimum sentence for all those charges combined, I'll be geriatric before I get out of prison. We might as well fight it,"

"You didn't let me finish," she glances at her legal pad. Scribbled and circled is the word 'NAMES??'. "They're only offering that deal if you also give up the identities of your co conspirators." I sit back in my chair with a groan. This suit is hot, but I've been told to keep it on to show respect to the courtroom.

"I change my answer. Absolutely...not. I'm not doing that. I refuse," I say, folding my arms and feeling the hard breath mint in my breast pocket, pushing against my chest. She puts a hand on my shoulder.

"They're dead, Monty. This could help you."

"They're not dead," I say. Doubting, even if for just a moment. It could have been a prank. Birch could have been the only survivor, telling me this so I could hold on. It could have been his brother-does he have a brother?—mimicking his voice and telling me what I want to hear, that this will all soon be over.

"They are dead. Dead to the court," she says. "You read it in the paper, just like I did."

"I know. Yet, I see the shame that I've brought to my family by being involved with this. I can't bear to bring that upon someone else's family, even if it would help me to get out of this bind. If I make the mistake of identifying them, then their lives would be ruined when they come back to the 352 world.

"I want to acknowledge that you're

still grieving. The pieces of them...whatever they are, aren't even in the ground yet. But you need to consider yourself. This is a dog eat dog world. How do you think I got to be where I am as a female attorney in *Utah?* This system is brutal and if you're not prepared to be as cunning as a fox at every turn, not prepared to fight with every ounce of your being, then it will consume you. The fact that I am here representing you is self-evident of that fact. Please, trust me."

Chapter 17 || Borderline

The cab of the tractor trailer is spacious, but it is obvious by the elbow in my ribs that we are well over capacity. I am one of the lucky ones, having gotten an actual seat. Mike, the largest of us, sits in the passenger seat with me between him and the driver. Wren is on my lap, Beet on his, and Manuel awkwardly crunched in a half standing position with one foot on the floor and one on the seat. The driver is a kind man with long eyelashes and a taste for Arabian instrumental music, which blasts so loudly we can barely hear one another speak. He sings in wordless hums, his lips shining with cosmetics.

"—so the housing is on property, too, right? I guess that's the excuse," Beet says, in the middle of a conversation with Wren. "After getting fired, you're told that you have 24 hours to completely move out of your employee apartment."

"I'm pretty sure that's illegal," Wren says.

"Par for the course. Nothing is illegal if the sheriff works for you," Mike says. The driver nods knowingly.

We continue like this for many hours. Eventually the music is turned down in both volume and subject until the sitar harmonics begin to lull us to sleep, and the conversations become fewer and far between. I awake to Beet shuddering, his face smeared against the closed window. The blasting air conditioning makes me drowsy. He shudders again, then slaps at his forearm with a shout.

"It's okay," I whisper, reaching around and putting my hand on his shoulder. "No fire. You're alright."

"A—yeah," he says, blinking and breathing. He shakes his head in frustration and takes a peek at Mike, who is still sound asleep. I turn to the driver.

"Do you want us to wear masks? We didn't even ask," I offer. He shakes his head.

"Masks are for the weak. I like the breath," he says, wafting air toward his nose. I nod and close my eyes, trying to figure out what in the world that means.

...

A few hours later, we stop in the middle of the desert. It seems to be somewhere along a highway-parallel road, streams of headlights zoom by. The blinking red beacons of radio towers in the distance. The driver opens the cargo doors in the back, I shiver. Hours of climate control and freon, and now the still hot desert air slaps my icy skin. 356 He shines a flashlight inside. Strapped down furniture. Bed frames, nightstands, stacks of old lumber. It smells like wood polish when I step inside. He lifts a board on the wood pile, it swings on a hidden hinge to open a spacious cavity that is well concealed. I note that this must be normal practice for him. He hands us bottles of water and a package of vanilla wafers to share. Most of us are able to fit inside with the equipment, but Mike and Manuel must hide inside a large bureau together. A cargo strap keeps it shut and secure to the wall.

...

More driving in darkness. The road noise sounds strangely boxed in after bouncing around the haul trailer and finally meeting my ears. We've been in traffic for a while, must be near the border. Despite the good shape of the trailer, I still see pin pricks of light coming through. This must be a testament to the lumen rating on the security lights.

We stop, the engine goes into low-idle. Voices outside, adjacent but not our driver.

"It's a measure of protocol, no cages. Ma'am, this is the last time I'm going to ask you to move along, you'll see your child when—"

Then, I hear the rear doors open and a metallic sounding boot steps inside. I know that sound—we've all seen the propaganda videos. The rust-proof aluminum paws walk forward, digital olfactory scanning and comparing to its downloaded database. A scratch on wood, outside. I can't help myself, I open the lid just enough to peek through and see it. A programmed K9 unit, utilized only at the borders, as far as I know. Soon domestic police forces will have them. It is pawing at a plastic lunch cooler, thrown haphazardly on the floor. It tips it over, a cured sausage spills onto the ground as well as a slurry of half melted ice. Out of the corner of my eye, a leather boot on the floor. Stealthily, I drop the lid and lay back down.

"Stupid dog, get out," someone says. A few bangs. What sounds like a hammer going through splintering wood. Someone opens the ornate crate next to us, with our extra gear. More importantly, our posters. I am grateful we decided to keep our firearms on us. Stomping, the sound of parchment being thrown. Then, the doors shut again.

More pavement. Frequent stops. Voices speaking in Spanish. Firm, but kind. The other side of the border.

...

Safely south of Nogales, the back door opens. Bronze sunlight from dawn shines in, the driver drinking from a thermos. I crawl out and topple to the floor, landing on my hands and knees.

"Oh, no no no," someone says. There is junk everywhere from the search. At least two good pieces of furniture are ruined. The cured sausage is gone. One of our backpacks thrown against the wall, its contents flung in all directions. It looks like a wild animal was wound up and set loose in here.

"Oh god," Manuel says, getting on his knees. One of the poster tubes is dented, a painting half unfurled next to it. A crease cuts into it with a muddy boot print on the white side. We gather around him and look down at it.

"Is that still going to sell?" Mike asks, saying aloud what we had all been thinking. Manuel sighs.

"It has to,". The driver hops inside and helps us to clean up the mess. He explains that he always picks up a few junk pieces to 'have a better chance at rolling the dice when they break something'.
I wonder if the lunch cooler was intentional, too. Manuel does his best to roll up the poster effectively, to uncrease it.

He exchanges a few hundred USD for pesos. We thank the driver vehemently before he lets us go next to a hotel. He and Mike even share in a hug.

Chapter 18 || Nacho Paintings

The hotel room here was nice, but not too fancy. Affordable cement and stucco, no continental breakfast but a few different bibles to choose from. That isn't a luxury we have in the US anymore. We walked and hitchhiked for the rest of the next day, with Manuel doing most of the talking and me nodding cordially next to him, catching every third word.

The vanilla wafers from the driver did not last long between our hungry bellies. We still have a few emergency rations, but decided to catch up on our meals by seeing what the local dumpsters have to offer. I led the charge, hopping over half walls and sifting through styrofoam plates until we finally hit the jackpot at a bakery that had closed for the day. I'm sure they gave out all that they could. All we found were burned orejas, the blackened sugar bitter in my mouth.

We made our way further into a town. After asking a man on a bicycle, we confirmed that we are in the state of Neuvo Leon, in Monterrey. It was only the middle of the day when we walked into the bar, the only worker there still polishing the glasses. What else would he be doing?

We sat down at a round table near the back, finally at a table again. We started with precious water. Beet, with a glass of ice. As it got later, the bar filled up and the sun outside sank lower until now, when the sky blasts a triumphant orange. It is getting louder, and Manuel speaks far too softly. Mike slurps down his third plate of chicken tacos, then asks me if I'm going to finish my nachos. I am.

"Well, he had to. The bike was trashed, he was trapped. As far as I'm concerned, he took one for the team," Beet explains.

"And you said it seems like he's not going to rat us out?" Wren asks.

"It seems that way. I don't think he would do that. That's why he was in Manuel and I's original draft. It's why you all were," I say.

"He has a record. They're not gonna let him walk, even if he gives up our names," Mike adds.

"But they could give him a plea deal," Manuel says. "A significantly reduced sentence. He might have already done that in secret, and not told any of us. There may be a hunt for us right now, and we would not know."

Mike winks at a girl sitting at the bar for what must be the fourth time. My guess is that she keeps intentionally looking away just as he makes a gesture. A man with a drooping ranch hat stares at me from behind sunglasses. He hasn't ordered in over an hour, so I check my watch. I worry that my   loan officer might be here to hunt me down, too.

Our conversation turns to go over the details of
our trip so far. We vocalize some of our individual
experiences to share the perspectives with those
that weren't involved. They explain what it was like
inside the dresser with the dog sniffing, we explain
what it was like in the lumber pile, and so on.
We also discuss how in the world we are going to
walk east across the Gulf of Mexico. Manuel says
that he has a plan, and that all we need to do is
follow and trust him.

Each of these conversations carry a tension
in them, a rope pulled taut with a blade dangling
over it. It feels like a balloon is bound to pop at any
moment, and send us to our graves.
We can keep running, but eventually they'll catch
up with us.

Eventually we work our conversation back
to the military base, and decide to hush our voices.
This quickly goes out the window when we realize
that nobody around us is speaking English. More
importantly, nobody is paying a bit of attention to us
in the dimly lit place.

"I have something to share," Manuel says,
propping his heavy bag on his lap and pulling out a
clipboard with some papers on it. He's got enough
literature in there to start a curriculum on our
little trip. He pulls out the roster, the one that was
sitting on the front seat of the transport truck, the
one that the driver's argued about and eventually
blamed each other for losing.

"Did you see it, Birch?" Beet says, handing
it to me. "About halfway down," he says between
chews. I scan the names, dated for the day we
escaped through the airport. It looks like they
were scheduling a pickup of a few more

people, and a few more cadavers. They all have a
section for 'condition'. Those that are dead have
a cause of death; cardiac arrest most often. The
occasional organ failure.

Then, I see her name again.
Maria Campos.
Condition: Critical.
Cause: Traumatic brain injury, major hemorrhage.
Traumatic is right. She was fine the last time we saw
her.

The consensus is clear. To me, at least. I hold the
brochure, still in my pocket, while everyone debates
their own deductions. I have the answer. But if I
share it, the horror show will be true. They have
enough motivation to finish the job. No reason
to tell them the rating of this whitewater. If we
fail, we'll get turned into test subjects and then
eviscerated by rockets. That's how that story ends.
Who knows what happens before we get shipped to
the base.

Mike winks again, this time more slowly and with a
stupid smirk on his face. A large man sits next to the
woman he was aiming at. Great... The man stands
up and approaches our table, threateningly saying
something to Mike, who takes another bite of his
food and pretends not to notice.

I nearly choke on my nachos when the man with the
sunglasses who had been staring begins walking over
to us. There are others in his way, who step aside
  without being touched. A shark through a school
of fish. An agent of the owner. It must

be. He reaches inside of his coat for something. A glimpse at a pistol grip and Manuel is on his feet.

"¡Oi!" he shouts, the boyfriend spins his head. A ringed hand on is placed on Beet's shoulder, across from me. A shout from somewhere else. Beet tries to stand, is forced back down.
Mike stands, chugging his beer in the man's face whilst being shouted at. He slams the empty glass down, grabs my full drink and launches it into the aggressor's mustache.
Mike catches a heavy punch to the jaw. Beet puts his feet on the edge of the table and kicks backward, carrying the sunglassed man with him. The aggravated crowd responds in anger, delivering blows with spurred boots to the man. Manuel leaps across the table and hauls Beet to his feet, Wren is gone somewhere.
Someone spins me around, I block a blow with my bracer, which cracks. Another catches me in the gut before I hit the sticky floor and crawl under the table to the other side. When I pop up, I see Wren ducking into the bathroom with our backpacks dragging behind her.
Chaos ensues. There's shouting and objects flying. A chair hits a picture frame which shatters and the leg punctures the drywall, while a cue ball sails through the air and catches someone on the bridge of their nose.
"Bathroom, now!" I shout, trying to force my voice over the cacophony of violence. Beet vaults over the table and sprints, then crashes into me. We fall through the door to the bathroom and slide across the tile. Wren stands upon a toilet, an open window leading outside just above.

She throws the last bag through when the door flies open once again, Manuel dragging Mike by the back of his stretched and filthy shirt. They use the chair leg that Mike was holding to barricade the door shut, then throw a garbage can in front of it for good measure. Breathlessly, we laugh and clap one another on the back.

One by one we are out the window and onto a dumpster below. It smells like old beer and fish. I sling my pack on and clip my hipbelt, looking down at the broken glass in the alleyway. Manuel is the last one out. He clambers over the edge of the dumpster slowly, tired. Burnt out.

Even here, the shouting from inside of the building is still audible. The metal door flies open, the boyfriend skitters out and stops, dust clouding around his boots. Mike glances behind him in a panic, grabs Wren and puts her in front of him as a meat shield. The man yells something, Mike takes a step forward. The man gets in my friend's face, practically spitting on him with their noses touching. Mike puffs out his chest and taunts the man. The man throws a punch, Mike ducks and punches back. Contact after contact and suddenly they're scrapping, shoulder near the beltline, bent over. Beet and I rush over, our backpacks slowing us. Mike ends up on the bottom and an elbow hits his temple.

"¡Ayuda mi, ayuda mi!" I shout at the man, showing him my empty hands. He grimaces at me and stops, I think out of confusion more than anything else. It was all I could think to say. We drag Mike back, he stands up and brushes himself off. The other man spits, then pulls a revolver out of his waistband. Manuel is the first to draw his pistol, the rest of us follow suit. My safety is even off, for what may be the first time on this trip. Manuel says something that sounds like instructions. The man rolls his eyes, curses, and throws the pistol at us. It slams into the broken glass and he takes off running in the opposite direction.

"You okay?" I ask. Mike nods and rubs his swelling cheek.

"That could have gone better," Wren says, picking up the revolver. Manuel takes it from her, dumping the bullets on the ground. He presses some release mechanism and the cylinder falls out. He takes this piece and drops it into the grease trap outside of the bar, with all the fryer oil. The body of the gun is hurled onto an adjacent rooftop, where a cat screeches in response.

"We have to get out of here," Manuel says, and we are off. We head east, out of town and into more flat desert. I can smell the ocean from here.

Chapter 19 || Observe and Report

She leans over to me again, her breath smelling like garlic and oregano.

"Make sure you look at the jury, but not in a homicidal maniac kinda way, alright?" she nudges me with her elbow. The prosecuting lawyer takes the stage, looking around. All is quiet except for Mary pouring a glass of water from the room temperature pitcher.

"Hello, I am David Fitzpatrick and I will be representing the state of Utah. During this trial we will be examining Mr. Montague's involvement with a still unidentified group of alleged criminals, his actions leading up to a robbery of one of Moab's most beloved resorts for his personal gain, and the brutal assault that followed while he attempted to escape with precious family heirlooms...from a family that he does not belong to. As you may well know, the defendant would typically be brought forth on a separate trial regarding the direct relation to the owner of the resort. In light of recent circumstances and the burden that our judicial system is currently under, we will be reviewing this case as a whole and complete incident. As such, I have agreed to represent not only the state of Utah but the spectacular Maroon Mesa Resort...where sandstone meets serenity," he winks at the jury. Found the eye.

"Hello, I am Mary Barclay and I will be representing the defendant, Cameron Montague, who fell under the manipulation and coercion of a group of misfits that did not have his best interests at heart—but fortune instead. Throughout this trial you will see that he was forced into participation by means of threats and force by a group of armed individuals that had experience in the industry of larceny. We will also see that my client is an upstanding citizen, a taxpayer, and an asset to our community here in Moab. Thank you."

...

The prosecution calls the first witness to the stand. The visa worker, the assistant that met us on the beach.

"Well, at first I didn't know who they were," she says, shuffling in the witness seat. "Mr. Montague quoted the exact wage I was making, and said something to the effect of 'we are leaving, sorry to be a bother'."

"And then what happened?" Fitz, the prosecuting attorney, asks.

"And then the general manager appeared, shouting that they were stealing something."

"After the general manager appeared—you saw Monty attack her?"

"No. I was instructed to recover the stolen resort assets, but I was frightened and I ran back inside the lodge to call 911," the visa worker says.

"And where did the general manager go?"

"I do not know, sir. She was there trying to stop them, and when I got inside and called the emergency services, the operator asked for a description of the individuals. It was at that point that I looked out the window and did not see anyone," she says.

"That is strange. So, what did you say when the general manager showed up in the afternoon?" the prosecution asks. I choke on my water, and straighten in my seat hoping that nobody noticed.

"The manager did not come back that afternoon,"

"The next morning, then?"

"Not in the morning, either."

"I see," says Fitz, taking a generous look at the jury before sitting back down. Mary stands to cross examine the witness.

"You mention that the manager did not show up for work, but something else did, isn't that right?" Mary asks.

"Yes, a note."

"What was on that note, Ms. Ramirez?" Mary asks, then holds up a sheet of paper in a plastic sleeve, written on in permanent marker. Blocky handwriting. She places it on the desk in front of the visa worker.

"It says something to the effect of 'Consider this an immediate resignation. Utah is just not for me," she says, nodding as if practicing something she had been reciting. The jury writes on their small notebooks. Ramirez, the witness, looks up toward the crowd for reassurance. A child looking for a parent at their ball game.

"Did this seem normal to you? Does this note align with the stresses of the job?" Mary asks.

"I—" she hesitates, looking to the crowd. A commotion behind me, I spin around and see a bailiff escorting someone in an expensive suit through the exit.

"That will not happen again," the judge says firmly. "Please, continue,"

"Yes, to be honest it does."

"Did anything about it strike you as odd, or off?"

"Yes. The position is extremely stressful. On average, our general managers last four months at Maroon Mesa. It isn't odd that she left abruptly, what is odd to me is that she said Utah is not for her. The landscape, the state itself, is the only thing that she claimed to like about the position."

"I see. The court appreciates your candidness. One final question for you. Between the date of the incident and today, did you see anybody that was involved near the raft?" she says. I wonder silently what she might be trying to get at.

"No, ma'am."

"So then there would be no possible way that anyone involved, aside from the general manager, could have left that note?"

"Hearsay, your honor," Fitz says, standing and sitting in one smooth motion.

"Sustained," the judge says.

"Thank you for your time," Mary says, brushing her blazer with her hand and retiring back to our table.

...

The next witness takes the stand, a deputy from the Moab Sheriff's Office. At the request of the prosecution, he shares his side of the story.

"After getting the call at approximately 18:42, I mounted my patrol vehicle and proceeded toward the last reported sighting. Via radio, I communicated with the law enforcement rangers at Arches National Park. I arrived on scene at approximately 18:51. Immediately, I saw the alleged perpetrators driving down the entrance road well above the posted speed limit, which is 25 miles per hour for a good reason. My siren and overhead flashers were already on, and at this point I amplified them to an increased volume to give the perpetrators a warning to stop. Based on the radio traffic, I concluded that I would be the first one on the scene, and that at least one pursuit vehicle was also on its way as backup. As it was relayed to me, the perpetrators had also commandeered an asset belonging to the National Parks Service," he says, speaking mostly with his lips.

"And what was that asset?" Fitz asks.

"The asset was an outfitted ranger truck designed for off-road utility and recovery, with a brush grill designed for pushing through dense vegetation. I knew that there was a chance they would be approaching in this vehicle, so I circumnavigated my truck to a position that placed me between the perpetrators and the many innocent civilians that were stuck in traffic on the highway, near the light. As I attempted to do this, one of the perpetrators attempted to accelerate and struck the brush guard on the front of my

373

vehicle. Immediately, I put the vehicle into park and grabbed my jump bag, prepared to render first aid."

"What happened when you got out to give first aid?" Fitz asks, leaning back in anticipation.

"Sir, I was never given the chance. You see, when I opened my door to exit the vehicle, I saw yet another perpetrator sprinting toward my position with what seemed to be aggressive intent. I quickly surveyed the group that came down on dirtbikes and determined that they were all armed with handguns. The perpetrator threw their body weight against the door, preventing me from exiting. Fearing for my own safety now that firearms were present, I lowered my window and produced my non-lethal, my stun gun,"

"Which is your dominant hand?" Fitz asks.

"My right, sir. As such, my service weapon is on my right hip, and my non-lethal is kept in an off-hand holster."

"And why is that?"

"So that there cannot be any mistakes. In critical moments like these, we rely on our rigorous training and muscle memory to keep everyone as safe as they can be, whether you're a fellow officer or an assailant," he says.

"You have been receiving some criticism from the public after video has been released, stating that you intentionally drove into the first biker. What do you say to this?" The prosecution asks. The deputy thinks for a moment.

"I say that there have been incidents in the past where we have made mistakes, and we could have done better. Now, we work hard with regular, updated training to make sure that we do not repeat any of those mistakes, and treat them as learning experiences.”

"Thank you. Let that be an example to all. Please continue, what happened after that?"

"Well, I quickly performed a scene assessment to see if I needed to engage my service rifle. It was at that point that I observed an individual in dirt bike armor, who I now know to be Mr. Montague, drive into a UTV that was attempting to bypass traffic by driving on the shoulder of the road. I produced my non-lethal weapon and attempted to incapacitate my attacker, who was at this point attempting to reach inside the vehicle to attack me. I was then disarmed and my weapon was turned against me. Seeing as our windows are reinforced, I engaged the automatic system that closes them and began crawling to the empty passenger seat. My plan was to exit the vehicle from the unblocked passenger door and attempt to gain control of the situation while I waited for backup to arrive."

"This sounds truly terrifying. It is a miracle you're here with us today. I do have to ask you something. Did it look like Mr. Montague drove into the UTV intentionally?"

"I—I'm not sure. I am a patrolman, not a detective. My job is not to investigate, but simply to observe and report," he says. "But in my unprofessional opinion, it absolutely could have been intentional," he says, and looks down at me. I try not to change my expression, the jury watches both of us as they scribble feverishly on their notepads.

...

The next witness is an older man,

someone I've seen before at accidents and lethal mistakes along the trail. Someone who deals with tourists more than they ought to, and the mistakes they make by not doing research and practicing land ethics. The coroner for the city of Moab takes the stand. The results have returned from the culture test, these things take time, we are told.

"And based on your long and developed experience identifying tissue samples, what conclusion did you reach?" Mary asks.

"As for the tissue samples that were collected on the railroad tracks on the night of the incident, my determination is that they are not human in nature," he says, looking at the jury. This is his big moment. "But rather, bovine."

"Then what's in those caskets in the funeral home, awaiting burial?" someone from the crowd shouts.

"Order," the judge answers.

"Order of beef, I'm afraid," the coroner says. "These things happen."

During the cross examination, Fitz tries to make the witness lay out what I really wish he wouldn't.

"Based on the results from the tissue samples, can you conclude that any human flesh was present?"

"No,"

"Therefore we can conclude that, in the absence of any human remains, nobody was struck by the train that night?" he asks.

"Hearsay, your honor," Mary says.

"I'll rephrase," Fitz says, glaring at my public defender. "In your professional experience, have you ever seen an incident where a human being died, and left no remains except those belonging to a cow?"

"No, never before."

"Thank you."

...

So that was what happened, then. The newspaper companies described photos that were too ghastly to share in print, allegedly photos of my maimed friends that had been creamed along the cargo rail. I am unsure why they failed to get ahold of the conductor of the train-they're not on the witness roster. Mary isn't sure either, but she thinks that due to the fact that it was a government train on a government route, the driver might have signed a non-disclosure agreement to keep whatever their operation was classified.

The next witness comes up, at first I'm not sure where I recognize her from. Then, it comes to me: snoring, stars, binoculars. Gwen, Birch's friend that invaded our space while we were preparing and warming up. She wears a casual version of something you might wear to an office run by hipsters, if that office also happened to be located inside the grounds of a festival.

"Did you know Mr. Montague before this incident?" Fitz asks.

"I may have seen him around town, but I did not know him personally," she says. I struggle in my seat, hoping she will not reveal their names.

"Did you know anyone else involved, personally?" he asks.

"No," she says. I relax a little, hoping that I'm invisible. I feel my father's eyes piercing into the back of my skull and feel him tensing up along with me.

"Who else was present while you were walking your dog near this...cistern?"

"There were three guys at first. One guy went down to the housekeeping building, he said he was visiting a friend. The other guy was asleep pretty much the whole time I was there, and the last guy was Monty. Er-Mr. Montague," she says, leaning into the microphone.

"What did you observe Mr. Montague doing?"

"He was—he was conducting reconnaissance with a set of binoculars," she says.

"Was he doing anything else?"

"He seemed to be relaying visual information through a radio, to another party that was not present," she says.

"What kind of visual information?" he asks.

"I'm really not sure,"

"If you had to make an assumption. What did it seem like?"

"It seemed like, Mr. Montague, was, uh, he was communicating information in relation to the police response on the property. And using a timer to do so."

"Critical information for a theft such as this to be successful, one would think. Based on your observations, for most of the night there were only three individuals at the overlook that provides a near complete view of the Maroon Mesa Resort, Mr. Montague, an unidentified male, and you. Is that correct?"

"I am not sure of the genders of the
  unidentified parties."

"Alright, let's keep it together. We are

in Utah, after all," Fitz chuckles to himself. Gwen
does not laugh. "Unidentified *individual*, then?"

"That is correct."

"And this unidentified individual, he—they
were sleeping for the duration of time that you were
there?"

"That is correct."

"And during this same amount of time,
you say that Mr. Montague was making and
communicating observations regarding police
presence, is that right?"

"Yes, that is correct."

"At any point, did it seem as though Mr.
Montague was acting under duress?" he asks. Gwen
looks at me with her mouth halfway open, then
looks back at the lawyer.

"No," she admits, her head leveling.

"At any point did you hear any threats to him,
through the radio, or otherwise?"

"No,"

"Did anyone produce a weapon or any other
intimidation device and use it in a threatening
manner?"

"No."

"Thank you," Fitz says, looking at Mary with
a cocked eyebrow. She nods to me, which brings
comfort. She stands and approaches the witness
bench for yet another cross examination.
"Would you please explain to the court what you
were doing at the cistern at that time of night,
considering the address on your driver's license is
over 20 minutes away?" Mary asks.

"I was walking my dog and going stargazing."

"You worked for Maroon Mesa about
three years ago, is that correct?"

"Yes, it is," Gwen says. Mary pushes her bottom lip up in a knowing manner.

"Do you still work there, or live on property?"

"No,"

"Were you coming to the area to visit a particular friend or acquaintance, or to meet someone specific?"

"No."

"And in what form did you obtain permission from the land owner?" she asks. The crowd shuffles, looking for the owner of the resort who hasn't bothered to show up to the trial for over a week. Probably drinking a martini in the Maldives before they disappear.

"In no form. I did not receive permission,"

"In the Moab Sun Newspaper, you told a reporter many of the same details you're sharing now. There's one more, though, that I think the court may like to hear. What were you consuming while you were...stargazing?"

"I smoked,"

"Yes, but what did you smoke?"

"A joint,"

"Which contains..."

"Weed," she says, through gritted teeth.

"Which is a federally controlled substance, and is illegal in Utah. Did you know that?"

"At the time, I-"

"Did you know that?"

"Yes." Gwen says.

"Mr. Montague's urine sample came back clean of any mind-altering substances. Do you know why that is?"

　"No."

"Because he was indicted on marijuana

related charges several years ago. As a condition of his sentencing at the time, he agreed not to consume any intoxicating substances other than alcohol while in the state of Utah. Would you please explain to me, then, why you repeatedly offered your marijuana cigarette to him?" Mary asks, faltering a bit but speaking louder in an effort to cover it.

"I don't understand the question, I had no knowledge that he was arrested for weed," Gwen says. Mary collects herself, getting the cards in order before she's ready to step off of the stage.

"Just to make sure we are on the same page, you trespassed onto a property that you did not have permission to be on, consumed an illegal substance, and witnessed strangers performing reconnaissance on the police?"

"—uh huh."

"And as a response to those strangers, rather than calling 911 or reporting it, you instead offered them a—what I believe is called a 'toke'—from your marijuana cigarette?"

"...yeah." Gwen says, folding her arms. The judge shakes her head.

"So you kept that information to yourself, despite the fact that nobody acted violently and there were no weapons present. You kept it to yourself for two days, until the newspaper offered a reward leading to the conviction of the thieves, is that correct?"

"Yes."

"Thank you," Mary says, coming to sit next to me with a smug look plastered across her face.

ACT III
LARGE & SPACIOUS BUILDINGS

Chapter 20 || The Rio Grande

Wren once told me that she had been on a river trip on the Rio Grande, and had likely rafted past the very section of river that we now relax on. Even though the trip was a few years ago, tensions at the border were high. The wall was still being built at that time, which now sits rusting and riddled with gaps. The dare, then, was to go to the opposite side of the river and cross the international border. Then, relieve yourself on foreign soil. Classy.

  We made improvised fishing rods when we first arrived this afternoon, out of reeds and shoelaces and bait with bits of food that we had left. The walk (more of a jog) out to here was hot, rough, and miserable. With Manuel's ability to change his dialect, we blend in a little bit better than the tourists. But I have no doubts that the agents of the owner should be able to find us if they look hard enough. Mike has his qualms with that theory, thinking that the man with

385

the sunglasses might be a government hitman or some such. We put enough distance between the bar and ourselves that I'll sleep well tonight, after an evening of much deserved rest. We haven't seen a town in many miles, and didn't even follow a trail to get here.   Manuel led the way, I guess he's been in this part of the country before. The sun sinks low and the air begins to cool. We splash in the water and dunk one another, tossing a bottle of Beet's supplements like a football because they float.

"You're scaring all the fishes away," Mike complains from the shoreline, sipping from a brown bag. I don't think he's serious; on the fire next to him are six healthy fish that he's skewered and is roasting. Next to him is a case of cheap beer, which he's just finished another can of. He crushes the empty can of schlitz and launches it into the water. Wren dives to catch it, then throws it back at him.

"I hope you know that when water gets trapped in your trash, it's a heavier load to carry. And we're not helping," she says. He shrugs and tosses the can into a growing pile.

I crawl out of the water and plop down next to the fire, letting the flames lick my chilled muscles. My rational brain is telling me that I ought to be on edge, that we shouldn't be relaxing, but I don't think we could have reasonably made it to the far side of the river today, and kept going. We're too tired. We've burned too many calories and need to make them up through rest and charred fish.

Wren takes a beer and presses it against the back of her neck, even though it can't be much

cooler than the air around us. Manuel searches for something in his bag, perhaps getting ready to give us another presentation. He knocks it over, a handful of passports fall out. I am the only one to have seen this. He looks at me and smiles.

"Just in case, you know," he says, packing them back away. I'm too tired to ask questions. As sketchy as he may be sometimes, I believe that if he had nefarious intentions he would have acted on them already.

"So can you tell me the plan yet?" I ask.

"Just hang in. Trust. I will get us there," he says, yet again. How many times will I have to ask before he explains how we will get across the Gulf? The poster tubes sit as the perimeter lines in a polygon surrounding Beet, who sits cross legged with a steaming drink in his hand. His back has been killing him, so we granted him voluminous but lightweight items. If I know him at all, he's drinking kratom. His eyes are closed, he breathes deeply. He hasn't been speaking much. The weight of the unknown and the responsibility to keep walking has been haunting all of us, but I haven't seen him sleep well in a week or more.

I admire the landscape, and note that perhaps this is a contributing factor as to why I feel so at ease. I haven't even had a drink yet.

I think about all of the explorers that have come down these same waters, and I wonder if they felt the same sense of ease despite the perils of their unknown journey ahead.

The river crashes softly against some rocks, yellow cliffs and domes surround us. Cactus populate every corner, small mammals jutting to and fro and night birds beginning to call. A cloud of bats fly overhead, darting erratically. Or, maybe they're nighthawks. I'm not sure, but I wish I had my bird book and a set of binoculars. Not that I'd be able to keep up with them, anyway.

In the morning we will swim across the river and hitchhike all the way to Corpus Cristie. We had the opportunity to buy phone chargers at the corner store, but opted against it as a group. Manuel made the point that if we are being hunted by someone, resort, government or otherwise, then surely they could see who's cell phones were on inside the resort the morning of the heist, but only if we were to power them back on, apparently.

So. That leaves us in the dark as far as Monty goes. I asked around when we were in town, but nobody down here seems to know anything about it. At the end of the day, I suppose Moab is still sort of a small town.

A stone falls behind us, we whip up and look. A strange dog, a metal one, stands there curiously. Its nose like the mouthpiece of a microphone, it sniffs forward and slides awkwardly, hydraulic legs locking. Paint scratched and chipped. On its chest, a D ring that has a long and ripped piece of webbing. It walks straight over to the fish, then turns its attention on Mike. He leans backward and puts down his drink. The article I read about these things said that unlike pitbulls, their jaw *is* physically capable of locking. And, with a programmable amount of PSI. "Hey buddy," Mike says, still leaning away.

"Those things are trained to sniff out drugs," Wren says, crossing her arms and shooting him an denunciatory look. Trained, or programmed? The dog sniffs his bare and dirty feet before nuzzling up to him. It lays on his lap, he grunts at the added weight. I approach and look at the blinking screen on its back, no larger than a nametag.

"Connection lost, independent mode," I say. I wish Monty was here. He'd know how to program it or rewire it to be free of its enslavers. We continue on our night like this might be the most normal thing in the world. Some of the models have cameras. I'm glad that this one does not.

Beet stands and stretches his back, Mike shoves a few beers and a carton of cigarettes that he restocked with into his bag. We all line up, criss crossed on the rough sand behind one another with him at the front. A massage train begins while we discuss the next phase of our plan.

Get to Corpus Cristie.

Hire a boat to cross the gulf faster than on foot.

Profit?

Chapter 21 || Society

It was a heartbreaking morning. We crossed at dawn, holding our bags over our heads and wading through the warm waters. Last to cross was Mike, who had snuggled with and developed a sort of relationship with the dog.

I expected Manuel to explain why he couldn't keep it. It has government tracking, it'll give our position away, etcetera. But, he stayed silent. I have long suspected that he has a soft spot for canids, even manufactured ones.

When it came time to cross, Mike walked backward into the water as the dog looked onward at him. It ran the shoreline back and forth with great speed, its rubberized paws slipping on the silty rocks. It gazed longingly, joints faltering as it ran its algorithm to decide on the next course of action. Mike made it to the other side, and it sat down, teetered backward, and launched forward into the water with impressive velocity. It splashed for just a flash before it sank like a stone, a puff of smoke shooting into the air. Mike covered his eyes, and we continued on without a word.

We finally made it to another town, where we stopped to buy some sandwiches from a gas station. Then, we humped our packs all day until we couldn't walk any longer, and found a table at another bar. Now, I sit and enjoy a bowl of peanuts and something called an IPA. Mike sits back down, with a lit cellphone in his hand.

"Where'd you find that?" Wren asks. He shrugs.

"Sweet talked the bartender. Told her I'm calling my brother in the service. Folks love veterans, especially 'round here," he says. "I just checked the news. Nothing about us, or the paintings. Says a ranger fell off the side of the White Rim, into the crack. Anybody know a Freddie Bauman?"

"Yeah, actually," Beet says, then slowly takes a sip of his margarita. We stare expectantly, until he sits up and starts speaking. "His brother owns that resort near Zion, he's the main competition for Maroon Mesa's expansion."

"Makes sense. Eliminating competitors," Manuel nods.

"Does it mention anything about Zion, or that feud?" I ask.

"No," Mike scoffs. Wren pipes up. "If it said anything about that, it would have to acknowledge that an expert in the outdoors fell into a crack so well defined that its got an interpretive sign next to it. That's like an astronaut taking off their helmet during a spacewalk; clearly coercion," she says, shaking her head. I take solace in the idea that she seems to be well converted to the mission.

We go over the facts again, each speaking from our own departmental experience and detailing the overspending that the resort does. There's no way they could ever hope to make the money back through traditional hospitality sales. There needs to be something more substantial feeding the beast from behind the curtains.

"I mean the cost of food is 110% there," Mike says.

"You mean they charge 110% what the cost is, for finished dishes?" I ask.

"No, I mean the cost of raw ingredients, not counting labor or utilities or...."

We then discuss the basic principles of money laundering... The dirty cash is produced by any variety of the nefarious methods available to someone like the owner. In the simplest form of this process, the extra income is cited as profit for their resort ventures, and is written into the books that way, too. The profiteer has complete control over most of it-how much to pay in taxes (if any), who is involved, and the ability to promote a failing league of businesses under the guise that they're pulling in millions more than they actually are. Maybe the owner isn't as bad at economics as we all think they are.

This conversation segues into peace, and the idea that perhaps there can never be peace when traditional business wars are waged.

As evening turns to night and our empty drink glasses pile up, the conversation turns away from atrocities committed by the ultra rich as Mike describes his sweet 16 to us, which was, apparently, the largest party ever held in

the town of Karns, Tennessee. I hang onto Mike's
words as he describes his party.

"So now we've got the *basket* of the hot air
balloon in the pool, and mom's gonna be home in
two hours, right?" he says energetically.

"What to do?" Manuel asks, his eyes dim and
smiling.

"Exactly. So I start calling around. All the
people that would have helped me were either in
the hospital or at the police station by this point, so
I'm stuck trying to pull this thing out with a bunch of
people I don't know, the people that just showed up
for the free booze. And I ask for help, but they're all
like *'Bro, I don't work for free'*. And that brings me
back to my point: capitalism will never work in the
long-term."

"I agree," Beet says. "I personally think that
you should be compensated for all work, but fiscal
compensation isn't the only way,"

"They *were* compensated," Wren adds,
sipping a Moscow mule out of a copper mug. "You
hosted a party for them and gave them free drinks,
how is that not compensation?"

"Exactly my point, man," Mike says. Beet
begins again.
"With an economy devoid of non-monetary trade,
we can only expect the divide between the major
classes to enlarge. A few more decades of this and
the only people that have anything to trade will be
the farmers. Then we'll see a migration of those
that are wishing for a more trade-based or wish-
based economy to areas with fertile soil, specifically
areas with sustainable practices, permaculture
394 farms, homesteads. Those that require artificial
inputs to be productive farms will be

grouped in with those that are willing to buy those goods-the rich. They'll have nothing but poisoned food to eat as they watch our country become balkanized."

"But," I say. "The food with artificial inputs would require less energy to produce, making it less expensive to buy the finished products. Just look at bleached flour versus organic whole flour. Most of us can't afford to buy organic if there's a cheaper option,"

"So we eliminate the cheaper option," Mike says. "Everything used to be organic. My dad told me that when he was a kid, there were worms in every other apple he ate. If not worms, then worm holes. Not the space kind, though. I don't know about y'all, but I've never once bitten a worm in an apple. Maybe there are some good things to come out of our farming systems,"

"I'd rather eat a worm than pesticides," I say.

"What's the only thing worse than finding a worm in your apple?" Beet asks. We look at one another and shrug. "Finding *half* a worm in your apple."

We share a laugh and get another round of drinks. I chuckle at the fact that Mike keeps talking about Mexico as if it isn't a capitalist country. Who's to say? He offers. Who decides that?

"Ah, man. I'm so glad to be back in the US," Mike sighs, reclining and putting his hands behind his head.

"You're forgetting that it is actually called the United States of Mexico," Manuel says. Mike puckers his lips, then bursts into a laugh.

"That's what I'm talking about, man," Beet says. "All these labels. That's just society,"

"Society," Manuel dictates.

"Society," Wren says, nodding.

"Society, *society!*" Beet says, growing in volume.

"Society, society!" Mike shouts, pounding his glass against the table.

We escalate, repeating over and over until it no longer feels like a word, but instead an anthem, a religious chant that embodies all we stand for.

"Keep it down over there, I'm tryna watch the game," someone barks from the bar counter, and we laugh.

"Okay, old man," I say, feeling a little lightheaded.

"Listen if you don't shut your mouth, I'm gonna come over there and shut it for you,"

"He's a society man with a society plan, what can I say," I muse, putting my hands up in surrender. The man huffs, pays his tab, and leaves. I feel a little bad, but we're just having fun. At least I can take comfort in the fact that we'll never see him again.

Just then, a flashy looking lady wanders over and stands near Mike.

"Hey, baby, looking for a good time? My friend over there says you asked her about it earlier, but she's turning in for the night,"

"Uh, I'm actually already having a good time," he says, looking up at her from his seat.

"I heard, it sounds like a charming conversation. What're you discussing?" she asks. He looks at us, then back at her.

    "We're just talking about how we're getting ready to bring some gnarly folks to justice. How we're ready to fight if anyone tries to stop us, and—ow," he says, looking down. Someone must've kicked him under the table.

"That sounds like fun, are you sure you don't wanna come back to my hotel with me? I've got a suite,"

"Mmmm," Mike hums, considering. Beet runs his finger along his mug, his eyes glassy. "Just, like, to hang out?" he asks, scratching the back of his head. Wren laughs in disbelief next to me.

"No, let's hookup," the woman says, leaning into him. He weighs it in his mind for a moment before nodding.

"Okay, sure."

"I charge $40 per session," she says. Mike sinks back into his seat, disappointed. I guess he's not used to having to pay for such services. He thinks for a moment before looking back up to her.

"That's great. I charge $50 so you can just give me a 10 and we'll call it even. Sound good?" he says, barely containing his amusement. The woman scoffs and walks away, fading into the background. Beet points at Mike from across the table.

"That's Capitalism 101, baby," he says. Mike grins and shakes his head, looking down.

"I thought she actually liked me for a second,"

"That is society for you, bro," Manuel says. Beet raises his mug, I follow suit and soon we all hold our drinks in the air.

"To society?" Beet asks.

"To society," we say in unison, and cheers. My drink goes down flat and cool, my glass empty and my heart full.

397

Chapter 22 || What Happened to James

When we arrive in Corpus Cristi we walk through a park on the water, with grass so green that I suspect it must be dyed. A set of gray buildings form an ugly skyline that detracts significantly from what this place could be. We march on a large green campus, the ground cover contained by a perimeter of sidewalks. The tourists are everywhere, refusing to pick up after their dogs and leaving empty drink cups on every corner. I reach over my shoulder and handle the cap on the titanium poster tube, just to make sure it is still secure.

A substantial breeze pushes into me, nearly causing my hat to go flying. My hand still throbs. I can't tell if the pain is getting less intense or if I am simply getting used to it. The humidity is high today, but that doesn't stop someone in military fatigues from walking around with a hotdog, pausing every few minutes for someone to thank them for their service. We arrive near the end of the marina, where we hope to meet someone that Manuel had connected with over the phone. He explained a few minutes ago that this was who he called at the payphone, which was met with little more than skeptical looks. In the absence of evidence to the contrary, the rest of the group remained silent.

"I'm the helmsman," a disheveled looking man says, sticking out a hand. Manuel meets it, we introduce ourselves. The man's collar isn't folded up or down, but bent between the two positions. "My name is Dorji Firth,"

"Thank you for helping us out," I say.

"No problem at all, happy to help. As one might expect, your arrangements aren't exactly in the lap of luxury. We've had to pick up extra men on account of the recent water traffic. I'm sure you understand," he says. Even from a meter away I can smell the whiskey on his breath. "Manuel and I have discussed, you'll ride with us the full way across the Gulf. Should save you a few days, at least, of walking. Give you a chance to rest the ol' peg legs."

I shuffle my feet. I think I'd rather just walk. The others seem to accept this plan more readily than I do. A sinking feeling in my gut. The helmsman walks us onto the ship, which is mid-sized and has a few shipping containers and rusted equipment lying about.

"Aside from the raw oil we've got in the hold, we connect retailers from one end of the Gulf to the other," he explains. "If you've ever ordered something to be picked up at a store, you utilized this section of the supply chain. Nothing high risk or particularly valuable, so don't get any ideas. I guess   you've already got that base covered, though," he says, looking at the poster tubes. A few armed guards amble about, looking at us through the corner of their eyes. Wren shifts uncomfortably. "Don't mind them. They're here to protect the cargo, not you. We've had quite a few...spooks, recently."

"Spooks?" I ask.

"Near-misses, threats. The Goodmen are out and about, could be aboard any of those ships out there. Everyone's on the edge of their seat, just waiting,"

"That's the same terrorist group that Carson mentioned at the dam, right?" Mike asks. I nod. Dorji takes a drink from his flask, then pockets it and shows us to our quarters. There is space enough for all of us and our equipment, but we are very much sardines in the way we have to lie down. Still, not a word of complaint. The room is windowless, with painted metal and a few bits of functional decorations about, such as fire sprinklers and caged light bulbs. The floor is cold and thuds loudly when I walk across it. Most of the day is spent eating the bits of groceries we have and staring mindlessly at the walls. It isn't long before night comes, and we all drift to sleep.

...

I awake to another shout: Beet. He rolls over uncomfortably and sighs, annoyed with himself I guess. After a few minutes of tossing and turning, he stands and steps over us, opens the door to head outside. I lay awake thinking of him, of his torture. I feel guilty, like I've opened this chapter for him while he was working on closing the entire book. Resolute, I slip my boots on without socks and walk outside.

A wet breeze drifts across the metal deck, the ship shifts slightly, water crashing below as we make our way slowly through the Gulf.

"Hey, did you see a ginger guy walk this way?" I ask one of the guards. More to make him aware of my presence (and avoid getting shot) than anything else. He points, I follow. I find my friend leaning over the side of the deck and looking down at the dark drink below. I lean on the railing next to him, he doesn't look up.

"You doing okay?" I ask.

"As well as I can be. I keep thinking of James, can't get him out of my head," he says. I push my body weight into him and let out a breath of air.

It happened at a low point for all of us, but possibly the lowest point in Beet's life. The working conditions were abysmal; 110 degree heat, ice makers in need of repair, air conditioners off to reduce power costs. Our 30 minute lunch breaks had been eliminated, us being forced to instead work 7.5 hours a day to avoid getting any sort of overtime pay, or full time benefits. God forbid.

Even 7.5 hours in conditions like those can erode the constitution of the strongest people, especially when clocking out was only a facade for the paperwork. In reality, we were expected to work upward of 12 hours, or risk being eliminated from the schedule entirely. Quiet firing, I believe they call it. Beet was working outside during that time, not given the option to work before the sun came up, but being forced to work in the middle of the day while guest activity was at a height to avoid the garden looking 'abandoned'. His health and sanity melted away in equal measure. His appeals to management hadn't been denied, just outright ignored.

Then, he was witness to the owner fornicating with an investor. This wouldn't have been an issue, had the owner not furiously bragged about being celibate during that period in their life. And so our hero spotted an opportunity. He called the owner on a personal number, and explained that harm would fall upon the investor if working conditions were not improved immediately. He was hung up on. Naturally.

His blood was already heated, but this brought it to a rolling boil. That fateful night, he located the guest cabin that the investor was staying in (at no charge). When Beet first told me this story, he continually reiterated that the cabin was empty. He checked multiple times, even turning on the lights despite the exposure that gave him in the desert night . This was to send a message about the seriousness of his threat on the phone. The curtains were the first to burn. Then the ceiling caught.

It wasn't a historical cabin, just made to look that way. The synthetic insulation burst into flame quickly, casting long orange light into the field. He ran, and hid behind a rock. He called the fire department. It would take them a good 40 minutes to get out there, anyway.

Out of the darkness, a pickup truck came barreling over the cryptobiotic soil. Out jumped James, one of the groundskeepers. James was never allowed to leave property once he signed his contract, one of his duties was to protect the buildings on site and make sure no harm befell them. To fail at any of your tasks at Maroon Mesa generally means a fate worse than firing, as we have learned over our journey so far. Fearing consequences from the owner, James rushed into the building to salvage what appliances and resort property he could. The television was pulled out, the fancy wines tossed into the smoking sand. In the headlights of the truck, Beet witnessed him trip backward out of the building, a molten comforter flaming and stuck to his arm. The building leaned, a support gave out. A blackened beam burst forth and struck the man, pinning him to the ground where he lay writhing and burning. Beet lept up to help him, then another set of headlights racing across the field appeared. And another. If it was discovered that this was his fault, he would be victim to consequences that none of us had ever seen.

And so he ran.

One might expect an incident such as this to reach the papers, or at least be mentioned on social media. But the fire was out within a few minutes, and James was driven to the hospital. In the end, the resort rumor system produced the story that it was caused by an old employee who had been known to put lit cigarette butts in flower boxes, and had once caused a small fire in this way. That night, the owner was out to dinner with that particular investor. Overnight, the rest of the grounds crew deconstructed the building and threw the remains of it into the furnace. Officially, James had to go out of town for a family emergency and utilize all the vacation days he had stacked. The ferocity of   the owner upon learning that a building was destroyed would be beyond any of these disadvantages. Once covered up, they never noticed that a building was even there. The night auditor at that time had the gall and charisma to convince that investor that they must have left their belongings in the adjacent cabin, because the building they're mentioning has never existed. It is just sand and rocks, see?

To this day, I believe that I am the only one with which he has confided this truth. I assume the owner forgot the phone call, and Beet left the state of Utah soon afterward. Here on the ship, he confides that he wants to use his money from this project to donate to James. He didn't get a dime from the resort, and did not have insurance at the time of the incident. He sits in the corner of a state run home, wheelchair bound and silent. No family. No friends except death waiting in the opposite corner.

The day that Beet was supposed to leave, he and I went to the free health clinic. I suppose that Beet intended to confess what happened. When we walked in the room we saw the man wrapped in casts and gauze, and Beet could not bring himself to do anything except gape for a few moments. And so no confession was given. He couldn't see, anyway, his eyes were wrapped. So we sat on stiff chairs next to the bed and red aloud from a library book. I don't remember which one, but what I do remember are the soft voices, the smell of disinfectant.

He looks at me sadly. Bluish smog drifts over the waters, red blinking radio towers all across the horizon. The lights from other cargo ships ambling every which way. It smells like rust. I tell myself that this mission is for the best, that it will bring Beet closure. This is the only way I can get to sleep tonight.

Chapter 23 || The Shell

I've been dreading it, but my time finally comes on the witness stand$_{11}$. It is roomier than I thought on the back side. There are several legal books in expensive looking bindings, tucked into a small shelf, and a microphone, a glass of water, a box of tissues that thankfully nobody has had to touch yet. Fitz walks up to the stand and I see him more closely than I ever have before. He looks professional, a hitman working for the state or the church or somewhere in between.

"We'll start this out simple. What are the names of your co-conspirators?" he asks. I blink and lean forward into the microphone. Water vapor from the previous witnesses still clings to it, smelling like old breath. I could rubber band a mask on top of it, I've seen that before.

"We all used fake names, which I cannot recall, as a matter of mutual protection," I say.

"Fake names are for playing house and stage productions. What you used to commit the crime was an alias. What was your alias? Or...can you not recall that either?"

"I was not granted the privilege of having one," I say, then continue before he can shoot another at me. "This is one of the things that the gang held over my head. Along with the threats of physical harm, I was threatened with exposure. They threatened to frame me if I went to any sort of law enforcement. They knew my name from the start, I didn't know theirs."

"Very well. How did you meet these people?" he asks. My neurons fire, trying to conceive a story while the words need to be leaving my mouth. Like trying to fill a sieve.

"They found me in the woods while I was photographing birds. They marked me because they knew that I worked at the resort in the past, and they needed that inside information,"

"Mr. Montague, most of Utah is public land. I find your statement of 'in the woods' to be quite vague. How did they know where to find you?"

"I was tracking a bird, a bird that tends to be in the same site each year," I say, the story failing to reveal itself to me as I speak. "I had been here in the past with dozens of people. It is a special place, and the gang must have spoken to one of those people to figure out where I was." Sounds reasonable enough.

"So everyone that wants to see this bird, they follow a track of feathers?"

"No, sir, there are other signs,"

"I'm no woodsman, but even I know that birds don't leave the nest unless absolutely necessary,"   he says, I shake my head. I see my dad in the pews, sitting on his hands.

"So how close were you to this bird's nest? You had to be extremely close in order to get a photograph, right?"

"I cannot say with any certainty. I'm unaware of where that bird's nest is."

"Then how did you find it?"

"I'm a wildlife photographer, I know how to find the animals I'm looking for," I say firmly. He grits his teeth and looks back at me. In the back, I see my dad practically rumbling out of his seat, his face red with anger.

"I find that answer vague and unconvincing, it seems to me that this must have been a predetermined meeting place. Unless it is at a nest, birds do not go to the same place twice," Fitz says. Mary stands.

"Hearsay, your honor,"

"Sustained."

"Let's take a step back. You're a wildlife photographer now?"

"Yes,"

"And what did you do before that?"

"As stated before, I worked at the resort."

"*You* worked at the resort you stole from?" he says, slowly rolling his tongue over the words.

"Yes," I say, wishing I could be at home in my bed.

"What was your position there?"

"A guide," I say.

"I see. You've left your large and spacious building to be here," he says, glancing at the jury.

Several of them nod in agreement. "Now, would you please describe for me the day of the incident, from your perspective?" he asks.

And I do, omitting all names for pronouns,

411

omitting anything about the general manager, except that she ran away shortly after the visa worker ran inside. All this with the creeping threat of a perjury conviction nestled at the base of my spine. The sword of Damocles, dangling above my head, shifting idly in the windless room, a touched starved windchime.

"At which point the gang members mounted the undamaged dirtbikes and fled the scene, leaving me behind."

"Then, critically, what did you do?" he asks.

"I produced my pistol and took cover behind a UTV."

"Yes. There are many people who believe that you hoped that the UTV would be destroyed in the crossfire, believing you were attempting to make a statement about their impact on the environment around Moab. Did any of these thoughts cross your mind?" he asks. No matter what I answer, I'll lose supporters. Some of which might be on the jury. Best to leave them in the dark if I can manage. I take control.

"I didn't want anyone to get hurt, that's why I dropped the handgun as soon as I saw the deputy approaching me," I say, Mary gives me a thumbs up. Fitz wasn't ready to get there yet, he cycles through his plan in his mind.

"Are you aware that the rest of your gang caused a completely avoidable traffic situation that could have injured many civilians and law enforcement personnel?"

"Yes,"

"Are you aware that your gang, during the same pursuit, later caused a deputy ranger to drive off the side of the Shafer Trail, plummet 300 feet amidst a landslide, and have to be evacuated via a *medical helicopter to Grand Junction?*" he shouts, I lean away from him. Mary, focused, standing.

"Objection-"

"Overruled." the judge speaks. The court reporter types feverishly to keep up.

"I was not present for the events that directly led to that incident," I say. Someone in the back stands up, points a finger at me.

"She's still in the hospital, too hurt to open her eyes and look at her daughter you disgusting—" she yells, my father stands and turns to face her.

"That's enough!" he shouts, they both sit back down before the bailiff reaches them.

"Order, order," the judge shouts, running her fingertips along her collar. She turns to me.

"Do you know those people?"

"I don't know the woman. The man is my father," I say. She nods.

"Let the record show that Mr. Montague, senior, is among the crowd and has expressed an outburst. If anyone else not directly involved with the case would like to speak their mind, I urge them to do so *outside* of this courtroom. We are here to seek truth and justice, not emotion. Anyone who disagrees and sees fit to act on such impulses is welcome to receive a charge for contempt of court. Now, Mr. Fitzgerald, please continue if you have anything further,"

"It's Fitzpatrick. But—thank you, your honor."

"So, Mr. Montague, despite the circumstances, in the presence of a police officer you still did not seek aid, even though you 413 were injured and were apparently under a threat to your life?"

"I sought aid by dropping my weapon and surrendering peacefully," I explain, hating that I have to articulate every detail, like he's a teenager suddenly pretending not to understand basic societal concepts.

"And did you drop your weapon and 'surrender peacefully' before the deputy had his service weapon aimed at you, and gave verbal instruction?"

"No I did not."

"No, instead you kept your firearm pointed *at* the deputy until your fellow gang members had fled the scene. Is that correct?"

"That is correct, yes,"

"And why did you do that?"

"I was told that if I interacted with any law enforcement officers I would be killed," I say. Simple. Serious.

"So I don't suppose you call pointing a firearm at law enforcement…interacting?"

"Objection,"

"Sustained."

"I'll continue," Fitz says. "At the time of the incident, did anyone else have a weapon drawn aside from law enforcement?"

"No."

"Except for you?"

"That is correct."

"And why is that?"

"I needed to blend in, sir," I say.

"You needed to blend in," he says, looking to the jury in a show of perplexity.

"Yes. I had no intent to fire the weapon at the officer. If I did, I had ample opportunity to, and did not take it. I was exercising my 2nd amendment rights. Utah is an open carry state," I say. I know this will be the hill on which I die. Get killed. He spins back around to me, ready for the execution.

"And where did you get this pistol?" he asks. I need to think fast, something he cannot prove.

"It was my pistol. My mother gave it to me before she passed," I say, the jury relaxes at these words, tilting their heads and looking at me. Why didn't I just say that they gave it to me? Maybe they can trace it back. Fitz backs up to the center of the floor, sizing me up. I'm grateful for the wooden box protecting me.

"This is not the first time that you are in this very courtroom, in that very seat, testifying for yourself, is it?" he asks. Taken aback, I blink.

"No, sir," I say. He smiles and clicks a pen.

"That is all,"

...

My father takes the stand, his face red and veins pulsing at his temples. I haven't seen him like this since my little league games, when he would shout at the umpires. I look around and see that the owner finally bothered to show up today. Immune to summons unless they're convenient, I guess. All of the seats at the prosecution's table are now full.

"Mr. Montague, how would you describe your son as a child?" Fitz asks.

"He's always been a good son,"

"Has he ever gotten into major trouble?" Fitz asks. Mary almost stands up, but spins her pen through her fingers instead.

"Like all kids, he experienced

the character challenges that come along with adolescence. He got into some trouble, but has worked hard to get out of it and has kept his nose clean ever since," my dad says, not breaking eye contact with me.

"Is there any doubt in your mind that he is guilty?" the lawyer asks. My dad falters on the wording, then grows more angry at the attempted trick.

"Nothing but doubt, counselor. My son is a good boy, he wouldn't do this voluntarily," he dictates. Good. If we've done a good enough job to convince him, then maybe we've got a shot at convincing the jury, too. Fitz takes the pistol I used from the evidence table. It sits in a clear plastic baggie, brass bullets still jangling around inside. My father was in the war, he has seen more weapons than he's had hot meals. They sicken him, and have never been allowed in the house. I wasn't even allowed to watch war movies growing up, or play the same video games as my friends. Fitz places the handgun on the desk in front of my father, who stiffens visibly and puffs out his cheeks. He doesn't want to look at the thing, afraid it will jump up and bite him.

"Can you please read the serial number on this pistol, the one that your son used?" Fitz asks, his eyelids relaxed. He smirks as my dad puts on reading glasses and leans forward.

"No,"

"Why not?"

"There is no serial number,"

"All legal firearms have serial numbers. What happened to the serial number on this one?"

"It's been filed off," my father says

softly.

"What was that?" Fitz asks, his smile growing uncontained, his teeth showing.

"I said that the serial number has been filed off," my dad says, staring hard at the gleaming lawyer. I know that look, and back my seat away from the table.

"One more time, I don't know if the jury quite heard you,"

"That's enough!" my dad rages, grabbing the baggie, cocking the weapon inside of it, and pulling the trigger. Two shots at Fitz; the bag explodes. Bullets clatter onto the table. Two shots at the owner, everyone dives on the ground. From the royal blue carpet I look up to see the bailiff jump to tackle my father, who has already dropped the gun and stuck his hands up. The handcuffs go on.

"It is loaded with blanks! It says so on—" he wrestles the cuffs, "—read the shell!"

Chapter 24 || Gullway

The ship moves smoothly through the currents, adjusting speed and heading occasionally to compensate for rogue vessels that don't seem to be heeding traditional right-of-ways or answering on the radio. There seems to be a great deal of interference coming from somewhere, as the guard's walkie talkies are barely working through all the static. I have little experience on salt water, but this is relayed to me through the comments of the guards, who seem frustrated because these incidents put them even more on edge.

An array of horns sound off; different pitches and volumes and distances. Our course adjusts once again to avoid a small sailboat aimed to cut us off. The various oil rigs suspended from the water make navigation even more difficult.

"It just doesn't make sense," one of the guards says, sticking a middle finger at the sailboat. The water is crowded, full of boats of all sizes and colors. I pray for them to speed up this journey, we're so close to the end, so close to finally delivering the packages. After we land, we'll sell the paintings as quickly as we can and hop on a plane back to Utah. We'll rescue Monty...somehow. I haven't worked that out yet. For now I need to focus on getting all of us there.

I cover my ears as the horn on the boat sounds once again, adjusting course now that the sailboat has turned around. Nearby, two vessels have a near miss, barely enough room between them for a gull to pass.

Beet speaks to me of his aspirations.

"I think I may finally be ready to talk to him. Once the dust settles, I want to go see him and tell him it was me,"

"I don't know that you should admit that, Beet. They could still try to prosecute you for arson, at the very least. You're lucky you weren't caught on camera," I say. He thinks for a moment.

"Maybe I'll visit and tell him it's just for old time's sake. Tell him I came into some money and I wanted to be—I don't know? Philanthropic?"

"It's been two years. I'm not sure he's healed to the point that he can talk. They said he never might,"

"Well that's what I need to do," definitively, swallowing. This wasn't a proposal. He wasn't asking for advice. I nod.

"Do you want me to come with you?"

Chapter 25 || The Price of Salvation

After a multi-day break, we return. During this period I am not allowed to speak to my father, except during his one allotted phone call, which he used to call me. No sense in trying to reach a new lawyer, a public defender is all we can afford. Otherwise, I might already be out of this.

They bring him back to the witness stand still in handcuffs and give him a chance to explain himself, no weapons in sight. When he appears, I'm already looking at the owner. A brief smile crosses their face, then a tear appears out of nowhere to promote the feigned cowering at the mere thought of being in the same room as him.

"Thank you for giving me the chance to explain. I would like everyone to know that I fought in the war, and I was in charge of munitions storage and distribution at my post. I know what a blank round looks like. I was simply trying to prove a point, I never intended to hurt anybody. The point is that the shells were blanks, they do not fire a projectile, just a powder that looks like a gunshot. Even if my son had fired at the deputy, which he did not, the only person harmed would have been himself in the return fire. This likely would have been lethal, considering how the situation had already escalated and there was not more than one officer present to provide additional protection for the deputy. My son had no reason and no intention to shoot anybody. The fact that the bullets are blanks proves the statement true," he says, looking at me pleadingly from so far away. Fitz stands up from his table, knocking over his water. The owner wimpers.

"It merely proves that his co-conspirators didn't trust him not to try to assassinate them. *Clearly,* the urge to do so runs in the family!" he spits.

"Order!"

...

The nights are the worst. During the day I am exposed to all sects of society that I loathe, I am sweating in my suit, and there's no comfort to be found. Yet somehow worse is the anticipation for the following day. At least when I am at the defense table I am facing my accusers, looking down the barrel of what is about to fire on me. Here, in my lonesome cell, I am left with nothing but predictions for tomorrow and the echoes of today.

It has to be close to midnight. There are two other cells in here, both empty. I've tried to make conversation with those that pass through here, but their occupation always has the nature of vagrancy. Nobody seems to stay except me. They took my belt, then my watch too. Once my father pulled his stunt, they came in and took my toilet paper, as well. Just in case I was planning to hang myself with that, I guess. Or maybe they revel in knowing that I don't feel truly clean, denied even the most basic of hygiene products. At least up on the mountain there were plenty of rocks around to use.

The door opens, the light that comes from the other side is equivalent to the light in here. I perk up, hoping to catch a glimpse at whoever they're dragging in now. It's a weekend, I'll take any entertainment that I can get. Probably someone got too drunk at Woody's and tried to climb up the roof again in a show of their free solo skills. Or maybe someone else drove a UTV into a mailbox again.

But this time is different. The deputy doesn't appear, walking in the shackled perpetrator. Instead, two nicely dressed men walk in. They look ordinary, someone you might pass on the street. Blue button up shirts, rolled up at the sleeves. Khakis, real leather belts. They both wear a white enamel pin of the holy cross on their chest, right above the breast pocket. I wouldn't have noticed it if I weren't sitting on the floor, angled for the light to reflect it. They come in and eye me with compassion; an animal in a cage. They remind me of my days canvassing for the church. Maybe that's why they're here.

"Hello," one of them says, pleasantly enough.

"Hey," I answer, standing up. The temples aren't open this late except for emergencies, or clergy.

"You're Mr. Montague," he says, I'm not sure if it is a question, so I say

"Yes,"

"We know. We're here to speak with you,"

"I deduced that, yeah," I say, crossing my arms and cocking my eyebrow.

"We have an offer for you," he says, taking his time.

"Maybe we could start with who you are?" I ask, wishing I had dosed the entitlement in my voice slightly lower.

"That's not imperative at this stage. All you need to know is that we represent a group that has a vested interest in your case, and we have a solution for you," he says. "We've spoken to your lawyer, and from what we understand, you aren't interested in giving up the names of your fellow gang members in exchange for a reduced sentence,"

"That's because I don't know them," I say, nodding. If I believe it, maybe they will. He smiles at me, breathes in, then back out.

"Right. We'll go with that. The names of your accomplices are irrelevant, that isn't why we're here. We have an offer for you that would be mutually beneficial. You see, we have some enemies. True sinners that are playing key roles in the way that things are being run. I believe that you used to work for one of them?" he asks, putting his hands in his pockets. The other one has a messenger bag, the flap tucked back against his hip. They must have been looking at the files in the hallway.

"Okay," I say, not sure where this is headed.

"We aren't asking for anything complicated. I know that you used to believe in many of the same things that we do, and even though you may have lost your way I hope that you retain some of the values that made you a good man. We don't want to see you rot in prison. We both know that before long, someone under the owner's influence will catch you with a sharpened toothbrush between the ribs, or you'll catch a loose brick to the back of the head when you're trying to shower," he says. I almost yell for the deputy, but my curiosity holds me silent and still. There is real, genuine, kindness in his voice.

"Listen," the other one says. "These sinners, we have their crimes listed, but we cannot surpass the burden of proof the way our current laws are. Do you catch our meaning?"

"I'm not sure,"

"He's saying that our government isn't designed to handle crimes against morality, it isn't set up to handle most of the real criminals. Did you know that one out of every 20 cases in the United States ends up with a wrongful conviction? That means that 5% of the people that spend their Earthly years in jail committed no crime," he says, shaking his head as if appalled at the system. "For the simple fact that the evidence provided is admissible or otherwise disproven. A shame, it really is."

"These sinners we speak of," the other man begins, "we want to give you their names. You will then give these names instead of the names of your gang members. You get your plea deal, we get to put away real criminals," he says, as if it is the simplest thing in the world. I stare back blankly. At first I want to argue, to provide some reason why this plan wouldn't work. It gets under my skin; it feels dirty.

"If you do this for the betterment of our community, we will look favorably upon you and your family in the coming war," he declares, his face solid as stone. I take a step back, freeze. Blink. What did he just say? I want him

to crack a smile, let out a laugh, elbow his buddy
and tell me he's joking. But he stands there like a
statue, the smell of some kind of nut coming off of
him. Pistachio shells, that's what it is.

"We're getting ready. One of the big ones is
coming very soon. What do you say, Monty? We have
some of the best health insurance in the country,"

"I—" I say, looking around the room for a
queue card. "I'm in enough legal trouble as it is. The
last thing I need is to be put on some watchlist,"

"You are already there, my brother," the
man with the messenger bag says, tolerance in his
voice. Pity, almost. "I certainly hope that you will
reconsider. For the safety of your family."

They stare at me for a moment more of
unbearable silence, their eyes dead like those of a
shark. Finally, they turn and walk out of the room,
their dress shoes clopping on the ground. I turn
around to face another wall, to change my view. I
hear the door shut and the electronic lock buzzing.
I sit on the stainless steel toilet and fight a stomach
ache from the white bread.

...

The next day I sweat in my seat, my cast
itching and biting me. I picture the dirt trapped
underneath it, bugs crawling inside and nipping at
my skin. They're getting all of the preliminaries
ready for the day, organizing the paperwork and
making sure everyone is on the same page. I
consider asking Mary, but she has a sharp edge to
her that has thus far remained sheathed. Without
a hint that they were about to do so, my legs
straighten and I am standing. My lawyer

looks up from her legal pad, then back down. I walk over to the bailiff near the chamber door. He wears a blue uniform like the local police, but nicer, more formal. Pressed. He stiffens as I approach, hand on his holster and the other stretched out to make me stop in front of him. Quiet talking from the crowd, I hope nobody notices I am up here.

"I need help," I say, showing my empty hands. My casted arm dangles limply, not like it would be much of a threat, anyway.

"I know, son," he says. "I don't think I can give you the kind of help you need,"

"Can we speak somewhere in private? Someone's threatened me," I say, leaning in. He looks like he's waiting for the punchline, like he's heard this one before. "I'm serious. The court is in danger," I say. He rolls his eyes and looks around, then gestures with his chin toward a door. He holds it open for me. When I first came out of the hospital there was talk about how to handcuff me. If my one good hand should be restrained against a belt loop, if I should be made to keep both hands in the air. For now, in between transports, my hands remain free. I wish the room in the back to be nicer. I wish for deeply stained oak, glossy banisters and leather bound books. But the room matches the rest of the building. Fluorescent lights, particle board tables and school chairs, walls painted a blue so faint it might be white if the sky gets cloudy. The window has a barrier on it, creating a barcode print on the royal blue carpet. He sits me down at the table and slaps a notebook down.

"Okay, we'll take a few details down. First I gotta send out a text message so they don't think you escaped while I was watchin' you," he says, whipping out a cell phone and typing quickly. He has the keyboard clicks audible. The sound of a text being sent, he pockets the phone and looks at me. "Alright, when did this happen?"

"Last night," I say.

"And who threatened you?"

"I don't know their names," I say, feeling foolish. I lean forward and try to make it look like I am engaged, hoping he will mirror me. He doesn't.

"Why don't you start at the beginning and tell me what happened?" he says. And, I do.

"So I guess to answer your original question, no. There's no physical evidence," I say, sitting back. He shakes his head knowingly, and the corner of his mouth turns up.

"No, there wouldn't be. They're good at preventing that when they want to," he says.

"Huh?"

"These men, are they in the room with us right now?" he asks, raising an eyebrow. I look around at the empty space.

"No, look, these are *real* people, this really happened," I say, exasperated.

The door opens, the two men from last night file in. Then, four more men in similar suits. They fill the room, one man shutting the door behind him and blocking it with his body. I stand in fear, a heavy hand on my shoulder, squeezing a pressure point. The weight of his digits lands me back in the chair. Across from me, an important looking man sits. His sideburns grow down further than I think they ought to, defying modern beauty convention. His eyes are a cerulean blue, when the sunlight catches them they hit me like a precious stone. He places his hands flat onto the cheap table, a string of rosary beads wrapped around one of them.

"Hello. Do you know who I am?" he asks. I shake my head, then look at the bailiff, who leans back in his new chair adjacent to me. He rips out the sheet of paper he wrote my testimony on, then slides it over to the man with the rosary. "I am Llewellyn Lynch. Most of my family just calls me Lynch," he says, I hear a hard candy clattering around in his mouth. "My brothers and I represent an organization. You likely know of us as the Goodmen," he says, inhaling. His breath seems loud in this otherwise quiet room, then I realize that it must be that nobody else is breathing.
He looks down and studies the paper, then folds it and places it into his breast pocket. I straighten up.

"I know that you used to hold some of the same values as me and my good men here, but it seems as though you've strayed from the path. We humbly came to you last night to offer a peaceful opportunity for a mutually beneficial agreement. I see now that perhaps it was unwise to be so trusting of a stranger. Now," he pulls out a set of printed glossy photos from a pocket, and places them carefully in front of me. No corners overlapping. Perfectly square. A chill runs down my spine. They are photos of my father sitting in his recliner. Photos of him at work in the paint shop. He is getting older, his awareness and paranoia not as keen as they apparently need to be. I lock eyes with Lynch after taking one last look at the photos, and realizing that there is no glare from a window. No atmospheric aberrations. These photos were taken recently, from inside of his home.

"I want to make sure that you understand what you're passing up here.

431

An opportunity to help our family grow, to bring forth a greener tomorrow. We have big plans, Monty, and we want you to be a part of them. Darkness is coming. Will you be a light?" he asks pointedly. I stare back at him, the hand left my shoulder a minute ago but still I feel the presence of someone behind me. Their breath on the top of my hair.

  "We have sources that tell a very different story of what happened the day of the shootout. Sources that don't speak of any diamonds, but paintings. Isn't that curious? Do you know anything about that?" Lynch asks. Still, I say nothing. "I have no qualms with what you and your friends did to the resort. In fact, I look up to you for it. The act took some courage, courage that most people don't have. We call that a testament. You're a hero to us, taking a stand against UTVs, the parks, and a private resort all in one day. Well, I couldn't tell my son a happier fairy tale," he smiles. His energy of amiability is in direct contrast to the watchmen that stand in every corner. He takes the photos of my father back. "You're fighting some bad, bad people that, quite frankly, are mentally inferior to those like you and I. I can tell. The only reason that they have so much money is because they were willing to exploit the *innocent* to get it, and it has stayed in their families for ages. IQ isn't hard to guess.... I can tell. People like the owner, they open their eyes in the morning and all they can see is *money money money* and *profit* and they can't stand not having what they want. They are *weak*. But you, Monty, you know what it's like to suffer, don't you? To not darkave what you need? In that way, you and I are alike."

432 Beneath the table, I stretch my leg out and ●———▸ my ankle pops. The muffled sound of a

UTV racing down the street outside. The window is closed, probably can't open it through the bars. They learned their lesson with Bundy.

"I met him once," Lynch says, leaning back in his chair. "At a convention for blue lives, of all things. Sometimes justice supersedes the badge," he pulls his suit jacket aside, a golden police badge glinting over his chest. Just below, a pin of the holy cross. "In those cases, we have to investigate outside of...traditional protocol. This is where God's light shines through and illuminates our path. Do you know what we found?" he asks. I shake my head. "Do you want to know?" I nod. "They're trading people," he says definitively. "Not sinners, not those who need to be saved. The good men standing around you have been bought, but I don't want you to think me a hypocrite. They were bought with sweat, commitment, and faith. This is the price of salvation. That is what we are working toward, for everyone. Certainly to complete our mission, with the current state of the public, finances simply must be involved. There is no way around that, and that is not the issue I'm speaking to you about. *Our* recruitment process involves taking either those that are willing, or converting those that sin. The owner and the sheriff, on the other hand, have no requirement, no discrimination other than those that are ripe."

I shudder at the word *ripe*, trying not to do so visibly. He continues.

"This is where our paths diverge. You see, the sheriff is a good man above all else. We used to be friends, even. He has done wonderful things to keep this community together through some of the most challenging of times. His actions of colluding with the owner on this project was the final straw for me. Sometimes we must disregard relationships to send a message in the hopes that a friend will find their way once again. Even though I still believe that he is a good man at heart, the sins he has committed are damning," he sighs, touches the rosary and looks at me. "That was a brilliant thing you did, taking those paintings. Cutting off Samson's hair," he says. I catch myself making a confused expression when he continues to talk for my benefit. "Their operation, where they trade innocent lives? It is a risky business. Most of the people of the same tier as the owner dabble in it for some time, but this isn't any information that you'll hear from the internet. The whole agenda is kept very quiet. The trades are made atop of scaffolding, so to speak. One strong wind, and—" he blows his breath at me. Minty.

"I'm not sure I completely understand," I say.

"Stick with me my friend," he says. "We'll get you up to speed. Sometimes these paintings are used as collateral for the trades. For the owner, they are kept as insurance for something that no front-facing agency would ever cover. If someone tries to expose all of the evil that goes on there, the paintings can be sold or traded to cover the cost of a bribe. If the threats don't work, that is. And, they usually work," he chuckles. "If not a bribe, then they can be used to afford legal fees. And by legal fees I of course mean gold coated ketamine and penthouse suites for those working on the trial. Large and spacious buildings for them all. Mr. Fitzgerald is certainly happy to be here, that much 434 is obvious."

I close my eyes, trying to comprehend

the enormity of his accusations.

"You look surprised. Without the paintings as assets, the owner has no cards left to play if anyone tries to prosecute for anything serious. They'll have to start selling their private jets and custom silverware. I know the human trafficking is awful, especially when you're not upfront about it, do it in public with witnesses the old fashioned way. None of this kidnapping and false letter business. This world isn't ready for that sort of thing, not yet.
Oh, come on. I know the rooms are expensive (how could you? The correct prices aren't listed online.), but did you seriously think that Maroon Mesa nets *millions* a year? It costs at least that much to upkeep the property. Which is half empty most of the time, might I add. I'm finding it hard to believe that this is a shock to you. When you worked there, did everyone just walk around under the spell of the owner?
Did nobody acknowledge the fact that general managers don't stay for more than a few months? The fact that the rooms are empty? I mean, it doesn't make any sense!" he says, throwing his hands up in the air. "They're all dumber than I thought,"

"It isn't that people don't notice," I explain. "We notice. We're suspicious. But you know what happens when we try to go to the police. Who do you want us to report it to? The Better Business Bureau?"

"Go on, please," he says, leaning forward and listening intently. I can't tell if he is mocking me or not.

"People have tried to go to the papers. They've tried to write about it. It isn't

about whether or not the owner can prove guilt
in court. The legal fees alone would completely
bankrupt any of their victims, but the fees would
not even be a fraction of the owner's wealth. Not to
mention taking the time off of work, the hits to our
reputations, and the threats to our family. People
have tried. And they've been ruined," I say. He
pushes his lower lip up and nods slowly.

"The owner is very good at cleaning dirty
laundry. That's for sure," someone against the wall
says. Lynch laughs, then looks at me.

"Listen, whether you knew this whole agenda
or not, you've kicked the beehive. And without our
protection, the swarm will come after you. Out
in the real world, or in prison. You won't be safe
without our help. The kniving tricks they're pulling
to destroy the southwest? Bears Ears? It is the same
story as back east, repeating and repeating and
repeating. We look up to you, you and your friends
took a stand against it. All in one day. It was real
clever, even if it was an accident. My family, my
brothers and sisters and I, are all planning something
big. Everything is coming together soon. I've flown
all the way out here from Florida to speak with you,
I've taken this time off of work. What do you say we
work together on this my friend?"

I blink back at him. Wondering, could this
be the 'client' we were contracted to deliver the
paintings for? I shake the thought out of my head
before it can take over. He slides a sheet of paper
over to me. A list of names[13].

"Memorize these details, these names, and
give them to the court the next time that someone
436 brings up the plea deal. They probably will
━━━━━━━ before today's session concludes. These

people are in the same circles as the owner of
Maroon Mesa, doing equally evil things to people and
to the land. You get to have a reduced sentence,
and at the same time put away some bad people
that are otherwise untouchable. People like that,
their voices don't get heard because there's no
dough behind them, no pull of the gluten. The
country is watching. We're watching. This is your
chance. You'll do a little time, but we'll make sure
you are well taken care of in there. It will all be
okay. And once this whole system collapses, we'll be
waiting for you with open arms," he says.

I look down at the sheet, then back up at him.
If they deliver the paintings, then I might not be
sentenced at all. Community service again. That's
not so bad. If my friends fail, or take too long,
I'll likely be killed in prison by one of the owner's
cronies before I've eaten my first meal. There are
eyes everywhere.
     "What do you say?"

Chapter 26 || Inextinguishable Flames

The night was sleepless. We stopped and dropped anchor a little after midnight, which according to one particular guard was not at all part of the plan, or the SOP. We have asked and pestered *Birch* everyone we can find, but nobody has any new information to share. We sit in our metal room, the door open and swinging noisily on its hinges when the breeze comes by. It smells like gutted fish. A propane lantern hangs from the ceiling, a cloud of moths crowding around it.

We sit in a circle, I produce the brochure and lay it in front of everyone. Manuel is the first to pick it up and read it, even though he's already done so. Then Wren, and so on. In silence, they look at me. Beet's face is bright red. Anger, embarrassment?

Manuel and I tell the full story of what we saw that morning. Through conversation and hard evidence, it seems that everyone in the gang had deduced their own conclusions, which were more or less close to what had actually

439

happened. But, the brochure is the nail in the coffin as far as I'm concerned.

"That proves it, then. Why have you been holding onto that without sharing?" Wren asks.

"I didn't—I didn't want to believe it," I say, rubbing my eyes. I look down at the crinkled and sweat soaked page once again. It has the names of individuals on it. Some ex-employees, some people I've never even heard of. Next to their names are headshots of them. Some look like they're from social media, others from security cameras or candid from across the room. Ages, weights, heights, languages are all listed along with some other markers. Tragically, at the bottom of each entry is a price.

"Couldn't we just have stayed in Utah and emailed a photo of this to the FBI or something?" Wren asks.

"No," Manuel says. "These paintings are condemnation of a crime themselves, yes, but they are also insurance. If someone tries to prosecute based on this brochure and the video we took, the owner will be able to pay for bribes, lawyers who work for the government—you understand. We have to make sure the paintings are secure before beginning any litigation. I do not know if you noticed, but we are being chased rather intentionally. They know we are going to east."

"I guess that makes sense," Wren says.

"Think of it like this," I say. "If you're trying to sink someone's raft, you don't just poke a hole. You take their repair kit and their air pumps too,"

"Right,"

440   Beet looks furious. His hands shake, I see ▬▬▬▬ melted candle wax on them. He gets up

and stands in the doorway, breathing audibly and trying to calm down.

There is brief talk of taking a lifeboat, or perhaps even my raft, and trying to get to shore and continue on foot. With all the water traffic, though, we agree that we'd be in great danger doing so. After a few minutes of deliberation, the helmsman appears and squeezes past Beet into our room. He holds a stainless steel flask in his hand and sways until he sits down on top of a crate.

"Oh what a night," he says. "I just came to tell ya that there's been some trouble on the gulf and we're following new Coast Guard orders."

The same shiver goes down Manuel's spine, I can tell when we look at one another. They've told us to stop because we're going to be boarded. Searched. The agents of the owner are finally coming to capture us and put an end to our masterpiece plan.

"What...kind of trouble?" Wren asks.

"Dunno, they won't share. With all the earthquakes messing about with the tide and water flows in the last few months, it could just be a seismic anomaly that they don't want us cruising over. Let's hope," he says, lifting his drink. "Could be a tsunami any day now. Just wish these jokers would stop clogging up the trade route. We about smashed into a dozen other vessels today on account of their ignorance. Anyway, I should probably get back topside. Who's steering this ship anyway?" he says, then a frightening laugh escapes him. He claps Beet on the shoulder when he leaves. Outside, the sound of helicopter rotors pounding the air into submission.

...

Most of the morning passes with us looking anxiously over the edge of the ship. A cool breeze arrives with the evening sunset. Below, the sea is full of smaller vessels once again. Our situation feels like a shaken can of soda that could burst at any moment. The tension in the air is palpable, I can reach out and grab it if I want to. The day is mostly clear, white and wispy clouds scraping the sky in groups.

Then, a shout from below. A collection of small skiffs ride adjacent to us, I stare down at them in disbelief. A grappling hook sails up toward me, nearly clipping me in the face. I jump backward, the line on it pulls tension and locks onto the perimeter railing.

"Boarding party!" shouts one of the guards. Boots scramble, the deep hum of the motors fires up to an abyssal roar. Manuel and Mike grab the grappling hook, trying to lift it off. Below, men on harnesses use their climbing gear to ascend. Behind, the anchor coiler comes to life and begins to retract the thick cable. The sound system crackles, a robotic voice booming.

"All personnel to your castle positions. All personnel to your castle positions. This is not a drill. Repeat, this is not a drill."

We look at one another and glance around, trying to figure out what to do. The anchor coil winds up so quickly that smoke spits out of it, smells like burning wires. A clang. The engines fully engage and the ship lurches forward quickly. A team of guards run up, aiming a fire hose down the wall. Someone down the line spins a wheel, water shoots out in a torrent. Screams below. A ladder comes over the other side. In the distance, oil tankers and rigs.

Honks below as our ship plows through other vessels in the way. The horn sounds above us. Manuel runs over and tries to push the ladder off. A guard leans over the side with a rifle, taking single shots at the pirates.

Promptly, the guard catches a bullet in the throat and falls overboard.

I stay away from the edge. More gunshots from somewhere, we back up toward the center of the ship. Next to me, a grappling hook flies through the air and sinks into the bulletproof vest of a guard. He drops his gun and tries wildly to rip it off of him, but is pulled over the side as he snatches at open air.

"Pirates?" someone yells from above.

"They're wearing *uniforms!* Does anybody know what's going on?" one of the guard shouts as she sprints by.

"This must be the organization that Carson warned us about at the Dam," Manuel says.

"The Goodmen?" I say.

"They're a cult, sure, but not terrorists." Wren says.

"I beg to differ," Manuel says, taking cover as an explosion booms from somewhere below. "They have been warning for months that something big was coming. It does not get much bigger than this."

A plume of water bursts from the sea below, sending a column of white high into the air.

"Are they a private military?" Beet asks.

"It certainly seems that way-" I start, interrupted by a flare of steam jutting

443

from a ricochet-caught pipe. It is challenging to think clearly. Alarms, sirens. Another ding in the metal behind me before my brain catches up. The Goodmen-whoever they are-are shooting *at* us. I drop down behind a spool of massive rope.

A man swings over the railing and scrambles to his feet, then dives behind a container. We produce our pistols and open fire when another arrives. Nobody manages to hit any of the targets. They hear our shots and begin firing back with increased accuracy.

"It is pointless, go up the stairs to the bridge!" Manuel shouts. Mike fires a few more shots and runs, we follow. Beet runs around the corner toward our room. The door to the bridge, where the captain and controls for the ship should be, is locked tight.

"Open up, it's your stowaways," I shout. I glance behind me, a Coast Guard helicopter banks severely and disappears out of sight. The helmsman appears at the door, then swings it open for us. We crash inside with Beet at my heels. He throws the poster tubes and the backpack with the raft on the floor.

"It's all I could carry," he says breathlessly. A bullet impacts the glass on the windshield, spider webbing in all degrees.

"Sir, they've done something to the rudder. We're locked on course," someone says.

"We've sucked in one of their skiffs, must be, blast—" the helmsman says. I look forward and see the oil rig coming closer and closer. On the side of it, two tankers docked parallel to one another. "Slow us down, we must be going 20 knots," Manuel commands.

"That's against protocol. We slow down, we only invite more of them on board," Dorji says. He pulls the steering wheel hard, leaning into it. "Best to try to break the rudder free,"

I look out the window, an overwhelming force of armed men race across the deck like ants. They're all wearing the same uniform, rushing up to the bridge. Carnage as the crew is cut to pieces by bullets and blades. The vessels in front of us, and the oil rig adjacent, grow to such a size that their figure entirely fills the windows.

"Slow down," Manuel says, reaching for the control. A guard pulls him backward. The helmsman sits down into a chair and puts a seatbelt on. The details on the side of one of the oil tankers becomes visible, I blink. This may be it.

"Brace for impact," the helmsman says calmly, leaning into the microphone.
The hit doesn't come immediately. I clench my eyes shut and breathe, waiting. It takes far too long.

The bow of our ship bites into the other hull with such stopping power that my feet lift off of the ground. I fly forward, my back slamming into the windshield and I roll to the ground already tasting blood in my mouth.

The ship in front of us keels to one side, black oil dumping out of its guts. The force of the slam somehow disconnected the other ship, which now drifts away.

"Major hull breach, reported, sir. Some kind of explosive. We need to get you to the life rafts," a guard says, crawling up against a counter.

"And we need to leave," Manuel says, opening the door and running out. I scramble to my feet and run after him, as do the others behind me. "This thing is going to sink, fast. We need to get to the oil rig," Manuel says, pointing. For that, we'd need to climb onto the larger vessel we T-boned, and then climb the metal framing of the oil drilling platform.

"Are you crazy? We can't climb that," Wren says$_{15}$.

"Trust me, just go up," he says. We look around, some of the soldiers are just barely standing. It looks like many of them have fallen overboard. Others with cracked bones, struggling to stand after having been thrown like ragdolls in the impact. The oil seeps out, the current against us. With the deck on an incline, we clamber upward until we reach the hull of the other ship. A leftover rope is here, hooked onto the upper railing a few stories above us. The other end disappears like a tar snake into the shiny black. Wren goes first: she is the fastest climber. We continue up, Mike climbing last with the backpack.

Atop is a scene of panic. The impact below propelled a piece of machinery through the deck of the ship, a fountain of wet black crude oil spouts forth. The space up here is expansive, shipping containers sliding on the now tilted deck. Further back the railing grinds against the lower platform of the oil rig, where we need to go.

We take cover behind a set of broken crates. Soldiers everywhere in a state of hysteria. Slipping and sliding and falling down and shouting trying to control the spill. With a metallic groan the ship angles harder, more things begin to slide. Soon, the angle is too much, causing us to fall into the river of petroleum. The stuff is thick and mucus-like, soaking my clothes in an instant. I try to stand, slip, and nearly lose my poster tube. We are spotted almost instantly. Yelling.

I can see the bridge from here, the crew hanged by their own ropes from the catwalk. This is not the Coast Guard, or even the US military. Is this who Carson warned us about? The Goodmen? Something else bursts, more liquid shoots out and rains down on us. We draw our weapons, three soldiers collect in front of us and aim their rifles at us.

One shot and we all go up in flames. We look at them, my safety is off. For sure this time. White eyeballs stare back, as terrified as we are. Alarms blaring, a helicopter in the sky. I'm done with this. I drop my gun on the ground. Mike pockets his. The ship lurches beneath us, a horn sounds. A frenzy of metal screeches. More men in the background working feverishly to address the fountain.

MIke pulls a cigarette out of his pocket and puts it in his mouth, pulls out his lighter. Tries to act calm. Then, slowly puts it back into his pocket and pretends that we aren't all staring at him.

"Just let us pass," I scream over the machinery. The soldier shakes his head.

"You are not one of us," he shouts back.

"We mean you no harm, we are just trying to get home," I say.

"Then repent," one of them says. "My Father's house has many rooms," he says. I remember that from Sunday school. John 14. I think. Think, *think!*

"Do not let your hearts be troubled," I say. "You believe in God; believe also in me."

He looks astounded, a dog thrown a bone.

"Let us pass," Manuel yells. The man lowers his weapon, we slip and run immediately toward the oil rig. At the edge of the ship, a water line is burst and spraying seawater like a fire hydrant. A divide on the ground between the water and oil, we look up. At least a skyscraper's worth of scaffolding and rusted, barnacled metal to climb. I almost vomit, my heart is pounding into my chest.

Behind us, a soldier barreling forward on the wet and uneven ground. A different one, he must not have heard the previous conversation. Wren and Manuel's guns are aimed at him, he skitters to a stop and almost loses his footing.

"Let us leave," I say.

"You're responsible for this, you're under arrest," he shouts.

"My brother in Christ," I begin, but he looks down his sights at me.

"You pull that trigger and everyone here goes up in flames," Beet says. The oily water drips down into my eyes, stinging. A golden sunset casts down upon us. I glance over the edge, the ocean waves are on fire. Rolling with the swells, they overtake the ship we just left. Only a matter of time. We need to leave. A squad of soldiers with weapons run at us from behind the aggressor, they'll be here any second. Mike opens his mouth.

"If you're going to fire that weapon, then just do it alread—"

POPPOPPOP!

A burst of bullets fly out of the soldier's gun. He erupts into flames instantly, dropping the assault rifle and swatting at the air. The fire 448 spreads without hesitation, without pausing for thought, the entire deck around him engulfed instantaneously. We dive backward into the spray of seawater, Beet slips and falls. I look back, the fire spreading to form a line and effectively cutting us off from the other soldiers. But it won't burn forever. The purple sky becomes choked with aggressive black plumes of noxious smoke.

We scramble to our feet, I put my hand on the first crossbeam and prepare to climb. I turn and see Beet with a worried look, his teeth chattering. His hair is soaked and fallen in his face. Black oil still running off of him like ink. His abdomen clenches, he falls against me into a hug. I wrap my arms around him, my hand touching something spiky and hot. Pull back. A bullet has ripped through his collarbone and exited through the back, shattering his shoulder blade and sending bone fragments through his skin.

"No, *no*," I say, pulling him back in and putting two hands worth of pressure on the wound. Between my chest and my hands, no blood can leave. He can't die. But I feel it streaming down my chest, soaking my shirt and my pants. Somehow, thicker than oil. This can't be my reality. I should be in Utah. Beet and I should be guiding on the Colorado together. This must be someone else's story.

He pushes me off gently and wipes water from his face, then delicately takes off his shirt, wincing in pain.

"I can't climb," he says.

"We'll carry you," I beg.

"No, you won't," he says, slapping his sopping shirt onto the deck and handing Manuel his poster tube.

"Then swim, we'll inflate the raft,"

449

I plead.

"Birch," Beet scolds. "It has come for me. Let me face it. I'm not going to die a coward."

"Beet," I say, all the air leaving my lungs. I can't see through my own tears, my eyes burning in pain. Wren stares at me, Mike stares at the ground, Manuel looks up.

The ship lurches again, forming a gap of a few feet between us and the oil rig. It slams back down and I almost lose my footing.

"Honestly? I can barely feel it. I drank some kratom this morning, my back feels great," he says. I stare in horror at the deep red oozing from the bullethole. There's no surviving that. "Here I am, covered in the embodiment of capitalism," he laughs, decidedly calm. "That fire's almost out. I'll hold them back while you climb. Don't waste your chance," he says.

"Let's go," Manuel says. Beet grabs him by his collar and pulls us all into a group hug, his freckled forehead against mine.

"Society, man, I'll tell ya," Beet jokes.

"*Fuckin'* society," I bleat through sobs. "Love you," he says. He pushes us back, salutes. Turns, disappears behind the wall of water and smoke. Wren spins me and puts my arms on the bars.

"Climb, we're sinking," she says. My brain shuts off, focusing only on the rusted metal inches from my face. I choke on my hysteria, turning my breathing into uncontrolled groaning as we ascend. Just like climbing a pine tree. Branch after branch after branch.

After we have some height I turn and look
  down at the chaos below. A bullet strikes the steel surface of the deck, sparking

and further igniting more flame. I see my friend sprinting, plowing into the soldiers making a run for us. His skin is on fire, he grabs a rifle and swings and—

Wren turns my head by force and reminds me to keep climbing.

...

At the top of the exhausting climb, we carefully drop onto a catwalk. I stare up and hold Wren's hand, I don't dare look down. The place is full of smoke, and the sound of grinding metal. A set of stairs leads us toward the center of the structure, into a bunk room. I collapse onto the bed, grabbing the dirty pillow and pulling it close to me. Why didn't I feel this way when we thought Monty was dead? Maybe because this is much more conclusive.

There is a small kitchenette—Wren searches the cabinets and passes out water bottles and a few small snack packages. Mike pulls out a soggy cigarette with quaking hands, puts it in the corner of his mouth. Wren spins and pulls it out, shoving it into her pocket. He sighs and leans against the counter, his face bright red with fury. He's a meteor sailing through the air, awaiting devastating touch down at some undetermined location and time. Primed.

Manuel takes our guns and washes them with soap in the sink, trying to get the black tar off with a sponge. They are, and always will be, extremely lubricated.

The entrance door is kicked open, we reach for our weapons and point at the man. A soldier, matching the uniforms from earlier.

His figure is covered in slick oil, dripping like ink onto the metal floor. He holds a large knife, a dagger, and creeps toward us until the others are pressed against the back wall and I am up against the headboard.

We shout, call, threaten, but still he moves forward.

"Stop, or this is yours," Wren says. I look at her. She's lit the cigarette and is threatening to flick it at him. His eyes loll back, he falls to his knees. The knife clatters down. Manuel kicks it under the bed.

"Didn't know you smoked," Mike says.

"I don't," Wren says. "I've got a whole pocket full of them. I do a lot of picking up after you, even though you might not see it. They kind of...leak out of you,"

"Dang, sorry, I didn't realize,"

Manuel is on the floor with the man, putting a tourniquet from our kit onto his leg. He's got a major laceration; blood mixed with petroleum leaks out onto the ground in a spreading puddle.

"I am with the Lord, the Lord is with me," the man says, mumbling. "Give me mercy, give me peace,"

"Please stop talking," Manuel says, annoyed. The moment he finishes wrapping the wound, he stands up. The soldier pulls a boot knife out, and has it on Manuel's neck instantly.

"Just drop your weapons," the man says, with more vigor that I would expect considering his injury.

The guns go back up, aimed at his head. The man sways, struggling to remain on his feet. Mike steps forward, only holding the pistol with one hand. Tears flow from the man's eyes, I watch silently and clench the bedsheets. Mike stops in front of him, placing the barrel of his gun on the man's forehead. I know he's angry, but I don't know if he has the guts to actually pull the trigger. The soldier speaks through a trembling jaw.

"And do not fear those who kill the body but cannot kill the soul. I do not fear, I—"

"And justice for all," Mike says. Safety off. Click. Boom.

The soldier's head whips backward, the knife falls. His boot loses contact with the slick floor and he slams down hard. He begins to crawl for the door, looking like a sea turtle scampering across a polished bowling alley floor. My ears ring from the gunshot.

Mike looks at his gun with curiosity, then fires at the floor. No indent, no hole.

"My gun is loaded with blanks," he shouts, then launches it at the back of the man's head.

Chapter 27 || Pyre

Within the hour, fire planes arrive and douse the flames with chemical agents dropped like carpet bombs. Bright orange helicopters pull castaways out of the water, news choppers fill the air. We were transported via a rescue vessel back to the shoreline, where a temporary hospital is set up. Glossy vinyl tents and the National Guard are here. Many of the terrorists involved are handcuffed, even more lay lined up in bodybags. I wonder where they'll be shipped off to.

They took the man that Mike tried to murder. I'm not sure where.

I look around from the cot that I sit on. They set up these temp hospitals in the early days of the virus, for testing and quarantining. Still, most of the uniformed staff wear masks and they make us wear them, too. Everything moves around me in a blur, I don't mind the obstruction in front of my face because I don't feel like I'm breathing anyway.

They separated us once we got to

the mainland, but we had enough time to come up with a cohesive cover story beforehand. The questions are about what I would expect. Are you Christian? How did you get where you were? What's in these tubes?

"They're posters...from Dave and Buster's." I say, hoping that the rest of the gang has gall enough to say the same. They re-wrap my hand while they ask me questions.

We were out sailing when it happened. Our boat was hit, started sinking, so we swam to the oil rig and climbed aboard. That's the story.

The interviewer seems to be hitched on the fact that none of us have any form of ID or any cell phones with charge. Eventually they give it up once they realize the trouble that the actual insurrectionists are giving; shouting prayers and pulling small knives from every pocket in their uniform. We get D-cont'd by being shot with a firehose. Bend over, touch your toes. Some sort of powder thrown on us and we're given old clothes. Some military, some must be from a donation stockpile. And then we are released...the others are waiting for me on a park bench, everyone except Manuel.

"How did your interrogation go, Mr. Bond?" Mike asks, a little too jovial for the occasion. I shrug, a bit of the powder falling off of me. A helicopter passes low overhead, then lands nearby. In the background, a news crew interviewing someone that still holds onto a life preserver and waves it for emphasis. Harsh flashlights and headlamps cutting through the night. There's a suburb back behind all this mess.

Manuel appears at the edge of the

facility, speaking amiably with a soldier, who pats him on the back and leaves with a wave. My friend walks over and tosses us each a peanut butter and jelly sandwich, which the others eat greedily. I don't have much of an appetite.

"Looks like you made some friends," Wren says.

"Yes, well, I also found the body of Turnipseed. If we want to take it, now is the time," he says. I shake my head, trying to stomach the idea. Mike picks up the raft pack, we sling the poster tubes over our shoulders and follow Manuel back into the city of tents. Although there are many people walking around with guns, there doesn't seem to be any sort of security perimeter. We stand idly for a minute facing one another, calmly looking behind the person opposite us to make sure that no eyes are watching. Finally, we bend down and pick up the body bag. Wren grabs the foot end, I grab the head end and we walk casually through the crowd. Maybe the donated military clothing helps, maybe it is the prostrated look in my eye and the general disposition of grief. We fit right in.

We walk for what must be a mile or two, until we're well out of the encampment, through the small town surrounding it, and back into the brushy desert. Hog tracks, prickly pear.

We followed the gulf most of the way here, and now there is a sort of shallow river pouring into the larger body of water. The flow is brackish and confusing, green and blue and sediment tan. There aren't many words exchanged, almost like we've all received an executive order that we must complete without question; this is our duty.

Soon the raft is dropped onto the sand and inflated by hand. Our intent is to paddle out to sea and drop his body out there, for the waters to claim it. He had confided this in me, if cremation was not an option. If the fire planes had taken only slightly longer to arrive, perhaps it would have been the only option. We pile into my raft, and push off from shore. Within a few moments we find ourselves being sucked backward, into the river and toward the mainland.

"Huh, it must feed into a water sink," I say aloud. The group, tired, nods in agreement. We let it take us, lily dipping our paddles to adjust course ever so slightly.

"Where are our guns?" Mike asks.

"I took the liberty of throwing them into the ocean," Manuel says. One by one, eyes close like garage doors. We slump against the inflated thwarts, the rhythm of the waves lulling us, the rubber cradling us.

...

I awake once the sun is already up, to a fly landing on my nose and trying to climb up my nostril. Nobody had bothered to beach us last night, I guess, because we're in an eddy on the side of the river bumping up against a sandy beach. My eyes are warm and puffy from the crying, my muscles sore. The rest of the crew is knocked out, I doubt we'll be making any progress today. Monty will have to wait. There's no sense in pushing so hard that we start to make mistakes, and yesterday was the roughest day of the entire trip so far.

In a moment of quiet anxiety, I fumble around until I feel the poster tubes securely in their place.

My eyes want to stay closed. I grip the side of the raft and roll myself down into the water. I splash onto the sand and shake my head, then push myself under the water. Stand up, sneeze, stretch. Something catches my attention on the raft: smoke. Mike is awake, but lying very still with a cigarette searing in between his lips. Or, maybe he's asleep somehow. I'm not sure.

I sit on the beach, in the shade of some sort of tree I can't identify, and watch the sun rise. While I wait for everyone to wake up, a heron patrols near a log. I wonder where the rookery is.

Once everyone is up, we drag the raft onto the beach and make sure Beet stays in the shade, in his body bag. I haven't opened it yet to make sure it is him, I am just going to trust Manuel on this one. The cost of discovering that he was wrong might be too much for me to handle. He and I take a short walk around the area to get our bearings. There's a rocky outcropping we climb up, and get a great view of the area. Surrounding us on all sides is hot, brushy sand. In the distance there is some elevation, but nothing to write home about. Climbing it certainly wouldn't be considered mountaineering. Maybe for a Texan, it would. It occurs to me that I've never met a guide from this state.

Just a few miles away, a small town glitters. Car mirrors, windows, shop doors all glint back at us like the business end of a rifle scope. A low veil of smog looms over everything. We make plans to stay the day at this site, then hike into town first thing tomorrow. It shouldn't take more than a few hours of walking to get there, and we won't have any bags or corpses to bring.

"Are you alright?" Manuel asks me, putting his hands on his hips and not looking from the town. He hasn't been his old self since we started this mission. It seems that the goal is the only thing on his mind, the only thing that impacts his decisions.

"I'll be okay," I say. "You?"

"I feel rotten," he says. I nod. There aren't any words I can share to console him. If there were, I'd be saying them to myself. I want to ask about the blank rounds of ammunition, but I bookmark it in my mind for a later conversation. Now isn't the time. I think of Beet's parents. Would they be upset at our plan for tonight, or would they be grateful? Certainly we cannot make the rest of the trip carrying a bodybag. I think that we are doing them a service, by preventing them from having to ID his charred cadaver anyway.

...

The night arrives. The large branches in our fire pit burn low, until only embers glow. We sit around, trying not to see the stars reflecting off of the vinyl body bag. This very same group of friends is responsible for helping me to build the raft. Plus two, of course.

I had been saving up for years to complete the project. Not saving up finances, but salvaged materials. The best place to find things is in eddys, where the water is low and slow. The best time to do so is right before the autumn rains, when the water is warm and at its shallowest. I've pulled all manner of things using these strategies. Most often vinyl stickers, a single flip flop,

and a lot of soaked headwear and empty sunscreen
bottles. After the Westwater take out, if one is
willing to hike out and patrol the sharp bends in the
river they can generally expect to find accidentally
jettisoned repair kits, lost paddles, and maybe even
a PFD. In order to get the materials for this project
though, I had to employ even more advanced
tactics. The method can only be completed where
there is a feature nearby that allows for significant
overwatch, such as a large rock or even a bridge
over the water. Dewey Bridge works well for this,
considering that the other qualification for a good
site is its immediate succession beyond a trafficked
rapid system.

Peering down with a set of field glasses, one
must look for disturbances in the water. Most often,
it looks like little more than a floating trash bag
with a bit of a rustle around it. A vessel must be
ready, for you to go down and recover the item. A
great deal of things can be found using this specific
method; whole thwarts, ripped segments of rafts,
burst air valves.

It took me about three years of doing this
often before I finally had enough materials to sew
them together into a raft. Lots of glue and seam-
seal, the first two editions burst as soon as any sort
of air pressure was added. In the end, it took most
everyone in the crew to make the final product. I
am proud of the raft, but it is ready for retirement.
It barely made it this far, and looking back with the
gift of hindsight tells me that using it as part of the
heist at all was rather risky. I think that one more
class IV wave would burst it into a thousand pieces.
It sits in the water, waiting, an ode to the
marvels that can be accomplished with a

good set of friends.

        We spent a few hours collecting timber when the sun was still up. Now, a mattress of kindling and fuel fills the raft, it looks like some sort of medieval transport craft. Nobody has spoken in over an hour. Wren makes eye contact with me. With that, we stand and I suppose it must be time at last. We gather on each side of the body bag, kneel and grab a fistful of plastic. Stand. He is much heavier than I think he ought to be. We place him respectfully onto the funeral pyre. Everyone steps back slowly, as if waiting for him to get up. The others look to me.

        I grab the chicken line near a D-ring and lean into it, pushing the vessel until I am wading with it. This is a large eddy, with the current still a good few meters away. A bird's nest of dried grass and bark is right where I left it, and greedily accepts the flame from my lighter.

The water is opaque, lit up and glowing green-gray in the firelight. I place the bundle into a cavity we prepared, and step back.

I sit down in the water, holding my knees to my chest, my head resting on my kneecaps and the liquid up to my breast.

The others join me on either side, some standing, some sitting down with me.

The raft catches a bit of wind and rotates idly, the extra air serving to accelerate the flames to the next level.It burns quickly now.

The body bag smokes and ignites, wisping away in smoke and exposing Beet's corpse in a revelation of volatile plastics. I hear the hiss of the raft as one of the thwarts melts open. I can see his body now. It smells like microwaved beef and hot vinyl.

His flesh is pale, this I know. But it is made golden by the burning light. The fire eats away, steam billowing off until bone is revealed.

The main body of the raft is compromised. A loud hiss and bubbles, it capsizes. The fire climbs, engulfing the pyre as it sinks and is slowly swallowed by the river.

The stars, light pollution and all, serve as watchmen overseeing our endeavor. Several planes fly by, carrying businesspeople, millionaires, normal folk. I wonder if they see us down here in our small little world, and if they wonder if we are enjoying our campfire?

It must not look like much from way up there, but to me this is everything.

...

For the following two days in court, I catch eye contact with those in the jury and crowd that I once thought of as strangers. They wait for my decision.
My father is on the witness stand again. I haven't been allowed to speak with him after he was detained, I don't even know if he is doing alright. Now, the prosecution is done with him and Mary approaches to cross examine.
"Mr. Montague, at what age did you teach your son to ride a bike?" she asks. My dad digests the question for a moment.
"Well, I tried with training wheels

463

when he was in about second grade. But even then he fell off.”

“And did he ever graduate to anything beyond training wheels?”

“No, I’m afraid not,” he says. Mary returns to sit with me, Fitz goes up to a wooden frame on the floor, and props a large map against it. I recognize it, a black and white terrain map of the area with my own highlighter across it.

“Ladies and gentlemen, this map was given to Mr. Montague, junior, after he was brought into the police station. Once given a highlighter, he was asked to retrace the route of the chase as best he could remember. The line begins inside of the park, when the gang mounted their dirt bikes and it continues until the intersection of the highway and the Arches main road, which you know as the collision point. This highlighted route covers over 12 miles of roadway that Mr. Montague traveled,” he says, then looks up at my father, who is straining to see it with his glasses on and is practically leaning over the desk. “Would you say that you find it striking that someone who cannot ride a bike can ride 12 miles without crashing?”

“Yes.”

A few more questions and Fitz sits back down, Mary approaches the stand once again.

“If it were true that he could ride a bike—even a motorbike—then it should stand equally true that he intentionally crashed into that UTV, ending the chase for himself and eliminating his position in the gang without injury,” she says, almost smugly, then sits back down. She glances at my broken arm. After a short recess, I am brought back to the witness stand. Fitz stands before me, greased hair shining brightly.

"Did you intentionally crash your dirtbike into the UTV?" he asks, directly. If I say yes, then I'm admitting to putting others in danger. If I say no, they might think I had no intention to surrender or be caught.

"Yes," I reply, trying not to shed any hesitation. He nods.

"Did you know that nobody would get hurt?"

"Yes," I reply.

"How?"

"I used to drive the same UTV as a tour guide. They're incredibly safe, I knew that even at a full speed crash, which this wasn't, nobody inside could be harmed due to the roll cage."

"Would you call that...professional expertise?" he asks. I narrow my brow.

"That's conjecture," Mary says.

"Overruled,"

"This tour guide job, where was that?"

"It was at Maroon Mesa," I say.

"The same resort that you participated in the heist at?"

"Yes, sir,"

"I know we went over it already, but could you please remind the jury what kind of work you did there?" he asks. Considering that I just mentioned I was a guide, I list the responsibilities of that position. Then, I go into detail about my long nights filling in for those that had been fired or quit due to the conditions that are so normalized in hospitality. Like most, I've worked in every department there. "So it might serve to say that you have professional expertise related to the resort, the equipment there, and how all

of it works?"
     "You could say that,"
     "Yes or no, Mr. Montague?"
     "Yes."
     "Thank you."

Chapter 28 || Monty

They bring up a few more witnesses; the time for the jury to vote draws closer and closer. One officer after another gives their testimony of the day. Even the conductor of the train made an appearance in the form of a written incident report. If someone recovered the branding off the cattle that was slaughtered, I expect I'd have to buy a rancher a new life of black angus. I just hope that I don't know them from high school or something.

Then, a witness that wasn't on the schedule. Both parties found out at the same time-when she was escorted through the door and propped up on the witness stand. I say propped, because they removed the witness chair and rolled the wheelchair up. Adjusted the microphone. She wears a neck brace, all of her limbs casted in plaster and her eyes black. She looks at me through swollen eye sockets, deep purple and red$_8$.

After questioning from Fitz, she explains the situation. She is the general manager, and saw part of the escape plan. She got hit pretty hard and doesn't recall most of it. Amnesia, documented by her doctor. She swallows and winces, then looks at me.

"Absolutely. There is no doubt in my mind that he was being held there against his will. And the fact that you disagree because there were no firearms present, counselor, only goes to show that you've never been threatened in your life. He treated my wounds. He gave me aid despite the rest of the gang wanting to leave me for dead. The paintings—the—" she trails off, looking a bit lightheaded.

"Paintings? I don't follow," Fitz says.

"I apologize. It's my pain medication—sometimes I forget myself. The picture he painted was one of generosity and genuine human compassion. He was my only advocate among the group. I can say, conclusively, that without his intervention I would be dead," she says, a tear building in her eye. I mouth 'thank you' to her. She smiles sadly. The jury retires, finally preparing their verdict.

Chapter 29 || Unobstructed Sky

Flying these days isn't like it used to be, even when I was a teenager. Between watch lists and blacklists and the price of flying, the amount of people boarding on airplanes has significantly dropped in the last few years. The amount of air traffic, though, remains the same.

Most airlines spend the money to keep their normal routes going, regularly flying entirely empty planes from airport to airport to maintain their earned priority on the tarmac, carved out over decades of cutthroat business. They hold out the hope that we will come out of this recession. That viruses will disappear and everyone will be able to take a week's vacation to Tahiti again.

But for now, the seats remain empty. Fuel burning and engines pumping more greenhouse gasses into the atmosphere.

Their only frequent flyers are the pilots

themselves.

Boarding the vessel is eerie, despite the harsh lighting and the hum of the pressurized cabin.

This is my first flight.

The part of airline travel that I've always dreaded was the fear of losing all my gear in luggage. I'm told by Wren that they make insurance for such incidents, but Mike insists that any sort of travel insurance is a scam.

The lack of any luggage or cargo makes our trip easy, the poster tubes get a seat all to themselves. Manuel even takes the extra precaution to buckle them in. He has lightened up, now that the major dangers seem to be behind us. Of course, that has been my continually disproven philosophy this entire trip.

The pilot, whom Manuel knows by only two degrees of separation, hands us some canned sodas and a box of pre packaged pretzels. A drink—no matter how sugary—is a relief. Before this there was only a $8 bottle of water at the airport cafe, which I refused. I look around. There is no hostess.

...

We take a greyhound from Atlanta to Clearwater without incident. We follow instructions from Manuel, who does not elaborate on how he got them. If I needed a final push to trust him completely, his role as a travel

agent during this endeavor has certainly proved
substantial.
 The meeting we have been anticipating for
weeks—it must be weeks, right?—takes place in
a half built skyscraper. There are painting tarps
billowing in the wind, stapled to bare concrete.
A humid thunderstorm rages outside, bits of mist
flowing through the gaps in the building and nesting
on my skin. I swat a mosquito, take a look at the
scaffolding.
       The sound of boots-I feel my butt clench and
I search for the nearest bit of cover. Manuel puts
a reassuring hand on my shoulder, but I can't help
feeling exposed standing in the center of this large
space. I hear high heels.
       "Are we about to get a cool duffel bag full
of cash?" Mike asks. "I've always wanted one of
those,"
       "No," Manuel smiles. "It'll be wired into your
account. This isn't the stone age."
       I am nervous, my heart pounding. What if
the client is the owner of Maroon Mesa? I want to
get this over with so I can get to Monty, so I can
apologize to him. My hand throbs. I haven't heard
from him since the phone call, but the internet is
going crazy about his trial.

...

       Back in Utah, I sit among the rows of pews
and stare at the back of Monty's head. He doesn't
know that we're here yet.
       "Are you sure they're coming? They said
they'd be here by now," Wren says, looking at
her watch.

"Trust that they will come. Have you ever dealt with the American government before? You should know better than to expect punctuality," Manuel says with a quiet breath of laughter.

Then, the jury appears. Someone from the posse reads through some legal numbers, something to do with paperwork and bookkeeping I assume. Monty stands with his lawyer. Even from here, I can see the sweat glistening on the back of his neck. Wren grabs my hand.

"We, the jury, find the defendant, Cameron Brigham Montague, guilty on the charge of reckless driving. We find him guilty on the charge of aggravated assault, disturbing the peace, and vandalism. We also find him guilty on the charge of conspiracy—"

The courtroom door kicks open, the bailiff reaches for his gun. Two women, two badges in his face.

"I'm with the CIA. We're shutting this down," one of the women says, before she can be interrupted. "Your honor, please excuse this intrusion. I need all counselors, the defendant, the jury, and all other parties bound to be here in the conference room, immediately,"

There is abrupt chaos as everyone stands, shouting begins.

"We're bound to be here, right?" I say, standing. We rush through the mahogany gates and jam ourselves through the door, shutting it behind us to keep the media out. The room is incredibly full and stifling hot, it smells like cologne and leather.

"Who are you?" someone asks me.

"Me? I'm, uh—"

"Birch?" Monty says from somewhere. He parts the sea of people, diving into a hug. The rest of the gang joins in, until he breaks off. After a brief reunion, the bailiffs gain control of the room and separate everyone into their own corners. We are graciously given a blind eye, and stand a good stance away. I hold my hat over my belt buckle. I see Monty's lawyer talking with the woman from the CIA who wears a black blazer with a cross pinned on it. Church and state?

The jury sits at a large round table, the two intruders at one head, standing. There is a pounding on the door for a moment, the bailiff turns the lock and it ceases.

"Hello, I know you all have spent the last few weeks of your valuable time here, and have finally reached a verdict. I apologize for what I am about to say, and I apologize that we could not arrive at this conclusion sooner. I am with the Central Intelligence Agency," she says calmly, like she's describing any other desk job. "For some time now we have been investigating the Maroon Mesa Resort, and its owner. The investigation began because of a generous tip from one of the workers there, who agreed to share information in exchange for legal protection. Immediately my comrades and I understood this case to be delicate in nature, something that would need to be unraveled slowly for fear of exposing ourselves and...forcing the turtle into its shell, as they say."

"Can you stop dancing around it?" someone from the jury snaps.

"I am granting you an explanation as a courtesy. If you don't wish to be a part of this historical case, you may leave. But please do so now, I have had a long trip here and I don't fancy being interrupted," she says. The juror leans back and crosses his arms, his lips pouty.

"The nature of these crimes relied on the import and abuse of exploited visa workers legally entering the United States of America, through a system called Finetrade, and working for the oligarchs that control the tourism industry in this region. In an ideal world, the visa program allows individuals to enter and work in our country without needing citizenship here. It aids our economy by providing affordable, dedicated workers, and these same workers return home having experienced our cultures and having developed skills that will improve their own countries upon their return. By colluding with parties in these origin countries, it seems that some individuals have found a way to exploit the system. To do so, they gave preference to visa applicants with few ties to their home countries, and especially to those without any surviving family to advocate for them. Upon arriving at their destinations, it seems that many of these individuals have disappeared," she says, then catches the eye of another juror who looks confused. "Although we have significant evidence that illustrates a verdict, the owner of Maroon Mesa's trial will still take place within the United States, and therefore I must express myself in a manner that depicts uncertainty of the conclusion of such a trial.

"These disappearances often go undocumented. The visas are still tracked, which leads to our databases focused on tracking illegal aliens, and inflates the numbers of those that appear to be residing in the country. Once our suspicions were high enough, we coordinated with the Peruvian government, who supplied us with a skilled agent that was willing to face the risks that came with such an operation,"

"Are you serious?" I ask, turning to Manuel. He smiles from ear to ear. I don't know whether to laugh or punch him in the face. The others turn to him, too, once they've put it together.

"Relax," he says, looking smug. "Our friendship was never fake."

Wide eyed, I turn my attention back to the woman.

"In partnership, our two great nations worked tirelessly in an attempt to expose this network of human trafficking. But there was a catch. A commissioned set of paintings resided in the Mesa, another target for our agent. In the vast and complicated criminal underworld, there are thousands of snares and traps that our digital investigators might set off. Should they do so, this set of paintings would go 'underground', where they could be used for any number of things. Had this happened, they most likely would have been used as collateral, either to bribe officials in the judicial system, or to escape the country and seek refuge somewhere beyond our reach.

"Additionally, these paintings were not the property of the owner, either. They were stolen by their family from a gallery in the 1980s, which only serves as a superficial motivation for our investigation. However, we were successfully able to replace the paintings with fakes. If the owner goes to sell them, then they will be exposed as a fraud to the market. Thanks to our agent and the team he recruited, the paintings are safely returned to the original owner, and the heinous and criminal insurance plan constructed by this network of traffickers is dismantled. Thanks to our agent, we are free to prosecute," she says.

Someone in the corner of the room stands and punches a bailiff, tries to leap across the table. "The owner's here?" someone says. Must have come in with the prosecution. A juror grabs the owner's pants, holds them against the table while the bailiff locks them in handcuffs. Screaming, shouting. The owner spits, kicks over a lamp as the bailiff drags them out of the room.

Things relax for a moment, while we wait for everyone to get settled once again. Monty walks over and hugs us again, and waves of relief wash over me. I was certain that he would be absolutely infuriated with me. I wonder if this will be something we bring up every year at holiday parties, or if we'll never speak of it again. His smile fades to a straight line, his eyes come into focus.

"Where's Beet?"

Chapter 30 || Meet me in Moab

The two 4x4 trucks that brought us here are parked and empty, side by side. Although we can see the river a few thousand feet below, at the base of the cliff, there is no sound but the wind. The sun sinks low in the sky, bringing the first breath of a blue twilight. A few clouds are scattered across the sky, a raven soars silently by.

"Were they Mormon?" I ask.

"No," Monty says. "I don't think so. There was something unnerving about them, though, but not the Mormon kind of unnerving,"

He scratches his head with the side of his cast. I look down at my hand. Over the last few weeks the swelling has gone down thanks to a stash of antibiotics Manuel brought from Peru. He disappeared for a few days, filling out paperwork I guess. I'm glad he's back though.

I still make an effort to keep the wound covered, given its ugliness. I don't want to throw any more dirt in there. Given the set of stitches I needed, I hope that it will heal into a formidable scar.

"So why not give the cops the names that those guys gave you?" Mike asks, dragging the cooler over.

"Well, I didn't know what was really going on. Those names could be anybody, you know? Could be some guy who cut him off in traffic. And I certainly wasn't going to give them *your* names."

"Thank you, man. Really," Mike says. We're at Dome Plateau, at the edge of a massive cliff on the side of the Colorado River. From here, we can easily see the disgusting set of resort developments that have slowly choked this valley as the years have gone on. In the distance, mesas galore. Castleton, the Preacher. Beyond, the La Sal mountains stand guard. Their timberline shows gray, just the faintest tip of white at the peak.

We take out the food to celebrate our victory, with just a few things on the back of everyone's mind. First comes the chips and dip, then the cured meat and buttered bread. Fruit salad, cold sandwiches. We share hard seltzers, except for Mike, who drinks a beer he brought with him.

I stand up and pour a drink into my camp mug, then raise it. The others meet me in a toast.

"For Beet,"

"It's about that time, huh?" Monty says. "For Beet."

And I pour the drink over the side of the cliff. By the time it splatters to the ground, it will be beyond my range of hearing. For a few minutes we share memories, our favorites, of him. That time   he wore the same kilt every day for the entire summer, or when he adopted the rat that broke into his apartment.

I've been avoiding thinking about his death. I'll be honest.

Maybe I'm still in denial.

I don't think anyone has notified his family, yet.

I have to make sure to do that.

Maybe it's a twisted viewpoint, but I hope that we would not have made it if it weren't for his sacrifice. If anyone is organizing this whole thing, I hope that he was the curveball that changed the ending of our story. That is what will let me sleep at night.

We pack away the rest of the food, and stow it into the cooler. We sit on a blanket thrown over the rocks and sand, waiting for Manuel. He drags a large bag out of the 4x4, and carries it over to us.
"I know I've had a couple drinks," Mike burps, "but I specifically remember you saying that it was *not* going to be in a duffel bag."
"Well, it did not seem right to do this electronically. After all we have been through,"
He unzips the bag, revealing stacks upon stacks of hundred dollar bills. I almost faint. Mike gasps, almost chokes on his drink. Monty pipes up.
"Without all that in your account, you're really missing out on potential interest. Think of the passive income. You gotta make your money work for you, and stop working for your

money," he declares.

"I don't think any of us are ever going to have to work again," Wren says, grinning sheepishly.

Manuel counts, tossing the stacks of cash with rubber bands to each of us. I organize mine in a grid, Monty tries to juggle his. All is distributed, each pile slightly larger than anticipated on the account that we operated under the expected budget, and that we lost a team member along the way. No pile of money sits in front of Manuel. Instead, an empty duffel bag.

"Are you...getting yours electronically?" Monty asks. He shakes his head.

"No, you do not worry about me. I did it for my country," he says. "Being rich would be nice, but I have been set up with ample compensation back home."

He displays a nice watch to us, and a new set of earrings that I hadn't noticed.

"Oh, and Monty, I forgot to tell you, but all of your legal and hospital fees are covered," Manuel explains. "You may still get a bill, but make sure you ignore it. I will make it right,"

"Thanks,"

"Of course."

"So...that's it?"

"I would like to know what the first thing is that everyone is going to do with their money," Manuel says. We think for a moment. I look out at the blazed orange sky, clouds like heroic navy vessels on patrol.

"I'm going to buy a new lens, and spend a few years photographing birds around the equator," Monty says. "And put the rest into a retirement account,"

"Maybe I would donate some of mine, invest some of it, and use the rest to buy some of the land that's left out here. Secure a place to protect it from the creep of urbanization," Wren says.

"Yeah, but I don't know that you'll be able to buy more than 5 acres," Mike says. "I'm gonna build a doomsday vault. Fill it with beer and cigarettes, ammo and stuff like that. Once everything collapses I'll be able to trade those things for well more than a few million," he says, then looks a little self conscious. "It's just a different type of investment."

"I think I'm going to finally take a vacation," I say. "A real one. For myself. And I'm going to pay off all my loans so that people stop trying to track me down. And then I'm going to retire and use my free time to volunteer, maybe at a dog shelter."

"I am really happy to hear that it will make a difference. I feel that I would be remiss if I did not thank everyone again, for all your hard work and for risking your lives. I know that you thought it was for the money, but it was for much more," Manuel says, then looks at each of us. Monty nods in solidarity.

"You're right," he says. He's got a funny look in his eye. "It was for much more than the cash," he says. He leans forward and pushes his pile of money into the center of the blanket, evenly spaced between all of us. "I want to donate my money to Beet's family. Help them get the headstone."

Wren adds her entire pile, without hesitation. "And with what's left, we can donate it to the volunteer groups that Beet was working with."

I look at Mike, who is looking back at me. I anxiously run my tongue along the roof of my mouth, tasting the echoes of the lemon-lime seltzer. I push half of my pile in.

"And with this, maybe we can work with Manuel's contacts, utilize the money to help those that had fallen into the trafficking program, and help victim's families get some closure, have proper funerals,"

"Yeah." Mike chimes. "What he said." He pushes his entire pile into the center of the circle. The others look at me, I concede and add mine to make the stack fully reassembled from its original state. I lean back onto the heels of my hand and breathe the cooling desert air.

"So we are all in agreement then?" Manuel asks.

"Yes,"

"Yeah,"

"Uh-huh,"

"Yep,"

"I knew we picked the right crew," he says, leaning over and happily clapping me on the shoulder. We pack the money back into the bag, he throws it in the vehicle once again.

"So what now?" I ask, putting my hands in my pockets. "We all get jobs at another luxury resort, get fired, then do this again next summer?"

For a moment, nobody answers. Monty comes over and pats me on the back, then shakes his head.

"I think it's back to work for a while. We've all got bills to pay," he says grievously.

"That's it?"

"Well, I'm signing up for a motorcycle training course. Just in case you have any bright ideas next time I see you,"

"Personally, I'm contemplating the idea of writing a memoir about this," Mike says.

That's not a bad idea.

We stand up and brush off the dirt, then walk over to the cliff's edge. The wind blows.

"Who's going to pay me back for all these drinks?" Mike asks, half serious. He runs to the 4x4 and grabs two 100 dollar bills from the stack, then shoves them deep into his pocket.

"Oh! I forgot," I say, jogging over to my bag and grabbing the bottle of liquor. I run back to the ledge and stand in front of the group. "We pulled this from a waterfall cache right before this whole thing started,"

"Where I was shooting?" Monty asks, appalled that he had missed it. I nod. "So *that's* what you were getting."

"Yeah. It's special," I say, holding the bottle at arm's length. The sepia liquid inside swishes.

"That is one old looking bottle," Manuel says.

"Probably handmade," I say. "I know I probably shouldn't have taken it, but it's from an old cowboy encampment, one of the ones along Westwater. I had a day off last spring, I was rappelling down the side of one of the cliffs and I found a crack only about as wide as I am. From the river, the rocks aligned in such a way that you'd never have seen it from any way but above. Even standing right in front of the entrance, the sheets of sandstone make it look cohesive. So, naturally I shimmied inside, flicked on my light. You should have seen the place. Cowboy furniture with paint still on it, bullets still on the table and hands of playing cards dealt. They must've left in a hurry. Well, on the table there were a few cups, which I'm sure were made of lead, and this bottle. I suppose I should feel a little shame, but it is hard to with the googly eyes y'all are giving me,"

"Wow, that's quite a story," Monty says, in a kind way that shows me he doesn't doubt the tale.

"I used to think that was one of the craziest stories I had to tell," I admit. "But this—this is one for the books."

I uncork the whiskey and waft it over my nose, like in the lab. It smells like pennies. It burns like hell going down the throat, I cough. They laugh and take a swig. Mike chokes and nearly spits it out, then forces himself to swallow and lets out a yelp.

"Phew, that's hotter than two fire hydrants fighting over a dog," he chuckles. With that last drink, nothing but a small sip remains. He looks at me for permission, I nod. He leans over the side and pours another one out for Beet. And I think of the serendipity of that moment, that we had all independently taken just the right sized sip, out of practice and tradition. Yet, we are one fewer than we ought to be.

We all get close together, forming a line to watch the disappearing sun behind the mountains. Below, the white caps of the Colorado thunder beyond our ears. A cool breeze carries a wisp of sand over the edge, catching the last rays of the sun and then dropping into invisible oblivion.

"Do you think we changed anything?" Wren asks.

"We only broke a single cog in the wheel," Monty says.

"We are here. We are together. And we're alive," I say. I wonder how Beet would pull us together in this moment. I stare forward, watching the landscape develop into indigo.

"All that matters is that we have done our best," Manuel says.

"And that is enough," Wren replies.

"We *are* alive," Monty says, as if it is a revelation. "Despite everything, *I am alive!*"

"*I* am alive!" Wren shouts.

"*I am alive—!*" we howl together, our voices echoing off the cliffside and unto time immemorial, to ricochet forever through the desert off of wind caves, tunnels, mesas and spires and juniper trees and through sagebrush and into the ears of every desert creature.

Above us, the first pinpricks of stars appear.

The sky wanes to the color of a deep wine, enveloping everything under the celestial blanket.

A streak of light across the sky—debris burning into terminal nothingness.

QR Code Appendix
QR CODE 1
QR CODE 2
QR CODE 3
QR CODE 4
QR CODE5
490

QR CODE 6
QR CODE 7
QR CODE 8
QR CODE 9
QR CODE 10

QR CODE 11
QR CODE 12
QR CODE 13
QR CODE 14
QR CODE 15
492

QR CODE 12
QR CODE 13
QR CODE 14
QR CODE 15
QR CODE 16
493

QR CODE 17
QR CODE 18

QR CODE 19
QR CODE 20
495

For Andre, who died due to the greed and gluttony that is inherent in the resort industry, who fell victim to the suffocation of our natural lands that inherently comes with urban development. He died at age 32.

For Alden, who like many of us was unequivocally in love with the desert. He passed in an act of stewardship toward this land. He was 29.

And for Roland, who was one of the silliest people I've ever met. In 2021, he disappeared leaving all of his earthly possessions behind at the resort-shoes, phone charger, diary. It has been two years, and little hope remains that he is still alive.

Like Roland, those of indigenous heritage are significantly more likely to experience profiling, violence, and targeted crime against them in their lifetime.

"More than four in five American Indian and Alaska Native men (81.6 percent) have experienced violence in their lifetime. And, overall, more than 1.4 million American Indian and Alaska Native men have experienced violence in their lifetime.

According to the National Crime Information Center, in 2016, there were 5,712 reports of missing American Indian and Alaska Native women and girls,
498   though the US Department of Justice's federal
⬤━━━━━━ missing persons

database, but the national information clearing-house and resource center for missing, unidentified, and unclaimed person cases across the United States, called the National Missing and Unidentified Persons System (NamUs) only logged 116 of those cases.

According to the Center for Disease Control and Prevention, the murder rate is ten times higher than the national average for women living on reservations, and the third leading cause of death for Native women. Additionally, this group were significantly more likely to experience a rape in their lifetimes compared to other women.

According to a 2008 report titled Violence Against American Indian and Alaska Native Women and the Criminal Justice Response: What is known, national rates of homicide victimization against American Indian and Alaska Native women are second to those of their African American counterparts.

Like other women, American Indian and Alaska Native women are more likely to be killed by their intimate partners compared to other offenders."
-From the Bureau of Indian Affairs

Pay attention. This may be a story, but real human lives are at stake.

Take care of yourself. Build your community until your friends become your family. No amount of wealth is worth losing a loved one—or worse; losing irreplaceable time with them.

Love your friends, and tell them that you do.

Acknowledgements

To try to cram my 'thank-you's between two covers seems a foolish endeavor to even attempt, yet I will try.

As mentioned in the beginning of this book, the characters traverse through vast landscapes and across environments that had been left abandoned since their original settlers moved on. Indeed, each path they walked had been stewarded by indigenous peoples for millennia before colonial invasion. I acknowledge and thank these groups for their undying care for the land and recognize an irreplaceable bond therein.

These groups include: the Navajo Nation, the Southern Ute Indian Tribe, the Hopi Tribe, the Las Vegas Paiute, the Ute Indian Tribe of Uintah and Ouray Reservation, the Ute Mountain Ute Tribe, the Kaibab Band of Paiute Indians, the Paiute Indian Tribe of Utah, the Pueblo of Zuni, the Rosebud Sioux, the Moapa Band of Paiute Indians of the Moapa River Reservation, the San Juan Southern Paiute, and others.

All characters in this book are based off of some of the best friends I have ever had, and the story is based off of some of our adventures together.

I would like to thank my partner who, for the last two years, has fielded questions such as 'what would you do if you found human molars while you were hiking in the desert?', and 'theoretically, how hard would it be to steal a ranger truck?'. Thank you for feeding me during long writing sessions, telling me when my analogies go too far, and encouraging me to push myself. Likely, you'll find her at the climbing gym, on trail, or riding a bicycle between those two.

Emily, a real-life park ranger and the greatest beta-reader to ever exist. I'll be the first to admit that this book only became a living thing once you cast your gaze on it. You can probably find her on a hike with her cat. Yes, she's one of those people.

Zuly, for providing insight and letting me know when my jokes actually land. You can probably find her pruning a coffee plant, drinking coffee, or studying coffee.

Annabelle, for channeling your inner English teacher in an effort to get me to correct my grammar. And, for reminding me that I don't need to challenge every bit of authority in literary convention. You'll find her making art powerful enough to make children weep.

Mike Hawk, for being truer to character than anyone else and being a trunk of inspiration from which I can sap. You can probably find him trying to fix his broken down truck in the middle of the desert somewhere, with too few tools but plenty of cigarettes.

Edward, for being perhaps the kindest and most forgiving soul I've met. Your heart is warm. You can probably find him cooking at a fancy restaurant in Peru, and bragging about how many different varieties of potatoes he gets to use.

Max, for giving me reality checks and always knowing what the best solution to a problem is. You've
encouraged me to try out so much that I otherwise
wouldn't have. You can probably find him somewhere in South America befriending the locals.

Beet, for keeping me in close contact with the other
side of myself, the side that doesn't know how to
type. You can probably find him on a commune on
one of the islands in Puget Sound, just a few miles
away from my tiny home. You didn't deserve what
happened to you in the book, sometimes the story
comes to life and demands a sacrifice. I hope you
can forgive me.

Finally, you. Thank you for reading my brain child
and being interested enough to make it all the way
to the end. You are why I do this!
You can probably find yourself reading this very line,
yes, the one you're reading right now. Weird, huh?
How did I know that?

<u>**About The Author**</u>
Cedar Elkheart is a Wilderness First Responder, Leave No Trace Master Educator, and was a guide in the Four Corners Region. He moved from Moab, Utah to the Pacific Northwest in an effort to distance himself from the impending climate disasters that are currently plaguing the region. Here, in a land with higher carrying capacity, he enjoys bathing in coastal fog and listening deeply to the hum of old growth forests. He lives in a converted ambulance on a homestead. He has two Bachelor's degrees in Wildlife Conservation and Sustainable Community Development with an emphasis on Sustainable Food Systems. He also has a Master's degree in Ecology , and is an ordained minister in the Four Corners Region. Presently he pursues a professional career instilling climate hope and tangible solutions to our man-made climate crisis. In his free time, he practices the traditional skills of firecraft, archery, tracking, threadwork, hunting, fishing, and more.

You can find more of his content by visiting his Linktree, at **https://linktr.ee/a.vulture.culture**. There, you will find links to his website, podcast, YouTube channel & more.

Other works by this author, and how they fit into The Timeline of This World (Ever Expanding):
1. The 21st Century Predator: Resilience for a Burning World
2. Birds of Paradise

For more of Llewellyn Lynch and the Goodmen, stay tuned. More is coming.

"Acts of creation are ordinarily reserved for gods and poets, but humbler folk may circumvent this restriction if they know how. To plant a pine, for example, one need be neither god nor poet; one need only own a shovel. By virtue of this curious loophole in the rules, any clodhopper may say: Let there be a tree - and there will be one."

— Aldo Leopold, *A Sand County Almanac*